THE HEIRESS OF LINN HAGH

The First Detective Lavender Mystery

by

Karen Charlton

The Heiress of Linn Hagh

ISBN: 978-0-9928036-0-5

karencharlton1@gmail.com

Alternatively, the author can be contacted through her website:

www.karencharlton.com

Visit Karen Charlton's website to learn more about her historical novels, *The Regency Reivers Series* and *The Detective Lavender Series,* published by Famelton Publishing (a specialist, independent publisher of historical fiction and fantasy.) While there, sign up for Karen Charlton's FREE monthly newsletter and join in discussion on her blog.

www.karencharlton.com

www.fameltonwritingservices.com

For my mother,

Carol James

who introduced me to the delights of Historical Fiction.

The book case in our family dining room overflowed with Georgette Heyer, Victoria Holt, Jean Plaidy, Catherine Cookson and some rather saucy novels featuring a lively wench called Marianna who had a thing for pirates.

This is where the story really began.

Thanks Mum.

XXX

Praise for

THE HEIRESS OF LINN HAGH

Worthy of Agatha Christie

"Forget the wham, bam, slash you ma'am of modern-day crime thrillers and return to a more sedate era in 'The Heiress of Linn Hagh', an engaging novel set in a time when ladies wore bonnets, highwaymen terrorised coach travellers and the Bow Street Runners were still, well, running.

Detective Lavender has no time for superstitious nonsense and is soon demonstrating a Sherlock Holmes-like determination in his pursuit of the truth. He's a well-conceived character, and in Constable Woods the author has created a perfect foil. Where Lavender broods and thinks, Woods is a man who would rather deal in practicalities. In short, they're a double act made in crime fiction heaven.

The plot has more than a touch of the old fashioned whodunit about it, and, in particular, the scene where Lavender reveals to an incredulous audience how the heiress got out of the locked room is worthy of Agatha Christie.

There's plenty of historical detail to give the story an authentic feel, and the wide-ranging cast of characters are well drawn and highly believable. Charlton is a skilled writer... It takes a lightness of touch to keep the reader intrigued without making them feel bombarded with historical context, and the author achieves this with aplomb."

Sandra Mangan

www.crimefictionlover.com

Fabulous, rollicking tale of intrigue and family secrets

"Karen Charlton's latest offering is a fabulous, rollicking tale of intrigue and family secrets. From the first page we are thrown headlong into Regency England with the introduction of Detective Lavender and his loyal sidekick Woods, amid the raucous and humorous arrest of a lady of dubious repute. The author's unique

ability to envelop the reader in the scene, to invoke the sights, sounds and smells of the Regency underbelly ensure an experience second to none. Wonderful language evokes the period and adds humour to characters that fairly leap from the page with their energy and eccentricities. Lavender's wry, intelligent approach to adversity is a perfect foil for the scheming and skulduggery he subsequently unearths.

Considerable, historical research blends seamlessly into this fascinating Northumbrian tale. The author plots the story expertly, with twists that will keep readers intrigued until the last page. Add to that a very mysterious and sensual senorita, and you have a recipe for a fabulous historical mystery that you won't want to end.

I, for one, am looking forward with great relish, to the next Lavender and Woods case."

B. A. Morton

Author of ***Wildewood, Mrs. Jones**, **Molly Brown** & **Bedlam.***

Atmospheric mystery

"Karen Charlton's 'The Heiress of Linn Hagh' is an absorbing glimpse into a Regency England far from London. Detective Stephen Lavender and his partner, Constable Woods, must deal with people who dislike any sign of authority- farmers and gypsies- and as they delve deeper into the facts of the case, they begin to understand why. I loved the way Lavender conducted his investigation and how he pieced the clues together. The comradery and humor he and Woods share is welcome relief from their dealings with suspicious townsfolk and supercilious gentry.

Although there was little doubt as to who instigated Helen Carnaby's disappearance and why, Charlton really made me wonder just how far those people would go to get what they wanted. All in all, a most satisfactory case for the detective...Charlton hooked me with her eerie, suspenseful tale and I didn't want to be pulled away from it for a second.

Now after seeing how Lavender and Woods can solve a case, I have only one thing to say: I want more!"

Cathy G. Cole - Kittling Books

A romp of a whodunit

"Karen Charlton's latest novel is a romp of a whodunit set in the wilds of an early 19th century Northumberland at the mercy of marauding reivers and lawless gangs. In the cerebral Inspector Lavender she creates a detective in the style of Edgar Allen Poe's erudite C.Auguste Dupin, investigator of the famous Rue Morgue murders--but his genial side-kick, Woods, owes much to Sherlock Holmes' Dr Watson. This dynamic duo--definitely worthy of their own TV series--delight us with their daring hunt for Helen Carnaby amidst the intricacies of family secrets, intrigue and deception. A cast of scheming women, gibbering lunatics and hostile gypsies entertain the reader as the pair unravel the mystery, and reveal something of their own softer feelings.
Surely this will not be the last we hear of their exploits?"

Moonyeen Blakey,

Author of ***The Assassin's Wife.***

CHAPTER ONE

London - October, 1809

The two-wheeled hackney carriage sped down Mile End Road towards Whitechapel, weaving in and out of more sedate vehicles, farm carts and barrow boys. It churned up the stinking waste and sprayed the startled pedestrians.

Beneath the hackney's black hood, a dark-suited man gripped his walking cane and braced himself as the carriage lurched violently from side to side. His sharp eyes scanned the crowds, seeking out familiar faces.

A never-ending tide of soot-blackened shops, brothels, dilapidated taverns and coffee houses flowed past the carriage as they raced through the crowded streets. He caught glimpses of shadowy figures lurking in the gloom of dank alleys between the buildings. The cries of the street vendors mingled with those of the drunks, rearing horses, and the constant rumble of wheels and clatter of hooves over the cobbles. For the man in the hackney carriage it was noisy, drunken and out of control.

It's good to be back, Detective Lavender decided.

When they slowed for the Whitechapel toll gate, he caught a familiar flash of scarlet. He rapped on the hood above him with his cane.

'Driver, stop here.'

In the centre of a ragged crowd of onlookers were two members of the Bow Street horse patrol. Instantly recognisable in their blue greatcoats and scarlet waistcoats, they had dismounted from their horses. One of them was Constable Woods. The officers circled a curvaceous and extremely drunk, young woman, who appeared to be on the point of passing out. Lavender climbed down from the hackney and watched the developing scene from the edge of the crowd.

Suddenly, the woman's legs buckled beneath her and she lurched towards the older, stockily-built man. Constable Woods caught hold of her beneath her stained armpits and broke her fall. Now on her knees, she flopped forwards and vomited down his breeches.

'Gawd's teeth!' he exclaimed. 'The doxy's gone and spewed down the leg of me damned boot.'

The crowd roared with laughter.

Woods frowned, lowered the rest of the limp woman onto the ground and whisked out his handkerchief to wipe his uniform. He glanced up sharply at his companion who hovered nervously above the prostrate female.

'Get on with it, Officer Brown - search her – you know what you're looking for.'

The younger man dropped down onto one knee and tugged at the drawstring of the faded reticule which was half-trapped beneath her body. She let out a great snore before obligingly rolling away into the pool of her own vomit. Her skirts were halfway up her legs, revealing the gaping holes in her stockings and the flapping sole of her boot. Officer Brown retrieved the tatty cloth bag, yanked it open and held up six shillings, a few pennies and a half crown piece.

'It's not here, Constable Woods,' he said. 'I think the strumpet has already drunk it away.'

''Tis not very likely in a mere two days,' Woods barked. 'I said search *her* – not fool around with her purse, you saphead.'

The crowd laughed again and some wag made a wisecrack about how the red, beaded bag matched the young officer's pimply complexion.

It was at this point, that the man from the hackney carriage stepped forward and joined his colleagues.

'Is there anything I can do to help, Constable Woods?' he asked. The bemused spectators regarded him curiously. One or two of them started with alarm and scurried away but few in the mob recognised him these days.

Woods beamed in delight.

'Detective Lavender!' He shook his hand vigorously. 'Well met, sir! It's been too long.'

'I agree. So, what do we have here?'

'We have been searching for this thieving trollop since yesterday.' Woods sighed. 'It's claimed she stole money from a rich merchant a few nights ago - while he slept in their bed in a bawdy house…'

'I think I know where the money is, sir!' the young officer interrupted, from his position on the ground. 'I heard the paper rustle when she moved.'

'Where, lad? Where?'

Constable Brown pointed nervously to the woman's ample breasts. 'I believe it's down there – between her habit-shirt and the bosom of her gown.'

'Well, get it!'

The young man blushed. His hand trembled above the two wobbling mounds of female flesh and the gaping cleavage.

'Go on, son!' someone jeered in the crowd. 'Give her a good fumble!'

There were howls of laughter.

'Oh, for Gawd's sake!' Woods snapped. He stepped forward, stooped low and thrust his hand down the bodice of the unconscious girl. He had a good rummage around.

The crowd loved it.

'Whayy!'

'Try the other end!'

'Don't forget her placket!'

'I'm glad to see that you've not lost your touch with the ladies.' Lavender grinned.

Undeterred by the irony of his colleague or the raucous leering of the mob, Woods' ruddy face was a picture of studied concentration. When he finally pulled back his hand from the woman's stained underclothes, he held up a crisp one hundred pound banknote. The crowd around Lavender emitted a sharp, collective intake of breath and the laughter subsided.

'That lush will get more than a whipping fer being drunk and disorderly,' Lavender heard someone whisper.

'Is the rest not there?' Disappointment flashed across Officer Brown's face.

'No. The trollop must have given it over to someone else fer safe keeping.' Woods straightened up. 'Never mind – if the numbers match those retrieved from the bank, then this should be enough to convict her. Let's get her back to Bow Street.'

The problem of how to transport the inebriated thief now made the constables pause. Lavender knew that normally they would have clapped her in irons and made her trot behind the horses.

'If I sling her over the front of me horse, she'll probably slide off and crack open her skull on the cobbles,' Woods commented.

'Perhaps I can be of assistance,' Lavender volunteered. 'I've a hackney carriage standing by and I'm on my way to Bow Street myself. Place her in the foot well. Woods, tie up your horse at the back of the carriage, and travel with me - there's a thing or two I want to discuss with you.'

Woods nodded, lifted the woman and carried her towards the hackney.

'Cor! She don't half reek.' He complained. His broad nose wrinkled in disgust.

Woods had no difficulty with carrying the woman. He was as strong and as agile as a twenty year old. His large build and great strength were fed by a legendary appetite. However, Woods did have a bit of trouble manoeuvring the woman's dead weight, to fit her into the tight space on the floor of the carriage, but he succeeded in the end.

The trollop didn't get any more attractive on closer acquaintance, Lavender decided. Her hair was dishevelled and matted at the back like a bird's nest.

Woods clambered into the vehicle beside the detective and he hackney swayed alarmingly with the extra weight. Lavender was squashed on the shallow seat, but despite this he was glad of Woods' company. He enjoyed working with him and made a point of singling Woods out when a case needed an extra pair of hands. Woods was honest, humorous and had the common touch, a quality he lacked. Besides which, Lavender was not thrown about so much in the swaying hackney, now that he was wedged between Woods and the side of the hood.

'She's in for a shock when she wakes up in the cells at Bow Street,' the constable commented.

'What is the full story? Who is she?'

Woods glanced down and Lavender saw pity flash across his weathered features.

'She's Hannah Taylor, a known prostitute and petty thief. She's been up to the beak before and went to a correctional institution. She must have thought she'd struck it lucky when she ran into this drunken merchant. He'd just returned to London, was flush with money and well in his cups. While he snored off the drink, Mistress Taylor, here, lightened his load to the tune of two hundred pounds. She took a one hundred pound note and two fifty pound notes from his pocket book and disappeared.'

'It's a shame that she doesn't have the other two banknotes on her.'

Woods nodded. 'She'll have to be questioned about their whereabouts. The merchant gave a good description of the woman who robbed him – I had an inkling the thief was her – he has also retrieved the numbers of the banknotes from Down, Thornton and Gill. Once we're back at Bow Street, I should be able match the number on the note with one of the numbers the merchant got from the bank. She'll be heading fer Botany Bay this time – at the very least.'

'That's good work,' Lavender said. 'However, you might have to let the blushing Constable Brown drag her to the gaoler back at Bow Street. I need your assistance on another case or two.'

Woods' eyes lit up.

'Heaven and hell! Where are we off to this time?'

'Back to Newcastle for a start. Magistrate Clennell has been in touch with Bow Street. Apparently, there is some more evidence come to light regarding the Kirkley Hall burglary.'

Woods' face fell with disappointment and Lavender understood why. That damned case had been the bane of their lives earlier in the year. Both of them were convinced they had found the thief, but the suspect, James Charlton, had been as slippery as a jellied eel and had avoided being sent to trial at the August Assizes. It was one of the few unsolved cases in his career as a principal officer. Their only consolation was that they had retrieved most of the stolen money – from beneath a redcurrant bush in the grounds of the Hall.

'And in addition to that,' Lavender continued, 'an heiress has mysteriously disappeared in neighbouring Bellingham.'

'An heiress, eh?'

'Yes.'

'Isn't it usually the case, when these pretty young gals disappear, they have eloped with some sponging rake?'

'Yes,' Lavender confirmed. 'However, I understand there are unusual circumstances surrounding this case – and I've been asked to travel to Northumberland to solve it.'

'Requested by name?'

Lavender nodded.

'It would seem the girl's concerned uncle is a close friend of Mr Clennell, the magistrate, and that the uncle is also familiar with the particulars of the Kirkley Hall robbery. Despite the fact that we failed to secure the conviction of James Charlton, we're still famous in Northumberland for recovering most of the missing rent money.'

Woods chuckled: 'So this uncle thinks that because we found the rent money – we should be able to find his missing niece?'

'Exactly. Are you willing to accompany me, Constable Woods?'

Woods glanced out of the carriage and seemed to be pondering for a moment. Lavender knew that Betsy, his constable's wife, would play merry hell at another lengthy absence. Their oldest two sons were a handful and difficult for Betsy to cope with on her own. Lavender knew the family well and if the truth were to be told, he was a little scared himself of the quick temper and sharp tongue of the tiny Mistress Woods. Yet he suspected that she wouldn't complain about the extra money her husband would earn in expenses.

'What're these mysterious circumstances surrounding the gal's disappearance?'

Lavender smiled and his face lit up like a mischievous school boy's.

'Oh nothing I'm sure we can't handle, Ned. Apparently, the girl vanished from a locked bedchamber.'

Wood's greying eyebrows rose sharply and a wide grin broke across his broad face.

'Is that all? Shouldn't take us long to fathom this one out, should it? We'll be back in Bow Street within a fortnight…'

CHAPTER TWO

Four weeks earlier…

'Do try harder to keep up, girl.'

Seventeen year-old Anna Jones scowled and shivered beneath her thin cloak. It was her half day off and she had not expected to be accompanied by her nagging mistress on her return to Linn Hagh. Miss Isobel had also insisted they leave the road and take the short cut back to the house through the woods. Anna hated this route, and Miss Isobel's presence made an unpleasant journey even worse.

Anna's fingers were frozen despite the knitted mittens her ma had given her. Stiffly, she adjusted her grip on the handles of the heavy bags and parcels she carried. Her shoulders ached from their weight. She tried to stifle the resentment she felt towards the woman striding next to her.

An unpleasant thought kept repeating itself through her mind. She had unexpectedly bumped into Miss Isobel in the market place in Bellingham. Had Miss Isobel been waiting for her to emerge from her ma's tiny cottage? Had it always been her intention to make Anna carry home her blooming parcels?

The sunset spread like a flaming quilt across the tops of the trees of Hareshaw Wood. The sky above was icily clear - another bitter frost would descend over the landscape tonight. The daylight took on a reddish tinge as they meandered through the meadow, towards the entrance of the dark woods.

"What on earth…?"

Miss Isobel had stopped suddenly. Another two women had emerged from the entrance to the woods.

Anna smiled. She was pleased to see that one of the women was Miss Helen, the youngest Carnaby daughter. She recognised the other girl as one of the gypsies, the 'faws,' who haunted these forests. Her bright shawl and ragged dress stood out against the gloomy backdrop of the wood and were in sharp contrast to Miss Helen's discreet, high-waisted mourning gown. Even from this distance, Anna could see the colourful band the faw wore around her black curls and the glint of her earrings.

As they approached, the gypsy girl glanced up, scowled and melted into the woodland behind.

'Helen! What on earth do you think you're doing talking to that trollop?'

Miss Helen sighed. 'Good evening, Izzie, have you had a pleasant afternoon in Bellingham?'

'Yes – but now all is spoilt by the shock of seeing the kind of company my sister prefers to keep. I ask you again – what is your business with the gypsy?'

'It was harmless enough, I chanced upon her during my walk and she offered to read my palm.'

'Superstitious nonsense. You would do well to avoid this tribe. Our brother doesn't want them encouraged. They poach our salmon and deer and steal our livestock.'

Miss Helen looked surprised. 'Our father thought highly enough of them to allow them to live on his land.'

Her sister snorted in contempt then swept past her and marched towards the trees. Anna scurried to keep up.

'Our father was a fool.' Miss Isobel threw the comment back over her shoulder. 'It's a wonder we all have not been murdered in our beds.'

Miss Helen said nothing but she fell into step beside Anna and smiled at the young girl. Anna instantly felt better. She hated it when the half-sisters bickered.

Anna leaned towards her and whispered: 'I hope the faw foretold a wonderful future for you.'

Miss Helen just smiled.

The trees now closed in around them and threatened to block out the light. Above their heads, the naked branches strained to touch each other with their bony fingers. The women were quiet as they trudged along the rocky path in single file. Ferns leaned over and lashed their waists as they walked.

No birds sang, the wind was still and nothing else moved in the tangled undergrowth. In the far distance, Anna could hear the sound of the cold water as it thundered over the rocks of Hareshaw Linn. Closer still she heard the laboured breathing of Isobel Carnaby and the occasional ominous creak of ancient timber. Miss Helen glided along like a ghost; her black, woollen dress and cloak made barely a rustle.

Now the women began to climb the steep path which led up to the waterfall. Anna's boots slithered on the ice and she struggled to keep her footing.

'Give me one of the bags,' Miss Helen said.

'Don't fuss,' Miss Isobel snapped. 'The girl is fine.'

Miss Helen ignored her, fell behind and took one of the heavy bags from Anna. Her other hand rose to her lips and made the sign for silence. Miss Isobel strode on ahead, oblivious to the exchange behind her.

They reached the black rocks at the base of the waterfall. Thick icicles hung like knives from the trees and the sides of the gorge. The waterfall had frozen over at its sides and so had the edge of the pool. A crescent of glittering ice spread out beneath their feet, enticing them to their doom. In sharp contrast to the whiteness of the crystallized water at the edge, ribbons of black swirled around the jagged rocks which rose like tombstones from the centre of the pool.

Anna shivered again. This was a place of death. Only last summer, some poor lass had thrown herself and her unborn bairn from the top of the waterfall onto the rocks below. Her broken and disfigured body had floated limply in the pool for days before it was found tangled in the reeds.

The path up to the top of the waterfall rose steeply; the slimy stone steps were treacherous beneath their boots. Gnarled roots reached out to trip them and patches of scree sent them slithering back down the hill. The spray from the waterfall caught on the drooping boughs of menacing trees and dripped down upon their heads. Anna wrinkled her nose at the pungent smell of rotting vegetation.

They stopped to rest when they finally reached the summit.

'Perhaps we should have gone by the road,' Miss Helen commented.

'Perhaps when you come of age, you'll use your inheritance and buy us a carriage and some horses,' her sister snapped. 'That will make the journey much easier.'

There was an awkward pause.

'Perhaps.'

Suddenly, something crashed through the dense undergrowth beside them and an unearthly howl rent the air. An ice cold chill shot up Anna's spine. A large creature thrashed its way towards them through the thicket of alder, hawthorn and bramble.

Miss Isobel squealed and clutched her sister's arm. Anna's ruddy cheeks turned pale beneath her freckles. She dropped her bags and covered her mouth with her hands in terror.

'Calm yourselves,' Miss Helen laughed. 'It's only our Matty.'

Matthew Carnaby, her mistresses' lunatic brother, lurched out of the gloom onto the path in front of them. Oblivious to his bloody scratches and torn clothes, the ungainly man grunted with pleasure at the sight of Miss Helen and lolloped clumsily towards her.

Miss Isobel stepped forward and slapped him sharply across his face. The confused man wailed, fell back and clutched his cheek in shock.

'Don't you ever scare me like that again, you pathetic saphead!'

She raised her hand to strike again but Miss Helen stepped in between her siblings.

'Enough, Izzie, he doesn't know what he does.'

Miss Isobel's anger now turned onto her sister.

'You've done nought but defy me and interfere with the running of this house and family ever since your return,' she yelled.

'Well, you won't have to suffer me for much longer.'

After what seemed like an age to Anna, Miss Isobel finally ceased glaring, turned and stomped off down the path.

'Come along, girl! Why do you dawdle so? Let's get these parcels home.'

Silently, Anna fell into step behind her. Miss Helen stayed behind a moment to comfort Master Matthew.

Now they neared the edge of the woods, but it didn't seem much lighter in the clearing which fronted Linn Hagh. The daylight had all but gone and there was still no sign of the moon.

Anna could just about make out the solid, oblong outline of the old pele tower with its distinctive castellated roof. Candlelight glimmered faintly behind the thin windows of Linn Hagh's kitchen and the bigger windows of the Great Hall on the floor above. The top storey of the tower was in total, freezing darkness. There, she shared a tiny bedroom with the cook. She shivered at the thought of the cold night which lay ahead.

Anna's young ears heard it again; the unmistakable sound of a large creature moving through the undergrowth in the woods beside their path – but this one moved with stealth. She spun around, hoping to see that Master Matthew had left Miss Helen's side. No. He still lurched like a drunk beside his sister.

Whatever, or whoever, followed them now was not Master Matthew.

Anna froze in fear and her mistress stopped with her.

'What is it girl? What's the matter?'

The forest filled with a sound far more disturbing than anything Master Matthew could make.

A cruel laugh echoed throughout the woods. It rebounded off the blackened trunks and rent the icy air around them.

Master Matthew let out a chilling primeval wail of terror and fled past Anna towards the hall.

'Run!' Miss Helen yelled - her voice full of fear. 'Run for your lives!'

Anna needed no second bidding. As more of the terrifying laughter rang in their ears, the three women screamed and ran for the safety of Linn Hagh. They clattered across the cobbles, scrambled up the flight of stone steps and eventually fell through the studded oaken door. Miss Helen slammed it shut behind them and shot home the great iron bolts.

Still trembling, Anna crossed the small vestibule to seek the warmth of the great range and the comforting presence of Mistress Norris, the cook. Master Matthew was there before her, cowering in his favourite corner.

'Gawd's teeth! What in hell's name is going on?'

Master George Carnaby was also in the kitchen. He had risen hastily and knocked over his chair, alarmed at the dramatic reappearance of his family.

'What devil's business is this?' he demanded of Anna.

His two sisters followed Anna into the kitchen. Miss Isobel collapsed onto a chair at the table. She was shaking and dishevelled, her eyes watered like an old woman's. Miss Helen leaned back against the kitchen wall and closed her own eyes. Her long lashes rested on cheeks now deathly pale. Both women breathed heavily.

'I say again – what in God's name is going on?'

Miss Isobel found her voice and pointed an accusing finger towards Master Matthew.

'That bacon-brained idiot scared us in the woods. He behaved like a fiend from hell.'

Master George laughed but the smile never reached his eyes.

'I thought you had more sense than that, Izzie.' He moved menacingly over towards his brother, his face contorted with cruelty. 'Fancy letting yourself be scared by this idiot.'

His boot lashed out. Master Matthew squealed, twisted and curled up into a ball on the floor. The vicious kick, which had aimed for his head, deflected into his rib cage. Anna winced as she heard it thud into his flesh.

Master Matthew screamed.

Anna began to cry. The cook placed a comforting arm around her shoulders and held her steady. Miss Helen and the two helpless servants winced as Master George delivered one vicious kick after another into the defenceless body of his sobbing younger brother. Miss Isobel laughed in delight and threw a withering, triumphant glance back at her sister.

Eventually, the two oldest Carnabys tired of their sport and left the kitchen to climb the stone staircase to the Great Hall above.

'We'll dine in half an hour,' Master George informed the cook, as he went.

Miss Helen went immediately to comfort her wretched brother.

'I'm so sorry, Matty' she whispered. 'I cannot stand up to them both.' Her cheeks were stained with the tracks of her own tears.

Mistress Norris sighed and moved over to the range, where she unhooked the great iron kettle from the metal contraption above the fireplace.

'Let's have a drink of tea. They's can wait fer their bloody supper.'

Miss Helen persuaded her brother to move onto a chair by the table. The cook warmed the pot and counted out spoons full of tea from the caddy. The familiarity of the routine began to calm Anna. The scalding drink revitalised her.

Eventually, Master Matthew's sobs subsided. He took the saucer of tea in his large, filthy hands and gulped it down like an animal. Every now and then he would groan and wince.

Anna looked away; she didn't want to shame the young master further by staring at him.

'I'll call at Doctor Goddard's in the morning and ask him to come and examine him,' Miss Helen said.

'Huh! They'll not thank you fer running up a doctor's bill,' Mistress Norris commented. Her eyes rolled up to the high beamed ceiling to indicate to whom she referred.

'I'll pay for it out of my own money.'

'I'll make him a poultice fer tonight, to tek away some of the pain. The Lord knows I've had plenty of practice with that particular recipe,' the cook added bitterly.

At last Anna found the confidence to speak.

'Miss Helen, why did your sister not tell Master George about the other gadgie in the woods? The one that laughed at us.'

'I don't know.'

'Master George could have taken his man and his gun and searched fer him.'

'Yes, I suppose he could have done.'

'The intruder will be long gone by now. Was it one of the faws, do you think? That laughter were creepy, weren't it?'

'I've heard that man before,' Helen Carnaby said, as she rose to leave. 'He is stalking me like a poacher.'

CHAPTER THREE

Dusk started to fall as the stage coach rumbled up the Great North Road towards Barnby Moor. Inside the cramped vehicle, which stank of damp body odour and burning oil wicks, the seven passengers began to droop with weariness. The road was in good condition on this stretch. The drivers kept up a steady pace and veered less to avoid ruts. The regular motion and the constant rumble of the wheels lulled the tired passengers towards sleep. Even the constant drumming of the rain on the roof of the coach had a rhythmic quality to it. One by one, they closed their eyes and began to nod.

Only Stephen Lavender and the shabby man who had joined the coach back in Newark remained awake. Another passenger, Mr Nathanial Finch - a retired bookseller from Sheffield - sagged in Lavender's direction. His weight pressed into the detective's shoulder. Lavender shuffled uncomfortably beneath the pressure. At the far end of their row of seats, the elderly Mistress Finch let out an unladylike snore.

Lavender's back ached with the long journey and the constant jolting of the carriage. He stretched his legs and tried to avoid kicking his dozing constable who sat opposite him. He envied Woods' ability to drop off to sleep in such an uncomfortable, upright position; it was not a skill he had ever mastered. Beside Woods, the Newark man pulled out a battered pocket watch and checked the time again.

It would be at least another hour, Lavender realised, before they arrived at the relative comfort of The Bell Inn. He glanced out of the mud splattered window into the foul weather outside but could see little beyond the condensation and the rivulets of rain which streamed down the pane. He tried to picture the vast expanse of barren fields and the snatches of woodland which he knew lined the road between here and Barnby Moor. It was an isolated area.

Still sleep eluded him.

He let his eyes feast for a while on the raven-haired Spanish beauty who sat next to the fidgeting man from Newark. Magdalena Morales was also trying to rest and leaned against her maid, who was fast asleep in the far corner by the window. Shortly after leaving London yesterday, the young girl had asked her mistress if she could sit next to the window. Doña Magdalena had smiled and changed places. At supper last night, in the tavern in Peterborough, the señora had resumed the haughtiness of her class and her race; she had been distant and evasive when questioned by the other curious travellers. But in this one small gesture of kindness towards her servant, Lavender felt that he had a glimpse of the real woman behind those beautiful violet-black eyes.

Despite her evasiveness, Lavender could tell from her frayed cloak, faded silk gown and elegant manner that she was probably another impoverished Spanish aristocrat who had fled her country after Napoleon's brutal invasion. Although her charming, deep voice was heavily accented, she spoke English well and clearly understood several of the idioms used by the other passengers. This indicated she had been in England some time. The only question that remained unanswered in his mind was the whereabouts of her husband. Here, or back in Spain?

He would not normally have cared, but an interesting magnetism had sprung up between them. Whenever he helped her down from the coach, her dark eyes smiled and the white skin of her neck flushed slightly. She paused in her speech when their hands touched as if savouring the strong grasp of a man. Last night at dinner, she had sought out his opinion on several occasions and had been noticeably less haughty with him than anyone else. Idly, he wondered how long it had been since the señora had lain with her man.

Her sensuous mouth dropped open slightly, revealing a glimpse of her moist, pink tongue. Her bosom began to rise and fall in the gentle rhythm of sleep. He leaned back against the cushions of the coach, half-closed his own eyes and allowed himself a few pleasurable thoughts about what he would do to Magdalena Morales if he ever had her naked in his bed.

He had nearly dozed off when the man from Newark reached out and gently eased the reticule from between the señora's limp, gloved hands. Slowly and carefully, his expert fingers began to feel the shape of the coins in her bag before replacing it onto her lap. His actions only took a few seconds but it was enough to tell Lavender exactly who and what he was; the man's greed had given himself away.

Lavender forced himself to remain rigid and still in his corner of the coach. He continued to watch the man through half-veiled eyes and tried to slow his own quickening breath. He scanned the contours of the man's shabby greatcoat, looking for the outline of his pistol. There was an ominous bulge by his right hip. It all made sense now: the uneasy fidgeting; the constant checking of the time. Lavender's brain raced. He desperately tried to remember if there was any place between here and Barnby Moor which was more heavily wooded, more secluded and more notorious for highway robbery than any others. He realised grimly that there were several.

The coach hit a rut and lurched violently. All the passengers jerked awake, groaned or sighed. The señora cursed quietly in Spanish.

Constable Woods woke up startled and blinking. When Mr Finch engaged the Newark man in conversation, Lavender leaned over and indicated to Woods that he wanted a private word with him. Beneath the murmurings of the other passengers, the rumble of the wheels and the persistent beating of the rain on the roof, he managed to discreetly whisper into Woods' ear.

'There's a toby man on board – him on your left.'

Woods' sleep-rimmed eyes blinked and stared back at him in confusion. A second later, his eyes glimmered with understanding and he sank back into his seat and nodded.

Lavender rose to his feet, braced himself against the rolling vehicle and banged loudly on the wood panelling above Wood's head, which separated the passengers from the driver. The other occupants of the coach glanced up in alarm.

'Ladies and gentlemen,' he announced loudly, as he sat down again. 'When Mr Woods and I introduced ourselves yesterday, we omitted to mention the fact that we're officers with the Bow Street Magistrates court. I'm Detective Stephen Lavender and this is Constable Edward Woods.'

'Good gracious!' Mr Finch gasped. His elderly wife leaned forward for a better look. Even with the dim and flickering light from the carriage's oil lamps, Lavender saw the man from Newark turn pale. His right hand began to slide beneath his greatcoat.

'I don't think so, my friend,' Woods said. He slammed the man back against the seat with one vicious punch and caught hold of the man's arms, pinning him against the cushions. The would-be thief swore and began to struggle violently.

Doña Magdalena cursed as she was knocked across her maid. Mistress Finch shrieked.

Lavender pulled out his own pistol, aimed it at the man's head and cocked it.

The passengers gasped at the sight of the weapon. Then a stunned silence descended over the coach.

‘Don’t make me use it.’

The struggling man froze and glared at Lavender.

‘What’ve I done? I’ve done nuffin!’

‘Oh yes, you have my friend. You’re a thief, a cove. While the señora was asleep you had a good feel of her reticule trying to work out how much money she was carrying.’

‘Cerdo asqueroso!’ Doña Magdalena twisted around and slapped the man sharply across the face.

The would-be thief flinched but continued to glare silently at Lavender. His cheek glowed where she had struck him.

‘But I don’t understand, Detective,’ Mr Finch said. ‘If he was going to steal her money why did he not just take it, there and then?’

‘I believe he is waiting for the arrival of his mounted friends, who are lying in wait for us further along the road. It makes it quicker and easier for them if they’ve planted one of their own on a coach they’re about to rob.’’

‘Highwaymen!

‘Dios mío!’

Mistress Finch shrieked. ‘May the Lord have pity on our souls!’

‘That’s just bloody guesswork – nonsense,’ their captive sneered.

‘I’m not prepared to take the risk,’ Lavender replied coldly. ‘Woods reach inside his greatcoat and remove his pistol – right hand side.’

There was a collective sharp intake of breath as another weapon was revealed. Lavender took it, cocked it and aimed the second gun at the thief. Woods hammered again on the back wall of the coach but the drivers failed to hear it – or heard it and failed to respond.

‘How many of you are there?’ Lavender demanded.

The thief stared sullenly ahead.

‘Where are they planning to hold up the coach?’

Still no answer.

‘We’ll get nothing from him,’ Woods said. ‘He still thinks his cronies will come to his rescue.’

‘We need to tie him up. Has anybody got anything we can use to bind him?’

The vehicle erupted with movement as the Finches and the señora scrambled around, reached up for their luggage and searched for bindings. Only Lavender, Woods and the man from Newark remained stationary. Woods resumed his vice like grip on the body of the felon beside him. Lavender’s eyes never left his face.

Without warning, the señora suddenly lifted up her skirts and held out a shapely, stocking-clad leg. Woods nearly choked, then beamed with delight. Even the thief seemed surprised.

'I have not any rope. Would these stockings bind him?'

'Thank you, Señora. They'll help.' Lavender found it hard to keep a straight face. 'Mr Finch, can I presume upon you for your belt and cravat? Unfortunately, I cannot move to get my own at the moment.'

The carriage appeared to be slowing down. Mr Finch whipped off his belt and Doña Magdalena calmly peeled off her stockings and handed them over before replacing her boots.

'Do we need more?' she asked.

'Yes.'

'Quitese las medias,' she instructed her maid.

'Well, don't think I'm going to undress for you, Detective Lavender,' protested Mistress Finch as the young girl dutifully followed her mistress' example.

'I think you English have an expression for times like this, do you not?' The señora's voice was light but Lavender heard the hint of reproach directed at the older woman.

'You say: '*When needs must...*'

'I think we may have enough now,' he said, as a second pair of warm stockings passed into his hands. 'Get him on the floor, Woods.'

The other passengers lifted their legs up onto the seats as Woods – with some help from Mr Finch – manhandled the cursing villain onto the narrow stretch of floor which ran between the two doors and attempted to bind and gag him. Their prisoner ceased struggling abruptly when Doña Magdalena stamped down hard with her boot on the back of his neck.

Immobilised and silent, he writhed uncomfortably on the floor beneath them.

Now Lavender reached up and banged once more on the carriage wall behind the drivers. This time the drivers reined in the horses sharply.

'Let's hope to God, we've not left it too late,' he muttered quietly to Woods, when he passed him the cove's pistol. He pointed to the far door on the other side of the carriage.

'Go that way. Identify yourself to the drivers first before you let them see your pistol – or else they'll shoot you. And if anything starts up – get the brake on and keep those horses calm. The last thing we need is the horses to bolt and overturn the coach.'

Woods nodded grimly and clambered across the prostrate man on the floor, towards the other carriage door.

As the vehicle slowed to a halt, Lavender threw open the door and leapt out. He nearly lost his footing on the muddy ground but steadied himself and moved quickly towards the front of the carriage. The rain lashed down in sheets in front of him, impairing his visibility.

'I'm Detective Stephen Lavender from Bow Street,' he yelled up to the drivers. 'We've restrained a man inside the coach – I believe there are toby men lying in-wait for us ahead.'

Two white, wet and scared faces stared down at him from the front of the coach. Muffled in scarves and hats against the dreadful weather, the drivers were soaked through. One of them had a blunderbuss in his hands. It was aimed at Lavender.

'Where's yer badge of office?' he growled.

'My tipstaff is packed in my luggage. You'll have to believe me. We're in great danger. There are toby men ahead.'

It was too late. A flash of powder illuminated the forest and a shot rang out in the night, echoing off the trees. The guard with the blunderbuss was thrown back in his seat as a musket ball tore through his shoulder. He screamed in agony. A horse reared in fright.

Four men on horseback now galloped out of the murky copse of trees where they had been lying in wait.

Lavender fired both barrels of his flintlock pistol. One of the highwaymen fell from the saddle and crashed onto the ground. As Lavender hurried to reload, he heard Woods fire his pistol. He risked a quick glance – a second highwayman slumped forward in his saddle and slid off his horse.

'Get the blunderbuss!' he yelled. The unharmed driver never heard him. He was struggling with the terrified horses which fought to free themselves from their restraints. The coach lurched violently.

One of the riders now bore down on Lavender as his frozen and wet hands fumbled to reload his pistol. He ducked down low behind the flimsy coach door, desperately hoping it would give him some protection from the shot which would inevitably come his way.

There was not enough time to reload and his powder was wet. He struggled to seat the balls in the rifling grooves. The horseman pulled up next to the coach and reined in sharply. Laughing viciously, he aimed his pistol straight at Lavender's head.

Another pistol shot rang out and Lavender felt the ball singe the top of his hair. A woman screamed.

For one brief, horrifying moment, he thought his attacker had missed him and shot someone behind him in the coach but there had been no powder flash. The next second, the highwayman collapsed forwards in his saddle. His pistol slid from his fingers and fell into the mud. The steaming horse began to prance beneath the inert body. Casting aside his own useless weapon, Lavender bent down, dodged the flailing hooves of the beast and retrieved the fallen gun. Stepping back, he watched in a trance as the robber slid slowly down the flanks of the horse and landed with a thud on the soft ground. The man lay still; dead.

Lavender glanced around quickly. The fourth horseman was now fleeing back into the shadows of the forest. They had shot three between them and the fourth had fled. The sound of galloping hooves faded away. Lavender's ears strained against the blackness of the night for more sounds of danger. He heard women sobbing in the lurching coach behind him; the frantic thrashing of the harnesses and bridles; Woods and the coachman shouting to the horses as they fought to steady them.

Two still, blackened lumps on the road revealed the whereabouts of the first two men they had shot and the third sagged in a heap a few feet away from him. A few tense minutes and it was all over. But who had brought down the cove that lay on the ground before him?

He moved cautiously over towards the prostrate man. The glimmering light from the lanterns in the coach enabled him to see the small hole in the man's forehead and the trickle of blood that seeped down over his mask. Sharply, he turned back to the heaving vehicle.

Magdalena Morales stood in the doorway of the coach, supporting herself with one hand on the door jamb. In the other she held a small, pearl-handled pistol. A wisp of smoke still curled from its barrel.

CHAPTER FOUR

When their carriage finally rattled over the cobbles under the archway of the courtyard of The Bell Inn, it was nearly two hours late. The concerned landlord and ostlers poured out of the inn and stables to assist them.

From his perch on the seat on the top of the coach, Lavender disarmed his pistol and allowed himself a sigh of relief. During the desperate dash to safety on the final leg of their journey, he and Woods had travelled on the outside of the coach with reloaded pistols. Woods had been seated beside the uninjured driver to render him assistance with the horses.

As the carriage raced frantically through the last of the forest, Lavender's nerves had been raw. He was mud-spattered, shivering and soaked to the skin. Yet despite his physical and mental exhaustion his mind still raced. His eyes had strained against the darkness for further signs of danger. He glanced sharply from side to side, barely blinking. It wasn't until they saw the welcoming lights of the small town of Barnby Moor glimmering ahead, that he had allowed himself to believe they would actually make it safely to their beds that night.

They had left the dead highwaymen and the still-bound man from Newark under a tree by the side of the road for later collection by the militia. The injured driver was bleeding badly from his shoulder wound and urgently needed the attention of a surgeon. They placed him gently inside the coach where Doña Magdalena had done her best to try to staunch the flow of blood.

When the story of the attack rippled around the crowd gathered by the coach, they became indignant and vociferous in their disgust and horror. Frantic hands reached up to help out the injured driver.

Lavender climbed down stiffly from the vehicle and moved to the coach door. Both Mr and Mistress Fitch needed his help to dismount; the elderly man looked very frail. Mistress Finch had fainted at the first sound of gun fire, and each time the Spanish maid had brought her round with the smelling salts, the woman had rambled deliriously and fainted again. She sobbed with relief as Lavender helped her negotiate the steps down from the carriage.

Magdalena's gloved hand rested in his and he glanced up at her framed in the doorway of the coach. Her cloak was stained with the coachman's blood and wisps of black hair had escaped from their pins and hung limply around her pale face. Yet when her dark eyes met his, she smiled warmly and that spark of mutual understanding and attraction flashed between them again. He guided her down the steps to the safety of the courtyard and didn't release her hand.

'You saved us, Detective,' she said simply.

'I wish to dine with you tonight, Madam,' he blurted out, in perfect Spanish, 'preferably in a private dining room.'

She flinched slightly from the force of his demand and raised her eyebrows but her smile never wavered.

'Por supuesto,' she replied. 'The hero of the hour must have his reward.'

'And so should the woman who saved my life. I'll call at your chamber at nine and escort you to dinner.'

She laughed, then turned sharply and swept majestically across the shining, wet cobbles towards the inn door, trailing her maid behind her. She had not turned him down, he noted. He didn't know what was more surprising: his own unusual forcefulness or the fact that she had not slapped his face. His spirits rose and he began to look forward to a cosy tête-à-tête over a pot roast with the feisty Spanish señora.

'Detective Lavender?' It was George Clark, the landlord. His hand was outstretched in greeting. 'Thank the Lord you and your man were on board this carriage tonight! God only knows, what would have happened if you had not been there to help.'

Lavender shook his hand, exchanged a few words and passed on a request for the local militia to be summoned. Only then did he allow himself to be led into the warmth of the inn. He joined Woods in front of the blazing fire in a private parlour and stripped off his soaking coat and hat. These were whisked away by a maid for drying. Another servant pressed a glass of brandy into his hand.

He drank it off in one gulp. As the amber liquid burnt the back of his throat and the flames of the blazing fire licked his frozen skin with warmth, he stopped shivering and felt the numbness recede. The barmaid refilled his glass.

Lavender caught Wood's eye. He raised his glass in a silent toast to a job well done. Woods followed his lead. They had defeated the toby men and lived to tell the tale. The fiery liquid flashed like jewels as the two men chinked their glasses in mutual appreciation of what they had achieved.

'I were worried for a bit,' Woods confessed. 'Four of them on horse-back and only three of us left able to shoot a gun after the driver were winged. For a moment or two, I thought our days might be numbered.'

'Oh, we were never in any danger,' Lavender joked lightly. 'There were more than three of us with arms, tonight.'

Woods glanced at him quizzically. Lavender smiled and quietly told Woods how Magdalena had shot the highwayman at close range, when his own weapon had failed him.

Woods raised an eyebrow.

'My Gawd! I realised the Spanish filly had a bit of spirit and a fine leg - but I never thought she would turn out to be an accomplished markswoman. Where did she learn to shoot like that, I wonder?'

'I intend to find out tonight. I'm dining with her at nine.'

'I'd proceed with caution if I were you, sir - and disarm her first - the señora seems to have a fine temper to go with her excellent marksmanship. Check she doesn't have another pistol in her boots.'

Lavender drained his glass and smiled.

'As always, Ned, you're full of helpful advice about the ladies.'

He had asked for a bath to be drawn in his room and was anxious to climb into it and remove his sodden clothes, but there was something still niggling him.

'Have you ever heard of the name Magdalena Morales before? I feel I should know it.'

Woods shook his head. 'No – but I dare say, I'll never forget it now.'

They were prevented from any further conversation by the arrival of the local constable and the captain of the militia. Both seemed competent and listened gravely as Lavender and Woods recounted their version of events. The militia were instantly despatched to bring in the prisoner they had left in the forest and to collect the dead bodies. A surgeon had been sent for to treat the injured coachman; the man was expected to live.

Relieved that others had now taken responsibility for the situation, Lavender went for his bath then dressed with care in his finest breeches and frock coat. His cravat and shirt were crumpled from their journey in his trunk but he doubted Magdalena would worry about that. The clothes of all travellers – including hers, no doubt – were usually patterned with a complicated array of creases. He imagined in her own room, haranguing her maid to smooth her gown, pass her perfume and fasten her stays. Not too tightly, he hoped.

The maid greeted him at the bedchamber door and modestly averted her eyes. Both women had also bathed it seemed; he caught a glimpse of a tin bath of tepid water, still standing in a corner of the large room. The maid's skin was scorched pink like a lobster's. Magdalena glowed radiantly as he bowed over her hand. She smiled, took his proffered arm and let him lead her downstairs to the back parlour which had been set aside for them.

The maid trailed silently behind them. Magdalena sent her to alert the tavern staff that they awaited their supper and Lavender asked the girl to bring back a bottle of the tavern's best Madeira.

As the door closed, he allowed his eyes to feast once more on the flawless beauty of the woman who had saved his life. The deep golden skin of her arms and throat reflected back the hues of the blazing wood of the fire. She was in the prime of her life; probably about thirty years old, with a body and features unblemished by disease or child-bearing. She had abandoned the sombre mantilla she had worn at supper yesterday. Now her hair was held in place by a tortoiseshell peineta. Her damson velvet gown was heavily embroidered and decorated with seed pearls; it flowed out luxuriously from her small waist over her plentiful hips.

'Señora, buenas noches,' he greeted her. 'I trust you've not suffered any lasting effects from our ordeal earlier today?'

'I confess I'm still a little shaken, Detective,' she replied, in English, 'and, sadly missing one pair of stockings.'

He remembered her faded and slightly frayed day clothes and wondered how straightened her circumstances were.

'A small price to pay for such a satisfactory outcome, I hope?'

One of her black eyebrows arched.

'I assume you're not a married man, Detective? Or if you are, then Mistress Lavender has failed to inform you of the high cost of silk stockings these days.'

He smiled.

'I'm not married. The kind of life I lead – the job I hold – means that it's virtually impossible to meet and court a good woman. I'm whisked away to all corners of the country at a moment's notice and am frequently out of London for unreasonably long periods of time. The gals tend to forget who I am by the time I come back.'

She laughed, led him to two stiff backed-chairs around at the mahogany table which dominated the cramped, low-beamed dining room and gestured for him to sit. She wore only two rings on her elegant hands, he noticed: a small garnet encrusted gold ring – and her wedding band.

'I must congratulate you on your English, Señora. You speak it better than most natives.'

'Likewise I must congratulate you on your Spanish. I had no idea until tonight you were fluent in my language. If I had known this before I may have been more guarded in my conversation with my maid while we were travelling.'

'No. You ladies were right: Constable Woods does snore loudly.'

She laughed again and he felt them both relax. The parlour was shabbily furnished with a couple of indifferent oil paintings in grimy frames on the white plaster walls. But the drapes were drawn across the leaded casement windows, and the cheerful blaze and crackle of the fire in the grate, along with the golden gleam from beeswax candles lent the room a charming intimacy.

'How long have you lived in England, Señora? I would guess several years.'

'Then you would be wrong for once, Detective. We only arrived this spring. I had an English governess for a while as a young girl. My father, God rest his soul, was a firm believer in the education of his daughters and fortunately, I was the kind of child who paid attention to her studies.' Her grammar and pronunciation really were excellent. Only her accent gave away her origins.

'Your esteemed father also taught you to shoot, I suppose?'

She smiled, ignored the question and turned the conversation back onto him.

'But what about you? How do you speak my language so well, sir?'

'I'm self-taught – but I've been several times to Spain in a professional capacity. Hopefully, these experiences took the edge off my appalling accent.'

'Indeed – your accent is good. You would pass for a native.'

There was a short pause. She put her head onto one side and eyed him curiously. The movement caused her embroidered, black satin girdle to fall away slightly at her breast. It allowed him a tantalising glimpse of her ample cleavage. He just hoped there was not another layer of stays to remove beneath that girdle.

'These trips to Spain - in your work for the British Home Department - they're top secret, of course?'

'Of course.'

'And should you ever forget yourself - and reveal the details to me - then you would have to kill me?'

'Of course.'

As she laughed, he noticed how the coils of shining black hair piled on her head were still wet from her bath. They gleamed in the firelight.

'You're very secretive, Detective, and you're very good at lying. There was no one more surprised than me when you announced you were officers with the Bow Street magistrates' court. I had completely believed your story that you and Constable Woods were grain merchants.'

'Oh, I think our light-fingered travelling companion from Newark, may have been more startled.'

A shadow crossed over her face at the memory. 'I hate to think of him - touching me - while I was asleep. What will happen to him? Will he hang?'

'He is a sly cove. Unfortunately, I think he will deny any knowledge of the highway robbery – or the villains who tried to rob us. Unless the magistrate can find any evidence to connect him to the highwaymen, he may not be charged with any crime. After all, he didn't actually steal any money from you.'

'Yes, of course, you saved me from robbery…Stephen.'

The use of his first name encouraged him. Their eyes met across the table and held. An hour ago, in his bath, he had finally remembered how he knew her name and had worked out who she was. He had vowed to himself to keep his distance - but he cursed silently as he realised that he was struggling to remain objective. He could not remember the last time he had enjoyed the company of such an attractive, intelligent woman. Her self-assurance was unusual for a woman, a Catholic and an immigrant, but it only served to make her more desirable in his eyes.

The door opened and the supper arrived along with the Madeira and the maid. He poured them both a generous measure of the wine then glanced over at the servant who had seated herself, self-consciously, in a corner of the room with her plate of food.

Magdalena intercepted his frown and smiled.

'You didn't really expect a woman in my position to dine with you alone, did you, Stephen? My reputation is about all I have left in this world, and in the absence of a duenna, my maid has to suffice.' Her voice was gentle, almost pleading with him to understand.

'Naturally, I'm disappointed, Magdalena – I wouldn't be a man if I wasn't. However, this can only add to my already considerable respect for you. You're without a doubt the most fascinating and resourceful woman I've ever met and I feel privileged to be able to get to know you better. After all it's not every day I meet a woman who secretes a pistol in her petticoats.'

She smiled at the compliment, ignored his last remark and changed the subject as she picked up her cutlery.

'Perhaps as we eat our lamb cutlets, you can tell me more about your forthcoming business in Northumberland. Or is that a state secret, too?'

'No. Not at all – it's a very worrying case.' He told her the few details in his possession about the mysterious disappearance of Helen Carnaby and became more and more animated as he talked; his work, his cases – the mysteries he solved – these were his passion.

'The poor girl,' Magdalena said. The soft candlelight emphasised the concern etched across her face, the sadness in the deep pools of her dark eyes. 'Do you suppose she has come to some harm?'

'I hope not – well not bodily harm, anyway. I just hope that it's a simple case of a silly young girl eloping with the man she loves.'

He enjoyed discussing the case with her. He imagined what it might be like to come home every night to supper with a beautiful, sympathetic woman with whom he could intelligently analyse his cases.

'Her reputation will be in ruins, of course – unless the fellah actually marries her.' He wiped a drop of gravy from his chin with his napkin.

'I see you're quite a pragmatic man, Stephen.' Her violet-black eyes now smouldered with amusement. Was she laughing at him?

'Absolutely. I'm not a romantic fool who believes a girl can vanish like a puff of smoke from a locked bedchamber. There has to be – will be – a logical explanation.'

'Ah, so you don't believe in supernatural spirits that can whisk away young women from their beds?'

'No, Magdalena, I don't.'

'Then your clients are very lucky. I've no doubt you'll solve the mystery very quickly.'

He felt very relaxed.

'Perhaps you'll write to me at my cousin's in Gainsborough and let me know how the case is resolved? I would be most interested. I'll write down the address.'

She beckoned to her maid and instructed her to pass paper, ink and a quill from a nearby writing desk.

'Certainly. In fact, I may be able to call on you on my way back to London and tell you the outcome in person. If that is permitted, of course - and your cousin will not object.'

She gave an unladylike snort of derision. The Madeira was helping them both to shed their inhibitions.

'My cousin is extremely elderly, deaf and forgetful,' she said. 'I don't think she will even notice your presence in her rambling house.' Her maid brought over another candle as she wrote down the address of her cousin. He watched her elegant fingers deftly wield the quill.

When she passed the parchment to him their hands touched briefly and he felt a spasm of excitement ripple through them both.

Damn that bloody maid. He leaned back in his chair and regarded her closely.

'Won't that be boring for you? Living with a deaf old woman out in the country side?'

'Yes, but unfortunately, I don't have any choice at the moment - except to accept her invitation.'

He slid the address into the pocket of his waistcoat and waited for her to explain her last statement. She didn't.

'Magdalena, I need to thank you for saving my life. What you did was both brave and selfless. I'm now forever in your debt.'

'It was - how you say it? Instinctive? I could see you didn't have time to reload your pistol. Besides which – you saved all of our lives today – and our money.' She flashed him a brilliant smile across the table but then it faded and she looked worried. 'Of course, I may now burn in hell forever because I killed a man…'

'You'll not go to hell for defending yourself – or for saving my scrawny neck by shooting a toby man,' he reassured her firmly.

She looked relieved and smiled again. 'I shall discuss this with my confessor.'

'I'm confident he will agree.'

They paused. He could see that she appreciated his assurance. It was time to ask the questions which burned at the back of his mind.

'I need to know why you carry a loaded pistol about your person.'

'Is it a crime in England, for a woman alone to protect herself? You've a dangerous country, Stephen.' Her smile had dropped slightly.

'But you're not *a woman alone*, are you, Magdalena?' he said slowly, conscious that he was about to shatter the charming image she had woven about herself. 'You've a husband and protector. I believe his name is Don Antonio Garcia de Aviles.'

She slammed down her cutlery onto the table. Shock and disappointment flashed across her face. Their flirtation was over.

'You know him?'

'No. But I've heard of him. I had also heard that his wife, Doña Morales del Castillo, had escaped to England. I rarely forget a name but I didn't make the connection between the two of you until about an hour ago. I believe De Aviles works undercover in your native country for General Sir Arthur Wellesley. I understand your husband has been an invaluable source of information in our fight against the French oppressors.'

'You're very well informed about his work.' Her voice had turned to ice. She rose suddenly and strode across the rug towards the fireplace. He remained still and calm but he knew he had destroyed her trust in him.

'So you think him as *husband and protector?* You think I'm not alone?' Her grammar began to slip. Her accent thickened.

'I don't know what to think. Why don't you tell me?'

She remained silent, glaring down into the flames. The contours of her curvaceous back were rigid in anger.

'Was he cruel to you, Magdalena?'

'Cruel?' Her voice rose sharply. 'No. Not by the way of Los ingleses, perhaps. But yes - I think he is cruel. What man would leave his wife and child to the French pigs? *Los cerdos franceses!'*

Child. He wasn't expecting that. Where was her child? He rose and joined her by the fire. He wanted to reach out and hold her but decided against it. She was angry and distressed. He had made a mistake mentioning her husband.

'When I escape here, he abandons us and sends me no money - and no words – for nearly three months!'

'Magdalena, what happened?'

She shook her head. She seemed close to tears and struggled to calm herself. He could have kicked himself for launching into an inquisition but the man in him was battling with jealousy; he needed to know the truth about her absent husband.

'No. Not now. Tonight I enjoy myself. Tonight I forget, dress up and dine with a man. Tonight I wanted to feel like a woman again.'

He paused, unsure what to do next. If that damned maid had not been in the room he would have taken her in his arms, comforted her and made her feel like a woman. Yet too many unanswered questions still hung in the air between them and she had made it plain she didn't want to talk about her husband or her life in Spain anymore.

To press her further would be churlish – the act of a detective – not the act of a friend and admirer.

'Listen to me, Magdalena. I can see I've distressed you.'

She began to protest but he silenced her.

'I'm going to leave you now but I want you to remember that I offer you my friendship. You saved my life today and I owe you a great debt. I sincerely hope you'll always regard me as a friend and a protector while you're alone in England. I am forever at your service, madam.'

With that, he bowed low over her hand and withdrew towards the door. She stared affectionately – and not a little ruefully, he thought - as he backed away. For a moment, he thought she would call him back – but she didn't.

When he opened the door, he turned and spoke quietly over his shoulder: 'I meant what I said about you being the most fascinating and resourceful woman I've ever met...'

The maid's eyes widened in surprise. Magdalena flushed.

'…I also think you're the most beautiful woman I've ever seen, Magdalena. Goodnight.'

He heard her gasp as he closed the door.

You are a bleeding idiot, he told himself as he stomped back up the stairs to his bedchamber and sank wearily into his bed. You could have had her. All you had to do was insist the maid was sent away and she would have been yours. Lonely, abandoned and desperate, she would have succumbed quickly to his advances. What was all that talk of wanting to be like a *woman* again? Wasn't that an invitation? Images of Magdalena's naked body, moaning and writhing in his arms filled his head. He turned over angrily, the frustration burned in his stirring manhood.

Yet, deep down he knew he had done the right thing. Magdalena was no tavern wench and the spectre of her absent and unexplained husband and child made things complicated. He was well aware that most of tonight's banter had only skirted across the surface of the truth. She had been a gracious and charming companion, indulging in a little flirtation with a stranger with whom she travelled. Earlier today, he had felt a kindred spirit with her as she played her part in foiling the highway robbery, yet still he felt he barely knew her.

Something bothered him. His instincts, which were rarely wrong, told him there was something unnatural about a lady who was so self-possessed and calm after she had just killed a man. Even her talk of burning in hell had been light-hearted for someone raised in Catholicism. Many women might have pulled the trigger of that pistol out of fear, panic and desperation, but most of them would have collapsed in hysterics afterwards, when they realised the enormity of what they had done. Magdalena had barely raised an eyebrow.

There was only one chilling explanation for her cool reaction; Doña Magdalena Morales had killed before.

CHAPTER FIVE

Four weeks earlier…

'Get doon from that ruddy window seat and give us a hand with this food!'

'But I want to see the snow!'

'Ye'll see plenty of ruddy snow in the winter,' the cook snapped. 'Snow in October! Who'd a thought it?'

Anna sighed and took one last miserable look through the patch she had cleared in the condensation of the window pane. Outside, the twilight sky was like gun metal behind the skeletal trees of the woods. Snow had been falling steadily since lunchtime. The foliage and outhouses were muted into a two-tone scene of soft white and dove-grey. In the distance the horizon and sky merged into one.

The snowflakes' merry waltz contrasted sharply with Anna's mood; on her side of the glass things were far from happy. For a start, Mistress Norris was in a foul temper, and Anna had also realised that a heavy snowfall might make it difficult for her to go and see her mother during her afternoon off. This meant another week trapped at Linn Hagh with the furious cook behind her and the feuding family upstairs. Mistress Norris said it would not settle for long in October; she hoped so.

Master George had invited some of his cronies round to dine and stay for the evening – an event which always flustered the cook. Anna knew from experience that the port would flow like a river, the house would become a choking fog of tobacco smoke, and their drunken carousing and gambling would continue into the early hours of the morning.

Miss Helen had already announced her intention to keep to her room that night – she claimed she felt unwell - and asked Mistress Norris to send up her evening meal on a tray. Miss Isobel, on the other hand, was thrown into a frenzy of excitement and had spent a long time in the kitchen fussing about crockery, table linen and the seasoning of the food. She had worked the agitated cook up into a foul temper with her interference.

'She's like a bitch in heat whenever Master George invites his friends to stay,' the older woman complained after Miss Isobel had finally left the kitchen to dress for dinner. 'Not that it will do her any good – she's got no money and nowt going fer her in the way of looks or character. Who'd want to marry that sour puss?'

Another copper saucepan crashed down onto the kitchen table. Anna climbed off the window seat which was hewn into the three foot thick walls of the tower, and hurried over to whip up the cream, anchovies and mace for the sauce. The master had ordered three courses for tonight and it looked delicious. A large silver platter of oysters sat in the centre of the table, surrounded by broiled chicken and guinea fowl. Syllabubs and a towering strawberry blancmange were already prepared for pudding.

'I just wonder where they get the money fer all this,' Anna observed. 'One minute they're telling us they don't have a farthing and cut back on the housekeeping; the next minute we're eating like lords.'

Mistress Norris shrugged. 'I reckon Master George has probably come lucky at the card tables at last.'

She nodded her grey head in the direction of Miss Helen's tray of food. Her dinner was already spooned out onto the china plates along with a napkin, silver cutlery and a cruet set.

'I coulda done without her fussing like this tonight, but I don't blame the lass fer keeping out the way. Tek it up to her, Anna – while the food's still hot.'

Anna smoothed her apron and carefully picked up the silver tray. She had to climb up two flights of narrow, stone steps to Miss Helen's room. The staircase ran up the side of the pele tower between two thick stone walls – one of them the outer wall of the building. A few lanterns hung from metal hooks, their candles flickered petulantly in the draught. Halfway up was a small landing and the entrance to the Great Hall. Anna paused quietly to readjust the balance of the tray.

The wooden door to the Great Hall hung partially open. Here the passageway was cold but she could feel the heat emanating from the log fires in the hall. The sound of slurred male voices and the chink of brandy glasses also drifted out onto the landing. She shivered and slid past the doorway unobserved.

Miss Helen's room was on the top floor of the tower, opposite the bedchamber where Anna slept with Mistress Norris. It was colder, smaller and more spartan than the three family bedrooms that led off the Great Hall on the floor below, but Miss Helen had made it pretty with knick knacks, lacy mats and paintings. She never complained about sleeping upstairs with the servants.

Miss Helen smiled when she took in the food but Anna thought she looked paler than usual in the glimmering candle light.

'Put the tray down there and leave it,' Miss Helen said. 'I'll eat it in a while.'

'You'll have te keep yer strength up, Miss. It looks like we're in fer a harsh winter this year.'

'Yes, the snow has taken us all by surprise. I can't remember it coming this early before.'

Anna smiled. 'You've lived down south too long, Miss, if you don't mind me saying. We've often had snow up here at the back end of October.'

'Whitby is hardly 'down south,' Anna.'

'Well it's a lot further south than *I'm* ever likely to go.'

'Who knows?' Miss Helen smiled. 'When I'm a rich lady next year and you're my lady's maid – who knows how far we shall travel?'

Anna beamed. This was the dream that kept her going and helped her get up at six every morning in this miserable house with a smile on her face. This was the dream she shared with Miss Helen. How many times had they sat here in this very room and planned their departure from Linn Hagh? For the last few months, Miss Helen had been secretly instructing her in the finer arts of hair curling, cosmetic powders and taking care of the beautiful clothes that hung unused in her wardrobe.

She glanced longingly at the closed doors of the cupboard and imagined the soft peacock blue velvet and shimmering coral silks which lay inside. Miss Helen had not touched these dresses since her mother died and she went into mourning, but Anna had been allowed to take them out, smooth out the creases and brush off the dust. Miss Helen had also been happy to let Anna continue to practise styling her soft, silky blonde hair.

'Will you bring me another scuttle of coal, before you start to serve dinner to my brother and his guests?'

Anna broke away from her reverie and glanced down at the blazing fire in the hearth. It was already quite warm in the room.

'I feel very cold tonight,' Miss Helen informed her. 'It must be the snow.'

Suddenly, Anna felt uneasy. Her dreams of escape vanished like the flame of a snuffed candle and she snapped back to the reality of her unpleasant role in the middle of the two feuding sisters.

'Miss Isobel is quite determined that you're only to be allowed one scuttle of coal a day.'

'Just for once, Anna – I'm not feeling too well. Don't tell her, please?'

'Alright – but eat your food. It'll mek you feel warmer.' Miss Helen skipped far too many meals in Anna's opinion. Yes, she knew that ladies of fashion liked to look after their figures but the growing number of untouched meals she had retrieved from Miss Helen's room recently had begun to alarm her. No wonder her favourite mistress looked thin, strained and pale.

'I can always rely on you, can't I, Anna?' the other woman said. Her voice sounded odd, almost pleading and she looked strange, desperate. For a minute Anna paused, then dismissed this fancy of her imagination. Miss Helen was just thanking her for the extra coal. That was all.

Anna just had time to deliver the fuel to the top floor and wash her hands before she started to serve the dinner. She lost count of how many times she ran up and down those stairs with platters of steaming food and jugs of rich, buttery sauces. It didn't help that twice she had to pull Master Matthew away from the main door as she ran back down the stairs. He opened the door and stood staring blankly out at the falling snow.

'Sort him out, Anna,' screamed the cook from the kitchen. 'The daft bugger's letting all the heat out!'

The master seemed very content and sprawled back in his chair, laughing crudely. Miss Isobel simpered coyly at the other end of the table and made sheep's eyes at some large bloated man with bushy whiskers. She wore one of the dresses which had belonged to Miss Helen's dead mother. Anna sighed. There would be hell to pay when Miss Helen found out about this tomorrow.

Their conversation made Anna blush.

'Damn shame your 'Ellen could not join us for dinner,' one of the guests slurred to Master George.

'Oh, never mind her,' said the bloated man with bushy whiskers. 'Young Izzie, here is enough of a woman for both of us.'

Miss Isobel dissolved into girlish giggles. Her sharp-featured face was flushed with the rich food and wine.

Finally, the pudding dishes were cleared away and the port decanter set upon the table. Exhausted and starving, Anna joined the cook, Master Matthew and the male servant, Peter, at the kitchen table for their own supper. Now the dinner was over, the cook had regained her good humour. She had saved them all a small portion of the chicken and guinea fowl which the guests had consumed upstairs.

'We'll hev a bit of that blancmange, as well,' she said, as she winked at Anna. 'No doubt we'll be back onto rabbit stew and scrags of mutton by tomorrow.'

Just after nine o'clock they dampened down the kitchen range and blew out all but one of the candles. For the last time that night, Anna's weary legs trudged up the staircase as she followed the cook to their room at the top of the tower. The laughter in the Great Hall became raucous and unnerving; she heard the constant clatter of dice being hurled across a board. The solitary candle they were allowed cast demonic shadows onto the soot-blackened stone walls around her. With a great sense of relief, she and Mistress Norris finally reached the safety of their room.

As they went through the door, there was a clang of metal from the other side of the corridor. The iron bar on the back of Miss Helen's door had been dropped into its staples.

'She's got the right idea, tonight,' the cook said. 'Tek the candle, lass, and I'll slam down the bar. We don't want any of them loose fish from downstairs thinking they can come up here and fiddle in our drawers, while we're asleep.'

'Will Miss Isobel be alright, do you think?'

The older woman snorted. 'I think that old tabby will be revelling in it. I doubt she'll bar her door. Mark my words – one of them cork-brains will end up making a cake of himself tonight.'

Anna was too exhausted to ask for an explanation. She collapsed into her bed and fell asleep in seconds.

There was ice on the inside of their window when they woke in the morning and the snow outside stood several inches deep against the walls of the tower.

'Don't worry, lass,' Mistress Norris consoled, as they warmed themselves at the great range in the kitchen. 'It won't last. It'll thaw in a couple of days – it's only October. Ye'll still be able to see yer ma on Saturday.'

Anna busied herself. She lit the fires and cleared up the mess left over from the previous night's drinking bout. The cook prepared kedgeree and bacon for the Master and Mistress and the guests. They didn't emerge from their chambers until nearly ten o'clock. They were all hung over. Master George was as bad-tempered as a bull with sunstroke. Only then, did Anna and Mistress Norris notice that Miss Helen had not appeared for breakfast. This was unusual because she was an early riser.

‘Maybe she’s suffering from one of her heads,’ the cook suggested. Sometimes Miss Helen would spend whole days lying in a darkened room. ‘Here – tek a bowl of porridge up to her room.’

There was no reply when Anna knocked on the bedchamber door. She turned the handle but the door was still barred from the inside.

‘I’ll leave yer breakfast out here, Miss, in case you want a bite to eat later,’ she called out.

As she descended the stairs, Miss Isobel caught her on the landing outside the Great Hall.

‘Don’t tell me that lazy chit of a sister of mine, has asked for more meals to be delivered to her room? Who does she think she is? The Duchess of Devonshire?’

‘She didn’t ask for food, Miss,’ Anna explained quickly. ‘I haven’t seen her all day. I think she may have one of her headaches again. She didn’t reply when I knocked on her door.’

‘Typical! We’ve a house full of guests and she behaves in this way. It’s the height of rudeness. It was bad enough she refused to join us last night. Heaven knows what Emmerson and Ingram think of this churlishness. Wait till my brother hears about this – she needs some manners whipped into her.’

‘Wait till my brother hears about what?’

Anna’s heart sank as Master George emerged from the Great Hall and joined them on the landing. His eyes were bloodshot in his ruddy face, his breath stank and his forehead was creased into a frown.

‘It’s our Helen,’ his sister replied. ‘She’s refusing to come out of her room.’

‘Is she, by God?’ Damn the disobedient wench! She needs reminding who’s master here.’

He turned and thundered up the stone steps, two at a time. Terrified, Anna sank back against the stone wall. Her legs had gone weak.

Master George hammered on the door to Miss Helen’s chamber.

‘Get yourself out here, now!’ he roared. His voice echoed down the stairwell. There was silence. He renewed his banging on the door. ‘Don’t you defy me, you bloody minx!’

‘What’s amiss?’

Roused from their lethargy by the shouting, the two guests now joined Miss Isobel at the entrance to the Great Hall. Silently, Anna slid down a few steps to make room for them on the landing. She was dismayed to see the brandy glasses clutched in their hairy hands; the day's drinking had already started.

Miss Isobel began to explain, but they were interrupted by Master George clattering back down the staircase.

'You!' he yelled at Anna. 'Fetch Peter up here with the axe. 'Isobel, get me the whip. I'll thrash the insolent bitch within an inch of her life!'

Horrified, Anna fled back downstairs to the kitchen. Peter, the manservant, was already on his feet in the kitchen. Master George's shouting had raised the whole house.

Her voice breaking with sobs of fear, Anna relayed the message. Peter turned pale as he went to fetch the axe; his expression was grim.

Upstairs, Miss Isobel was explaining to the guests what had happened. Anna could hear her excited voice as she dramatised the whole event.

'Good fer you, George,' one of the guests slurred. His voice was heavy with cruelty. 'No damned doxy should be able to defy a man in his own house.'

'It's a while, since I've seen a good whipping,' the other commented. 'Mind you don't mark her pretty flesh too much though, George – steer clear of the face.'

Anna put her hands over her ears to try and block out the sound of the lascivious laughter which followed. Mistress Norris came over and put her arms around the terrified girl.

'Come away,' she said, her own voice breaking with emotion. 'There's nothing you can do to stop it – ye'll only get a good thrashing yerself if you try to interfere.'

But Anna couldn't tear herself away. Peter returned with the axe and trudged heavily up the stairs. Anna pulled herself away from the arms of the cook and followed. The Carnabys and their guests crowded onto the top landing. They shouted angrily for Miss Helen to come out and hammered on the door.

As the terrified maid neared the top of the building, she heard the sound of the axe being swung into the heavy oak door, again and again. Her legs nearly gave way beneath her when it stopped. She heard Master George reach inside, lift up the iron bar and hurl it clanging onto the stone flags of the bedchamber. The door was forced open. She waited for the sound of Miss Helen's screams.

None came.

Dimly, she heard Master George swear in surprise. Then silence. The wardrobe doors were forced open then slammed shut.

One of the guests burst into laughter:

'The damned bitch has done a runner!'

The next second, Master George and Peter raced down the stairs. Anna flattened herself against the wall as they tore past.

'Search outside!' Carnaby yelled. 'Search all the outbuildings - the chit can't have gone far in this weather.'

Miss Isobel appeared at the top of the stairs.

'George!' she called out.

He stopped abruptly and stared back.

'The room was barred – barred from the *inside.'*

Her brother paused but failed to understand. Fuddled with drink and anger, he leapt down the stairs two at a time and disappeared into the kitchen below. Miss Isobel and the guests followed him downstairs. Her starched skirts swished past Anna, cutting the air like glass.

Left alone at the top of the hall, Anna moved nervously towards Miss Helen's room. She sidestepped the shattered wood and splinters in the open doorway and entered the bedchamber.

The coal embers still glowed in the hearth and the tray of food lay on the dressing table, untouched. The room was empty. Miss Helen had gone.

CHAPTER SIX

Friday 19th November, 1809

The coach finally arrived in Bellingham just after nine o'clock. Their tavern, The Rose and Crown, was an ancient Elizabethan coaching inn with exposed stone walls and a rabbit warren of smoky, tap rooms on the ground floor. A flight of narrow wooden stairs led up to their room and both men had to stoop beneath the low-beamed ceiling of their bedchamber. The room stank of damp, but close inspection of the sagging mattresses revealed they were dry and free from fleas and bugs. As the porter dumped their trunks on the uneven wooden floor, Lavender breathed a sigh of relief. Despite the limitations of their new accommodation, at least they wouldn't have to climb onto a bone-rattling stage coach again for a few weeks, and he would be able to give his aching limbs a chance to recover.

They went down to dine in the main room of the tavern, where a motley collection of local farmers eyed the two Londoners suspiciously. They ignored them and concentrated on the food, which they were relieved to discover was both plentiful and passable. Woods was soon ordering a second helping. Lavender read a copy of *The Newcastle Courant* while he waited for his own food to digest.

Despite the lateness of the hour, he had sent a message with a potboy over to the residence of Mr Armstrong, their new client, announcing their arrival.

'I don't suppose he will want to see us tonight,' he told Woods, 'I get the impression he is quite elderly.'

He was right. A message came back from a Miss Katherine Armstrong that her father had already retired for the night, but Mr Armstrong would be pleased to receive them at his home on the High Street at 9 o'clock sharp the next day.

'That's settled then.' Woods said, clearly relieved. He beckoned a serving girl over to their table and helped himself to a third helping of the mutton stew. 'At least we'll be able to get a good night's sleep and start fresh in the morning.'

'Yes.' Lavender replied, more sharply than he had intended. 'And in the meantime poor Helen Carnaby faces another night of God-knows-what, while we sleep comfortably in our beds.'

Woods paused guiltily with his spoon halfway to his mouth.

'D'ya reckon there's something we can do tonight?'

Lavender smiled grimly and shook his head. The dreary travelling, the incident with the highwaymen and his unresolved encounter with Magdalena, had affected his mood. None of this was the fault of his cheerful constable.

'Other than setting off into the freezing pitch-black night, and searching this unfamiliar and treacherous countryside for a body? No, my friend. There is nothing we can do at the moment. See here.'

He laid *The Newcastle Courant*, on the table in front of Woods.

'This is last Saturday's paper.'

Woods examined it closely. The first entry in the *Hue & Cry* section was an offer of a reward for the safe return of Helen Carnaby.

> ***'One Hundred Pounds Reward.***
> *Whereas, Miss Helen Carnaby, the sister of Mr George Carnaby of Linn Hagh, Bellingham, in the County of Northumberland, was during the night of Thursday the 21st day of October removed from her home at Linn Hagh, Bellingham by persons unknown. Whoever therefore will, after this notice, provide information to safely reunite Miss Carnaby with her grieving family, and apprehend the offender or offenders, so as he, she, or they may be brought to conviction, shall be paid a Reward of ONE HUNDRED POUNDS upon his, her or their conviction, by applying to Mr George Carnaby, Linn Hagh, Bellingham.'*

'Good grief,' Woods said. 'The poor gal has been missing for nearly a month.'

'Yes,' Lavender said. 'We should have been summoned to this crime weeks ago - before the trail went cold.'

'D'you think she was kidnapped and taken for ransom? You said she's wealthy.'

'If the girl has been kidnapped and there is no ransom note, then her chances of survival are indeed very slim. The perpetrators of the crime will have disposed of her by now.'

Woods grimaced.

'However, if no corpse has been found,' Lavender continued. 'Then there is still hope that we are not looking at a murder. One thing is for sure though, if a young woman who has not reached her majority disappears with a man – whether voluntarily or involuntarily – then he could face a series of charges brought by her family. At the conclusion of this case, it's highly likely that someone will be transported.'

He sat back and realised that the smoky warmth of the inn, the good food and the prospect of a challenging new case had started to lift his spirits. This was what he needed to get Magdalena out of his mind: hard work.

When they entered Mr Armstrong's substantial house on Bellingham High Street the next day, they were shown into a front parlour cluttered with brightly-upholstered and mismatched furniture, ornaments and children's toys. Despite the clutter the house was comfortable, the furnishings in excellent condition. A good indication of the financial stability of this family, Lavender thought.

'Hello, young fellah,' Woods said, as a small boy suddenly popped up from behind the sewing boxes, books and cushions piled on a sofa.

The child, probably no more than three, stuck out his tongue, dashed out from his hiding place, veered past the clothing and blankets that littered the wooden floor, and clattered past them into the hallway. Another crowd of noisy young lads raced down the stairs, whooping at the top of their voices. They quickly disappeared into the back of the house. Two young girls leaned over the banister above the stairs and giggled at them as the maid took them across the hallway into Armstrong's study.

'Do shut the door firmly on your way out, Parker.' Armstrong's tone was plaintive as he instructed the maid. The old, white-haired man seated in front of the fire sighed deeply when the door finally clicked shut. Lavender could understand why. The young lads had returned to the hallway with reinforcements and wooden swords. They appeared to be enacting one of General Wellesley's victories.

'Damn those French dogs!'

'To Vimeiro!' they screamed in unison.

Peace eventually descended into the room and Lavender could hear the steady tick of the French clock on the mantelpiece.

'Thank goodness for that.' The elderly man was wrapped in plaid blankets. He held out a gnarled, arthritic hand towards Lavender. 'Their father is with Colonel Taylor in the 20th regiment of Light

Dragoons. A re-enactment of the Battle of Vimeiro is a daily occurrence in this house.'

'It was splendid victory,' Lavender said, smiling. 'No wonder your grandsons are proud of their father.' He shook Armstrong's hand and introduced him to Woods. Next he handed over a sheaf of papers from Magistrate Read in Bow Street.

Armstrong's hands shook slightly as he held up his monocle to read the invoice in his lap. Lavender knew that their client had run a successful legal practice for many years. Despite his obvious frailty, the old man's eyes were sharp as they scanned the invoice. 'Everything seems to be in order.' Armstrong's voice had lost its whine and become steady and authoritative. 'I'm glad you're finally here.'

'I'm sorry for the delay, sir,' Lavender said. 'I was detained on important Home Department business in Nottinghamshire.'

'Never mind, at least you've made it here. Let's just hope you can bring this case to a speedy resolution – and a happy one. Please take a seat.'

Lavender sat down in the armchair opposite Mr Armstrong. Woods pulled up another chair and sat behind him.

'Perhaps you would like to tell us how far the local constables have progressed with investigating Miss Carnaby's disappearance?'

'They haven't,' Armstrong's tone was sharp. 'The local constables have not discovered anything. No one knows what happened to my niece, or where she is.'

'Surely someone must have seen or heard something unusual on the night of her disappearance – or in the following days.'

'Not that we've discovered. My family and I are all very distressed – and bewildered by these events – as are the constables who have already investigated the case.'

'Can we start from the beginning, sir? What exactly happened at Linn Hagh on the night of the 21st October?'

The elderly man sighed as if he was weary of retelling the story.

'I'm sure George and Isobel Carnaby will be able to tell you the details better than I, when you visit Linn Hagh. However, I understand there was a dinner party; a couple of guests stayed for the evening. Helen had excused herself and retired to her room. The servants heard her bar the door just after nine. The next morning, when Helen didn't appear, her brother – fearing his sister may have taken ill – broke down the chamber door. The room was completely empty.'

'Was the window closed?'

'Her bedchamber is at the top of the tower. When you see Linn Hagh you'll understand why no one would consider escaping from the window. Her bed was still made as if she had not slept in it and a tray of food from the night before lay untouched on the table.'

'Uh-oh,' the noise which escaped from Woods' gaping mouth was involuntary, but audible enough to be heard by the sharp ears of the old man.

'Yes, exactly, a very strange state of affairs. I trust you're not a superstitious man, Constable? I'll be very disappointed if you report to me in a few days' time that my great-niece has been spirited away by the fairies.'

'Of course not, sir,' Woods reassured him. 'There's bound to be a simple explanation.'

'We shall make it one of first priorities to establish how Miss Carnaby managed to leave her room with the door barred,' Lavender said, quickly. 'It will be a significant step in establishing if she left the room voluntarily - or was forced.'

'Good. None of the addled-brained constables around here have managed to explain this mystery. Unfortunately, because of the unusual nature of Helen's disappearance, there has been a resurgence of old superstitions and folktales in the town. It's a small, tight-knit community, Detective, with a high rate of illiteracy and a lax approach to church attendance. The situation is not helped by the unpopular presence of a band of faws in the neighbourhood.'

'Faws?'

'Gypsies. A travelling band of tinkers. Baxter Carnaby – Helen's father – had always been far too indulgent with them and allowed them to camp on his land. There have been mutterings of witchcraft in the town since Helen's disappearance – linking it to one of the gypsy women.'

'Has their camp been searched?'

'Yes. This was one of the first things the local constable arranged. His men came away with nothing – except the curses of the faws ringing in their ears.'

'What other steps did the local constables take to track down your niece?'

'I've arranged for the local man, Constable Beddows, to call on us at 10 o'clock. He will escort you to Linn Hagh and furnish you with further details of his enquiry.'

The door opened and a middle-aged woman came into the room. Round-faced and plump with a kind smile, wisps of curly, grey hair escaped over her forehead below her lace cap.

Lavender and Woods rose hastily to their feet.

'Detective Lavender, Constable Woods – may I present my eldest daughter, Miss Katherine Armstrong? Katherine runs the house for me since my dear wife died.'

Lavender bowed over Miss Armstrong's hand. She smiled, nodded courteously to Woods and then moved over to her father and straightened his blanket.

'Please excuse me, gentlemen, I've just come to check that Papa is not tiring himself too much.'

'Don't fuss, Katherine,' her father whined. She ignored his protests and poured out a measure of dark red medicine from one of the bottles on the rosewood table beside his chair. He took the drink, swallowed it back in one and grimaced at the bitter taste. His daughter sank gracefully onto a padded stool next to her father's chair. Lavender instantly felt that she was a pleasant and likeable woman.

'Helen's disappearance has been so distressing for him.'

'I'm sure it must have been very upsetting for everyone,' Lavender observed. 'You seem a close family. How was Miss Carnaby related to you all?'

'Helen's grandfather was my older brother, Thomas Armstrong. She is my great-niece. You may have heard of Thomas? While I happily settled for a steady career in law, my brother was a shrewd business man and an entrepreneur. He made a fortune from various enterprises.'

Inwardly, Lavender congratulated himself. It was important to him that he was always thoroughly prepared for every case and he usually carried out meticulous research on his clients before he met them. The good citizens of Northumberland would be amazed at how many parchment documents containing their details were now being held and filed down in the dusty offices of the burgeoning British Home Department in London.

'Was your brother, Thomas Armstrong, of the Newcastle shipbuilding yard of the same name?' he enquired.

Armstrong looked impressed.

'Yes! He had successful interests in several shipping lines and coal mining ventures. He amassed a fortune. Sadly, his son and heir died in infancy, which left him with only one child – a daughter named Esther. Helen's fortune comes down the maternal line – from her mother and my brother.'

'This George Carnaby you mentioned – is he your great-nephew?'

'Heavens, no. They share the same father but had different mothers. George Carnaby is nothing to do with the Armstrong inheritance; he is Helen's half-brother. I've a copy of my own brother's will, Detective - if you think it would help with your investigation?'

'Yes, thank you, it would be helpful but I'll pick it up another time,' Lavender said.

'Esther was my cousin,' Miss Katherine told him, as she rearranged her father's blankets. 'We were very close as girls and we've always been very fond of her only child, Helen.'

'Yes, Esther was a lovely woman,' Mr Armstrong looked sad. 'Unfortunately, she died earlier this year, in February.'

'That was why Helen came home from school in Whitby,' Miss Katherine explained. 'She came to nurse her mother in her final few weeks.'

'School? Exactly how old is Miss Carnaby?' Lavender started with alarm. Had he missed something here?

'She is twenty years old. When she finished her education, Helen stayed on as a pupil teacher for a while. She only returned to Northumberland in February when her mother became seriously ill.'

Ah, a pupil teacher. That explained it. For one awful minute he thought he had misread the information and he was looking at child abduction.

'Several of my sisters have sent their daughters to the same school,' Miss Armstrong volunteered. 'I understand Helen was well-liked and very popular with the pupils.'

Lavender nodded and glanced at the clock. It was nearly ten o'clock.

'Before we leave you to set off for Linn Hagh, I need to ask you if you have a likeness of Miss Carnaby.'

'Yes, we've a small portrait of her.' Miss Armstrong rose to her slippered feet and padded over to the great mahogany desk which stood by the window. She removed an oval-shaped frame from one of the deep drawers.

Woods leaned forward and both men stared at the portrait in Lavender's hand. A very pretty, fair-haired woman smiled back at them. Her skin was luminous and her vivid blue eyes gleamed with warmth.

'She is beautiful,' Lavender said. 'Were either of you – or any of your family – aware if she had any admirers? A beau, perhaps?'

Mr. Armstrong shook his head. 'We've been through this several times with the Constable Beddows. As far as we know, Helen was not romantically attached to any young man. She was greatly distressed after her mother's death and has just quietly lived at Linn Hagh since then.'

Lavender nodded again but a new thought struck him and his forehead creased into a frown. 'Why did Miss Carnaby need to work? I understood she was quite wealthy. Surely she didn't need the money?'

The two Armstrongs stiffened and glanced quickly at each other across the stuffy room. 'I believe Helen wanted to teach at the school,' Miss Katherine said carefully. 'She enjoyed it and liked the independence she gained from having her own income.'

'She doesn't come into her inheritance until her twenty-first birthday at the beginning of January,' Armstrong added. 'Until then, she is still financially dependent on her half-brother, George Carnaby.'

Lavender had the curious impression that these answers had been rehearsed – or at least discussed beforehand. The Armstrongs delivered those lines with the wooden amateurism of the set of actors he had recently had the misfortune to watch at Vaux-hall gardens. Betsy Woods had dragged both him and Ned along to the play. Woods had nodded off in his seat and started to snore loudly. Lavender's hand moved instinctively to rub the spot on his arm where Betsy had battered her husband with her fan.

Lavender noted this slight change in the demeanour and tone of the Armstrongs, but he didn't comment. His face remained inscrutable, his voice neutral.

'Exactly how much is Helen Carnaby due to inherit in January?'

'My brother's fortune is invested for her. It amounts to around £10,000.'

An involuntary whistle escaped from Constable Woods' lips.

CHAPTER SEVEN

'What's that?' Woods asked in surprise. 'A castle?'

They had rounded a bend on the lonely road from Bellingham and caught their first glimpse of Linn Hagh. Woods reined in his horse and paused to admire the towering, cresselated, stone rectangle which reached up into the brooding sky.

'It's a pele tower,' Lavender drew up beside him. 'An ancient family home, common in these border regions. It's fortified, of course.'

'How's that work, then?'

'The walls will be three feet thick and the roof is made of stone. The building was impregnable even to fire. You see the bigger windows of the first and second floors? That's where the family lived. Animals would have been stored in the building on the ground floor and there would have been no staircase in those days – just a wooden ladder up to a trapdoor in the floor above, which would have been hastily pulled up if they were under attack.'

'Seems like a lot of trouble to go to.'

'It was necessary. This area was completely lawless until the union of the nation under James I. Before that, roving bands of reivers – from both sides of the border – pillaged and stole at will. Even royalty was nervous about travelling around here.'

'Aye,' their escort, Constable Beddows, agreed. 'Rough lot around these here parts.'

Lavender and Woods didn't reply. Their relationship with Constable Beddows had not got off to a good start when he had turned up at Mr Armstrong's house with horses for the London officers.

'That's a right pair of queer prancers you expect us to ride!' Woods had exclaimed in disgust as he ran his hand down the quivering, bony flank of the smaller nag.

'Constable Woods is the finest horseman in the Bow Street Horse Patrol.' Lavender told Beddows. He had trouble hiding his smile.

'Is he now?' Beddows shuffled uncomfortably and his eyes would not meet Lavender's. 'I see our northern horses are not good enough fer you southerners.'

‘I’ve seen northern horses,’ snapped Woods. ‘On our last case up here we ran into the Duke of Northumberland himself - and he had a right set of gallopers on his carriage. Don’t tell me you can’t get decent horse flesh in this part of Britain.’

Beddows thin mouth had gaped open at the mention of the Duke of Northumberland. Then it slammed shut.

They conducted most of their slow journey to Linn Hagh in silence. Both constables were sulking: Beddows was smarting from the criticism he had received from Woods and Woods was fuming from the perceived insult of being given a couple of inferior horses.

However, the sight of Linn Hagh seemed to have roused Beddows back to his purpose.

‘It was snowing on the night of her disappearance,’ he announced. ‘All footprints had been completely covered.’

‘What effort did you employ to try and find Miss Carnaby?’ Lavender asked.

‘Well, George Carnaby and his guests searched the outbuildings of Linn Hagh and the surrounding area on the morning of her disappearance.’ He pointed at the single storey buildings just visible behind the pele tower. ‘Later, us constables undertook a lengthy search of these here woods. We gave her description to the local toll gate keepers and the landlords of the coaching inns. Everyone was questioned to see if they remembered the lass passing through on the night of the 21st or the morning of the 22nd. But damn me, she has disappeared without a bloody trace.’

‘And this Saturday you posted a reward notice for her, in the *Hue & Cry* of the local newspaper?’

Constable Beddows bristled with pride.

‘Aye, that were my idea. I had a rum job persuading George Carnaby to pay fer it at first, but eventually he agreed.’

They rode up an overgrown, meandering path through meadows, where a few scattered sheep bleated mournfully. As they drew closer to the hall, they could see the dead moss clinging to the side of the stone building. Rusty farm equipment lay scattered around the entrance amongst the weeds. Window frames were rotten and warped. The whole place looked neglected and reeked of decay.

‘I can see someone’s got a fire blazing in the forest, over yonder,’ Woods commented.

The other two men paused and glanced to their right. A thin spiral of black smoke swirled and disappeared into the leaden sky above the tree tops.

Constable Beddows spat onto the ground.

'It'll be them damned faws.'

'Ah, the famous gypsies,' Lavender said. 'So that's where they camp. I think we'll have to pay them a visit at some point, Woods.'

'Ye'll not find owt,' Beddows informed them, sharply. 'We've already searched their camp.'

'Is there another way to Bellingham, besides the road?' Lavender asked.

'Aye, there's a path through the woods but it ain't no good fer horses. Damned woods are full of beggars and faws.'

'Oh?'

'Bellingham is a market town, Detective. Every week we're swamped with beggars come to tap the crowds. They doss in the woods on a night. There are caves along the side of the gorge.'

To enter Linn Hagh they had to climb a narrow flight of worn sandstone steps to a studded, oak door. Grains of silica glistened in the sandstone staircase and the weathered walls around them. The frail wooden banister swayed dangerously beneath their grasp. Lavender hammered on the door with his cane, then used it to point upwards to a lip of stone above their heads. He turned to his Constable.

'That is where they poured out faeces and boiling water onto anyone trying to break their way in.'

'Charming,' said Woods.

They were greeted by an elderly serving woman, with frizzy grey hair and a scowl. She wiped her hands on her dirty apron and informed them that everyone was out except the master. She let them into a small, paved vestibule and swayed arthritically up the stairs to announce their arrival.

Lavender noted that only one room led off from the vestibule - a large, gloomy kitchen.

Eventually, the woman returned and told them that the master would see them now.

'Thank you, my good woman,' Woods said with a charming grin.

The cook seemed taken aback at his politeness. Lavender smiled to himself as they mounted the staircase. It was Wood's job to ingratiate himself with the servants whenever they investigated a crime. His constable had made a start.

George Carnaby sprawled inelegantly across a faded armchair in front of the huge stone fireplace which dominated the backroom of the Great Hall. A large grey cat sat purring in his lap. He was a plain man with a tanned, rugged face and close-set brown eyes. His unkempt, dark hair was rapidly greying and loosely tied back with a black ribbon. His slack mouth drooped at the corners. He didn't get up to greet them when they entered the room.

'I had no idea you would be calling today. Armstrong told me he had employed Bow Street runners of course, but he had not let me know you had arrived. You could have let me know, Beddows,' he snapped at the constable.

The local man flushed and shuffled uncomfortably beneath Carnaby's glare.

'Shall I fetch tea for yer guests?' the serving woman asked.

'That won't be necessary, thank you,' Lavender said. 'I would prefer to get straight on with the investigation.'

The elderly servant hovered for a moment, as if she preferred to get her instructions from Carnaby. But he remained silent, so she bobbed a curtsey and disappeared back down the stairwell.

Carnaby indicated that the officers were to join him around the fire but he didn't offer them a seat. They stood and waited patiently while he groped in the pocket of his waistcoat for a silver snuff box.

'What do you want to know? No doubt Armstrong and my man Beddows have filled you in on the details of the night of the 21st.'

My man, Beddows? Lavender frowned.

While Carnaby took his snuff, Lavender allowed himself a quick glance around. The vaulted wooden ceiling which towered over their heads was crumbling with woodworm. He could just make out the grimy rectangles on the bare stone walls were tapestries and oil paintings had once hung. This family was selling off their heirlooms. He smelt mould beneath the wood smoke.

'Mr Armstrong and Constable Beddows have already given me their version of events but perhaps you can tell me in your own words what happened?'

'Nothing new to add, really. We rose late that day, and when we realised no-one had seen my sister, I went to find out what had happened to her. She'd not been well the previous day, so naturally I was concerned. She'd barred her door, and when we couldn't rouse her – I broke it down. But she'd gone – like a bloody spirit in the night. We've been searching high and low for the damned gal ever since.'

He scowled, took another pinch of snuff then wiped his nose with the back of his shirt sleeve. Lavender recognised the rich and expensive aroma of Macouba.

'What do you think happened to Miss Carnaby?'

'Damned if I know. That's your job to find out, ain't it, Lavender? The bloody minx has probably run off somewhere just to give us all the trouble of looking for her. '

'Were you aware if she had a lover or an admirer?'

Carnaby flushed and a muscle twitched in his neck. 'If there is one and he's part of this, I'll thrash the bastard within an inch of his life when I catch him. She's been under my protection since our father died, and I'll have no bloody fortune-hunters seducing my baby sister.'

'We've found no evidence of a man in her life,' Beddows soothed. 'I'm sure that our reward advert in the *Hue & Cry* will bring forward some information – with or without the help of these London detectives.' His voice was high pitched. Lavender could not tell whether it was with nerves or affectation.

'It might have been better if you'd included a full description of Miss Carnaby in the advert,' Lavender observed, wryly. 'Fair hair, blue eyes, five foot two inches tall – or something like that – so the readers of *The Newcastle Courant* would recognise her if they saw her.'

A stunned silence descended into the room and Lavender could see Carnaby's neck begin to twitch again.

'You bloody sap-head, Beddows,' he growled. 'You made me pay for an advert – and didn't write the damned thing properly?'

'How was I to know?' Beddows began to bluster beneath the glowering fury of the owner of Linn Hagh. 'I've never dealt with a case of a missing lass before.'

'You're an addled-brained idiot, Beddows! If you fell in a barrel of women's dugs you'd climb out sucking your thumb.'

Lavender had seen and heard enough.

'Can you point us in the direction of Miss Carnaby's room?'

The master of Linn Hagh threw a final contemptuous glance in the direction of the local constable and then rose to his feet.

'I'll take you,' he said. 'I won't have any bugger wandering around Linn Hagh on their own.'

'I'll get back to the horses.' Beddows sniffed and left.

The door of Helen Carnaby's room was a mess. The upper half had been completely smashed away by Carnaby's axe. The bottom half was spiked with light-coloured jagged shards where the blade had sliced through the age-blackened wood and revealed the natural patina beneath. Someone had made a half-hearted attempt to sweep up the mess, but splinters still crunched beneath their boots.

Lavender pointed at the door on the other side of the dark corridor.

'What room is that?'

'It's where the female servants sleep. We've two of them. The cook - you've met her - and a maid. '

Lavender followed Carnaby and Woods into the bedchamber, closed what remained of the door and began to examine it. Behind him, he heard Woods slide up the sash window.

Two iron staples were screwed into the rough stones on either of the door and another two staples were widely spaced on the back of the door. These were needed to hold the weight of the heavy metal bar which was designed to lie along them. The iron bar leant against the wall. Lavender picked it up and tested its weight. Next, he lowered it down onto the four staples. He noted its snug fit against the wood. The door would never have yielded an inch once the bar was dropped in place, although, it clearly did not stand up to a determined man with an axe.

'The last line of defence,' he said.

'Eh?' Carnaby growled. His eyes flitted coldly between the two officers.

'Oh, I was explaining to Constable Woods earlier about how pele towers were designed to protect families from the border reivers. See here, Woods? If raiders has breached the pele tower and were storming through the building, the family could bar themselves into one of these rooms in a last desperate attempt to save themselves from rape and murder.'

'Charming,' Woods said.

'Very interesting, Detective,' Carnaby yawned. 'But how did my sister get out of this room when it was barred from the inside?'

Lavender lifted the bar off the staples, dropped one end onto the floor and ran his hand across the flaking, rusty surface. His fingers caught against a globule of candle wax. He scratched it off with his nail and pocketed it discreetly.

'I've no idea at the moment, Mr Carnaby. I'll have to give it some thought.'

'Was anything missing when you checked the room after your sister's disappearance?' Woods asked.

'Only her cloak and hand muff,' Carnaby said.

'Nothing stolen?'

'No. Not that we could see.'

'So she didn't wander outside in the freezing snow in her nightgown,' Lavender said, with some satisfaction in his voice.

'No, the maid who sorted her clothes said that her nightgown was still here and Helen had disappeared in the same dress she had been wearing the day before.'

'Which suggests she never undressed for bed on the night of the 21st.' Lavender dropped down onto his haunches and began to scan the dusty floorboards. He gently shifted piles of sawdust and splinters with his fingers. He felt Carnaby's dull eyes bore into his back. He leant forward onto his knees and began to inch his way towards the iron bed frame, sifting patiently through the debris on the floor.

'And whatever happened,' he called back over his shoulder. 'Miss Carnaby – or who ever took her – remembered to take warm clothes for when she left the hall.'

'Might not have done her any good,' Carnaby observed, dispassionately. 'It was a foul night and snowed heavily. No late night coaches run from Bellingham. Cloak or no cloak, unless she got inside somewhere quickly she'll have bloody perished.'

'Where's the maid servant now?' Woods asked.

'She's on her half-day but she'll be back soon. Both servants heard my sister put down the bar on the door just after nine that night.'

'And no-one else saw or heard anything?'

'No.'

'Has this room been cleaned since Miss Carnaby's disappearance?'

'She was expected to clean her own room. The servants had enough to do without running after her.'

'What kind of a young woman is Miss Carnaby?' Woods asked.

Lavender appreciated the distraction his constable was causing. Carnaby was clearly irritated with the questions and his attention was now directed entirely at Woods.

'We hadn't seen much of her for the last ten years, while she's been away at school. She came back to nurse her mother while she was dying.'

'How would you describe Miss Helen's character?'

'She's a spoilt piece,' Carnaby snapped. 'She always wanted extra coal for her fire - or different food from the rest of us. She ran the servants ragged with her demands and drove Izzie to distraction.'

'Izzie? Is this your other sister, Miss Isobel Carnaby?'

'Aye, that's right. Izzie runs Linn Hagh for me. Helen was the baby of the family and the only child of my father's second marriage. My father and his silly wife doted on her, spoilt her - and that school she went to filled her head with fancy ideas.'

Lavender lifted the trailing bedcover and moved to inspect beneath the bed. There, next to the cracked chamber pot, he finally found what he was looking for – the stub end of a candle. He pocketed it stealthily, slid back out and stood up.

'Where is Miss Isobel Carnaby now?' he asked.

'She's also in Bellingham at the Saturday market. She'll be back before dark if you want to talk to her. Sometimes she comes back with the maid.'

'No. We'll probably call back here next week and talk to her then. We'd better get back to Bellingham now.'

'Send word if you plan to come here again,' Carnaby growled.

Lavender brushed the filth and the sawdust from his coat and breeches. 'Constable Woods tells me that those horses Beddows provided are a poor show, and at least one of them is likely to die beneath us on the way back to town. I'd like us to be able to walk back before dark falls if that happens. I understand the woods around here are riddled with robbing gypsies and beggars?'

Carnaby shrugged. 'My father was soft. He should have burnt those bloody faws off his land a long time ago.'

'Mmm, that is what everyone keeps saying. But he didn't; your father let them stay – and so have you,' Lavender observed. 'I wonder why?'

Alarm flashed in Carnaby's eyes.

'Don't you want to see the rest of the Linn Hagh?' he asked, hurriedly. 'Save you the trouble of coming up here again.'

'Not today.' Lavender smiled. 'Today I've seen and heard enough.'

CHAPTER EIGHT

Anna was halfway back to Linn Hagh when she saw the three horsemen on the road ahead of her. In the failing light she couldn't make them out at first, but as she drew nearer she recognised the slight figure and untrimmed sideburns of Constable Beddows. He was talking to the dark-haired man riding beside him. This man wasn't listening to Beddows; he was watching Anna approach. She pulled her cloak tighter, stared straight ahead and quickened her pace.

'Miss Jones?' The man had a funny accent. She stopped and turned towards him. His features were mostly hidden beneath the shadow cast by his hat but he had a long, sharp nose.

'Miss Jones, I'm Detective Stephen Lavender from Bow Street in London. Mr Armstrong has employed me to try and find out what has happened to your mistress. I need to talk to you.'

Anna recoiled slightly. George Carnaby had threatened all the servants with dismissal if they talked to the authorities without either him or Miss Isobel present. Yes, she wanted to find out Miss Helen was safe, but as the miserable days since her disappearance had dragged on into weeks, Anna had become more and more reconciled to the fact that her favourite mistress had fled without her. All the dreams she had shared with Miss Helen had vanished into that snowy night, along with the only person who could help her escape from her wretched existence as a drudge at Linn Hagh. Anna's moods had swung between depression, anger and frantic concern for her former mistress.

The detective dismounted from his horse and turned to face her. He was dressed almost entirely in black from the sole of his mud-splattered boots to the tip of his hat. Only his spotless, white cravat broke up the severity of his attire. Above its whiteness, his skin looked pale in the poor light as it stretched tightly over his high cheek bones. A pair of sharp, brown eyes scrutinised her dispassionately. Constable Beddows remained on his horse but the other constable dismounted and moved to the side of the detective. Now two strange men were watching her closely.

'I need to hear in your words what happened on the night of the 21st October.'

Anna felt intimidated and stepped back away. Her foot slipped on the mud and she struggled to keep her balance. A large hand shot out and grabbed her arm.

'Easy there, lil' lady,' another foreign voice said. 'We don't want you falling.'

Her rescuer let go of her arm and he grinned at her. He had large round moon of a face.

'It's Anna, isn't it? Pretty name. One of my daughters is called Anna. I'm Constable Woods.'

He was a bigger man than the sour detective and broader, but he had a friendly smile.

'Can you tell us what happened, treacle?'

'The master says we're not to talk to anyone about it - except at Linn Hagh.'

There was a surprised pause. The two men regarded her closely. For a moment she thought the detective was going to shout at her. Then the constable laughed softly.

'So that's the way of it, is it? Well, don't worry, lil' lady, we won't make you go against the wishes of yer master. I tell you what, why don't you climb up onto my horse and I'll give you a ride back to Linn Hagh? I promise not to ask you *any* questions about Miss Carnaby's disappearance.'

Anna remained sullenly silent. As much as she hated her life at Linn Hagh, she and her mother needed the money from the job. But her eyes flicked curiously at the waiting animal. She'd never been on a horse before.

'My daughter – your namesake – she loves to ride on me horse. She's only small yet, and I lead it and walk beside her. I'll do the same for you.'

'Ye'll be safe enough, girl,' Constable Beddows snapped. 'Apparently, he's the best horseman in London.'

Anna nodded silently and allowed herself to be led towards the animal. She gasped as the constable suddenly grabbed hold of her waist and swung her up sideways into the saddle. He lifted her with ease and she grasped hold of the mane to steady herself as the beast snorted and took a step or two. The smell of wet leather and the strong odour of the horse surrounded her. The animal was warm beneath her skirts.

'This is how ladies ride,' Constable Woods said. 'You're a proper lady now, with a horse and a handsome escort back to Linn Hagh.'

Anna giggled. Constable Woods was not handsome. In fact, he was quite old. He had short-cropped grey hair beneath his hat and his teeth were a bit black but the grin that lit up his broad face made him look friendly. He pulled the reins over the head of the beast and pointed to where she could hold on.

'Ready?'

She nodded, then gasped again as they began to move off. She felt a long way from the ground and it took her a moment or two to get used to the swaying of the horse but she loved it. Woods turned the horse around and they slowly began to return to Linn Hagh. The detective and Constable Beddows continued their journey to Bellingham.

Constable Woods was chattering on about his daughter again.

'She's a natural on a horse – just like you – she's fearless and she's got the poise for it. I reckon she'll become a better rider than either of her elder brothers.'

As the animal plodded along, Anna asked him a few questions about his children which he answered enthusiastically. She was enjoying herself and marvelled at how strange everything looked from horseback; it was a completely different view. Within a few minutes he had her laughing when he told her about one of the scrapes his two lads had got themselves into. Next, he told her how their furious mother had grabbed the broom and whacked both of the rapscallions out of the house. Anna's face fell.

'What's the matter, treacle? My wife didn't hurt them really. Why so sad?'

'You remind me of my da. He died five years ago in the explosion in Mr Carnaby's mine. It used to be lively and fun like that in our cottage. When Da died, all the fun went out of the house. My brothers moved away to work in other mines and my ma has been unhappy ever since.'

'That's sad,' Woods said. 'It hurts when you lose someone you care about. Mr Armstrong has told us what a kind young woman Miss Carnaby is. I'm guessing you were sad when she disappeared?'

'Yes, it broke my heart. You and that scary Detective will find her won't you?'

'Course we will, darling. Can you tell me a bit about what she's like?'

'She's lovely to work for, kind, gentle and funny. She looked after her mother really well when she was dying. She wanted to take her mother away to the seaside in Whitby, to let the sea air help her get better, but there wasn't enough money. I think she hoped her ma would last out until she got her inheritance in January, but she didn't. Miss Helen was very sad after she died.'

'Did Miss Helen make any other plans for after her birthday - when she would come into her money?'

'Oh yes, we talked about it all the time,' Anna said brightly. 'She wanted to move back to Whitby – she liked it there.'

'And she was going to take you with her?'

'Yes, she wanted me to be her ladies' maid. Sometimes Miss Helen would ask me to come to her room and style her hair.' Her voice grew wistful as she remembered. 'She has a beautiful, tortoiseshell brush and a sparkling set of jewelled hair pins. I would try to copy the styles Miss Helen showed me in pictures from some old pamphlets. I were a bit awkward at first: I dropped the pins often and tied her hair up too loose because I were frightened I might hurt her. But I got better and was quite good at the end.'

'Did you help her with her dresses and clothes?'

'Oh yes, she has some wonderful gowns.'

'Did she not take any of them with her when she disappeared?'

'No. I used the laundry list to check everything carefully. I was very careful. She disappeared with only the clothes she was wearing that day. Nothing else was missing – except the old blue dress I knew she had given to the faw – but I didn't tell Miss Isobel about that.'

'Sorry?' Woods exclaimed. 'She gave an old dress to one of them gypsy women?'

Anna suddenly felt alarmed. Had she said too much?

'Yes, it was a *very* old dress – too small for Miss Helen. Should I have told Miss Isobel about it?'

'No, treacle, not at all – and don't worry I'll keep your secret. Was Miss Helen friendly with this gypsy girl then?'

'I've seen her talking to her a couple of times. Her name is Laurel Faa Geddes.'

'Wasn't Miss Carnaby nervous about roaming around these woods and fields on her own?'

'She didn't used to be. But she had got it into her head lately that someone were following her, intent on harming her.'

Sharply, Woods pulled up the horse to a standstill.

'Did she tell anyone?'

'Yes, her brother - but Master George said it was her imagination and she were being silly, but I know it was true – I heard this gadgie following us in the woods. He has a horrible laugh. I thought it best not to say anything to Constable Beddows, if the master didn't think it were important.'

They reached the bend at the bottom of the long drive which led up to Linn Hagh. Darkness was falling rapidly, but Anna knew that in a moment the pele tower would come into view and they would be visible from the house. Constable Woods realised it too.

'I'm going to have to leave you here to walk back to the hall on your own, Anna. Will you be alright?'

'Of course.'

His strong arms reached up and lifted her down. She felt sad; she'd enjoyed herself.

'Listen, treacle, that scary detective and I are going to find out what happened to Miss Helen - but we might need a bit of help from you.'

'Oh? He looks so serious.'

'He can be - but he's very good at his job. I need you to trust us both.'

'What do you want me to do?'

'First of all, if you hear or see anything which you think might be important, I want you to tell me, yes? Anything at all – no matter how small – just like you've done today. You can read and write, can't you?'

'Yes.'

'Well, leave me a note at The Rose and Crown in Bellingham if you can't find me. And I need you to search out the laundry list and go back through Miss Helen's wardrobe to double check everything is still there.'

Anna was confused, but she nodded in agreement.

'We'll be back up to Linn Hagh in a few days' time. Can you do that for me, treacle?'

'Yes.'

'Right now, take care of yourself and remember that if anyone has seen us together, you've done everything Mr Carnaby asked; you haven't told me a thing about the night Miss Helen disappeared. Do you understand?'

She nodded happily, waved good-bye and skipped off down the road and around the bend.

Woods swung himself up into the saddle and watched her disappear into the gloom, his mind going over the details he had gleaned. Helen Carnaby had turned out to be an enigma, he realised. Adored by her doting uncle, kind to her young servant and vagrants - yet scorned by her half-brother as a spoilt brat. She was also an intelligent young woman with a bright future who was plagued by irrational fears. Or were they irrational?

The old horse moved restlessly beneath him. He shivered slightly as a cold breeze moaned through the creaking timber of the ancient woodland. Night had fallen quickly as they had travelled back to hall. He could barely see the road in front of him. His own breath began to billow out before him in white clouds. The persistent drizzle had ceased and the temperature had plummeted. He was suddenly conscious of how remote the area was and the darkness and heavy silence of the woods which lined one side of the road.

A sharp crack in the forest made him reach for the highwayman's flintlock in his coat pocket. His horse whinnied nervously. He cocked the pistol and paused. Memories of the attack near Barnby Moor flooded back into his mind. Silence descended again.

'Sod this,' he muttered beneath his breath and turned the horse around. 'Time to see what you're made off, you old piper.'

Woods spurred the animal into a gallop and thundered back towards the warmth and safety of Bellingham.

CHAPTER NINE

Lavender made straight for the blazing fire in the tap room of The Rose and Crown and warmed his frozen hands. He called for a glass of brandy and began to remove his outer garments. He was staring thoughtfully into the flames when Mistress McMullen, the landlady, appeared at his side with the brandy and some startling news.

'Ye've got a lady visitor.'

For one brief dramatic moment he thought it was Magdalena.

Had she followed him here? Why? Was she in trouble?

He felt his rush of excitement fade to disappointment when the ample figure of Mistress McMullen stepped aside to reveal the equally rounded Katherine Armstrong standing behind her.

He flushed as he bowed and greeted her.

'Miss Armstrong! What a pleasant surprise. How can I be of assistance?'

His client's daughter regarded him quizzically through her warm, brown eyes.

'Good evening, Detective Lavender. I came to bring you this.'

She pulled out a bundle of stiff parchment from her hand muff and offered it to him. He recognised the seal of legal documents.

'It's the copy of Thomas Armstrong's will you asked for.'

Lavender suddenly became aware that the landlady was hovering. On top of that, the noisy dice game to his right had been suspended with the cup poised in mid-air. Most of the large group of drunken farmers at the far end of the tap room, now watched them curiously. When one of them let out a curse, his neighbour elbowed him in the ribs and told him to 'mind his language.'

'Do you have a private room where we could go?' Lavender asked the landlady.

Disappointed at being excluded, Mistress McMullen mumbled that a fire had been lit earlier in one of the private parlours and she led them to it.

'Evening, Miss Armstrong.'

Several of the farmers nodded respectfully as the small, stout, middle-aged woman glided past their table.

Katherine Armstrong was well wrapped up against the cold in a purple, fur-trimmed pelisse over her brown dress. She wore stout boots and a domed velvet bonnet which matched her coat. Her funny-shaped hat, decorated with artificial berries, reminded Lavender of a plum pudding. This was a good image for her, he decided: rich, full of goodness, traditional and probably only remembered by her family on Christmas day.

They moved to the barely-warm dining room at the back of the inn. Lavender recovered his wits and shoved Magdalena out of his mind. They sat down in the chairs by fireplace where a few red embers still glowed in the grate. The landlady poured half a scuttle of coal on the fire and then left them in peace. Katherine Armstrong declined the offer of refreshments.

'This is most kind of you to deliver the will personally, Miss Armstrong,' Lavender said. 'However, I would be remiss in my duty to your father if I didn't point out that your reputation may suffer if you're seen entering a public house without a chaperone.'

Her kind eyes twinkled with mischief and amusement and the lined corners of her mouth turned up in a smile.

'At my age, Detective, I would be most grateful if a whiff of scandal would attach itself to my name. I fear I've been far too good and far too boring for the last forty years.'

Lavender smiled and took the dry, parchment from her hand. He undid the tapes which bound it and spread the thin pages out on his knee.

'It's rather complicated,' she informed him as she peeled off her gloves. 'My uncle's assets were vast. I thought it might help if I stayed to explain it.'

'Thank you. Fortunately, I've had some legal training. I studied to become a barrister at Lincoln's Inn.'

Katherine Armstrong's face registered surprise.

'But you never practised as a lawyer?'

He put down the documents in his hand, his face serious.

'That was my father's dream for me, Miss Armstrong. Not mine. My ambition had always been to become a policeman, like him. My father worked for thirty years for the magistrates at Bow Street – he knew both the Fielding brothers well. I'm fascinated by the law – but I wanted a more active occupation.'

'Do you regret the choice you made?'

'Not at all.' He smiled. 'I think my current role is far more stimulating than that of a legal barrister.' His mind flashed back to the attempted robbery of the stage coach at Barnby Moor. 'In fact, sometimes the responsibilities of being a police officer are a little *too* exciting. I do regret though, any pain my decision may have caused my father.'

She nodded, and then smiled.

'I'm sure he is very proud of you. After all, you've paid him a *huge* compliment, following in his footsteps.'

He had long since realised that women were the more curious of the two sexes. They were never happy until they had determined someone's pedigree and 'placed' them in society. Perhaps now she would be more open about the Carnabys.

He turned his attention to the documents before him. By the time he had finished reading a frown creased his forehead.

'I confess that I don't understand, Miss Armstrong. What happened to your Uncle Thomas' fortune when he died? Why didn't his daughter, Esther Carnaby, inherit it? Why was she passed over in favour of *her* daughter, Helen?'

'This is why I thought it might be useful if I stayed and explained,' she said. 'My Uncle Thomas was unhappy when Esther married Baxter Carnaby.'

'He was Helen Carnaby's father?'

'Yes. Baxter Carnaby was a decent man, of course - popular and well-liked in the local community.'

'But?'

'But he had made an unfortunate first marriage.'

'How so?'

For a moment Miss Armstrong struggled to find the right words. Her hands fidgeted in her lap. Clearly some dark family secret lay behind her torment. When the words came, they came out in a rush. Her voice hardened.

'His first wife – Martha - was a mad woman.'

'A mad woman?'

'She was hysterical, an insomniac - and prone to violent fits and rages. Baxter had no choice but to send her to an asylum for the last years of her life. She became a danger to all around her – including herself and her own children. Poor Baxter had a terrible time with her in the years before he had her committed.'

'These children would be Miss Helen's half-brother and sister, George and Isobel Carnaby?'

'Yes – and the other one – the lunatic, Matthew.'

'There's *another* brother?'

'Yes, he's a simpleton – backwards.' Her voice had softened a little with compassion. 'Matthew's a harmless fellow but the Carnabys keep him out of sight. I'm not surprised you didn't come across him on your visit there today.'

'No. We saw no-one of that description. Tell me, is he dangerous at all?'

'Heavens no! A softer, gentler, young man you could not hope to meet. Matthew has the mind of a child – and cannot speak, nor write as far as I know. Baxter had a string of nursemaid's for him when he was younger but I don't think he ever went as far as to employ a governess for his son. Matthew was very young when his mother was committed to the asylum. Tell me, Detective, do you believe that madness is inherited?'

A little taken aback, Lavender paused for a second before he replied.

'No. I don't believe it is. I've seen plenty of evidence to the contrary.'

Miss Armstrong nodded thoughtfully.

'My father believes it is, but I'm not convinced.'

'Anyway, you asked about my uncle's fortune. Following Esther's marriage to Baxter Carnaby and Helen's birth, he visited my father at his legal chambers and remade his will. He was not happy about the thought of Baxter Carnaby – or his elder children - inheriting his money. He settled the whole lot on his only grandchild, Helen. Baxter and Esther could have the interest on his investments but the full amount of £10,000 was to be given to Helen when she came of age - or when she married - whichever came soonest.'

'Were Helen's parents happy with this financial arrangement?'

'They seemed to be. Baxter Carnaby wasn't a fortune hunter - he was genuinely in love with Esther. At the time, his own interests - his coal mine, and so forth - were doing quite well. Baxter and Esther received the interest on my uncle's investments, which amounted to about four hundred pounds a year, to supplement their own income.'

'What happened to the Carnabys' income in the following years?'

'Unfortunately, Baxter's mine exploded shortly before his death and it had to be closed. His personal income plummeted after that. I believe Esther sold jewellery and other family heirlooms recently, to support the family at Linn Hagh.'

'Who gets the £400 a year now?' Lavender asked.

'George Carnaby - their eldest son.'

'It may be useful to see the will made by Baxter Carnaby himself.'

'Baxter used a lawyer in Newcastle – Mr Agar, I believe. He'll have a copy but I've never seen it myself – and I doubt my father has. He had retired from his practice at the time of Baxter Carnaby's death four years ago.'

Lavender paused and regarded the greying woman by his side with new respect. She was clearly a woman with a keen mind, humour and compassion.

He found himself comparing her with Magdalena. Katherine Armstrong had none of Magdalena's sensuous beauty, but the two women shared intelligence, humour and a clear disregard for propriety. He felt that Katherine Armstrong would probably like Magdalena if they ever met, and the thought warmed him towards the woman in front of him.

'Why do you need to see Baxter Carnaby's will, Detective?' she asked.

'Unfortunately, it's always necessary to know who has the most to gain in difficult circumstances like this. The Carnaby family finances are complicated. I take it that George Carnaby – her half-brother - would inherit Miss Helen's personal fortune, if anything unfortunate should happen to her?'

'Yes, he would.' She paused before asking: 'Do you think Helen's inheritance had something to do with her disappearance, Detective Lavender?'

'It's too early to say, Miss Armstrong,' he replied, gently. 'I only met George Carnaby briefly. What kind of a man is he?'

'Not very bright,' she said, sharply. 'George is genial enough in public but he has always been a bit shifty as far as I'm concerned. He lives the life of a country gentleman with his horses and his gambling, but he has never had the money to sustain that lifestyle. According to my own brothers, George can be a brute with his horses at the hunt. He pushes them to extremes and he'll lame a horse rather than miss out on being in at the kill.'

'So tell me again, Miss Armstrong, was Helen Carnaby happy at Linn Hagh?'

'No, she wasn't.' She sighed and fidgeted nervously with her gloves in her lap. 'I believe that was one of the reasons she decided to stay on at the school in Whitby.'

Ah, at last – the truth.

'Do you or your father have any reason to suspect that George Carnaby may have been involved in some way with his sister's disappearance?'

Lavender's question hung in the air for the moment. A flurry of grey curls bobbed around her face when she shook her head.

'No. He seemed as alarmed and shocked as the rest of us at the time. On top of this, I understand Constable Beddows has verified with the two guests who stayed with them at Linn Hagh on the night of her disappearance that Carnaby drank with them until the early hours of the morning. He had to be helped to bed. I'm not an expert in the drinking habits of men, Detective, but it seems unlikely to me, that a man who is that far gone in his cups could then orchestrate Helen's mysterious disappearance.'

Lavender nodded.

'I totally agree, Miss Armstrong,' he said. 'Their inebriation would have hindered them from staging her mysterious escape from Linn Hagh. I believe it to have been a very elaborate hoax.'

Her eyes lit up with hope.

'Have you some idea already how she got out of that locked bedchamber.'

He realised he had said too much.

'It's early days yet, Miss Armstrong, early days. Tell me, did Miss Helen have any close female friends of her own age in the neighbourhood?'

She watched him shrewdly for a moment before answering.

'Yes, one of my nieces, Cecily. She and Helen were at school together in Whitby. Cecily has been quite distraught about Helen's disappearance.'

'Would it be possible to speak to Miss Cecily?

'Yes, she will be at the house, tomorrow afternoon. We're having a little family gathering to celebrate Papa's birthday. Please call after lunch and I'll introduce her.'

She rose to leave. Lavender hurried to his feet.

'We shall be delighted to pay our respects to your father on the occasion of his birthday – and perhaps we'll have some news for him.'

'Cecily is now Mistress Nicholas Derwent,' Miss Katherine informed him while she fastened the top button of her pelisse. 'She married Captain Derwent of the Northumbrian Fusiliers about a month ago. They married just before Helen's disappearance. Cecily was most upset to return from her honeymoon and discover Helen had vanished.'

Her pleasant round face contorted with pain.

'I do believe that Cecily's wedding was the last time we saw Helen.'

CHAPTER TEN

Lavender walked Miss Armstrong back to her home, then returned to The Rose and Crown and made himself comfortable in a seat near the fire in the smoky tap room. He settled down to read while he waited for the return of his constable. However, he had trouble concentrating on the slim, leather-bound volume in his hands. Apart from the noisy game of dice to his right, he was also distracted by the mutterings of the large group of drunken farmers on his left. These hard-featured men had retired to the tavern after completing their business at Bellingham's Saturday market and seemed intent upon drinking the tavern dry. He had noticed several small flocks of forlorn sheep, penned up outside the inn in the dark and had commented on them to the landlady.

'Aye, they'll belong to Isaac Daly or Jethro Hamilton,' Mistress McMullen told him. 'They're good lads - regulars, like, here on a Saturday after market. Mind you, after a few ales they've bin known to tek home the wrong flock of ewes.'

That would explain the dogs, thought Lavender. The farmers' end of the taproom also contained half a dozen tired and hungry sheep dogs. They sprawled across the flagstones like a matted, black and white carpet and the whole tavern reeked of wet dog, the smell trapped beneath the low, beamed ceiling. Occasionally, a farmer would throw a scrap of food onto the floor, and a vicious fight would break out between the animals. A yell and a sharp kick from a hobnailed boot would end it; the curs would scurry, yelping, into a corner.

These distractions made reading impossible, so Lavender amused himself trying to identify 'Isaac' and 'Jethro' from the rest of the rowdy group. It didn't take him long. They all wore dirty, thick jackets, neck cloths and the collarless shirts of labouring men but each had distinguishing features. Isaac was the tallest of the group, lank-haired and thin-faced. The most powerfully-built amongst them was Jethro Hamilton. He had piercing blue eyes, several days' stubble on his strong jawline and the confident, deep voice of authority.

Suddenly, their boisterousness subsided, only to be replaced by dark mutterings about some group or other who were giving them problems. He heard the phrase 'thieving bastards.' He picked up his book, but he had barely read half a page before he was interrupted again.

'Hey – you. Detective gadgie from London.'

Lavender glanced up and found most of the farmers staring coldly in his direction.

'Yes, Mr Hamilton.'

The big farmer recoiled in shock.

'How d'you know my name?'

'I'm a detective, Mr Hamilton. It's my job to know things.'

The tavern erupted with laughter. 'The bugger's bin eavesdropping,' someone commented.

'Well never mind that,' Jethro said firmly once the laughter had subsided. 'Ye've bin looking fer that missin' lass from Linn Hagh, haven't you?'

'Yes.'

'Hev you found her yet?'

'No.'

'Give the gadgie a chance,' one of the older men said. 'They've only bin here a day.'

Jethro ignored him and pushed ahead to his point. 'Hev you searched that faw camp?'

Lavender put down his book.

'Constable Beddows has already searched the gypsy camp; Miss Carnaby is definitely not there.'

'Phaow,' Jethro sneered, 'Beddows couldna find a tup in a sty full of porkers.' The other men laughed in delight.

'You mark my words, Detective; one of them faws will have stolen that lass. The buggers steal owt else around here that's not nailed down.'

'Aye.' A murmur of agreement spread around his table. Faces glowered and the mood darkened.

It was at that point that his frozen and ruddy-faced constable returned. Woods slumped down on the settle opposite Lavender, called for a glass of ale and rubbed his ice-cold hands in front of the blazing fire.

'Since when was one of your daughters christened, 'Anna?'' Lavender chided him quietly. 'I've stood god-father to at least one of them, and I'll swear your girls are named Rachel and Tabitha.'

Woods grinned then gulped back his ale. He belched loudly and wiped away the froth from his mouth with the back of his sleeve. 'It were necessary to stretch the truth a bit to put the gal at ease,' he said. 'Since you always frighten the young gals.'

'I'm a detective,' Lavender said. 'I'm supposed to frighten people.'

'What's that fancy book you're reading?'

'It's *Candide* by Voltaire.'

'Spanish?'

'No, French actually.'

'Now *that's* frightening.'

'Anyway, what did you find out from young Anna Jones?'

Quietly, Woods related the details of his conversation with Anna to Lavender. He told him how Helen Carnaby had complained about being stalked through Hareshaw Woods.

'Anyway, I think we should put out a few feelers towards Whitby,' finished Woods. 'By the sound of it, Miss Carnaby is rather partial to the place – and that gypsy girl is definitely worth talking to.'

Lavender nodded. 'I'll ask Miss Armstrong for more details about that school she went to – and her friends in Whitby.' He told Woods about his earlier conversation with Katherine Armstrong.

'So have you worked out how the gal got out of that locked room, yet?'

Lavender smiled. 'I've got one or two theories. I just need a bit more evidence before I declare them. Tell me, Ned, what do you think of what we've learned about Helen Carnaby so far?'

Woods thought for a minute, took off his hat and undid the buttons on his greatcoat.

'She's obviously a clever young woman – they wouldn't have had her stay on at that school unless she was clever. This also suggests that she's not afraid of a bit of hard work.'

'Unlike her brother,' Lavender observed. 'I get the sense that George Carnaby is headed for ruin.'

'By the sound of it Helen Carnaby likes her feminine fripperies, dresses and hair pins, and such like.'

'And that's what's confusing me,' Lavender said. 'I'm not an expert in women's clothing or - as you keep pointing out to me – women in general. But I do find it hard to accept that a fashionable young woman would abandon all her clothes if she left her home voluntarily. The girl didn't even take her nightgown with her. Yet none of the evidence suggests that she was forced to leave by another. Even if she had been drugged, I hardly think anyone could have got her out of that building unnoticed – not if they were carrying an unconscious woman.'

‘It’s a long way from civilisation and it would have been difficult carrying bags of clothing – never mind an unconscious gal - in the snow,’ agreed Woods. ‘One thing’s for certain, she didn’t leave by the window or up the chimney. That second floor room in the tower is far too high for a ladder and the chimney is too narrow for even a nipper to climb.’

The two men fell silent for a while. Woods took of his coat and ran his fingers through his thick, damp and dishevelled hair. Lavender called over a barmaid and asked for their supper.

‘I think we may have been asking the wrong questions, Ned.’

‘What do you mean?’

‘All of this investigation has been focused on *how* did she get out of the locked bedchamber and *where* has she gone. I think we need to try to establish *why* she wanted to leave in the first place?’

‘What do you mean?’

‘Does it not strike you as strange that she has disappeared now, just weeks before her twenty-first birthday, when she was entitled to access her inheritance? In six weeks’ time, she will be an independent woman with ten thousand pounds, and could have walked out of Linn Hagh forever. Why go now - with nothing but the clothes on her back? Even if there was a lover waiting for her out there – which everyone seems to doubt – all he had to do was bide his time until January and then marry the girl. There would have been nothing that George Carnaby could have done to stop their marriage after she came of age – ‘baby sister’ or not.’

‘Do you suspect foul play?’

‘Possibly – but not from George Carnaby. Ignorant brute that he is - he seems as irritated and confused by her disappearance as the rest of us. But there is one thing I am sure about.’

‘What’s that?’

‘Helen Carnaby was scared of something.’

CHAPTER ELEVEN

Sunday, 21st November 1809

Lavender and Woods arrived at St. Cuthbert's church in Bellingham a good half an hour before the rest of the congregation. Lavender said he wanted to examine the graveyard before they joined in the service and he intended to watch the worshippers as they arrived.

St. Cuthbert's was only a couple of streets away from The Rose and Crown in a low-lying spot next to the River North Tyne. There had been a sharp frost overnight and the roads were treacherous with ice. The sky had cleared and weak northern sunlight smiled down on them as they slithered down the hill towards the small twelfth century church, which stood apart from any other building.

'Well, I'll be damned,' Woods exclaimed. 'Even the church's got a stone roof. Don't tell me that those bloody reivers used to burn down the church, as well?'

'Repeatedly.' Lavender smiled. 'And did you notice the strong buttresses alongside this one-storey building? They're to support the weight of the stone on the roof.'

The isolated graveyard went right up to the very edge of the silent river. Beneath their boots, the long grass of the churchyard, which had frozen into icy spikes, crunched like glass.

Edged with ice, the North Tyne River was black with peat, slow moving and deep. Barely a ripple shimmered across its surface. The trees on the opposite bank and a nearby stone bridge were perfectly mirrored in its glassy surface.

After a while, they began to search for the Carnaby graves. It didn't take them long to stumble across: *'Martha Carnaby, 1752 – 1784, beloved wife of Baxter Carnaby.'*

'It must have been hard to love a mad woman,' Woods commented.

Lavender bent down, reached out with his gloved hands and pulled away the tangled briars and weeds at the bottom of the gravestone. 'I see that Baxter Carnaby was buried with his first wife,' he said.

'Was he?'

'Yes, look here.' *'Also, Baxter Carnaby, 1749-1804, beloved husband of the above'*

'There's a lot of 'beloveds' in there.'

'Mmm,' Lavender agreed. 'Somebody was determined to make a point. I guess this is George Carnaby's doing. I doubt his grieving step-mother would have been happy with this arrangement.'

He paused for a moment and re-read the inscriptions. 'I see that Baxter Carnaby was a widower for four or five years before he remarried and had his last child, Helen, in January 1789.'

'Is that significant?' Woods asked.

'It might be. Most men I know who are left with no wife and three young, motherless children usually remarry quite quickly.'

'According to Mr Armstrong, the mad first wife was in an asylum for several years before her death. The poor bloke had probably just got used to the peace and quiet.'

'Yes, you may be right. Now, if Baxter Carnaby is here with his first wife, where is Esther Carnaby –the second wife – buried?'

It took them a while to find her. Esther was buried in a remote corner of the graveyard with a plain headstone which bore the simple words: *'Esther Carnaby, 1764- 1809.'* A small posy of wilting wild flowers lay across the grassy mound in front of the headstone. Lavender bent down and picked them up.

'Helleborus. How long have these been here, I wonder?' He stared at the dying flowers and frowned while he tried to remember how long they lasted after they were picked.

'A couple of days, perhaps?'

They didn't get chance to discuss the flowers further. The congregation started to arrive for the service. Lavender and Woods stood at a discreet distance and watched family after family drift through the low door of the ancient church. Both Isaac Daly and Jethro Hamilton had been transformed into respectability by the Sabbath. Sober, combed and besuited – if still a little bleary-eyed - both farmers were accompanied by their wives and a gaggle of lively young children.

The Carnabys arrived in a carriage with two other men. Poor Anna sat shivering beside the driver. Woods winked at her discreetly but she ignored him and looked away. George Carnaby climbed down first and hailed Lavender to join them.

'I didn't know they had a coach and four,' Woods commented.

'They don't. It must belong to one of the other men.'

'Lavender,' George Carnaby said abruptly. 'This is Mr Ralph Emmerson and Mr Lawrence Ingram. They were guests at Linn Hagh on the night of my sister's disappearance.'

Lavender made a short bow.

'Yes, it was a rum do, that,' the man called Emmerson commented. 'Quite the mystery.' He had thick bushy sideburns and a bristling ginger moustache. His wool waistcoat strained over his huge belly.

The other man, Ingram, helped a plain, dark-haired woman climb out of the carriage.

'Miss Isobel Carnaby, I assume?' Lavender bowed again. 'Pleased to meet you, ma'am.'

'Yes, that's Izzie,' Carnaby said.

The woman looked pleased with Lavender's manners but her dark eyes examined him shrewdly.

'George tells us you want to speak to us regarding the gal's disappearance,' Ingram said. He was thin with a poor complexion and lank, greasy hair. Flecks of dandruff spotted the shoulders of his expensively tailored coat.

Lavender nodded. 'When would be convenient, sir?'

'Ingram is staying over at Greycoates Hall with Emmerson at the moment. I'm riding over there tomorrow,' George Carnaby said. 'You can call on us all at 11 o'clock.'

'Certainly, sir.'

The Carnaby's party swept past him into the church. The corpulent Ralph Emmerson offered his arm to Isobel Carnaby. She simpered like a young girl while he escorted her inside the church.

The next family group to arrive were the Armstrongs. There were dozens of them. Lavender suspected that the entire family had turned up in Bellingham to celebrate Mr Armstrong's seventieth birthday. They swarmed up the path to the church chattering noisily. Two middle-aged men - clearly his sons – helped the frail Mr Armstrong along the icy flagstones.

A gloved female hand tapped Lavender lightly on his arm with a prayer book. Sharp-eyed Katherine Armstrong had spotted them at the edge of the crowd.

'Don't forget you promised Papa that you would call on us after dinner,' she reminded him.

He bowed again.

When Woods and Lavender finally entered the heaving church, they managed to find a seat right at the back amongst the poorer members of the congregation. But despite the squash, Lavender still had a good view of the family pews ahead, which contained the Carnabys and the Armstrongs.

The service began with a desultory hymn accompanied by three screeching fiddle players and a breathless man on a harmonica.

Lavender grimaced as the congregation and musicians massacred the music, but he distracted himself by scanning the faces and backs of the rest of the congregation. Beside him, Woods belted out the hymn in a rich deep baritone that bounced off the vaulted roof and white plastered walls of the church. He was surprisingly tuneful. Only the wealthy, literate church-goers at the front had hymn books. Most of the people around Lavender and Woods just shuffled or chatted during the song, although several were clearly mesmerised by the singing policeman from London.

After the last notes had died away, the vicar gave out a few notices: the fee charged for the family pews was to be increased by two shillings; Mr Armstrong was to be congratulated on reaching his seventieth birthday; new worshipers were welcome (here his gaze seemed to linger on Woods.) Next, the sullen man launched into a tirade about several church members who had not attended a service for three weeks. Woods and Lavender shuffled uncomfortably.

The vicar took around the collection plate himself. Lavender tossed a few coins into plate and looked away. Woods made the mistake of pausing over his handful of change trying to select an appropriate amount and then looking up at the vicar. The small man glared back. Hastily, Woods tipped the entire handful of coins into the plate.

Lavender recognised the theme of the sermon instantly; like many others in the Church of England, the vicar in Bellingham was upset at the number of his flock who had left to join the Methodists. The man spat out his disgust with vitriolic fervour.

'I see this coming up everywhere—a belief in simplicity, services held in the open air – or a lazy resting in squalid homes because the worshippers are too slothful to attend church! Bible reading under taken by the unordained and uneducated who then lead their misguided followers in prayer. Children are baptised without holy water! Worship for God undertaken without altars, fonts or churches consecrated by a bishop and blessed by God!'

'He's upset,' Woods whispered.

'This is veneration for modesty that borders on the hypocritical!' shouted the vicar. 'A veneration so profound, that we must not venture upon a remark, for straightway of sinners we *are* chief.'

Now the clergyman lowered his voice until the tone became deep and menacing. 'Here is the essence of Lucifer, peeping up under the garb of a decent respect for sacred things. It is impossible but that this creeping Methodism must spread, when we - who are watch-dogs of the fold - are silent and let them be.'

Suddenly, he brought his hand crashing down onto the pulpit.

'It's the Devil work, I tell you!'

He roared so loudly that a small girl began to cry.

'Lucifer himself is gently and smoothly turfing the road to perdition for these fools, and making it as soft and smooth as possible, that those converts to Methodism may travel down to the nethermost level of hell!'

'Blimey!' Woods said, when they stumbled, blinking, back into the wintery sunlight an hour later and headed back towards The Rose and Crown. 'It's a while since I've heard a service where so many folks are damned to hell.'

'I'm glad you enjoyed it,' Lavender said, smiling. 'Because you're going back again tonight - for the evening service. With any luck, you'll get to hear it again.'

'What?'

'Mistress Norris, the cook, was not with the Carnabys. I guess she has remained at Linn Hagh to cook their dinner and will probably attend the evening service. I need you to question her away from Carnaby.'

'If she has any sense, she will sneak off to join the Methodists,' Woods muttered, grimly.

CHAPTER TWELVE

It was mid-afternoon when they called on Mr Armstrong. The rooms of the large house overflowed with chattering, well-dressed Armstrong relatives and gangs of noisy, rampaging grandchildren. Led by the maid who had answered the door, they manoeuvred their way down the packed hallway past a large group of men in scarlet uniforms, whose brass buttons and leather boots gleamed. Most clutched china plates of food in one hand and had their regimental hats tucked beneath their arms. Interspersed between the men, women floated around in a sea of muslin, perfume and bonnet ribbons.

The elderly Mr Armstrong had retired to his study for some peace and quiet but he greeted the policemen warmly and pretended to be annoyed with his guests.

'I had ten children of my own, Detective,' he pouted. 'And looked forward to the day when they all left and I could have some peace and quiet. Unfortunately, Katherine seems determined to move them all back in again.'

'Nonsense, Papa,' Miss Armstrong chided. 'You know how much you enjoy company.'

'What news of Helen?' Armstrong demanded.

'In a couple of days, I believe that I may be able to explain to you – or demonstrate to you - how Miss Carnaby got out of her locked bedchamber,' Lavender said.

Father and daughter looked startled and leaned forward with their mouths opening, to demand more information. But Lavender had not finished.

'However, it's still too early to be sure and I need a couple more days. Please bear with me. I'm sure of one thing, though. I believe that she walked out of that room unharmed and went of her own volition. I suspect that wherever she is, she is probably safe.'

He paused. Miss Armstrong glanced at the silent, grim face of her father.

'That is some comfort - is it not, Papa?'

'Yes,' Armstrong said shortly, but he still looked despondent.

'I need to know if the authorities in Whitby and her friends there at the school, were alerted to her disappearance.'

'It was one of the first places we checked.' Armstrong told him. 'I had a lovely letter back from the Headmistress of the school who told me that no one had seen anything of Helen since she returned to care for her mother last February. Apparently, Helen had been invited back in September to resume her position at the school but had declined.'

'So she chose to stay at Linn Hagh instead?'

'Yes.'

'I also need to ask you if anyone in the family has visited Esther Carnaby's grave recently?'

Katherine Armstrong threw up her hands in frustration and blushed.

'Oh, I forgot!'

'What did you forget, Miss Armstrong?'

'It was Esther's birthday three days ago – I meant to visit the grave and leave some flowers. But with all the fuss of arranging this party for Papa it went clean out of my mind.'

Lavender pulled the small bunch of wilting flowers out of his pocket and held them out. 'So you're not responsible for laying these at her grave?'

She took the flowers from him and examined them closely.

'No, no.'

'Would somebody else in the family have remembered Esther Carnaby's birthday and perhaps taken these flowers?'

She shook her head sadly. 'I doubt it, Detective. We've all been so busy – and I was the closest to Esther. Poor Esther.'

'What about Miss Isobel at Linn Hagh? Do you think she may have taken them to her step-mother's grave?'

Katherine Armstrong snorted in an un-ladylike manner. 'Highly unlikely, Detective - Izzie Carnaby was not kind to poor Esther.'

For a moment silence descended upon the room. Lavender was conscious of the buzz of indistinct conversation and laughter emanating from the hallway outside.

'I don't suppose,' Miss Armstrong said slowly, 'It could have been *Helen* who laid the flowers at her mother's grave?'

Lavender could sense hope rising like sweet smelling bread dough. Even Armstrong suddenly roused from his torpor, lifted his head and looked keenly at Lavender.

'Good God!' the old man exclaimed. 'That would mean Helen is still somewhere in Bellingham - and walking around.'

'These flowers could have been laid on that grave by anyone,' Lavender warned. 'I would be very grateful, if you could discreetly ask your other relatives if any of them have visited Esther Carnaby's grave in the last few days. We've got to eliminate all other possible explanations. Please send me a note at The Rose and Crown with your findings.'

Katherine Armstrong nodded.

'I think we need to keep this a secret between ourselves. If anyone else finds out about this latest development and goes to St. Cuthbert's looking for Miss Carnaby, they may frighten her away. Whatever it was that scared her away into hiding in the first place is clearly still worrying her. In the meantime, Woods and I will stake out the graveyard – particularly at night – and keep our eyes open for young ladies.'

'Whatever you think for the best,' Katherine Armstrong murmured.

'You've done well, Lavender,' Armstrong commented. 'That is the first lead we've had in our search for Helen.'

'It may still come to nothing,' Lavender warned.

'I hope not.' Armstrong sighed. His voice cracked with emotion and his eyes moistened. 'I want Helen found so badly.'

There was an embarrassing pause while the old man struggled with the anguish that wracked him. 'I blame myself for her disappearance,' he said.

'It's not your fault, Papa,' Miss Armstrong soothed. She reached out and stroked his bony hand.

'I cannot accept that, Katherine. You see Lavender, on the last occasion I saw Helen – at Cecily's wedding – she asked us if she could come and stay here for a while…' His voice trailed away with grief.

Miss Armstrong squeezed his hand tighter then turned to Lavender.

'Helen never said why,' she said. 'Unfortunately, two of my sisters are staying with us at the moment with their children – their husbands are fighting in Spain. We just didn't have the room.' She looked as miserable as her father.

'I still blame myself,' Armstrong said. 'I should have recognised that Helen was in trouble of some kind and welcomed her into our home. I've failed her in her hour of need.'

'Neither of you should blame yourselves,' Lavender informed them. 'George Carnaby was responsible for his sister after his father's death. He is the one who has clearly failed her.'

Mr Armstrong went for a rest in his bedchamber and Lavender and Woods had a private interview with Cecily Derwent, the young woman whom Miss Armstrong had told them was close to Helen Carnaby. Unfortunately, the distressed Mistress Derwent could tell them very little else to their advantage; she was as baffled as everyone else. No, Helen had not confided in her that she was unhappy at Linn Hagh or given her any indication that she was planning to run away. Nor had Helen ever mentioned a secret lover – or any young man at all – to her closest friend in Bellingham.

Lavender was disappointed. If Helen Carnaby's confidante and cousin – a young woman who claimed to be like 'a sister' to the missing heiress – had been excluded from her plans, then Lavender doubted if anyone would have been privy to her thoughts in the days leading up to her disappearance. Anyone else, that is, except the person who harboured her.

Lavender and Woods began to make their way back through the heaving crowds towards the front door, but they were suddenly called back into the study by a flushed and excited Katherine Armstrong.

'I've just remembered something,' she told them. 'This Wednesday – the 24th – is the anniversary of Baxter Carnaby's death. If Helen is still in Bellingham and placed the flowers on her mother's grave on her birthday…'

Lavender finished the sentence for her.

'…Then it's likely that she might return on the 24th to visit her father's grave.'

'Yes, Detective! Exactly!'

The evening service at St. Cuthbert's was every bit as grim as the service Woods and Lavender had sat through in the morning. However, Lavender had been right; the Linn Hagh cook attended the service. Woods watched her for a while, then set his face in his most pious expression, rubbed his hands for warmth and tried to block out the rants of the vicar by admiring the pointed gothic arches and windows of the old church.

It was pitch black when they finally left the building. He watched Mistress Norris pull her shawl tightly round her shoulders then scurry down the road in the direction of Linn Hagh. He began to follow her at a discreet distance, but suddenly the vicar seized his arm.

'Your piety has been noted, my son,' the reverend declared, loudly.

Woods thanked him and shook the elderly cleric's hand. Unfortunately, the vicar wanted a few more words; the man was curious about how long they intended to remain in Bellingham. It was several minutes before he could break away. By this time, Mistress Norris had disappeared from view but there was only one road to Linn Hagh – he doubted the cook would try to return home through the woods.

When they had left the lights and coal-smoke laden air of Bellingham behind, he caught up with the woman and hailed her. She stopped and stared suspiciously in his direction.

'What you want?' she asked when he moved to join her.

It was a clear moon-lit night; freezing cold, but brighter than the previous night when he had thundered back from Linn Hagh in near-blackness.

'Good evening, Mistress Norris. I saw you in the church and thought to myself, why this poor lady has a long and arduous trip back to Linn Hagh in the dark! I presumed to come and offer you me protection fer your journey.'

'Where's yer horse?' she demanded. 'Am I not to get a ride on that?'

Ah, obviously Anna had been talking.

'I'm afraid that wind-bag of a horse is back in the stables – or possibly on its way to the knackers yard where it belongs. However, I'm happy to walk with you ma'am, and should we be attacked by gypsies or vagabonds - fortunately I'm armed.'

'Ye've a pretty way of speaking,' she said. 'Despite yer funny accent, but if you try to tell me that ye've got a daughter named Gladys like me, I won't believe you.'

'Er, no. Sadly, I don't have a daughter named Gladys. Charming name,' he lied.

She snorted, turned away and set off back towards Linn Hagh. For a woman so badly affected by arthritis she was very quick on her pins. He fell into step beside her.

'I have three daughters: Rachel, Tabitha - *and Anna*,' he told her, with his fingers crossed behind his back. 'And two sons: Eddie and Dan.'

'And your wife – what does she think about you gallivanting all over the country and leaving her alone with the bairns?'

'To be honest, Mistress, my Betsy hates it. She appreciates the money my job brings home, but she struggles without me help with the lads.'

'Handful, are they?'

'Yes.'

An owl hooted deep inside the woods. He waited for her next comment.

'You're lucky,' she said. 'Despite the trouble you're having wi your lads.' Her voice had softened, become wistful. 'We never had any bairns. When my husband died I had no one to turn to. I were real grateful when Mistress Carnaby took me on at Linn Hagh. I'd have been in the poorhouse, else.'

'Was this Martha Carnaby or Esther Carnaby.'

'Esther, of course. Martha Carnaby were too mad to run her own home properly. I've bin at Linn Hagh fer twenty years.'

'Ah, you must have seen the younger Carnabys grow up.'

'Miss Helen, maybe – but Master George were nigh on fifteen when I first went to Linn Hagh and Miss Isobel weren't that far behind him. They were already far too wise fer their years at that age – they'd seen too much, I reckon,' she added. 'Master Matthew were a Nick Ninny even back then.'

Woods paused at the unfamiliar phrase but decided to push on with his questions while she was in the mood for talking.

'Do you like working at Linn Hagh?'

The cook laughed bitterly and quickened her step. When she slipped on the ice, Woods reached out to steady her but she shook off his hand, stopped and turned to face him in the darkness. By the silver light of the moon he could just make out sour expression on her face.

'Of course, I don't like werkin' there, Constable. What woman of my age wants to traipse around to a remote place like that and werk fer fourteen miserable hours a day? But I'm a widow, see? I hev no choice - and I'll never get another position if the Carnabys let me go. I'll end up maunding my way around Bellingham market with the other beggars.'

She spun round and set off back towards Linn Hagh. Woods hurried to catch up with her.

'Are you saying you're scared to talk to me because you think Carnaby will dismiss you if he finds out?'

She didn't reply. She set her face and she stared straight ahead.

'I don't understand,' Woods moaned. 'Surely Carnaby wants his sister found safe and well? Why is he so reluctant for us to talk with his servants?'

She snorted in disbelief, stopped again and stared at him: 'You never know what goes on behind a closed door of a family home, Constable – and you and that detective gadgie hev not even scratched the surface yet of life at Linn Hagh.'

'Why? What goes on at Linn Hagh?'

'Let's just say, that Miss Helen is a lot safer and better off where she is now.'

'Where is she? What do you know about her whereabouts and what are you talking about?'

The woman shook her head. 'I don't know where she is now.'

'So what did you mean?'

She sighed and leaned towards him.

'I'll tell you this - and this only. There were a drover at the market in Bellingham a few weeks back. He comes here with his sheep every month or so. He claimed he'd seen Miss Helen talking with a man on horseback in the week just before she disappeared. He said they seemed close.'

'Did he know the man?'

'No.'

'Did he describe the rider?'

'No.'

'Did this drover report this valuable piece of information to Beddows, Mr Armstrong or George Carnaby?'

'I telled him not to.'

'What?'

'I telled him not to. You see, Constable. I don't know how Miss Helen got out of that bedchamber, but I do know that even if she were snatched out of that room by a ruddy bogle, the lass will be a lot better off with the little folk than living with the Carnabys.'

With that the woman clammed up and refused to say another word for the rest of journey back to Linn Hagh.

CHAPTER THIRTEEN

Monday, 22nd November 1809

'A bogle is a mischievous little person, in northern folklore, who frequently causes trouble for humans,' Lavender told Woods at breakfast the next day. 'Obviously, Mistress Norris has been listening to those who say that Miss Carnaby has been spirited away by the fairies. I would like to hear more about the man on horseback seen by the drover.'

'She were very reluctant to say more,' Woods said.

'Well, she is going to have to identify this sheep drover if nothing else,' Lavender said firmly. The superstitious nonsense which the locals attributed to this case was beginning to irk him, and he had slept badly. 'This is the first lead we've had – anyone has had – that there is a lover lurking somewhere in the background. You can ask Mistress Norris for more details when we go up to Linn Hagh after breakfast.'

Woods glanced up from his porridge in surprise. His spoon hung loosely in the air.

'I thought you told George Carnaby you would join him, Emmerson and Ingram at Greycoates Hall at eleven o' clock?'

'I lied,' Lavender snapped. 'It seemed the best way to get Carnaby out of the way for the morning. He is trying to control us every step of the way in this investigation. We need to interview the servants away from his intimidating presence. If the cook still won't divulge the name of that drover, I'll take her into custody until she tells us the whole story. There's a girl missing, possibly in danger. It's about time, the inhabitants of this town started to take this investigation seriously.'

Woods said nothing, but continued to eye him curiously across the breakfast table.

'As for the woman's accusation that we've barely scratched the surface when it comes to understanding this family,' Lavender continued. 'I think she may well have a point. However, last night I wrote to the lawyer, Mr Agar, for a copy of Baxter Carnaby's will – so that problem may soon be rectified. If there is anything amiss in the Carnaby family we will soon know of it. Pass the salt, please Ned.'

Today Lavender decided they would walk to Linn Hagh through Hareshaw woods. It was damp, eerie and silent. The foliage was a swirling mixture of evergreen and muddy brown. The ancient woodland became darker and denser as they followed the overgrown path which snaked beside the stream. Gnarled fingers of skeletal trees creaked overhead and their moss-covered trunks fought against the steep incline of the gorge. For many, this fight with gravity had been too much and their bark had split like Chinese paper lanterns.

Lavender could tell that his constable hated it. Woods started at every noise, his eyes flicked sharply from one side to another every time a branch creaked and strained in the wind, his hand hovered instinctively over the pistol in his pocket.

Lavender smiled for the first time that day and thought about the irony of the situation. Woods was completely at home in the crime-ridden and festering maze of the London slums, where a cut-throat lurked around every corner; yet his constable was uncomfortable and lost in the countryside. The man was spooked by trees.

Now a dense patch of willow weed, eight feet high, reared up either side of the path. It formed a sea-green tunnel above their heads, where the tips of the plants reached out and touched. The men trudged through in silence.

Suddenly, Lavender heard an animal – a large animal – grunting and pushing its way through the weed towards them. He stopped. Dead branches cracked beneath the feet of the creature. The towering plants were forced violently apart and splayed out across the path in front of him.

A grotesque parody of a man, half stumbled, half fell onto the ground before them. Blinking in the weak sunlight, the strange wild-haired creature stared with uncomprehending eyes at the two Londoners. His right cheek twitched in fear and his slack mouth fell open. There was only one explanation for this sorry creature.

'Mr Matthew Carnaby?'

Whimpering and shuffling, the man's hand plucked at his torn and filthy woollen coat before he nodded.

Lavender watched with pity as the poor creature shrank back and lowered his head. Great scars snaked up the right side of his face, across his temple and into his hairline; white valleys of scar tissue, where the hair no longer grew, criss-crossed his close-cropped dark head. Puckered flesh distorted the corner of his eye and dragged it down into a grotesque shape.

Now, a coffee-coloured dryad glided out of the forest of willow weed and joined Matthew Carnaby on the path. Two identical pairs of blue eyes watched the police officers with distrust. The wood nymph wore a red scarf around her black curls topped with a wreath of laurel. Silver hoops glinted at her ears when she turned her head to Matthew Carnaby. Silver rings flashed on her fingers. She pulled a dirty shawl tighter over her old dress and reached out for Carnaby's hand.

'Away, Matty,' she said and she led him back into the forest of willow weed.

'Miss Geddes?'

But it was too late. The towering weeds swished back like a curtain as they disappeared. The plants swayed and were still. Lavender heard again the distant roar of the waterfall and a crow cawing mournfully in the tree canopy. It was as if Matthew Carnaby and the gypsy girl had never been there. The ancient woodland had just swallowed them up.

Isobel Carnaby was not pleased when Anna told her that the London detectives were at the door of Linn Hagh and seeking admittance. She snapped at Anna to wait a few moments while she took off her apron and tidied her hair. By the time Anna showed Lavender and Woods into the Great Hall at Linn Hagh, the young girl could see that her mistress had made some attempt to brush and pin back the tendrils of wiry hair that escaped from her cap and she had added rouge to her sallow cheeks.

The small, sharp-featured woman glared coldly at the detective when he bowed low over her hand.

'I'm sure that I heard you promise my brother you would meet him, Ingram and Ralph Emmerson up at Greycoates Hall, this morning.' Her voice cut through the air like ice.

'Please pass on my apologies to your brother, Miss Carnaby. Unfortunately, something important came up.'

'Really? In your investigation into my sister's disappearance?' Her dark eyes regarded him shrewdly.

'Yes.'

'What is it?' she demanded. 'Do you know where she is?'

'I need to see the Miss Carnaby's bedchamber again before I report back to Mr Armstrong. He has been most insistent.'

There was a short pause while Isobel Carnaby tried to assess this unexpected situation – and the man before her. Anna, who had remained quietly at the back of the room, did the same. As the bright morning light filtered through the dirty mullioned windows of the hall, Anna decided that the thin detective was not as scary as she had first thought. He had a quiet determination in his voice. The phrase: 'before I report back to Mr Armstrong' particularly impressed her.

Anna hoped that Miss Isobel would not show herself up and try to bully these policemen, like she did Constable Beddows. There was something different, something alien about these unknown men from London. They didn't fit into the usual order of things in Bellingham – even she could see that.

She had the laundry list Constable Woods wanted, secreted down her bodice. It rustled slightly as she breathed.

In the end, Isobel Carnaby dropped her harsh tone and became the charming hostess.

'Of course, Detective, anything I can do to help. Naturally, I want my little sister returned to the bosom of her family as soon as possible. You say you want to start with Helen's bedchamber?' She moved towards the staircase.

'Actually,' Lavender's voice brought her to an abrupt stop. 'I wonder if you could just explain to me the layout of Linn Hagh. I didn't have time to study the whole building on our last visit.'

'Certainly,' she said, and waved her hands in the direction of the three closed doors which led off the Great Hall. 'It's quite simple. There are three bedchambers on this floor: mine, my brother George's and a guest room. Upstairs, there are two further bedchambers; one where the female servants sleep and Helen's room.'

'Did Miss Helen object to sleeping on the same floor as the servants?'

Isobel Carnaby seemed genuinely surprised.

'No, why should she? You have to remember, Detective, that Helen has hardly been at home over the last few years. She returned in January to nurse her dying mother, and my brother and I were surprised that she stayed here after poor Esther died. I understand that the school in Whitby had offered her a teaching position again for September last. She is always welcome at Linn Hagh, of course - it's her home - but she is not in any position to complain about her bedchamber being on the same floor as the servants. She seemed happy to fit in with our arrangement.'

'Of course,' Lavender said. He fell quiet.

In the silence that followed, Isobel Carnaby began to bluster.

'Mind you, she did manage to complain about other things. The food was never to her liking – she always wanted something different. Her room was too cold. She needed more coal for her fire…'

'Did she ask for extra coal on the night she disappeared?' Lavender interrupted sharply.

Yes she blooming well did, thought Anna. *And she would be asking for it again if she had been here today.* Once the master had left the Great Hall that morning the fire had been allowed to die out as usual. It was cold now and Anna shivered beneath the thin cloth of her black uniform.

Miss Isobel cast an accusing glare across the room at Anna, who squirmed beneath it.

'Yes, it would seem that she had persuaded our maid to give her an extra scuttle full of coal that evening. This didn't come to light until we discovered her room empty – with coals still hot in the grate. Is that significant, Detective?'

'It may be.'

'Let me show you…'

'Where does Master Matthew Carnaby sleep in Linn Hagh?'

Isobel Carnaby paused halfway across the room and froze to the spot. Her face turned ugly with anger.

'Mr Armstrong told us about your unfortunate younger brother,' Lavender continued, smoothly. 'I believe we've just come across him out in the woods.'

The colour returned slowly to Isobel Carnaby's cheeks.

'Yes, yes, Matty – poor Matty,' she sighed. 'He should have been placed into an institution years ago of course, but my father was soft – and my brother – is also a kind-hearted man. Matty takes a simple pleasure in roaming Hareshaw Woods, he enjoys flowers and birdsong. It would have cruel to have locked him away.'

Anna was horrified at how convincing she sounded.

'He sleeps downstairs in a small room off the kitchen. It's warm in there for him and Cook and Peter, our man servant, can keep an eye on him: Cook watches him during the day and at night, Peter sleeps in the next room.'

'Do you think Mr Matthew Carnaby knows anything about Miss Helen's disappearance?'

Miss Isobel paused, thoughtfully.

'We asked him of course…'

Asked? thought Anna. *You all screamed your heads off in his face and then threw him outside into the snow to go and track her down like some sort of human bloodhound.*

'…but he has no speech and fails to understand the simplest of things. My sister was kind to him - in a distant sort of way - but he barely seems to have noticed her absence over these last few weeks.'

Safe and unseen, behind Miss Isobel's back, Anna shook her head sadly. Matthew Carnaby had wailed for days and roamed from one end of the parish to the other, trying to find Miss Helen.

CHAPTER FOURTEEN

Stephen Lavender crouched down onto the floor of Helen Carnaby's bedchamber and pretended to carry out another examination of the debris still littering the floor. He slipped his hand into his pocket and pulled out the candle stub end he had found there two days ago.

'Do you make your own candles, Miss Carnaby?' he asked.

'Yes, in the autumn we render down mutton fat and make tallow candles.'

He kept his back to her.

'Do you have beeswax candles at Linn Hagh?'

'A few, I keep a few in our cold store for when we entertain guests. We used beeswax candles the night Emmerson and Ingram stayed – the night Helen disappeared.'

'So that is why, Miss Carnaby used beeswax candles up here in her chamber – because you had guests?'

The smile dropped from Isobel Carnaby's face.

'No. Helen should not have lit beeswax candles up here. I was most clear about that. They're so expensive to buy from the chandler and are solely for use in the Great Hall when we are entertaining guests. Helen should have burnt tallow candles up here in her room.'

Silently, Lavender held up the creamy candle end towards her. She snatched it from him.

'This will not do!' she exclaimed. 'Yet again she defied me!' Her face contorted with anger.

'Would you like to check how many of your beeswax candles are missing?' Lavender suggested quietly.

'Yes! Yes!' She flew out of the room. Lavender followed her down the stairs of the pele tower. When her bony arms reached out to steady herself against the stone walls, Lavender thought she resembled an ungainly and vengeful black bat.

Isobel led him through the smoky kitchen and into a back store room. She yanked the lid off a large tin box and pulled out a handful of beautifully-crafted creamy beeswax candles, each item an almost exact reproduction of its neighbour. She laid them out on a shelf, then painstakingly counted them before she reached for the housekeeping ledger where she kept her records.

'Six!' she exclaimed. 'Six! The thoughtless wench took six of our most expensive candles for use in her bedchamber.' Her hands shook with rage when she replaced the precious items in their box.

'I can understand how distressing this must have been for you,' Lavender said sympathetically. 'Did Miss Helen exhibit other acts of selfishness?'

But Isobel Carnaby would not be drawn at that moment. She flushed and pressed her thin lips angrily together. Wisps of her hair escaped their pins and fell untidily across her creased forehead.

'Would this be a good time for you to show me Master Matthew Carnaby's bedchamber?' he asked.

She threw open another wooden door behind him, gestured him inside and returned herself to the kitchen. While he searched languidly amongst the stinking rags which covered Matthew Carnaby's bed and the curious collection of rocks, dead plants, sprigs of laurel leaves and driftwood which littered his floor, Lavender heard Isobel Carnaby snarling at Mistress Norris. He could not make out the cook's reply but her voice sounded indignant as if she defended herself from accusations of negligence or complicity. He hoped that Woods and the maid had finished their search upstairs.

As soon as Lavender and Isobel Carnaby disappeared, Woods spun round to Anna.

She had already pulled the laundry list out of her bodice.

'Good gal,' Woods grinned. 'Let's just check and see that nothing has been taken in the weeks since her disappearance, shall we?' He pulled open the doors of the closet and the crushed material of her gowns splayed out and swayed in the draft. Anna held up the list and began to check off the dresses with her finger.

'I don't know how you and that Detective gadgie think she gets in and out of her bedchamber unseen,' she grumbled. 'I can tell you…'

She stopped and frowned - glanced at the closet – and then back at the list.

'Is something missing?' Woods asked hopefully.

Anna's frown deepened.

'There's two dresses gone.'

'Ah,' Woods sighed with relief. This was more evidence that Helen Carnaby was still alive – and somewhere nearby.

'What about the linen?' he asked. 'Undergarments and so forth.'

Anna moved towards the dresser and opened the top drawers. A few moments later, she glanced up.

'Her two best sets are missing.'

Woods nodded and smiled.

'Unfortunately, I think I may know where they are,' she said. 'You're not going to like this.'

'Oh?' His face fell.

'Follow me.'

She led him down the stone staircase back into the Great Hall. There was still no sign of Miss Isobel or Detective Lavender. Anna moved swiftly across the flagged floor towards the bedchamber at the back of the hall. She entered the middle room and Woods realised at once that she had taken him into Isobel Carnaby's bedchamber. The dressing table was scattered with hair pins and powders, a heavy scent hung in the air. Woods compared the richness of the furnishings, bed hangings and ornamentation of this room with the spartan little garret of Miss Helen upstairs. Anna threw open the doors of Miss Isobel's dark, mahogany closet, sighed and pointed to two gowns hanging there.

'That's them,' she said. 'Miss Isobel's taking Miss Helen's clothes again.'

Woods swallowed his disappointment.

'What about the undergarments?'

Anna opened a drawer and nodded. 'They're here.'

He glanced down at the delicate lace chemise which lay across the top of the drawer and fingered the ribbon laced through it. Something silver caught his eye at the bottom of the drawer.

'We had better get back,' Anna warned.

Woods pulled aside the clothing and found a small tin snuff box. He smiled.

'Does Miss Isobel take snuff?'

'No, that's where she keeps some of the seasoning.' She was becoming nervous; her eyes kept straying towards the open door.

'Seasoning?'

Woods flipped open the lid of the snuff box and sniffed the crushed, pale green vegetable matter in the small box.

'Yes, sage and such like.'

It smelt like finely chopped sage. He dipped his finger into the seasoning and licked it. Yes. Sage.

'We should go.'

He went to replace the tin snuff box in the drawer but at the last moment hesitated and slipped it into his coat pocket. Anna was too distracted to notice.

'Quick! They're coming.'

They left the bedroom, closed the door and reached the centre of the room just as Lavender and Isobel Carnaby entered the Great Hall. She collapsed into one of the faded chairs in front of the fireplace, her face puckered with anguish.

'Fetch your mistress a glass of brandy,' Lavender instructed Anna. 'I think she has had a shock. Would you like a fire lit in the hearth, Miss Carnaby?'

Isobel shook her head about the fire and apologised to the detective for making such a fuss. When the brandy arrived, she drank deeply.

'I'm sorry, Detective,' she said again. 'It's just so upsetting to think that Helen has been defying my instructions over yet another housekeeping issue.'

'I can understand it must have been difficult for you to all adjust since her return…'

'Very much so!' Isobel Carnaby interrupted. 'Yet who would see it from my point of view? Helen was like a stranger when she returned last February. She was unused to our ways and unaware of the pecuniary problems we've faced since our father's mine closed. She had been cosseted since she was a child and safe in the knowledge that one day she would be a very wealthy young woman. My pleas for economy and frugality in the household just fell on deaf ears.' She drained her glass and sighed heavily.

Lavender nodded sympathetically and held out the brandy decanter towards her. 'Another brandy, Miss Carnaby? I think the circumstances decree it might be acceptable.'

'You're very kind, Detective.'

Woods grimaced inwardly as he watched Lavender fill Miss Carnaby's glass with more of the fiery amber liquid. The old tabby could certainly put it away, he noted. Both of them were acting out a part: Lavender was the embodiment of calm, reassuring solace; Isobel Carnaby, the distraught little housekeeper, nearly hysterical over a couple of missing candles. Lavender's concern was no more genuine than the sly-eyed woman's distress. Fascinated Woods watched the charade unfold before his eyes.

'It's often the difficulty with second families,' Lavender agreed. 'And younger children always tend to be spoilt.'

'You're so understanding, Detective.'

‘Do you have any family portraits, Miss Carnaby?

‘Not of Helen,’ she snapped.

‘No, I meant of yourself - your brothers and your parents.’

She rose and smoothed down the creases in her bombazine dress with one hand, while the other still clutched the brandy glass. She led them to one of the few remaining oil paintings in the room.

‘Well, I’m not sure how it will help you in your search for Helen, but that was painted when we were very young. Happier times.’

Woods and Lavender glanced up into the soot-blackened frame at the dark painting. Baxter Carnaby, clean-shaven and thin-faced beneath his tightly-curled wig, stood stiffly behind his family, who were seated on a rose-coloured chaise lounge. He looked like a severe and worried man. Woods had the impression that Carnaby’s vivid blue eyes were glaring down specifically at him. Behind the family, the unmistakable, deep-set mullioned windows of Linn Hagh peered out over the grounds of the pele tower - grounds which looked like they were tended far better then, than now.

Reluctantly, Woods shifted his gaze to the dark-haired, bright-eyed woman who smiled and gazed boldly out the canvas. The mad first wife: Martha. Woods stared into the dark pools of her eyes, and searched for signs of the insanity which he knew would soon overtake her. He could see none. Beside Martha Carnaby, a small boy in a miniature version of his father’s jacket, waistcoat, breeches and stockings stood bashfully at the end of the sofa. He clutched a wooden sword. Another child, perhaps three years old and enveloped in the short shift and tumbling curls of the nursery, stood by her knee. A baby of indeterminate gender lay swaddled in lacy blankets in Martha Carnaby’s arms.

‘Delightful,’ Lavender said. ‘A lovely reminder of happier times. Is this you, Master George and Master Matthew in the portrait?’

Whether it was the strong drink, or her mask of deceit slipping, Woods could not tell, but Isobel Carnaby’s eyes suddenly slid away from Lavender’s gaze.

Yes, she confirmed. Those were her two brothers in the portrait.

Woods could have sworn he saw the corner of her thin mouth twitch in a slight smile.

‘It’s always sad for young children when they lose their mother,’ Lavender continued. ‘I can only hope that your step-mother treated you kindly?’

Isobel Carnaby shrugged her shoulders.

‘She always favoured her own daughter.’

‘Tell me, do you ever visit her grave?’

'No, not recently. Why do you ask?'

'No particular reason,' Lavender lied. 'I just noted on Sunday that Esther Carnaby's grave was very overgrown compared to the careful tending you obviously give to the grave of your own parents.'

The mistress of Linn Hagh snorted and bristled with self-righteousness. 'Huh! Typical! Helen can't even tend her own mother's grave properly!'

CHAPTER FIFTEEN

The gypsy encampment near to Linn Hagh had clearly been established a long time. Lavender's eyes flitted quickly across the traditional tents that crept across the muddy ground like ragged, gaudy caterpillars. Most were ranged in a rough half-circle, with their backs to Hareshaw Woods. The faded blankets and felts laid over the arched hazel rods of the tents were damp and torn. He could smell the rot and decay. A few small carts rested on wheels which had sunk deep into the muddy ground. One had lost a wheel entirely; its back corner balanced on a cairn of large rocks. Cluttered and littered with debris and abandoned articles, the camp sprawled across the field. There was a rough-hewn stone pig sty, a privy, and some sort of meeting house which leaned precariously to one side.

A series of large, circular and smoking hearth fires blazed in the centre of the arc formed by the tents. Gaunt, dark-skinned women stirred food in charred pots hung over these fires and glared suspiciously at the two men as they approached. Black-coated and sloe-eyed, the women looked dirty and hungry. Other women lounged on small stools at the entrance to the tents. They paused with half-made reed baskets in their laps and stared sullenly at the two Londoners.

A crowd of curious, ragged children raced over holding out their filthy hands, begging for coins in a gabbled breathless mixture of English and Romany.

'Spare a copper, mister.'

'Gi' us a groat!'

Lavender smiled but kept his hands still and firmly placed over the pockets in his greatcoat. Woods did the same. Lavender's eyes scanned the encampment, looking for a man who might answer the description he had been given back in Bellingham of Paul Faa Geddes, their leader.

An elderly man climbed stiffly from his seat by the fireside, a piece of tin and a pair of hand snips hung limply from his cold, arthritic fingers. By his feet lay sheets of metal, ornamental cake stands and plain pastry cutters. Another younger man rose quietly, picked up a dead goose and disappeared inside one of the tents. For a brief moment Lavender wondered if the elderly man was the leader of the faws, but then a crowd of six swarthy gypsy men came out of a wooden meeting house at the edge of the camp.

Now Lavender realised who was in charge. Paul Faa Geddes had the same swarthy complexion, high cheekbones and penetrating dark eyes of his kinsmen, but he stood half a head taller and had a vicious scowl etched across his scarred and leathered face. Broader than the other men, his long black hair fell down from beneath the brim of his hat and draped around his shoulders. A silver ring dangled from one ear.

'What d'you want?'

'Paul Faa Geddes? I'm Detective Stephen Lavender from London. I'm investigating the disappearance of Miss Helen Carnaby.'

'Aye, we've seen you coming and going from the tower.' He had the same unusual accent used by the girl they had met earlier in the wood.

'We're working for Mr John Armstrong of Bellingham - Miss Carnaby's uncle. We're not working for her brother.'

A faint shadow of amusement flitted across the brawny gypsy's face. 'It don't mek no difference to me who you're werkin' for.'

'Fair enough,' Lavender said crisply. 'I don't want to disturb any one. I would like to speak to your daughter, Laurel Faa Geddes.'

The swarthy tinker spat contemplatively onto the ground. 'She ain't my daughter.'

'I need to speak to her.'

'Well, you can't – she ain't here.'

Lavender paused. The gypsy glared at him arrogantly.

'I'm concerned about the safety of Miss Carnaby. I need to find her as soon as possible. I believe that Miss Geddes can help me.'

'*Miss Geddes?*' one of the other gypsy men queried. 'Be that our Laurel he's tokkin aboot?' A snicker of amusement rippled around the group.

Paul Geddes lifted his hand for silence.

'You mean well – but you know nowt,' he said. Then he turned his back, walked away. The interview was over.

Lavender became suddenly conscious of an angry hissing and muttering to his right. An elderly woman glowered at him and Woods from the nearest stone hearth while she chanted. The language was Romany, the words indecipherable, but the intention was clear; she was cursing them.

A fair amount of daylight remained so Lavender decided that they would return to Bellingham through Hareshaw Wood. He told Woods he hoped to catch another glimpse of the Geddes girl. They paused for a while at the top of Hareshaw Linn and watched the water thundering down onto the slimy, fossil-strewn rocks below.

Woods shivered. There was something unnatural about this desolate forest. The overhanging sandstone cliff face dripped dampness and misery onto them as they passed beneath it. The tangled briars of the undergrowth, sliced into the flesh of their legs like glass wire. Felled trees took on the shape of prehistoric monsters when glimpsed out of the corner of his eye - and always, always he had the sensation of sharp eyes boring into his back like a pair of daggers.

Dusk fell rapidly as they wound their way back to the town. Candles glimmered softly in the windows of the houses and the smell of roasting meat and coal fires drifted in the air around them.

Woods sighed with relief when he felt and heard the hard cobbles of Bellingham beneath his boots. His legs ached and he had to drag himself through the last few streets to the tavern. Even the welcoming warmth of The Rose and Crown did little to cheer him. It was as if Hareshaw Woods had sucked the soul out of him.

Back in the comfortable tap room, Lavender ordered their supper and tried to engage him in a conversation about Isobel Carnaby, Linn Hagh and the faws, but Woods struggled to concentrate. Lavender's voice drifted in and out.

'What did you notice about that family portrait of the Carnabys?' Lavender asked.

'They were a set of funny looking nippers,' Woods commented moodily. He fought back a sickening wave of dizziness which threatened to swamp him. 'Isobel Carnaby looked more like a lad when she were a toddler.'

'She's not the most delicate or feminine looking woman in England, is she?' Lavender grinned. 'She's as flat as a cake board and almost as angular as one.'

'I know it's hard to tell with those fussy pantaloons they made little 'uns wear in those days, but I thought at first Miss Isobel was a lad.'

Lavender eyed him curiously.

'Mmm, a rather indifferent portrait painter, I suspect. I also noticed that the artist had given the oldest child - George Carnaby - the same blue eyes as his father. This was wrong of course – George Carnaby has the dull, mud brown eyes of his mother and sister. Ned, are you feeling alright?'

'No.'

Woods staggered to his feet. The nausea made him sway. His upper body, his stomach, his gullet and his mouth burned like they were on fire. He staggered out of the tap room, out of the back door of the inn and reached the stinking privy just in time. He vomited up the entire contents of his stomach.

He groaned and retched again, dimly aware that one of the other customers of the tavern had just left the adjacent privy and was grinning at him through the open door.

'One of them Bow Street runners is foxed in the privy.' Isaac Daly declared loudly when he returned to the tap room. He was in such a rush to report Woods' indisposition that he was still buttoning up the front fall on his breeches as he hurried back inside.

'Ohh! It looks like yer constable's a bit of a toss pot,' Jethro Hamilton goaded Lavender across the tap room. 'Has he bin having a sip or two from his hip flask while he's supposed to be helping you find that missing lass? I'm guessing that Mr Armstrong won't like to hear about this.'

Lavender looked up alarmed.

'He hasn't been drinking,' he retorted, coldly.

'He ain't touched his veal, either,' Mistress McMullen, the landlady commented. Lavender glanced down at the pewter plate beside him and frowned. She was right; Woods had hardly eaten a thing.

'He likes his food an all, does that one,' Mistress McMullen continued. 'I reckon that summat's amiss.'

Grim-faced Lavender sat silently, while the woman continued to prattle on about Woods.

'They've bin up to the faw camp, today,' she told the farmers.

The mood instantly darkened amongst the gang.

'He'll have bin cursed by that young witch.'

'Or the old hag.'

'Oi, you - detective gadgie - you didn't happen to see me missing goose, while you were up there, did you?'

Jethro Hamilton slammed his tankard down onto the table. 'This here town's crawling with bloody constables and detectives – yet still them damned faws thieve and threaten folks into handing over what's not theirs to own.' An ugly murmur of agreement rippled around the tap room like poison.

Tight-lipped, Lavender got to his feet, left the bar and went upstairs. Woods was not in the bedchamber. Increasingly alarmed, he hurried back down and went out the back of the building. The freezing night air hit him sharply in the face as he stumbled outside then groped his way through the blackness towards the privy. His boot slammed into something solid lying across the path.

Woods was unconscious at his feet, sprawled in a pool of his own vomit.

He had no choice but to ask the help of the amused farmers from the bar to get the heavy constable up the narrow stairs and into bed. Most of the men remained convinced that Woods was drunk, but they helped him, nevertheless. Lavender sent for the doctor. Mistress McMullen stoked up the fire in their grate and did her best to clean up the constable.

Dr Robert Goddard was brisk, efficient and surprisingly confident for such a young man; Lavender estimated that he was in his late twenties. A handsome man with gleaming, wavy, chestnut hair tied back with a ribbon at the nape of his neck, his presence threw Mistress McMullen into a flurry of excitement.

Goddard felt Woods' forehead, opened his mouth and peered down his throat. He then lifted his eyelids to examine the colour of his eyeballs. Finally, he took his pulse. When the doctor turned over Wood's wrist, something caught his eye and he called for a candle to be brought closer to the bedside.

The flickering light revealed the blistering hives that had swelled across the top of Woods fingers. Doctor Goddard raised the candle to Woods' pale and clammy face. More raised, red welts were visible around his mouth.

The doctor touched them and the semi-conscious man moaned.

'Dear me,' he observed. 'I do believe the constable has ingested something which has caused his illness.'

'Well, it's not owt he's eaten at my inn,' Mistress McMullen snapped. 'You tell him, Detective' she demanded of Lavender. 'Yev both had the same to eat today and there's nowt wrong with you.'

'Calm yourself,' the doctor soothed. 'No-one is blaming your excellent cooking. For heavens, sake I've eaten here often enough myself, Mistress McMullen.'

'They've bin up at Linn Hagh as well,' the indignant woman pointed out. 'Perhaps they had summat bad to eat there.'

'Perhaps.' The doctor smiled. 'Although I'm sure that Gladys Norris would not appreciate you saying that. Tell me, Detective, did you travel back through Hareshaw Wood or did you take the road?'

'We used the woodland path on the way back. Is that significant?'

'Only in so much as whatever he has taken such a bad reaction to, he has had it in his hand as well as his mouth. I just wondered if you investigated any strange looking plants. The woodlands around here are full of natural poisons.'

'No.'

'He'll hev bin cursed – that's what it is! They've bin up to the faw camp. Tha'll need fairy ointment to cure him.'

Lavender frowned. He had been grateful for the woman's help earlier but now she irritated him. Sensing, the detective's impatience, Goddard smiled and intervened.

'Would it be possible to have a glass of brandy, Mistress McMullen? Doctoring is thirsty work.'

The woman scurried away down the narrow stairs in a flurry of indignant petticoats, and Lavender breathed a sigh of relief. As if on cue, Woods groaned and groggily opened his eyes.

'What happened?' he croaked.

'Don't try to speak,' the doctor instructed. 'Your tongue and throat are quite swollen. You've passed out with shock and the difficulties you've had breathing. I'll give you a salve to rub into your hand and face for the blistering. Otherwise, sleep it off, my good man.'

Woods nodded and closed his eyes gratefully.

'He's had a bad reaction to something,' Dr Goddard told Lavender when he handed him his bill and a small glass bottle from his bag. 'But he has a strong constitution. I think he will live.'

CHAPTER SIXTEEN

Tuesday 23rd November, 1809

Woods slept fitfully that night. When Lavender checked on him the next morning, he found his constable still groggy and pale. The sores around his mouth were still inflamed, itchy and shining beneath the doctor's salve.

Lavender told him to stay in bed and rest. He decided to pay a visit to Greycoates Hall to interview Gorge Carnaby's two drinking companions.

But before he left the room, Woods called him back and reached into the pocket of his coat, which had been slung across a bedside chair. He fished out a small silver tin and slid it across the quilt towards Lavender.

'I found it in Isobel Carnaby's underwear drawer - yesterday,' he croaked through his swollen throat. 'I found it when I searched the closets with Anna. I stuck my finger in and licked it.'

Lavender raised his eyebrow. He flicked open the lid and stared at the flecks of green matter inside the tin.

'What is it?'

'I don't know – I thought perhaps that doctor might be able to tell us. Anna said she thought it were sage - for seasoning.'

Lavender nodded.

'You enjoy your rest, Ned. I'll call on the doctor and see if he can identify this. In the meantime, try to keep your hands out of women's underwear. This is the second time you've had a good grope amongst the lingerie of strange women in the last few weeks. You're obviously developing a dangerous habit - and I doubt that Betsy would approve.'

When Lavender approached Doctor Goddard's house on Bellingham's main street he noticed that the drapes were still closed. The maid, who showed him into the gloomy parlour, explained that Dr Goddard was in mourning for his late mother. Lavender nodded and remembered the black cravat and armband the doctor had worn the night before when he had attended Woods.

It was a small but comfortable home. There were just a few rooms on the ground floor: one across the passageway where the maid told him Goddard saw his patients; a dining room and the parlour where he now stood waiting. The mismatched furniture reminded him of his own bachelor rooms in London, a place he seemed to hardly see. A pretty French clock ticked away gently on the mantelpiece between two pot dogs. Lavender held open the window drapes and looked out down the street. The windows offered a good view of St. Cuthbert's graveyard down the cobbled hill, he noted. That reminded him; one of them need to stake out the graveyard at midnight – tomorrow was the 24th – the anniversary of Baxter Carnaby's death.

The doctor appeared and gestured for Lavender to take a seat. Goddard wore a black frock coat and breeches along with the black cravat. Only a mauve silk waistcoat broke up the darkness of his attire.

'You're lucky to have caught me,' the doctor said coldly. 'I'm on my way out this morning. I'm busy sorting out my late mother's estate. Your constable has not taken a turn for the worse, I trust?'

'Quite the contrary,' Lavender reassured him. He could sense that the doctor was unhappy about something.

'Constable Woods is making an excellent recovery; fortunately, he has the constitution of an ox.'

'So, why are you here?'

Lavender ignored his rudeness and pulled out the small silver tin from his pocket.

'I called by because I hoped you might be able to help us identify this.'

A frown creased across the doctor's broad forehead. He sniffed the small specks of plant material in the tin suspiciously.

'Woods claimed he tasted some of this yesterday,' Lavender told him. 'He thought it was sage. I wondered if it was significant, in the light of his illness.'

'Where did he get hold of it?'

Lavender paused surprised. He usually asked the questions. 'What do you think it is?' he persisted.

'It's shredded digitalis leaves.'

'Foxgloves?' Lavender paled.

'Yes, their leaves. It can be mistaken for sage. It's one of the most virulent poisons.'

'Poison.' Lavender sank down, uninvited, into a chair next to the fire and pushed back the hair from his forehead.

Why did I not see this before? He thought. *Poison: the preferred weapon of murderous women.*

'Where did you find it?' Goddard asked again.

Lavender met the other man's steady gaze. Goddard had impressed him in their brief acquaintance with his humanity, humour and intelligence. His current antagonism was out of character, and probably due to his emotional state following his mother's death. He made a snap decision to trust him.

'From a drawer in Isobel Carnaby's bedchamber.'

'Good Lord.' Horror flashed across the doctor's handsome face. He walked over to the fireplace and rested his hands on the mantelpiece.

'Do you think – is it possible? – that Isobel Carnaby used this poison on her sister?' The doctor's voice was sharp. He looked wretched. Lavender's mind raced.

'Possibly. I don't know for sure,' Lavender's tone was grim. 'But no-one keeps poison unless they've used it – or plan to use it. You're the family physician, Doctor Goddard – did Miss Helen ever complain of ill health to you?'

'Not once.'

'Perhaps Helen Carnaby also had her suspicions. We've found out that she often left her meals uneaten and was generally regarded as fussy about her food. I'm increasingly convinced that Helen Carnaby was terrified of *something* at Linn Hagh and was desperate to escape.'

He could only see half of the doctor's face, but he watched him closely for his reaction. The man was tight-lipped and frowning as he continued to stare down into the fireplace. His broad shoulders were rigid.

'Maybe the poison wasn't meant for Helen Carnaby.' Goddard eventually said.

'What do you mean?'

The doctor turned around to face Lavender.

'Esther Carnaby died last February because of complications caused by perforated ulcers in the oesophagus – or so I believed. In the end, her heart could not take the strain anymore and it gave up.''

'What is the significance of this?'

'Like you witnessed last night with your constable, the symptoms Esther exhibited - weakness, dizziness, vomiting and fainting – are exactly the same as digitalis poisoning. The end result of consistent digitalis poisoning - is heart failure.'

The two men stared at each other across the room. The clock ticked patiently on the mantelpiece as the seconds passed and the two men absorbed the full horror of the idea slowly taking root in their minds.

'Are you suggesting that Isobel Carnaby may have also poisoned her step-mother, Esther?'

'It's quite possible given her symptoms,' the wretched doctor said quietly. 'I'm appalled to think that I may have missed this.'

'How long have you been physician to the Carnaby family?'

'About three years.'

'In your professional opinion, do you think that Isobel Carnaby is capable of murder?'

Goddard shook his head a little, shrugged his shoulders and raised his hands in a gesture of helplessness. 'She is not insane like her mother was if that is what you mean. She is completely rational.'

'Mmm, insanity may be your area of expertise, Doctor, but the murderous and the evil are mine. You know the family far better than I. Could Isobel Carnaby sink that low, do you think?'

Goddard shrugged and emitted a hollow laugh.

'Like you said yourself, why else keep digitalis if you don't intend to do some harm with it?' His tone was bitter. 'For the record, she is in good company – George Carnaby thrashes the living daylights out of his younger brother Matthew. He is a sadistic bastard. I've regularly been called to Linn Hagh by Miss Helen to try to help the boy Matthew with his injuries.'

'Dear God,' Lavender gasped. 'At last we are beginning to scratch beneath the surface of the truth about this family. Are you aware if George Carnaby ever whipped Miss Helen?'

The doctor grimaced, frowned and sank down into an armchair. 'I don't know…I doubt it.' He looked nauseous at the thought.

Lavender eyed him shrewdly.

'You're being very helpful, Doctor. I appreciate this. Is there any way of finding out if Isobel Carnaby tried to poison her step-mother?'

'None that I can think of. Not now. Not now she is dead.'

'I wonder if Helen Carnaby had any suspicions about her half-sister's intention to harm her mother. It would have been difficult for Isobel Carnaby to poison Esther once the sharp-eyed Helen came home from Whitby.'

Goddard said nothing. He continued to frown and stare into space.

'What if we exhumed Esther Carnaby's body?' Lavender asked, sharply. 'Would you be able to anatomise the corpse and uncover evidence of digitalis poisoning?'

The doctor gasped and snapped his full attention back to Lavender. 'You could – you would - order an exhumation?' he asked.

'If I had evidence that there was just cause; then yes.'

For a moment, a flicker of hope lit up the doctor's eyes. Then it died.

'No. No. I would not be able to tell if she had been poisoned. Digitalis is a natural product; it would have long since dissolved back into the mud of the grave. That kind of science – it is beyond the medical profession.'

Lavender was disappointed but he didn't give up. 'Mmm, Isobel Carnaby would not know this, of course. I wonder how she would react to the *threat* of an exhumation?'

Goddard's hazel eyes widened. 'I should imagine that it will alarm her – if what we suspect is true,' he said.

The two men mulled over the idea for a moment. Then Lavender stood up and pulled on his gloves.

'I've taken up more than enough of your time, Doctor, especially as you've personal matters to deal with in Newcastle. Please accept my condolences, by the way, on the sad loss of your mother.'

'My mother lived in Morpeth,' Goddard said, absentmindedly.

'Ah, all roads lead to Morpeth this week. I shall be there myself on Friday at a pre-arranged appointment with Magistrate Clennell. I'll be honest with you, Doctor, I shall now also be discussing with him the possibility of acquiring a warrant for the arrest of Isobel Carnaby on suspicion of murdering her sister.'

The doctor's mouth gaped open in surprise.

'I'm not sure that there is sufficient evidence for a warrant, but I shall certainly make enquiries. I trust I can rely on your discretion? No hint of this to the Carnabys – or anyone else for that matter?'

Goddard nodded glumly.

Lavender chose his next words carefully.

'In the meantime, Doctor Goddard, I'll share with you my opinion on another matter. If Miss Helen Carnaby is still alive, in good health and in hiding – I sincerely hope that she has the sense to remain where she is until I've had the chance to sort this out.'

Lavender took a short stroll around the graveyard of St Cuthbert's church before he picked up his horse at the stable. He spotted a large clump of rhododendron and elder, which would give good cover yet be an excellent vantage point during their long vigil observing Baxter Carnaby's grave.

Ralph Emmerson and Lawrence Ingram were already half in their cups by the time Lavender reached the Elizabethan Mansion, Greycoates Hall. Both men were red-eyed and sprawled languidly across the sofas when Lavender was shown into the drawing room. Dark and oppressively hot, it stank of liquor fumes, stale cooking and unwashed men. Platters of half eaten food lay on the soot-stained Persian rug at their feet. A whippet moved between them, sniffing and licking at the leftovers.

Emmerson glared at Lavender from beneath his bushy ginger eyebrows. 'You were supposed to call on us yesterday, God damn it,' he said.

Lavender tore his eyes away from the stained waistcoat protruding from Emmerson's open topcoat and he bowed his head slightly. He had met their type before many times in the drawing rooms of London; the spoilt, indolent sons of wealthy fathers.

'My apologies, gentlemen, Mr Armstrong had a pressing matter he wished to discuss with me at the same time. He's paying the bill, of course, so I had to humour the old man. I trust I didn't cause you great inconvenience?' His apology sounded false to him – which it was - but the two drunken sots could not tell the difference.

'George Carnaby were right put out that you failed to show up,' Emmerson told him.

'Carnabys allus put out about something or another,' the lanky Ingram pointed out and the two men laughed at some shared joke.

'Again my apologies, gentlemen – and I promise not to take up much of your time. I just have a few questions about the night Helen Carnaby disappeared.'

They fell silent and stared coolly in Lavender's direction. Ingram pushed his long greasy hair out of his eyes to see the detective better.

Lavender asked his questions, but their responses did nothing to add to his knowledge about events on that fateful night.

'I don't know if we'll be of much help, man, we were all three sheets to the wind – including Carnaby,' Ingram confessed.

'Yes,' Emmerson agreed. 'I were that out of it, the Devil himself could have arrived and pitchforked everyone into hell and I would have heard nothing. What do you suppose has happened to the damned girl, Lavender?'

'Oh, the usual,' he replied airily. 'I'm sure the strumpet's run away with a lover. She'll probably turn up spoiled and abandoned on the road to Gretna Green soon enough.'

'Really?' Emmerson's piggy eyes widened in surprised. 'Well, Carnaby will be put out by that bit of news.' He turned to his companion. 'God's strewth, it looks like you've had a narrow escape there, Ingram.'

The dark man nodded and bits of dandruff detached themselves from his scalp and landed gently on the velvet collar of his coat.

'How so?' Lavender asked.

Emmerson raised himself slightly then pointed a sausage-like finger at Ingram.

'Ingram's the heir to Baron Widesbeck,' he slurred.

An expectant pause hung in the air. Lavender had the distinct impression that he was supposed to know the peer and the significance of the statement. He didn't, but a reaction was needed if he was to keep these two idiots talking.

'My heartfelt congratulations, sir.'

Ingram nodded, then sighed and looked pained.

'The old guy has told him to get a wife and get her knapped,' Emmerson continued. 'The old Baron wants more heirs.'

Lavender winced inwardly at his crudeness.

'Ingram was considering Carnaby's offer to take his younger sister…'

Offer?

'…But it's a bloody good job you didn't, Ingram. If Lavender is to be believed, it turns out the damned girl is a courtesan and a wanton jilt.'

'Damn good looking gal, though.' Ingram's voice was full of regret and self-pity. 'I'd have enjoyed docking with her.'

'That little ruse of Carnaby's failed as well,' Emmerson said. 'Thanks to that ruddy door bar.'

Ingram nodded, sadly.

Lavender's eyes flashed between them both.

'What 'little ruse' was that?' he asked. But the two men would not be drawn and fell silent. Even their fuddled brains knew they had said too much; they had all but admitted that George Carnaby had been prepared to turn a blind eye to the rape of his sister. Lavender was filled with revulsion, but the professional within him forced his face to remain impassive and his tone light. He decided to change tack.

'It's hard to find an honest woman these days,' Lavender said, careful to add a sympathetic note. 'How much was Carnaby prepared to pay you to marry his sister?'

Emmerson threw back his head and roared. His great belly shook with laughter. Even the doleful Ingram managed a wry smile.

'Pay Ingram? You've got it wrong there Detective – Carnaby doesn't have two shillings to rub together most of the time. No. He said that for five hundred guineas he would make sure that there was no fuss in the church - that the girl would walk down the aisle *docile*, like.'

I'm sure he did.

'She were worth ten thousand, as well,' Ingram said sadly. 'You don't find many gals around here with that kind of chinks.'

'It's a good job Mr Carnaby still has another sister to sell off.' Lavender's tone was heavy with irony.

'What, Izzy? That hatchet-faced old trot?' Emmerson laughed. 'Now Carnaby would have to *pay us* to marry that stale maid!'

Lavender bowed and left the men to their crude jokes about Isobel Carnaby. Their ribald laughter still rang in his ears when he crossed the gloomy hallway and walked out of the building towards his waiting horse. For one brief moment, he felt a twinge of sympathy for the eldest Carnaby daughter. Then he remembered the digitalis; the woman had probably murdered her stepmother. He sighed and felt the cold air bite into lungs.

He had had enough. Carnaby's cronies disgusted him. They had nothing new to add to the evidence he had already accumulated and his understanding of the characters involved in this case. It had been a wasted trip.

That George Carnaby was prepared to force his pretty sister into marriage with Ingram, and let the cad rape and impregnate her, didn't surprise him. He had already decided that Carnaby was the lowest form of low life, who would sell his soul to the devil for five hundred guineas – never mind his sister. Yet still the thought disturbed him.

He paused for a moment before he mounted his horse, enjoyed the animal's warmth next to him and stroked its neck.

He wondered at what point the idea of murdering his sister had entered George Carnaby's mind. Or had it been Isobel Carnaby who had first suggested the evil deed? After all, why settle for five hundred guineas from Ingram for an arranged marriage, when they would inherit the full ten thousand pounds if she was dead?

He shook off the low spirits which threatened to overwhelm him, climbed onto his horse and whipped her into a gallop. The icy wind blasted his face. He hunched low over the neck of the beast, and his thoughts turned back to Magdalena.

Had hers been an arranged marriage, perhaps? He knew that this was common practice amongst the Spanish nobility. If Magdalena's marriage had been arranged, then she must have agreed to it. Somehow he couldn't imagine anyone forcing Magdalena to do anything she didn't want to do, even her father whom she clearly idolised. She didn't have the browbeaten demeanour of a depressed woman trapped in a miserable marriage, so it must have been an amicable arrangement if nothing else. A wave of jealousy surged through him.

He blocked out all thoughts of her husband and allowed his mind to dwell on the better parts of the evening he and Magdalena had spent together. His thoughts warmed him while he raced back through the desolate winter landscape towards Bellingham.

CHAPTER SEVENTEEN

Woods managed to get down the creaking wooden staircase of the tavern about ten in the morning. He still felt faint and queasy and his stomach complained of hunger. Mistress McMullen fussed around him like a mother-hen but seemed relieved when he ordered a mug of tea and a hearty meal of ham and eggs to make up for the supper that he had failed to finish the night before.

Unfortunately, once the greasy food arrived he experienced the unusual sensation of losing his appetite. Determined that his mind played tricks upon him, he picked up his cutlery and ate it anyway. Ten minutes later, he rushed back in the privy and regurgitated his first meal of the day. Unabashed, he returned to bed for a while then came back downstairs and tried again. This time he was more successful. Although plagued with the burps, he managed to keep down breakfast number two and felt far more like his old self. He sighed happily, closed his eyes and tried to rest his aching limbs on the hard wooden settle in front of the fire.

A few of the local farmers had begun to drift into the tavern for a mid-day meal. Most of them laughed and jeered when they saw Woods by the fire.

'Why if it ain't Constable Guzzle Guts!' Jethro Hamilton jeered.

'Still bowsey with the brandy are you, Mr Bow Street Runner?' Isaac Daly enquired with mock solicitude.

Woods ignored them and kept his eyes closed.

The farmers huddled in a corner over their drinks. Their mood changed and they soon began complaining bitterly about the faws.

He had just nodded off when Mistress McMullen shook him awake.

'Ye've got a lady visitor,' she informed him. 'So ye'd better stop yer snoring and wake up sharpish.'

Bleary-eyed, he glanced up to see Katherine Armstrong watching him quizzically. He struggled to his feet, knocking his leg on the table in the process.

'Miss Armstrong – ouch – what can I do fer you? Detective Lavender is visiting Greycoates at the moment.'

She nodded and opened her mouth to speak.

'Miss Armstrong! Here again in the tavern?' yelled Jethro Hamilton from across the smoky room. 'Second time this week -

and to see *another* gadgie? Folk'll start talking, ma'am, mark my words!'

'Oh I do hope so, Mr Hamilton, I do hope so,' she retorted, smiling.

The farmers laughed but it was not unkind. Woods sensed that this community held Katherine Armstrong in high esteem. The farmers had returned to their conversation but Mistress McMullen offered Miss Armstrong the use of a private room to talk to the constable.

'There's no need – I've only come to relay a quick message.'

'Oh yes?' Woods eyebrows' rose.

'Please inform Detective Lavender that my father has decided to add another twenty guineas to the reward money of George Carnaby's offer for information about Helen's whereabouts. I don't know if it will help but he is determined to do everything he can for Helen.'

'That is most generous, I'm sure,' Woods said. 'I'll pass the message on to Detective Lavender when he returns.'

She thanked him and moved away a few steps, but then she turned back, her forehead creased.

'Detective Lavender…' she began.

'Yes, ma'am?' For a moment he thought she was about to question him about their progress on the case. He hesitated. Lavender didn't like revealing information to the clients until he was ready.

'Is he the usual sort of detective who operates out of Bow Street?'

Woods smiled, relieved. Dealing with questions about his enigmatic superior had become part of his job. Everyone was curious about Lavender.

'No, ma'am. He's part of a new breed of detectives – all educated and very clever.'

'Yes, I can see that. My father and I were pleasantly surprised when we met him. We'd assumed he would be more – what shall I say – more bullish, perhaps?'

'He's the quiet type, ma'am – a great thinker and very clever. He's also successful; he usually gets his man.'

She paused to rearrange her bonnet and pat her grey curls.

'Well, let's just hope that on this occasion he gets the girl – in this case, our Helen.'

'He'll do his utmost, ma'am.'

'Yes, I'm sure he will.' She looked like she was about leave but still she paused. 'Is he married?' she asked.

'No ma'am.'

'Now that surprises me. He is an attractive man.' She stared at him calmly, clearly expecting more information.

'He were once betrothed to a lovely young gal back in London – a school mistress.' Woods spoke quickly, unsure about where this line of questioning was heading.

'What happened to the engagement?'

He wondered how much time Katherine Armstrong had spent watching her father question his clients or grilling witnesses in the dock. She definitely had the knack. Her steady brown eyes never left his face, and she timed the silences which lay between them with a precision that forced him to answer.

'The poor gal died two weeks before the wedding.'

'How?'

'Cholera morbus. She'd visited a sick pupil and picked up the disease there.'

'Poor girl,' Katherine Armstrong echoed. 'That is a tragic story. Detective Lavender must have been devastated. It can take years to get over a loss like that.'

Woods nodded. 'It has, ma'am,' he said, simply.

Finally, she seemed satisfied and turned to go.

'Good day to you, Constable – give Detective Lavender my regards.'

When Lavender returned just after one o'clock, he ordered a mug of tea from Mistress McMullen then joined Woods in the tap room. Jethro Hamilton and his cronies had disappeared and the room was now deserted.

Lavender told Woods about his trip to Greycoates and Woods relayed the message passed on to him by Katherine Armstrong.

'Twenty guineas? Well, that's something. It might bring forward some information. From what we've learnt about George Carnaby's finances over the last few days it's obvious that the man will not pay the promised two hundred pounds for news about his sister. He doesn't have it – as I'm sure everyone in this town knows.'

'Miss Katherine seemed a bit put out that you weren't here,' Woods commented with a wink. 'I think that ye've got yourself a bit of an admirer in that lady.'

'Mmm, I doubt that.' Lavender smiled. 'But *you* definitely have an admirer in Bellingham. When you were taken ill last night, the good vicar called into the tavern to see if he could be of assistance. He was most concerned to hear that his most talented baritone was sick.'

'He'd have been after reading me the last rites.' Woods scowled and shuffled uncomfortably. 'Business in his graveyard must be slow.'

Lavender smiled.

'His services might have been needed. Doctor Goddard tells me that the vegetable matter you ingested was digitalis.'

'Foxgloves, eh?' Woods now looked impressed. 'It'll take more than a few weeds to put me in a wooden surcoat.'

'The problem is Ned, they didn't intend to poison you - that was an accident. The poison was intended for Helen or Esther Carnaby, possibly both of them.'

Woods listened with amazement as Lavender related Doctor Goddard's fears about the death of Esther Carnaby.

'Who'd have thought it?' Woods shook his head. 'I mean, neither George Carnaby nor his sister, are pleasant people – he's a cock-sure bully and she's a sly old tabby – but killers! Are they in this murdering lark together, d'you think?'

'Yes, I think so.' Lavender sighed. 'They must be. Fortunately, Helen Carnaby seems to be more intelligent than the pair of them put together. It's obvious to me that she has a lot of discretion for a young woman; it's just possible that she gulled them both and escaped from Linn Hagh unscathed.'

'I still find it hard to believe that they would try to murder either their step-mother or their half-sister for money.'

'Greed combined with desperation is an unhealthy mix,' Lavender said darkly. 'I believe the older Carnabys are becoming more and more anxious as Helen gets closer to claiming her inheritance. This ridiculous scheme to 'sell' her in marriage to Lawrence Ingram is another sign of that desperation. The loss of four hundred pounds a year will hit them harder than we thought. As the cook at Linn Hagh hinted, no one knows what goes on behind the closed doors of a 'respectable' family home.' He ran his hand over his head and pushed back the hair that had escaped from its binding. 'Unfortunately, I suspect that we've only just begun to scratch away the scabs which cover the festering sores of life at Linn Hagh.'

'Poor gal,' Woods said thoughtfully. 'Then there is the fellah she reckons stalks her through Hareshaw Woods. He scared her. Where does he fit into all this, I wonder?'

‘I don’t know.’ Lavender shook his head and frowned. ‘We need to examine those caves at the edge of the gorge and see if we can find him. I think in light of this new evidence we need to take the threat to Helen Carnaby’s life seriously. She was obviously scared to death – the fact that she had asked for refuge from her uncle is further proof of this.’

‘I just wonder why she never returned to that school in Whitby in September.’ Woods commented. ‘She’d have been safe there. Both Katherine Armstrong and Isobel Carnaby told us that she had been invited to return. All she had to do was bide her time at the school for a few months until she came of age, then claim her inheritance and move away.’

Lavender smiled.

‘I think that that sheep drover may have the answer to that question.’

During their trip to Linn Hagh the previous day, Woods had excused himself to use the privy. On his return to the Great Hall he had managed a few quiet words with the cook in the kitchen. Lavender’s threat to take Gladys Norris into custody had worked; she called Lavender a few choice names in his absence, then gave Woods the name of the drover who had seen Miss Helen with her young man. The man they now sought was called Abel Knowles.

‘There is a lover lurking in the background of her life,’ Lavender continued. ‘She didn’t want to leave the area. Young women in love can be very foolish and stubborn.’

‘How d’ you know this?’ Woods smirked.

Lavender ignored his interruption.

‘When we find the lover we’ll find the girl. I just hope that we get to her before the older Carnabys do.’

‘I’ll seek out Knowles the sheep drover at the Wednesday market tomorrow,’ Woods said.

Mistress McMullen arrived to collect the used crockery from their table, which ended all hope of more private discussion.

‘I’ve ordered a couple of horses from the stables,’ Lavender said, as he rose to leave. ‘Are you feeling up to returning to the gypsy camp, Ned? I’m determined to track down that Geddes girl today.’

Mistress McMullen dropped the dish she held. It crashed down on top of the other crockery and shattered as it fell. Startled by the clatter, both men glanced up.

‘Is something amiss?’ Lavender asked.

‘Nowt. Nowt at all.’ Her hands shook as she picked up the broken shards of crockery.

Lavender moved towards her, took hold of her plump arm and forced her to look at him.

'What on earth is the matter with you, woman?'

She flushed, averted her eyes and tried to pull away.

'Nowt.'

Lavender held onto her with a vice like grip.

'Are you withholding information from an officer of the law?' His voice was menacing.

She squealed and struggled against his grip. 'Gerroff me! You're hurting.'

Lavender tightened his grip.

'Is it Jethro Hamilton and Isaac Daly? Do they intend to cause trouble up at the gypsy camp?'

She wouldn't look him in the face. 'It's nowt to do with me. I said fer them not to do it!'

'Do what?'

She ceased struggling and dropped her voice.

'There's talk about burning them out.'

Lavender's colour faded. He let go of the woman abruptly and turned back to Woods.

'Let's move quickly, Ned. If we ride like the devil, we may just get there before they do.'

CHAPTER EIGHTEEN

In the heavy drizzle, the faw camp looked even more desolate than it had in the weak sunshine of the previous day. The rain had driven the gypsies undercover and the camp was almost deserted. A few curious faces peered out of the entrances of the dirty tents, and the embers of the abandoned fire hearths sizzled and smoked in the damp.

'What do we do?' Woods asked as they dismounted. 'Knock at one of them cloth tent doors?'

'Just wait,' Lavender said. 'They know we're here and what we want.'

Sure enough, a few moments later, Paul Faa Geddes walked out of the woodland. He chewed his tobacco slowly and eyed them with an irritating insolence, which was difficult to ignore.

'We still need to speak to the girl Laurel Faa Geddes.' Lavender's tone was abrupt.

'You and your kind need to leave our women folk alone,' Geddes said.

'Why? Who else has asked to speak to Miss Geddes?'

'You can tell George Carnaby to keep that damned idiot brother of his away from the gal, fer a start. It ain't right.'

Lavender stared at Geddes coldly. Yes, gypsy women across the country were known for their low morals, easy ways and frequent arrests for prostitution, and the poverty of this group was glaringly apparent. But he had seen Matthew Carnaby and Laurel Faa Geddes together only the previous day and had gained the impression that their relationship was innocent. Matthew Carnaby might adore the girl but he was not an unwelcome stalker. Geddes was either misguided or he was faking this moral indignation.

'What is it that you think she can help you with?' Geddes asked.

'I believe she knows something about Miss Carnaby's disappearance, her current whereabouts, what happened on the night she fled and the man she is with.'

Geddes laughed. A large wad of stringy tobacco bobbed on the saliva between his teeth. 'Say she does know sommat, why should she help you? When did yer kind ever do owt to help ours?'

'Can you see into the future, man?' Lavender asked. 'Do you have the 'sight'?'

Geddes' eyes widened. His rugged face contorted into a scowl.

'I see you don't,' Lavender continued. 'Well, fortunately for you, Geddes, I can predict the future - and it doesn't look good for you and your kind right now.'

He pointed down the road towards Bellingham.

'At any moment, a gang of angry farmers will appear on that road – intent on doing you harm. As representatives of the law, we're the only people standing between you and them.'

'Ye've set us up?' Geddes spat out the accusation with his tobacco.

'I didn't have to,' Lavender told him sharply. 'You've managed to upset them all by yourselves - with your constant thievery from their farms. Petty theft is a matter for Constable Beddows. We're here to find a missing girl – but right now we find ourselves in the wrong place at the wrong time. I would urge your people to arm themselves quickly. You may need to protect your homes and your families – I believe they intend to burn you out.'

A look of horror now flashed across Geddes' face. He spun around and hollered out instructions in his alien tongue. Men and women appeared from nowhere and the deserted camp filled with movement, screams and panic. Faces pale with fright, the gypsies scurried from tent to tent like a colony of beetles scooping up possessions and herding children towards the safety of the forests. The elderly hobbled painfully after them.

When the panic had subsided and the area cleared, eight men remained. They pulled out their knives with a flash of steel and ranged themselves silently in front of their ragged homes.

It would not be enough; the farmers would easily outnumber them. Despite the drizzle, the whole place would go up like a tinderbox if the farmers got near enough to the camp with their torches.

Lavender wondered how many gypsies remained in the flammable tents, too sick or too stubborn to flee.

'We're going to have to help them,' he whispered to Woods.

The two officers moved away from the camp and positioned themselves halfway down the slope between the gypsies and the road. Woods glanced in the direction of Linn Hagh, where the smoking chimney stacks rose silently above the trees.

'Should we go to Carnaby and ask for his help?'

'I doubt we'd get any help from him.' Lavender's tone was bleak. 'A lynch gang of farmers attacking the faws will play right into his hands. From what we've learnt of his cruelty he'd probably just come out to watch.'

A crowd of twenty farmers appeared round the bend on the road. Angry and determined, they marched purposefully towards the gypsy camp. Brandishing pitchforks, scythes and flaming brush torches, they moved as one, the still air amplifying the thud of their boots. The once friendly men of The Rose and Crown and St. Cuthbert's parish church were now a seething mob and hard-faced as granite.

When they saw Lavender, Woods and the faws ranged against them their pace faltered. They stopped about thirty yards below the encampment, pointing and murmuring amongst themselves.

'Make sure your pistol is primed, Ned.' Lavender said.

'I'm ready.'

Lavender left Woods with their horses and walked down the slope towards the mob.

Jethro Hamilton scowled angrily as Lavender approached. His hair, heavy and wet from the ceaseless drizzle, was plastered against his head.

'What d'you want, Detective?' he snapped. 'This ain't yer quarrel. I reckon ye'd best gan back to Bellingham and yer investigation.'

'I'm afraid it is my quarrel, Mr Hamilton. You see, I'm an officer of the law and I cannot stand by and watch you burn the homes of these people and put their lives at risk.'

'What you tokkin aboot? They ain't *people* - they're bloody thieving scum who live like animals!' The other men roared approval.

'D'you hear that Geddes? You're all parasites – leeches! Not one of you bastards has ever done a decent days work in your damned life!'

'You tell them, Jethro!' Isaac shouted. The rest of the men growled and cheered encouragement. The menacing noise echoed back from the trunks of the ancient woodland, where the frightened women and children cowered in the undergrowth. The flames of the torches cast flickering demonic shadows across the contorted faces of the mob.

'They do nowt but steal from those of us who work our backsides off from dawn till dusk – and we've had enough. We've had enough, I tell ye!'

'Then take your grievances to the proper authorities,' Lavender urged. 'Complain to Beddows – get the magistrates to issue writs for arrests.'

'D'you think we haven't tried? Beddows is useless - useless. Enough tokkin. Come on men, let's do what we set out to do!'

Hamilton stepped forward and the pack of farmers began to surge up the hill.

Woods fired his pistol into the air.

Startled by the blue powder flash and the sharp retort, the farmers stopped. A nervous horse whinnied and a whole colony of rooks rose shrieking into the sky. Lavender sensed the faws stiffen behind him. In the short silence which followed, Woods lowered his gun and aimed it at the chests of the nearest group of farmers.

'The next one of you joskins that moves - gets the second barrel.' Woods' deep baritone voice had never sounded more threatening.

Lavender pulled his own pistol out of his pocket and made it visible to the farmers.

'Listen to me!' he yelled. 'On Friday I have a meeting with Magistrate Clennell in Morpeth. On Friday I'll take your complaints to him and, if you furnish me with evidence of the crimes committed, I'll seek warrants for arrests on your behalf.'

The farmers jeered, unconvinced.

'I'll help you with the due process of the law but I'll *no*t stand by and watch you burn innocent children and women to death.'

'You're on their bloody side!'

'No,' Lavender retorted. 'I'm on the side of the *law* – and although you can't see it – I'm on your side as well, Jethro Hamilton. Every one of you is a decent, law-abiding man. Not one of you wants to spend time in gaol for arson, or hang for murder. None of you wants to bring terror and death to the innocent.'

'You know nothing about us!' Hamilton's face glowed red with fury and frustration.

'I know more than you think. I've watched you with your own children in church, Hamilton. How are you ever going to face your sons again, if you terrorise or kill these faw children today? How long do you think they'll survive out here without their homes in the middle of winter? And you, Isaac Daly - can you go back home and face your own family after this?'

'You've no idea what we've had to put up with!' Daly yelled.

'Yes, I do know – and I also know that the faces of these terrified gypsies will haunt your dreams if you harm them.'

'Bollocks!' Daly snapped but his voice had less force now.

'You've all got kin that respect you,' Lavender announced loudly, 'And for good reason. There's a woman in labour up there in one of the caravans. Harry Hurst - your wife is pregnant, isn't she? And near her time?'

The farmer addressed as Harry Hurst looked startled, then nodded.

'This faw woman can't be moved and her aged mother refuses to leave her. Are you going to burn these women out, Harry Hurst? Are you going to listen to their screams and think it's a job a well done to burn alive a pregnant woman?'

Hurst grimaced, turned pale and glanced down at his boots.

'In another tent an old woman lies dying; her terrified husband is beside her. Is this the end you'd like for your own parents, Fred Jamieson, to have them writhing in agony in the flames? Is this what the men of Bellingham do to their elders?'

The farmers shuffled uncomfortably beneath the rain of accusations. Lavender's words hit home; he picked them out as individuals, not creatures of the senseless mob. His evenings of quiet observation in the tap room of The Rose and Crown now bore fruit. He knew them. One by one, he named them and re-humanised them. Gazes dropped before his fierce glare, arms holding torches and weapons were lowered.

'Go home, the lot of you,' Lavender said. 'Gather the evidence you have and bring it to me at The Rose and Crown. I give you my word as a principal officer with the Bow Street magistrate's court, that I'll seek redress for your wrongs through the Northumbrian courts.'

'Aye.'

'He's right.'

'Let's gan home, lads.'

'There's bugger all we can do while they're standing there with pistols, anyhow.'

The famers began to fall back.

Only Jethro Hamilton stood his ground. His face contorted with frustration; his stubborn jaw bones rigid beneath his tanned skin.

'If you do come back wi' a warrant,' he complained, 'Them bastards will just tek off and disappear before you can serve it.'

Lavender dropped his voice and leaned forward.

'Isn't that what you've been wanting for the last twenty years, Hamilton? For them to just go?'

The big farmer said nothing.

'Do as I say, Hamilton, and you won't regret it. You cannot lose out now. I'll sort out your problem and I'll see you in church next Sunday – not as an arsonist and murderer – but as a proud man and a decent Christian. You'll be able to hold your head up and look your wife, children and neighbours in the face.'

Hamilton stared at him. His blue eyes were like ice. Then he broke his gaze, turned and followed the others back down the road towards Bellingham.

Lavender breathed a huge sigh of relief. He pushed his damp hair off his face. His hands were frozen but he daren't put away the pistol and retrieve his gloves just yet. Behind him, he heard the faws begin to shout amongst themselves and move around their camp. Woods joined him as he gazed at the retreating farmers.

'Nicely done, sir, if you don't mind me saying so.'

Paul Faa Geddes appeared at their side.

'D'you think they'll be back?'

'I've no idea,' Lavender sighed. 'That depends on how much you folks continue to harass them with your thievery.'

'That's falsehoods they've bin saying agin us.' Geddes whined. His insolence had vanished.

Lavender scowled. 'We're going down to the gorge to investigate those caves in the sandstone rocks. Tell us where they are - and send that Laurel girl down to speak with us when she turns up.'

'All right,' Geddes grovelled. 'But you'll have to come back and protect us. This ain't right. We've a right to be left alone here. It's yer job to protect us.'

CHAPTER NINETEEN

They left the horses tied to a tree on the main path and scrambled up through the undergrowth towards the crumbling cliff face of the gorge. The vegetation petered out and they struggled up a boulder-strewn scree slope towards the fissures in the rock. There was only one cave large enough and dry enough for human habitation. A trickle of green water leaked out from the edge and formed stagnant pools in the mud at the entrance. The officers approached cautiously. Lavender pushed aside a small bush at the entrance. They peered into the gloomy interior and waited until their eyes became accustomed to the darkness. It was deserted. A blackened stone circle in the centre of the uneven floor contained the ashes of a dead fire. A pile of mouldy rags lay heaped in one corner.

Carefully, Woods examined the jutting shadows at the back of the cave while Lavender dropped to his haunches and raked around amongst the ash and the debris at the edge of the fire.

Outside, the rain continued to fall softly onto the bushes. Woods stood for a moment and tried to imagine what it must be like to sleep here on this cold earth floor with only these stinking rags for bedding. Even with a fire for warmth and comfort, the place was desolate. The walls were slimy with damp; the silence and isolation oppressive.

'Do you ever get the feeling in these here woods that you're being watched?' he asked.

Lavender glanced up. He never doubted Wood's courage for a moment but he knew that this brooding woodland had affected his constable in a way that the familiar, heaving streets of the capital never did.

'Constantly,' he said. 'This forest is full of eyes – most of them fixed on us.'

Woods nodded with relief and moved across to an uneven floor to the pile of rags in the corner. Lavender watched him lift each one carefully and shake it out. A flash of dull metal glinted and fell amongst the stones on the floor. Woods reached down and scooped up a rounded pewter button.

'What have you found?'

Woods held out the button for inspection. A couple of black threads hung limply from the back.

'From an old coat, I should think,' Lavender said. 'Black. Possibly military.'

'Does this help us?'

'I don't know. Most of the market towns in England have second-hand clothes stalls which sell surplus army greatcoats. They're warm and favoured by farmers and beggars alike. This might be of more interest, though.'

He rose stiffly to his feet and showed Woods a thin taper of blackened parchment. Burnt at one end, the tightly folded taper looked like it had been torn from a pocket book. Lavender took off his gloves and unfolded the flimsy material. The burnt end disintegrated in his hands as he did so.

He groaned with frustration and moved over towards the better light at the entrance of the cave. Woods joined him and craned his neck to peer down at the faint spidery writing. The only two words which remained decipherable were *Redesdale arms.*

'Redesdale: that's the next valley along.'

'I bow to your greater knowledge of the local geography,' Lavender said. 'I assume that 'arms' refers to another tavern or inn - perhaps in Otterburn?'

'I don't know that much,' Woods confessed.

Lavender continued to stare at the thin strip of parchment in his hand.

'This is not a taper used to light a fire.'

'Was it used to get a light from the fire for a pipe?' Woods suggested.

Lavender knelt down on the floor and continued to feel along the uneven ground. His fingertips pushed through the soil and ash with meticulous care.

'Ha!' he said.

He lifted a few strands of stringy brown matter from the ground and sniffed them cautiously.

'What is it? Tobacco?'

'Yes.'

'I were right about the clay pipe. We've got a mysterious beggar in a military greatcoat who smokes a clay pipe.'

Lavender nodded, searched again and lifted more matter to his nose.

'There's more - there's snuff. This bit is snuff. Macouba snuff, to be precise.'

'Ain't that a bit pricey for a beggar?'

'Yes – it's the brand preferred by George Carnaby.'

‘So why is a penniless beggar, who sleeps in a cave, smoking George Carnaby’s snuff in his pipe?’

‘I don’t think he does. I think Master Carnaby paid a visit to the rogue who slept here. Carnaby takes his snuff everywhere; he even took it in church on Sunday.’

‘But why were George Carnaby here? Did he warn him off or encourage him?’

‘I don’t know but this is Carnaby’s land. He could have a thousand feasible explanations for being in this cave. However, I think the landlord at the Redesdale Arms in Otterburn is worth a visit.’

They went back out into the grey drizzle and slithered back down the scree slope to their horses. There was still no sign of the gypsy girl so Lavender suggested they bide their time and take a walk along the gorge. It was hard going with the animals.

Eventually they reached the icy edge of the pool at the base of Hareshaw Linn and stared across the gleaming black rocks to where the water thundered and foamed down the waterfall. Their faces were soon wet with spray. Lavender could see the look of dislike on his constable’s features and sense his discomfort.

‘Be careful Detective or the grindylows will nab you!’ The young woman’s voice had a musical quality, like the trilling of birdsong.

Lavender spun around. Laurel Faa Geddes stood behind them. She had appeared out of nowhere – as silent as a padding cat. One silver-ringed hand rested lightly on her hip. She grinned. Her vivid blue eyes sparkled mischievously.

‘I’m not familiar with the grindylows, Miss Geddes.’ Lavender smiled. ‘Perhaps you’d care to enlighten me?’

She pointed a grimy finger towards the reeds at the edge of the brackish pool. ‘They live down there, in the watter. They’ve long, sinewy arms and grab you to drown you, if you’re not careful.’

‘Sounds like a few of the trollops I’ve met down the London docks,’ Woods observed.

She ignored him and fixed her attention on Lavender who back stared at her, taking in every detail. The girl dropped her head to one side and grinned. Her teeth flashed like small white pearls in brilliant contrast to her dark skin. Luxurious black curls tumbled down from beneath her headscarf and the laurel wreath which adorned her head.

‘How old are you, Miss Geddes?’

She laughed lightly.

'We don't keep track of the years that come and go in my world. Where's the point in that? There's no cake with candles fer me at a year's end. All I know is that I were born cursed.'

'Cursed?'

Lavender left the dampness of the water's edge and climbed a few steps up onto path beside her. She edged away slightly. As she moved, he caught a fleeting glimpse of white circles of flesh through the holes in her stockings above her ancient boots. The ragged hem of her dress was only just a decent length. Briefly, he wondered what had happened to the dress Helen Carnaby had given her. No doubt she had sold or pawned it

'Aye, a bairn born at midnight before the Sabbath is allus born under a curse,' she informed him.

'For a young woman born under a curse, you seem very comfortable with it.'

'What's the point of fussing?' She shrugged and smiled again. 'I keep a sprig of holly fer luck – and you cannot alter what's written in the stars.'

'Is that what your mother tells you?'

'Me ma's dead.'

'And your father?'

'So what is it you're wanting from me, Detective?'

Her self-assurance suggested that she was in her twenties, he decided; it was difficult to judge. Her playful manner belied her years but the harshness of her life had aged her prematurely. Already, fine lines had formed around her vivid blue eyes.

'I need your help to find Miss Carnaby.'

'What if she don't want to be found?'

'For her own safety, I would still like to know where she is,' he said, quietly. 'I can protect her. I know her life is in danger and she feels threatened. I need your help to eliminate that threat.'

'Seems to me like you already know all there is to know then, Detective - but perhaps I can help you a bit more - if I can see the colour of yer silver.'

For a moment Lavender was confused.

'She wants money,' Woods volunteered. He had come to join them up on the path.

'Aye – and from you, too,' the girl said.

Sighing, the constable reached into his pocket for some loose change. Then he turned over his large hand and the girl skimmed the silver coins from his palm. She held his hand in hers and traced her finger across the lines etched across his palm.

'Why, I see you're a big round robin redbreast of a fellah, Constable Woods!' she teased. 'And there's plenty of chicks in yer nest back in the old oak tree – I see four with yer jenny wren.' Woods' face erupted with surprise then he froze. His hand still lay in hers.

'Is this how you earn your living, Miss Geddes?' Lavender interrupted. 'Telling fortunes to the gullible?'

Woods flinched. Laurel turned away from Woods but kept hold of his hand. She was not laughing now.

'I hev the sight. I can see things others can't. I can help. I'm not a whore if that's what you think.' Her expression was sincere, if mildly irritated. She spoke with the voice of a parent trying to explain something to a willful, young child then turned back to Woods.

'You need to watch out fer the hairy beast with a ring through its nose – and bless you, sir!' Her face fell.

'What is it?'

Lavender could hear faint alarm in his constable's voice.

'Yer youngest daughter will break yer heart.'

Woods laughed awkwardly and pulled back his hand.

'Very interesting,' he said, nonchalantly. 'We'll see about that.'

'Is this why they call you the 'young witch' down in Bellingham, Miss Geddes?' Lavender asked. 'Because of your sight?'

'Is that why you're here, Detective?' she parroted his question. 'To arrest me fer witchcraft?' Amusement flickered at the corners of her pretty mouth.

It was Lavender's turn to smile. 'Witchcraft ceased to be an act punishable by law in 1735,' he told her. 'No, madam, as I've already said: I'm here to seek your help to find and protect Miss Carnaby.'

'Then it's yer turn to cross my palm with silver, Detective.'

Lavender paused. This was all nonsense of course, but he recognised a challenge when he saw one. He would get nothing from this girl unless he went along with her game. He took off his glove, plunged his hand into his pocket and held out a palm full of silver sixpences.

'Why what clean hands you have, Detective!' she complained. 'You oughtn't to wash them so often – you keeps yer luck in the grimy lines of yer hands.'

She fell silent and screwed up her face in concentration. Lavender could see that reading his palm was not so easy for her; she looked troubled. Her voice lost its lightness and lowered in tone.

‘I see the still black waters of the Tyne run deep in you, Detective. Folks only see themselves mirrored when they look into the darkness of yer eyes – they never see you. But who is the woman with the jet black hair and the red-stoned ring? She’s crept under your skin like the Queen of Elphame, seeking comfort beneath a rock. She’s a shape-shifter and she’ll ensnare you.’

‘Enough.’

Lavender withdrew his hand sharply.

‘Watch out fer the man with the burnt face – he’ll threaten yer happiness,’ the girl continued unabashed.

‘Tell me what you know about Helen Carnaby’s disappearance, the man she is with and the other man – the one who camps out in the cave in this gorge.’

‘He’s a bad un.’ She scowled.

‘Which one?’ he queried. ‘The lover, or the vagrant in the woods?’

‘Him.’ She jerked her thumb back towards the sandstone cliffs. ‘He’s bad, allus watching, allus prowling around – watching…’ She shivered and pulled her shawl tighter over her thin shoulders.

‘Can you describe him?’

But her mercurial mind had already moved on.

‘They’ve a lot of bad blood up at Linn Hagh, there’s bin evil there. On the day she left I heard them shrieking and screaming. They think the thick walls of their tower protect them - but I know what goes on. He were going to beat her.’

‘Who?’

She spat at the ground in disgust.

‘Him, Carnaby. He were going to flay her - like he does to Matty. He wanted her to come out of her room.’

Lavender grimaced.

‘What is your relationship with Master Matthew Carnaby, Miss Geddes?’

Her eyes widened in surprise then her face softened with compassion.

‘Why Matty is my friend, he’s a sweetie. We’ve grown up together in these woods.’

‘Did you used to take care of Matthew Carnaby when he was a baby and his mother was…ill?’

She shook her head and the silver hoops in her ears flashed in the fading daylight.

‘Matty’s allus bin bigger than me. I never knew him as a bairn.’

‘Where’s Miss Carnaby, Laurel?’

She laughed, threw back her glossy black mane and gave him a dazzling smile.

'You know where she is – you're toying with us all,' she accused, playfully. 'You're a clever 'un – with a bit of the sight yerself - and if you weren't too sure, you could allus hang a ring on a red silk thread and dangle it o'er an article of her clothing.'

'What good would that do?'

'You have to say: *'Av mi Romani mal, dawdel dur chumbas.'* Then what you seek you shall find. Remember me words, detective, remember me words...''

With that, she turned and climbed swiftly up the steep side of the ravine, gliding over the fallen logs and rocks with the nimbleness of a fawn. The bracken parted before her as she moved then it swished quietly back into place after she passed. She blended back into her natural habitat like a wood nymph.

'Wait!' Lavender called.

She stopped, turned back and pointed further downstream to where a rickety bridge crossed the black water.

'Over there – on the other side,' she pointed. 'Behind the cracked sycamore that snarls like serpent - there's a path that'll lead you back up to the road. You can take the horses that way.'

He took his eyes off her for one moment to follow the line of her finger but when he turned back she had gone. She had melted back into the latticework of timber like a dryad and vanished as mysteriously as she had arrived.

CHAPTER TWENTY

'So how did she know that 'robin redbreast' is the nickname of members of the Bow Street horse patrol?'

Lavender sighed. Woods had been animated and full of questions since their encounter with the gypsy girl. Lavender found it hard to keep him objective.

'I've no idea. She could have heard folks talking about you, the horse patrol – or your scarlet waistcoats - in Bellingham market. This is how these people operate. They listen and pick up signs.'

'What about my home on Oak Road? How could she know about that? Or my four little nippers?'

'It was all a coincidence, Ned. She talked generally about birds: robins and wrens. Birds nest in trees – oak trees sometimes. As for the number of little Woods back at Oak Road, well just how many times have you talked about your children while you've been in Northumberland?'

Woods paused and screwed up his face with concentration.

'Twice: once with Anna and once with that cook – Norris.'

'Both times while travelling along this road?'

'Yes.'

'Well, there's your answer. As we said earlier, all eyes in Bellingham have been watching us since we arrived. No doubt every ear has been tuned in our direction, as well.'

'Hmmph.' His constable was not convinced. Woods thought for a moment and then tried a different tack.

'And what about them things that she said about you?'

'Well, I'm obviously more 'black' and 'mysterious because I don't go blabbing around town about my personal life.'

Woods eyed him slyly.

'She knew about that Spanish señora, all right – and neither of us have talked about her since we came up north. She wears a red garnet ring on her left hand. I know that because I saw it.'

'Well done, Constable Woods,' Lavender snapped. 'Let's get you promoted to principal officer.'

'Now, there's no need to get testy.'

'I'm not getting testy.'

'Yes, you are.' Woods tone had become that of a parent admonishing a naughty child.

Lavender sighed. It had been a stressful twenty-four hours and the day was not over yet. They were nearly back at Bellingham and probably faced an angry encounter with the farmers in The Rose and Crown.

'Look at it this way, Ned. Women are generally either dark or fair – the gypsy had a one in two chance of mentioning the correct hair colour of a woman I've met recently. As for the ring? All women wear rings. It's nothing more than coincidence and luck. She has had a good day with us, that's all. Tomorrow she'll get it wrong with someone else, and they'll laugh in her face and demand their money back.'

Woods didn't seem convinced, but he fell silent as they entered the livery stables, dismounted and handed over the reins of their animals to a groom. Stiff from their journey, they trudged up the icy cobbles towards The Rose and Crown.

The streets of the Bellingham were deserted. The smell of smoke from the brick chimneys descended onto the town like an invisible cloak. There were no street lamps; only the occasional warm pool of light from bare windows spilled onto the road to provide light against the encroaching starless night. Their breath billowed in clouds before them. Woods pulled his coat tighter around his shoulders and voiced the niggling fear which bothered them both.

'Let's just hope we're still welcome after that little stand-off at the gypsy camp earlier.'

'Mmm,' said Lavender. 'I wonder what will happen next? I had better send a note to Beddows and alert him that he has some serious trouble on his patch – though I doubt he'll care.'

Lavender was prepared to organise a private dining room for their supper that night in order to avoid another confrontation with Jethro Hamilton, but to his surprise the main bar of the tavern was deserted. A few elderly men were hunched around the gaming tables, intent on their endless dice game, but apart from them, Mistress McMullen and a sullen barman, the tap room remained emptier than Lavender had ever seen it before.

The two officers sank exhausted into the comfortable chairs by the fire and removed their gloves, scarves and hats.

'I hope to God, Hamilton, Daly and their cronies are not back at Linn Hagh, burning down the gypsy camp.' Lavender sighed.

'If they've any sense they'll just stay quietly at home tonight,' Woods said, grinning. 'They probably feel a bit embarrassed after you talked them down.'

Lavender and Woods ordered their supper and enjoyed a glass of brandy. The fiery liquid warmed their insides.

'What I don't understand,' Woods said. 'Is where does this gypsy girl fit into the mystery of Helen Carnaby's disappearance? Why is she important?'

Lavender smiled. 'I think she may have helped Miss Carnaby with her dramatic exit from Linn Hagh. I still wait for proof,' he volunteered, as he sipped his drink. 'But I also think Laurel Faa Geddes is Baxter Carnaby's natural daughter – a half-sister to the Carnabys at Linn Hagh. '

'What!'

'Didn't you see those eyes, Ned – those vivid blue eyes? The same blue eyes are in Helen Carnaby's portrait and Matthew Carnaby's face.'

'With respect, sir, she's a gypsy gal – she could be *anyone's* daughter.' Woods looked stunned.

'True, but I believe when we finally get hold of a copy of Baxter Carnaby's last will and testament, from that lawyer in Newcastle, I think my theory will be proved to be true. I expect it to tell us that his natural daughter, Laurel Faa Geddes, is entitled to remain with her people on the land of Linn Hagh for the duration of her natural life. This is the only explanation for why those gypsies are still tolerated up at Linn Hagh.'

'But Mr Armstrong never said nowt about it.'

'I don't think Mr Armstrong knows. What occurs at Linn Hagh – stays at Linn Hagh. It is guarded by its isolation and a small army of loyal, tight-lipped servants.'

'Well! That's a turn up fer the books!' Woods looked impressed. 'So old Baxter Carnaby had a by-blow with one of the gypsy women?'

'Exactly. Linn Hagh is so remote from civilisation, anything could have happened up there - and I suspect that it probably did. Judging by the fact that Laurel Faa Geddes told us that she is younger that Matthew Carnaby, I suspect that the liaison between her mother and Baxter Carnaby happened in those five years between his two wives. Maybe during the time when Martha Carnaby was in the asylum - but definitely before he met and married Esther Armstrong.'

'Do you think the other Carnabys know?'

'I'm sure they do. If I'm right and Baxter Carnaby has tried to protect or help his natural daughter in his will, then they'll be well aware of her existence – and probably very frustrated by it. I've no doubt that if he had been given a free reign, George Carnaby would have turned the faws off his land years ago. The gypsies know about it too. That's why their leader is uncomfortable with her friendship with Matthew Carnaby; he claimed it 'wasn't right.''

'What do you mean?'

Lavender laughed softly and swirled the amber liquid around in his glass.

'While the faws may be a tribe of easy virtue and turn a blind eye to prostitution in all its forms amongst their women folk, even gypsies are not comfortable about the prospect of incest. Matthew Carnaby may be backward and a simpleton but he is still a man, and he is obviously devoted in his simple way to his own sister.'

Mistress McMullen appeared with their supper before Woods could question Lavender further. She also had two letters for the detective.

One of them was a note from Katherine Armstrong. He read it quickly as he ate. It told him that she had been unable to discover any other member of her family who may have left the flowers on Esther Carnaby's grave.

'We'll stake out the grave of Baxter Carnaby from midnight, as we promised,' Lavender said. 'We'll split the watch and if the ghostly Miss Carnaby makes another appearance in the graveyard of St. Cuthbert's, then one of us will be there to witness it. Eat heartily, my friend, it looks like we're in for a long and cold twenty-four hours.'

The other letter was from Magistrate Read in Bow Street, in response to the note Lavender had sent him after his encounter with Doña Magdalena at Barnaby Moor. Lavender opened it, put down his fork, frowned and tapped his fingers irritably on the table as he considered its contents.

'Trouble back home?' Woods queried.

'Not exactly.'

'Oh?'

Lavender paused while he mulled over the contents of the letter. His face flushed as he struggled with the conflicting emotions the news in the letter invoked. Woods waited patiently.

'We may not have returned Helen Carnaby to her family yet, but it does appear that I've solved one mystery this week.'

'What do you mean?'

'We now know the reason why Doña Magdalena has not heard from her husband for the last few months.'

Woods paused with his fork halfway to his mouth. He raised his eyebrows and regarded Lavender with renewed interest.

'Her husband, Don Antonio Garcia de Aviles, was killed at the battle of Talavera at the end of July. He fought under the Spanish General Cuestra.'

'God's strewth!' Woods put down his cutlery.

Lavender didn't know how to react. Despite his casual dismissal of Laurel Faa Geddes' words, his encounter with the gypsy girl had unnerved him; she'd been right. Magdalena had gotten underneath his skin and it was not just gratitude for saving his life that he felt towards her.

The death of her husband now changed everything. Left vulnerable and helpless in a hostile, alien country, Magdalena probably also faced financial ruin. He felt an impulsive urge to leap onto the next mail coach, race down to Gainsborough and protect her. This alarmed him; he was not a man given to rash behaviour. One thing was for certain, he needed to bring this case in Bellingham to its natural conclusion. He now had pressing business further south.

'What else does the letter say?' Woods asked.

Lavender shook himself and tried to think rationally.

'The Home Department has tried to contact Doña Magdalena for some time to pass on the news of her husband's death. Unfortunately, they've been unable to locate her. This doesn't surprise me. She has been flitting from the charity of one set of Spanish émigrés to another for months.'

Woods nodded.

'Magistrate Read asks me to convey the news to her myself if I know of her current location.'

'Then I guess, you'd better write to the señora tonight,' Woods said, simply.

Yes, thought Lavender. *He's right. A letter is what is called for – no rash gestures. Give the woman some time to grieve for her husband.*

'While you writing to her, I'll get a nap and then I'll take first watch in the graveyard.'

CHAPTER TWENTY ONE

The rain turned to sleet and then snow as Woods trudged down the hill towards St. Cuthbert's just before midnight. This is a dismal trip, he thought as he stared at the flurry of snowflakes that danced down in his narrow window of vision between his hat brim and the top of the wet scarf which swathed his face. He was wearing every item of clothing he had brought with him – including two pairs of trousers and the thick socks Betsy had knitted for him, but he still knew he would be frozen before long. He had forgotten how bloody cold it was up here in the north east of England.

He pushed open the creaking, iron gate and walked across the lonely graveyard to the rear of the church. In the dim moon light he could see the fine layer of unblemished snow which had settled over the ground. No one had been this way in a while. He turned around and watched the falling snow cover his own tracks.

He went to the back of the church and sought the straggly patch of bushes Lavender had told him to find. There, amongst the perennial willow weed and a couple of stunted elders, was a large rhododendron bush. Carefully, he pushed aside the waxy, lance-shaped leaves and tried to force his way between the boughs. They did their best to resist him. Suddenly, they yielded and he found himself in a large, dry space. The branches sprung back behind him.

Careful not to take out his eye on any unseen branches, he scooped up as much loose foliage as he could find and heaped it onto the damp soil to make a nest. Next, he took out his blankets and made himself as comfortable as possible on his pile of leaves and twigs. By breaking off a few more branches of the bush, he was able to make a gap big enough to peer through.

Before him, the black walls of St. Cuthbert's were silhouetted against an even blacker sky. Baxter Carnaby's grave was just about visible. If the missing heiress did decide to pay her father a visit on the anniversary of his death, then Woods would be able to see her. Personally, he felt that even the most devoted of daughters would quail at venturing out on a night like this.

Sighing, he realised that he was in for a long and futile wait. He settled down and allowed his mind to think back to Lavender and his Spanish señora. Was the untimely death of Don Antonio Garcia de Aviles a blessing in disguise for his friend and employer, or a curse?

It was never a good idea to go mooning around after another man's wife but Woods was not convinced that the newly widowed señora would make Lavender happy.

The man had been moody and tight-lipped when they had left Barnby Moor after his encounter with the highwaymen and the señora. He had sat brooding in the corner of the coach for the rest of their trip north. At supper in the taverns he had been taciturn and distracted.

Woods had heard him stomp back to his bedchamber after dining with the señora and had got the distinct impression that their meal together had not gone well. He had tried a bit of gentle ribbing, but Lavender would not be drawn on what had transpired between them. Woods suspected that the detective had had his fingers burnt – or at least slapped. Hardly surprising, he thought; that señora was a feisty filly and would be a handful for any man.

Lavender's professional reputation, university education and obvious intelligence opened up the doors of many upper class drawing rooms, but Woods suspected that even as an impoverished widow, the señora would still be out of Lavender's reach. The principal officers were fêted in London by the ton; their novelty and rarity meant they were welcome everywhere as guests, from Almack's to private boxes in Vaux-hall Gardens.

But, in the eyes of high society, none of these things would make Lavender good enough for the aristocratic señora. His friend and colleague aimed too high. This dalliance was doomed to fail. At the end of the day, Stephen Lavender was still a working police officer and the son of a Bow Street runner.

What Lavender needed, he decided, was a good, homely woman like his own Betsy. Indeed, Betsy had tried to introduce Lavender to a couple of eligible gals back home in London on the few occasions when he had dined with them. The young women had sighed and reported back to Betsy that the detective was charming, polite, but very, very distant.

Betsy told him that Lavender was an attractive man for a gentleman in his mid-thirties. A bit thin in the face and body perhaps and in need of some good home cooking, but he was tall, dark, wealthy and fastidiously neat and clean. Unfortunately, the man was also married to his work.

Back at The Rose and Crown, Lavender stared miserably at the black-edged parchment on the table in front of him, twirled his quill and felt hopelessly to the task ahead.

Beside him on the table, lay the letter from Magistrate Read. In another attempt to put off the inevitable, he picked it up and read the last paragraphs again:

'...I do not know how you came to meet Señora Morales, Stephen, but should you know of the current whereabouts of de Aviles' widow, I would be grateful if you would pass on the unfortunate news of her husband's death and ask her to contact me at Bow Street for further information.

While rendering us some good service at the start of the French occupation of Spain, de Aviles turned out to be as vainglorious and inconsistent as the rest of his aristocratic countrymen. He had no reason to be fighting at Talavera and indeed, had been dispatched on an altogether different mission by General Sir Arthur Wellesley. However, I will strive to give a good report of him to his widow.

Regarding this lady, I would also urge caution on your part. There are reports that she and her servants shot their way out of Spain, despatching two of Napoleon's officers and half a dozen infantrymen who had been sent to arrest her. It may very well be that the female is the more deadly of the species when it comes to the de Aviles family...'

Oh, Magdalena, he thought sadly. *No wonder you wanted to 'forget.'* With a heavy heart he took up his quill and dipped it into the inkwell.

My dearest Magdalena,
It is with great sadness that I must inform you ...

In his bush in the icy churchyard, Woods was freezing, shocked and indignant.

He had been shivering in his cramped position in the rhododendron for only an hour, when a drunken couple burst through the iron gate of the graveyard. Laughing raucously, they clutched each other for balance and slithered down the path towards the rear of the church where he was secreted. They passed a brandy bottle between them, raised it to their lips and drank. The woman sought shelter from the flurries of snow behind one of the buttress pillars, but the man continued to move towards Woods.

For one terrible minute he thought he was about to be discovered but the drunkard stopped three feet away and stared glassy-eyed at the trunk of a stunted elder tree. Woods could still see the unpleasant, crooked grin stretched across the face below the hat.

The next second, Woods heard the unmistakeable sizzle of an arc of warm urine hitting frozen holy ground. The acrid stench nearly made him retch.

Damn it, he thought. *I'm going to have to sniff that for the next seven hours.*

The drunken sot now wove his way back round the gravestones to his doxy and took the brandy bottle from her. She meanwhile reached for the unbuttoned front fall on his breeches – the strumpet's intention was obvious.

'God's strewth,' Woods groaned between gritted and chattering teeth as the fumbling commenced. It had ceased snowing, the wind had dropped and he had an unimpaired view of her attempts to box the Jesuit.

Cursing beneath his breath, Woods closed his eyes. Unfortunately, he couldn't close his ears. After several embarrassing minutes of grunting the couple briefly fell silent. Woods risked a look. That was a mistake.

The woman's ministration to her companion's member had only inflamed his sodden passion. Now he had hitched up her skirts and had her pressed up against the consecrated wall of the church. She squealed like a stuck pig with every thrust and Woods had to endure another painful twenty minutes of their noisy and intoxicated lust.

He shuffled uncomfortably on his damp blanket, pulled his hat further down over his ears and tried to imagine the expression on the face of St. Cuthbert's vicar if the man ever got to see what his parishioners did in his Saxon churchyard. The cleric had a lot more to worry about than the insidious rise of Methodism.

Finally, the rutting couple broke apart and readjusted their clothing. Woods saw the glimmer of metal in the moonlight as coins changed hands. He sighed and waited for them to leave. The trollop pulled her shawl tighter around her shoulders and staggered off into the night, but her customer now slumped down in the shelter of the wall and took another swig from his bottle. A few moments later, he had fallen asleep and began to snore loudly.

Great, thought Woods. *This is the last thing I need.*

If the nervous Helen Carnaby did creep out in the middle of the night to visit her father's grave, the first thing she would see was a frozen stiff only yards from where Baxter Carnaby was buried. If that didn't scare her away nothing else would. For a moment he considered breaking his cover and trying to shake the tosspot awake to send him home, but then he decided against it. Tough as they were up here in this county, even a Northumbrian could not sleep out of doors on a November night without cover; nobody was that immune to the cold, were they? The man would probably wake up soon and stagger back to the warmth of his home.

He didn't. When the first red smudges of dawn glowed above the eastern horizon and the smell of smoke drifted down from the silent town towards the isolated church on the marshy ground by the river, the man still slept in the graveyard, curled up against the sandstone wall of the church.

Bleary-eyed, stiff and sore, Woods shuffled around in his confined space. He was frozen to the bone, fed up and hungry. He had kept awake all night – thanks to the annoying and incessant screech of a tawny owl. Helen Carnaby had not shown up. Well, not yet anyway. Fortunately, he knew that Lavender would soon be along to relieve him.

Somewhere down the valley, sheep began to bleat. Crows called to each other from nests in the tree tops then rose, circling and wheeling, in pairs and groups of three before they headed down to their favourite feeding grounds. Down by the silent river moorhens squabbled in the reeds. Slowly, daylight spread across the frosted earth and the church with the strange stone roof. Trees, distant rooftops and tombstones took form out of the indistinguishable mass of blackness. It promised to be a brilliant day with a sky of white light and ice blue arched over the world, but Woods was not in the mood to appreciate the shimmering clarity of the northern winter sky.

The church gate squeaked again and a heavily-veiled young woman entered the graveyard.

Woods forced his teeth to stop their noisy chattering. It was her.

She didn't take the direct route which would have led her straight to the unconscious drunk; she went the long way around the building. For a moment he had doubts. Perhaps it was someone else? Then he remembered that her mother's grave lay on the blind side of the church.

Eventually, she appeared round the corner and glided over to Baxter Carnaby's grave, the hem of her black gown damp with melted frost and dew. She reached out a gloved hand to touch her father's headstone. Even with her veil, Woods knew it was Helen Carnaby. Her silvery-blonde hair was clearly visible beneath the material. He could see the compassion etched across her shadowed and thoughtful face. Her youth, poise and grace all gave away her identity. The small posy of helleborus she carried – the twin of the one they had found on her mother's grave - was yet another clue to her identity.

Quietly, he waited and watched. Lavender had been quite clear in his instructions: watch her and follow her back to her lair; at no point startle her or alert her to your presence.

Out of the corner of his eye, Woods caught the unexpected flash of silver.

Instinctively, he turned his head. He swore.

The drunken wretch from the previous night was now on his feet, his gaze fixed on Helen Carnaby's back. His eyes blazed with madness in a face consumed with hatred. He held a gulley knife in his right hand. He raised it and began to advance on the oblivious young woman.

'For Christ's sake! Run, Miss!' Woods yelled.

He forced his stiff limbs into action and struggled to his feet. He tore off his gloves, fumbled inside his pocket for his pistol and crashed through the bush into the open, fighting the excruciating cramp in his leg.

'Run gal!'

But Helen Carnaby was rooted to the spot, still unaware of the danger behind her. She stared at him in alarm - as did her attacker – both of them shocked at Woods' sudden appearance from the bush. For a brief second, the three of them were held there, motionless in a triangle of fear: the woman, the killer and the grimacing constable with the agonizing cramp. Then Woods aimed his pistol at her attacker.

Helen Carnaby gasped, turned and finally saw her would-be assailant and his blade. She screamed. The villain turned on his heels and sped back up towards the road.

'Stop, you bastard, or I'll shoot!'

Woods tried to give chase but his legs folded under him. He crashed down onto the icy ground with a resounding thud. His pistol fired as he fell. The shot ricocheted off the deep-set church windowsill with a puff of dirty sand and shattered the stained-glass window. Its retort echoed around the still valley as ancient glass slithered noisily to the ground.

Woods scrambled to his feet and staggered awkwardly over to the deserted road. The murdering rogue had vanished.

He returned to the rear of the church. Helen Carnaby had also disappeared. Swearing, he moved down the overgrown path which meandered off into the distance beside the black river. It was empty and edged with the towering willow weed that swayed lightly in the breeze. If she was there he would never find her.

'Damn and blast it!' he cursed.

An angry exclamation behind him made him turn sharply. Still brandishing his smoking pistol, he found himself face to face with a furious, indignant and breathless man in a billowing nightshirt.

It was the vicar.

CHAPTER TWENTY TWO

'Can you describe him?'

Woods sat huddled in a dry blanket before the blazing fire in the empty tap room of The Rose and Crown and shook his throbbing head. His frozen hands still trembled as he sipped at a steaming bowl of hot chocolate.

'His hat was pulled down low - and to be honest, sir – I'd not paid him any attention. I just thought he was a befuddled rat, sleeping off the liquor. But his eyes! Full of hatred and viciousness – they were light coloured.'

He sipped some more of his beverage. Lavender and Constable Beddows observed him quietly and took in his words.

'What about his coat? Did you get a good look at his coat?'

A flash of recognition now jolted through Woods' exhausted brain. The hot chocolate slopped dangerously towards the edge of the bowl.

'Yes!'

An image of the man silhouetted against the moon and only three feet away, urinating against the tree, now came vividly to mind.

'It were dark but I'm sure it were an army greatcoat – with capes. I couldn't make out the colour, mind.'

Lavender fell back satisfied, his expression grave.

'What's the significance of that?' Beddows demanded.

'We've found evidence that a beggar who camps out in one of the caves in the gorge wears a military greatcoat.' Lavender informed him.

'A beggar, eh?' Beddows spat on the floor of the taproom. 'Damned town is crawling with them.'

'Ah, but this one is a tall, light-eyed, with a hat, and carries a clay pipe and a kitchen knife in his pocket,' Lavender informed him. 'So perhaps he might not be too hard for you and your men to track down? Woods will be able to recognise him when you arrest him.'

'He don't sound like one of our regulars. Never seen a gadgie of that description afore.'

'You need to find him – and quickly,' Lavender said.

'I don't rightly know…' Beddows began to bluster.

'Well, I do,' Lavender snapped. 'You need to gather up your men and find this madman before he succeeds in harming someone. If it hadn't been for the quick thinking of Constable Woods you would have had the murder of a young woman in your church yard to contend with.'

'He could have just been out to rob her – a silk snatcher.'

Lavender frowned. 'Either way, I think it's time for you to take some action, man.'

Beddows scowled and scratched the stubble on his chin. His fat jowls wobbled as he started to protest.

'I only have a couple of beadles – and we're needed in Bellingham today at the market.'

Lavender turned around now and faced the local man squarely. His eyes narrowed and in a voice heavy with irony, he asked: 'Why? Are you expecting the sheep to organise a riot?'

The local man blinked at Lavender's tone but continued to doggedly argue his case. 'The stall holders expect us to be on hand like, in case there's trouble. There's a lot of drinking goes on market day in a town like this, and petty theft.'

'And no doubt these stall holders palm you a dawb or two to keep you here and watch over them.' Woods observed, cynically. 'We have the same thing with the constables all the time down at Smithfield meat market.'

'What you accusing me of?' Beddows small eyes flashed angrily beneath his bushy eyebrows. 'I've never tekken no dawb!' His colour rose in his cheeks.

Lavender cut him short.

'Your parish seethes with crime and violence, man. I'm visiting Magistrate Clennell tomorrow and will make sure that I report to him the level of lawlessness I've uncovered in Bellingham, and your inability and reluctance to deal with it.'

Beddows shuffled and looked away. 'There ain't that many of us,' he whined.

'There's enough to restrain one villain. I want you to take your men to the gorge and see if the rogue has returned to the cave – afterwards, I want you to stop, question and search every man at the market today who answers the description I've just given you.'

'This were a quiet town afore you two arrived and began to stir things up,' Beddows whined.

'Nonsense,' Lavender retorted. 'Things were already stirred up before we got here. You've got a missing girl, remember? The one you couldn't find. I've been shocked to discover the extent of sin and depravity in Bellingham: couples copulate on consecrated ground; farmers take the law into their own hands. Now this – attempted murder in broad day light. And in all this there is no sign that you, the beadles or the night watchmen do your jobs. I'm sure that Magistrate Clennell will be as disappointed as I am with this report.'

Beddows pulled out his gloves and slunk away towards the door.

'Alright, alright,' he growled. 'I'll get the beadles and we'll search the gorge.'

'I don't want a word of this to George Carnaby, do you understand me? This is nothing to do with him.'

Beddows stopped on his way to the door and stared back at Lavender in surprise. Then he turned to Woods.

'So who were the lass that were nearly stabbed?' he asked. 'If it weren't Carnaby's sister?'

'I don't know,' Woods lied. 'Just some village girl – she fled terrified after I scared off the cove.' He had given this story to the incandescent vicar but had managed to whisper the truth to Lavender when they returned to the tavern. Baxter Carnaby's grave had never been mentioned.

After Beddows left, Lavender sighed and sat down beside Woods on the fireside settle. He lowered his voice and ran his hand through his hair.

'Are you sure it was her – Helen Carnaby?'

Woods nodded and described the girl and the helleborus she carried.

'What are we going to do?' Woods asked. 'The foxgloves were one thing – but this murdering bravo is another. That girl is in great danger. Who do you suppose he is?'

'I don't know,' Lavender sighed. 'But I've no doubt that George and Isobel Carnaby are behind this latest attempt on their sister's life.'

'How did they know she would have been there?'

Lavender grimaced.

'I fear I may have given them the idea of someone staking out the graveyard. Isobel Carnaby is sharp-witted. When I asked her if she had visited the graves of her parents I could see an idea forming in her mind.'

'Oh,' murmured Woods.

'Yes, I think it may be my fault. I made a mistake. The trouble is I've no evidence yet to prove the older Carnabys are connected to this. We need to find this cove and question him. I also doubt that Clennell with give me a warrant on Friday to arrest the Carnabys. Despite the stain of madness, they're an old family and respected landowners hereabouts.'

‘They’re cunning buggers, that’s for sure. What shall we do?’

‘For a start,’ Lavender said, decisively, ‘you’ll get some sleep. In the meantime, I shall try to track down Abel Knowles, the sheep drover and I shall pay a visit to the Redesdale Arms in Otterburn.’

‘I can come with you.’

‘No, you get some sleep, Ned. Tomorrow we shall go to Linn Hagh and demonstrate to the impatient Mr Armstrong how his great-niece got out of a locked bedchamber.’

‘I still think it’s shocking,’ Woods commented. ‘We expect the scum and tagrag of the Seven Dials and the rookery of St. Giles down in London to murder their grandmothers for their last shilling - but out here? Amongst the gentry?’

‘Ten thousand pounds is a lot of money to a lazy man with no other income,’ Lavender observed, cynically. ‘The Carnabys are desperate. All that stands between them and the money is a sister they barely know – a girl they’ve disliked since she was born.’

‘I still think it’s harsh – and difficult to believe.’ Woods fought back a yawn.

‘I agree. But God knows what depravity George and Isobel Carnaby witnessed when they were children, growing up as they did with an insane mother. Who knows what example they were set - or what is ‘normal’ for them.’

Lavender rose to his feet and picked up his gloves and cane.

‘Ideally, I would like George and Isobel Carnaby and their hired assassin behind bars at Hexham gaol by the Sabbath. Only then will I feel it’s safe for Miss Helen to come out of hiding. ’

Something about the way Lavender looked made the exhausted Woods start with surprise. His raised his eyebrows and a smile large spread across his broad face.

‘That gypsy gal were right - you know where Helen Carnaby is, don’t you?’

Lavender smiled.

‘I’ve a fair idea. She’s safe – well, from murder, anyway.’

Woods gasped, pushed off the blanket and started to rise.

‘I’ll come with you.’

Lavender held up his hand and shook his head.

‘I don’t think so, my friend. You need to get some sleep.’

Reluctantly, Woods fell back into his seat.

As Lavender reached the door, he turned back and grinned.

‘By the way, Ned, make sure you stay out of sight of the vicar for a while, otherwise you could find yourself denounced from the pulpit.’

'Eh?'

'It turns out the man was rather partial to his stained glass windows.'

'Humph!'

'Don't dismiss him lightly,' Lavender winked as turned to go. 'You've fallen from grace. One letter to the Bishop - and you could be in great danger of excommunication.'

Bellingham market square heaved with people. The racket made by the lowing cattle, barking dogs and shouting drovers and auctioneers was a shock to Lavender's ears. The rank smell of animal excrement filled his nose when he left The Rose and Crown. As the crowds surged around him, he surveyed the chaos with dismay. It would be impossible to find Abel Knowles, the mysterious sheep drover in that writhing pack. Carefully, he wove a path between the steaming piles of manure which littered the cobbles, past patient flocks of tethered sheep and enquired of every farmer he met the whereabouts of 'Knowles the sheep drover.' Most of the farmers just shrugged, or else pretended not to understand his accent.

Beddows had been right. There was a good deal of excessive drinking associated with market day in Bellingham. Drunken beggars sat mournfully at the edge of the crowds, empty bottles by their side, hands outstretched, and their voices whining. Gaudily dressed whores hovered in groups outside the public houses. Here and there, he caught the flash of dirty scarlet as discharged soldiers hobbled on their crutches through the crowd.

What he didn't see – and he was grateful for this – was any sign of Constable Beddows and his men. Good. That meant Beddows had gone to search Hareshaw Woods for the man who had tried to murder Helen Carnaby. Lavender examined every face but there was no sign in the market of any man who answered the description of the murdering cove. No doubt he was lying low somewhere today. Could he possibly be at Linn Hagh, being sheltered by the Carnabys? Lavender dismissed the idea. George Carnaby would not associate himself directly with this would-be assassin.

'Have you lost sommat, Detective?' A familiar voice cut through the babble of the crowds and halted him in his tracks.

'Aye, he's lost his constable.'

A ripple of laughter.

'And his pistol.'

'Aye.'

Jethro Hamilton, Isaac Daly and a third older, rugged and scowling farmer leant over the wooden gate at the entrance to one of the sheep pens, eyeing him coldly. He noted again how powerfully built and hard-featured these men were. Despite their prejudice against the faws, they were the kind of allies he needed, not idiots like Beddows. Lavender's brain raced and he tried to calculate how much damage his stance against them yesterday had done. Beneath the growling, they were decent men. There was still a chance that this situation could be turned to his advantage.

'I need your help.'

'What's this, then?' Hamilton snorted, ironically. 'Have ye come to tell us that you can't manage to deal with them faws without us?'

The other men sniggered.

Lavender moved closer. He could smell the body odour and the stench of farm animals which emanated from their thick, dirty jackets.

'I seek two men. One of them is innocent and has information which could help me. The other is dangerous, and could be a threat to your wives and daughters.'

'Oh aye?' Hamilton pushed his thick, blond hair back out of his eyes.

'Firstly, I need to find Abel Knowles, the sheep drover. He is not in any trouble but I think he has information about the missing woman, Helen Carnaby.'

'And the other?'

The farmer's faces were hard and expressionless, but he had their attention.

Lavender described the mysterious beggar who had tried to murder the 'young woman' in the churchyard. He gave them just enough detail to understand that the man he sought was a dangerous threat.

'That's Beddows' job – rounding up villains.' The older man spat onto the muddy cobbles by their boots. Lavender ignored him. Hamilton was the natural leader of this group; where he led, the others followed.

'Apparently, he's got a lopsided grin which gives him a leering expression – and his eyes – his eyes are light in colour.'

'Sounds more like Carnaby's idiot younger brother,' Daly suggested.

Hamilton remained silent, his face thoughtful.

'If you can spread the word that we seek this man,' Lavender said, 'And keep an eye out for him - I'd be grateful.'

'Ye've a cheek asking favours from us,' Hamilton finally said. 'What's in it fer us, anyhow?'

'Safety in Bellingham for your families - and Armstrong has offered a twenty guinea reward for further information. In the meantime, my offer to take your grievances to Magistrate Clennell on Friday still stands.'

The glimmer of a wry smile traced the edges of Hamilton's mouth.

For a moment there was silence.

'Abel Knowles ain't here,' Hamilton suddenly informed him. 'He's driving sheep to Newcastle market this week.'

'Thank you.'

'You ought to stick to searching fer that missing lass, Detective. Tha's gonna be busy if you try to rid this parish of all its crime,' Hamilton suggested. "Half this bloody town's guilty of sommat.'

CHAPTER TWENTY THREE

Lavender called briefly at the Armstrong's home before continuing on his way to Otterburn. Miss Katherine and her father had already heard about the 'incident' in the churchyard earlier that morning. In a small town like Bellingham, news like that spread like wildfire. They listened gravely as he recounted what had happened to Helen Carnaby as she stood beside her father's head stone. Miss Katherine turned pale when he mentioned the knife.

'Who is this murdering devil?' Armstrong asked. His thin arm thumped the side of his chair angrily. Miss Katherine reached out and took his arthritic hand in hers to soothe him.

'We don't know.' Lavender gave them description supplied to him by Woods.

'It doesn't sound like anyone from around here,' Miss Katherine frowned. 'We're a small community, Detective, strangers are quickly noticed.'

'And your constable is sure it was Helen?'

'The woman was heavily veiled - but he is certain. The second bunch of helleborus and her interest in Baxter Carnaby's grave convinced him it was Miss Carnaby. It couldn't have been anyone else.'

Miss Katherine shuddered and fear flashed across her face.

'Thank the Lord, Constable Woods was there. I dread to think what would have happened to Helen if he had not been present.'

'Do you suspect that George Carnaby had a hand in this?' the old man asked angrily.

Lavender hesitated for a moment, before he nodded. Slowly, he relayed to them his suspicions about George and Isobel Carnaby. However, he refrained from revealing the concerns voiced by Doctor Goddard about Esther Carnaby's death. They had enough to take in at the minute, he decided.

He explained about the poison they had found at Linn Hagh, the man who had stalked Helen Carnaby in Hareshaw Woods and all the other little details which led him to believe that Helen Carnaby had been in fear for her life.

The Armstrongs were horrified.

'But I've no evidence at the moment to prove that George and Isobel Carnaby have tried to murder their sister – or to connect them directly to this would-be killer. I was going to suggest that we all took a trip up to Linn Hagh tomorrow morning, so I could demonstrate to you how Helen escaped from the locked bedchamber, but I'm not sure it's appropriate now.'

'Nonsense, Detective. Of course it's appropriate,' Mr Armstrong snapped. 'We'll leave here at ten for Linn Hagh. Carnaby is no threat to us. I'm not scared of the brute.' His grey, lined face set with determination.

'I would like to see George Carnaby's expression when he realises how Helen tricked him,' Miss Katherine said. Lavender could see the cold anger in her eyes.

'So would I, ma'am,' he confessed. 'But I need you both to understand that I don't intend to confront Carnaby as yet – I need more time to find evidence which links him to this would-be murderer.'

'We understand. We shall be discreet,' she reassured him.

Lavender nodded, satisfied. Armstrong might be elderly and frail, but he was a retired lawyer and could practise discretion. Katherine Armstrong also had his trust.

'And as for dear Isobel, well! I suppose that as long of neither of us eat or drink anything that comes out of her kitchen we shall not come to any harm!' she snapped. 'Foxgloves! Pah!'

Katherine Armstrong accompanied him out into the spacious hallway. As soon as the door closed on her father's study she dismissed the maid and walked alone with Lavender towards the door. She lowered her voice to an urgent whisper.

'Have you any idea where Helen is hiding, Detective? I'm so frightened for her.'

He could see the concern etched across her gentle face.

'Yes. We've heard rumours – but nothing I've been able to substantiate yet – that she had a lover, an admirer. I suspect she is with him.'

A wave of alarm now flashed across Miss Katherine's features.

'Have they eloped?'

'I don't know. The fact that they've not returned to Bellingham openly as man and wife, suggests to me that something has gone wrong with their plans – very wrong. But of course, George Carnaby will be furious and create trouble for any man who dares to marry his sister without his permission. He may still bring charges against him. Perhaps that is why they're still lying low? They may wait until she turns twenty-one in January.'

He paused while she struggled to digest this latest information. He could see her fighting to supress her shock.

'So Helen could be living in mortal sin, unmarried - *with a man*?' she whispered.

'Yes.'

'Good grief! Please don't say a word of this to my father.'

'I won't,' he reassured her. 'Miss Armstrong, I know that this is a lot to take in, and I know you're concerned about the scandal which will follow. But I'm still convinced that Helen is safer where she is at the moment, while we try to catch this murdering rogue who stalks her.'

'I see you're a practical man, rather than a spiritual one, Detective,' she observed.

'Yes. I believe that we face far greater dangers in this world than 'mortal sin.' I genuinely fear for Miss Carnaby's life.'

She paled, set her mouth in a firm line and nodded as he moved to open the door.

'Find this terrible man, Detective, and find him *quickly* - please!'

Woods woke up just after one o'clock and came down to the tap room for food. He still felt a bit groggy but as the warm chicken, bread and a large slice of meat and potato pie filled his growling stomach, he began to feel better. He washed down his food with a glass of ale and belched with satisfaction.

Their business in the market concluded, a few of the usual gang of farmers began to cluster around the low wooden tables. The blank-faced bar man in a dirty apron drew flagons of ale from a large casket and exchanged them for a few coins from the farmers' cold and grimy hands. Mistress McMullen bobbed around the room, refilling brandy glasses out of a chipped ceramic jug.

'It does my old heart good to see you back enjoying yer food again,' she told Woods as she piled a second helping of pie onto his plate.

He smiled at her solicitude. He knew full well that her attentiveness was prompted more out of relief that he had not pegged it on her premises during his mysterious 'illness', than out of genuine concern. Nevertheless, he chatted amiably with the woman and complimented her on her cooking.

After she had left, he closed his eyes, enjoyed the warmth of the fire as it licked his face and settled himself down for a fireside snooze. A genial hum of conversation hung over the far end of the bar, where the farmers discussed the price of corn and beef.

Still exhausted and sore from a night staking out the graveyard, he needed more sleep. This is the toughest part of police work, he decided: the night shifts. Three weeks ago he had spent two bitterly cold nights down at the East India docks with other officers, desperately trying to avoid freezing to death, while they waited for a gang of pilferers to appear. Then his mind drifted to back to the expenses he was earning from this case and a broad grin spread across his face.

His pleasure was to be short-lived. He had only just registered the angry stomp of riding boots heading his way across the flag stones when George Carnaby's fist crashed down on the table in front of him. The crockery leapt and rattled. All conversation died.

Woods jerked awake and tensed.

'Easy there, fellah!' he drawled.

Carnaby's lip curled and he scowled. '*Mister* Carnaby to the likes of you. Where's that damned fool Lavender?'

Woods could not decide whether Carnaby's face was red with exertion or anger. The man wore a stained riding coat and buckskin breeches and clutched a bloodied horse whip in his right hand. Briefly, Woods wondered how hard the bastard had driven his poor horse on the ride into town and the thought angered him. Woods shoved his clenched fists into his pockets.

'*Detective* Lavender is away on *Mr Armstrong's* business,' he said, slowly.

Carnaby's eyes narrowed and his hand tightened on his whip. 'All business concerning my sister is also my business,' he snarled between gritted teeth. 'I cannot fathom why you haven't reported the attempt on her life this morning. And why your detective instructed Beddows not to tell me anything about it.'

Damn that ruddy Constable Beddows, thought Woods. *The blithering idiot has gone straight back to Carnaby with the news.*

'I'm sure Detective Lavender had his reasons. For the record, I could not be sure that the lass in the graveyard were your sister. She could have been anyone. It were barely dawn.'

'Well, that doesn't surprise me. You're both a pair of incompetents. Nor am I impressed to discover that you've also questioned my cook behind my back.'

Another one who can't be trusted, Woods thought. *Damn the bloody cook. What about Anna? Was she still his friend?*

'You can stay away from Linn Hagh and my servants, do you hear? I shall complain to Armstrong about your cack-handed methods.'

Woods had endured enough. Gentry or not, this cock-sure braggart thrashed his younger siblings and had tried to murder one of them. Disgust rose in his throat like bile. The whole tavern had fallen silent now, everyone watched the two men closely. Woods pushed back the table, its legs screeching in protest along the flagstones.

Carnaby fell silent in surprise when Woods stood up and squared up to him. He stared Carnaby straight in eyes. The two men were the same height. Carnaby may have been ten years younger, but Woods was broader and more confident in a fight.

'I'll bid you a good day. This interview is over, *Mister* Carnaby.'

Carnaby's plain face contorted with rage as he sized up the defiant man before him.

'Don't you try to dismiss me, you insolent dog! You're nothing but a pathetic excuse for a policeman. I've a good mind to -'

'To what?' Woods shouted. 'Use yer riding whip on me? Come on then, man, try it.'

Startled, Carnaby edged back slightly.

'Why you!'

Carnaby began to raise his arm but then stopped mid-way when he caught the glint of iron flint in Wood's eyes.

'If you raise that whip at me, *Mister* Carnaby -' The constable's deep voice was loud, calm and dangerous. '- I'll take it off you, snap it and slam both ends up between your blind cheeks and into your arse.'

There were howls of delighted laughter from around the tavern. Woods stared straight ahead, his face rigid. His eyes never left Carnaby's face.

'You tell him, Constable!'

Carnaby's face flashed with a mixture of confusion and fury. Then he broke eye contact with Wood's and turned on his heel.

'Stay away from Linn Hagh!' he shouted over his shoulder as he stormed out of the tap room.

'There's never a dull minute in this here tavern since you gadgies came to join us!' Jethro Hamilton was laughing his head off.

'You London detectives have a real charming manner,' Isaac Daly added. 'One hell of a way with words!'

Woods paused to let his racing heart calm down, while the public house continued to comment and laugh around him. He reached down for his glass.

That's buggered it, he thought.

He shrugged and drank off the last of his ale.

What's done is done, he reasoned, as he burped up the gas. Lavender has nearly got this case in the bag and George Carnaby should be in gaol by the Sabbath. Too tense to return to his afternoon nap, he decided to ride out to Otterburn and try to track down some evidence about the murdering bravo who stalked Miss Helen.

Meanwhile, Lavender had changed his plans.

Katherine Armstrong's words rang in his ears as he left her home: *'Find this terrible man, Detective – and find him quickly - please!'*

She was right. Catching the thug who had tried to murder Helen Carnaby should be his main priority. He primed his pistol and set off on foot through Hareshaw Woods towards Linn Hagh. The dense woodland remained as silent and secretive as ever. Apart from the distant roar of the waterfall, he could hear the steady drip of condensation from the naked branches arched above his head. He saw no-one. Yet, no matter how quietly he trod along the muddy path, he still felt someone else watched him, someone who was quieter and slyer than him.

The ground around the caves in the gorge was heavily trampled. He had no doubt that Beddows and his beadles had been there before him. The pile of rags within the cave had been disturbed and carelessly tossed to one side, but the ashes of the fire were cold and there was no sign that new fires had been lit, or that the murdering beggar had returned to his lair.

Fighting back his disappointment, he resolved to pay another visit to the faw camp. He reckoned the gypsies owed him a favour.

Paul Faa Geddes listened quietly when Lavender described the man they sought. His weathered, rubbery face contorted as he chewed his tobacco.

'I knows the gadgie you mean,' he said at last. 'He's camped out in them woods, on and off like, fer a few months.'

'Do you know where he is, now?' Lavender asked.

Geddes barked out a question in Romany over his shoulder. The other gypsies, lurking beside the tents, shook their heads.

'No. None of us have seen him fer several days.'

'Have any of you ever talked to him? Can you tell me anything about him at all?'

Geddes shook his head and watched Lavender dispassionately from the depths of his penetrating dark eyes.

Lavender could feel frustration and disappointment descend on him like a cold winter fog.

'Keep your women close and keep your eyes open,' Lavender advised him. 'This man is a murderer. There's a twenty guinea reward out from the Armstrongs for his capture.'

When he turned to go, Paul Geddes grabbed his arm and stopped him.

'What?'

'I'll tell you one thing fer nowt,' Geddes said.

'Oh yes?'

'This gadgie knows Hareshaw Woods like the back of his hand. He slips through the trees like a spirit. Every time one on us gets close to the fellah, he disappears.'

Lavender's brow creased with surprise.

'Surely no one knows Hareshaw Woods better than you and your people?'

'We know them well,' Geddes conceded. He spat his tobacco down onto the ground. 'But this gadgie roams the woods like he were *born* here…'

CHAPTER TWENTY FOUR

Thursday 25th November, 1809

Linn Hagh was in turmoil. Miss Isobel was in a right mood.

Mr Armstrong had sent word that he, Miss Katherine and the London detective would arrive at eleven to demonstrate how Helen Carnaby left her locked bedchamber. This threw Miss Isobel into a panic; she raced around the Great Hall scooping up discarded riding boots, dragging Anna in her wake.

'Put that dirty crockery onto a tray and take it downstairs,' she instructed. 'Then sweep up that mud and remove the cobweb by the window.'

'I don't know why you're fussing so,' said Master George, from behind his newspaper. As usual, he was sprawled across his favourite chair in front of the fire. 'The Armstrongs and their pet detective want access to Helen's bedchamber, not this room.'

'This place is a pig sty,' snapped Miss Isobel. 'Half the furniture is broken or faded. I can't have Katherine Armstrong think that this is how we live. The woman's tongue is as sharp as her nose.'

But it is how you live, thought Anna as she gathered up the last of the brandy glasses. *Why try to hide it?* She tried to work out how long it had been since the Carnabys had entertained a lady at Linn Hagh but quickly gave up. Miss Isobel did not have any friends, and she couldn't remember any guests in the last year apart from Ingram and Emmerson.

'You should have told them: no.' Miss Isobel complained. 'Told John Armstrong to bugger off.'

'Now, now, that's not very lady-like,' admonished her brother. 'Talk sense, Izzie. We can't afford to offend the likes of Armstrong; that starched old fox still has a finger in every pie in Bellingham. He's got influence.'

'And why do they want two of my beeswax candles taken up to Helen's room?' she demanded. 'And two scuttles of coal? I've barely got any candles left after Sister Helen's acts of thievery. It's broad daylight. What do they want candles for?'

'How should I know?' the master snapped. 'I just hope Armstrong is not foolish enough to bring along that insolent dog of a constable. If that sod tries to set foot on my property I'll flay the bastard alive.'

I'd like to see you try, thought Anna, triumphantly. She had no idea what her favourite policeman had done to upset George Carnaby but her master had returned from town in a right mood yesterday, ranting and cursing his head off about the constable. She had been delighted to see him so put out.

From a window in the Great Hall, Anna watched the Armstrong's coach wind slowly up the weed-strewn drive of Linn Hagh. It was just before eleven. Master George sat up, brushed fragments of snuff off his stained shirt and hastily buttoned up his waistcoat.

'Izzy!' he roared.

To Anna's annoyance, Miss Isobel emerged from her bedroom in Helen Carnaby's favourite high-waisted dress of soft, turquoise satin. She arranged herself across the chaise longue like she was about to pose for a portrait. With her sallow skin and wiry, black hair she looked like an old crow decked out in peacock feathers.

Anna stomped down the stairs to the great oak door of the pele tower. Its weight strained against the creaking iron hinges when she opened it.

The elderly Mr Armstrong struggled up the steps to the entrance to Linn Hagh, aided by his coachman and the detective. Lavender glanced up at her.

'Hello, Anna.' He smiled. She ignored him and scanned the coach hopefully for a glimpse of Constable Woods. There was no sign of him. She sighed.

The guests paused in the vestibule opposite the entrance to the kitchen and stared up the gloomy, well-worn stone staircase of the ancient pele tower.

'It's on the top floor, I'm afraid,' Lavender said.

'Perhaps we shouldn't have come,' Miss Armstrong suggested. She wafted past Anna in a cloud of perfume and a swishing, plum velvet pelisse, her faced etched with concern for her father. She had an odd shaped hat balanced on her grey curls and an over-sized fur hand muff.

'Nonsense,' the old man said. 'I'm determined to see this through until the end. I'll understand what happened to poor Helen even if the effort kills me.' His gnarled hand shook as it gripped the top of his walking stick.

'Would you like a cup of tea, ma'am?' Anna asked as the party began their laborious ascent of the main staircase.

Miss Armstrong paused and fixed her intelligent eyes on the housemaid.

‘Has your mistress been anywhere near the kitchen this morning?’

‘Er, no, ma’am,’ Anna replied, confused. ‘It’s just been me and cook in there since yesterday.’

‘Very well. In that case, Father and I will take a cup of tea.’

Anna bobbed a curtsey, suppressed her curiosity about Miss Armstrong’s strange comment and dashed into the steamy kitchen to ask Mistress Norris to make tea.

Next, she hurried past the Armstrongs up the stairs and announced their arrival to Master George and Miss Isobel in the Great Hall.

It was all very embarrassing. The Armstrongs remained on the landing in the doorway to the hall, an action that forced the Carnabys to leave the warmth of the fireplace and walk over to join them.

‘Katherine! It’s been too long! How delightful to see you,’ Miss Isobel gushed.

‘Likewise, I’m sure,’ Miss Armstrong replied, coldly. ‘This isn’t a social call, Izzie. Detective Lavender has something to show us in Helen’s bedchamber. He will demonstrate how she escaped from a locked room. Perhaps we could go straight up?’

George Carnaby moved towards Mr Armstrong with his hand held out in greeting. The old man ignored him, turned his back and hobbled towards the next flight of stairs. His walking stick tapped angrily across the flagstones.

‘Let’s get on with it,’ he said over his shoulder.

Miss Isobel gasped at his rudeness and exchanged an angry glance with her brother.

Silently, they all followed the guests up the remaining stairs. Anna hovered on the landing outside the Great Hall, unsure whether to go up or not. She desperately wanted to see how Miss Helen had got out of a locked room but didn’t want to risk a public rebuke from her mistress.

‘We’ll need your help, too, Anna,’ the detective shouted down. She didn’t need a second invitation. She picked up her skirts and raced up behind them, her boots clattered noisily against the stone.

In the cold, narrow corridor between the two top floor bedchambers, the detective had stopped before Miss Helen’s room, its battered door still missing the top half chopped away under the fury of George Carnaby’s axe. The bottom half remained a forest of jagged shards and splinters.

'No, this won't do.' Lavender shook his head. 'I'd forgotten how badly damaged the door was. We shall have to use the servant's bedchamber for the demonstration.'

Without asking permission, and much to Anna's dismay, he turned around, lifted the latch and opened the only intact wooden door on the landing. It was the room she shared with the cook.

Lavender stood back politely to allow the Armstrongs to enter.

Well, at least he's got some manners, Anna thought tartly.

By the time she entered, Mr Armstrong had collapsed exhausted onto the thin, fraying quilt which covered her own little bed. Miss Armstrong lowered herself gracefully onto the other bed in the room. The springs squeaked alarmingly beneath her weight. At this point, Anna noticed the artificial berries on Miss Armstrong's velvet domed bonnet.

Toss some brandy on her, set fire to it and she'd flare up like a Christmas pudding, she thought. Neither Katherine Armstrong nor Isobel Carnaby could hold a candle to Miss Helen's style, grace and elegance she decided. Her heart ached for the missing woman.

Miss Isobel lurked at the edge of the room with her brother. In Miss Helen's peacock gown, she looked out of place and gaudy against the plain, white-washed walls of a humble servant's room. Anna saw that she was shivering and fought back her natural impulse to offer to fetch her shawl. Her mistress' sharp eyes took in every detail of the small pile of personal possessions on the dresser: Anna's hairbrush and comb, her bible and the heap of stockings waiting to be darned.

'Don't worry, Anna, we won't be in here any longer than necessary,' the detective said suddenly. She flushed slightly and wondered how he had been able to read her mind so well? His severe expression broke and a slight smile lifted the edges of his lips. He looked quite nice when he smiled, she thought, even though it was hard to see the expression in his dark eyes beneath those hooded eyelids. He had what her mother called 'good cheekbones.'

'Perhaps you would be so kind as to fetch in the two scuttles of coal outside on the landing and start a fire for us?' he asked.

Anna needed no second bidding. She dropped to her knees, arranged the kindling and struck the tinder box she carried in her apron pocket. The fire blazed. Delighted, she fetched the scuttles and heaped a shovel full of coal into the flames. As the fuel settled into place a cloud of black coal dust rose lightly into the air. A fire in their bedchamber! With any luck, the embers would still be glowing tonight. For once she and Mistress Norris would not shiver but sleep comfortably in their narrow beds.

She stepped back and nearly clapped her hands with joy when Detective Lavender picked up the second scuttle and hurled most of its contents noisily into the grate.

'I must protest, Detective!' Miss Isobel exclaimed over the clatter of the coals. 'Is it really necessary to waste two scuttles of fuel on the servants?'

'It's completely necessary, Miss Carnaby.' He spoke with confidence and to emphasise his authority over the proceedings, he picked up the poker and gave the smoky heap a good prod. The temperature in the cold garret began to rise as the flames took hold and the coals glowed red. Anna could barely contain her delight.

'I'm trying to recreate the conditions in this room on the night Miss Helen disappeared,' he explained. 'Now, if I remember rightly, Anna was the last person to see or speak to Miss Helen before she vanished, is that correct?'

'Yes,' Anna confirmed. 'I brought up her meal on a tray and she asked me fer a second scuttle of coal.'

'When did you take this to her?'

Anna paused and tried to remember. She remained by the fire and relished the steadily increasing heat.

'It were before everyone sat down fer the first course. I know this because as soon as I had washed the coal dust of my hands I had to take up the oysters.'

'We sat down to eat at seven o'clock, Detective,' Miss Isobel informed him.

'So we know that Miss Helen was inside her room at seven o'clock. That is the last time she was seen.'

'She were still here just after nine o'clock, sir,' Anna pointed out. 'Cook and I heard her put down the bar on the door when we came to bed just after nine.'

'Be quiet, Anna,' Miss Isobel snapped. 'Speak when you're spoken to.'

Anna dropped her head and sulked.

'Ah yes, the door and the bar.' Detective Lavender ignored Isobel Carnaby and moved over to the entrance of the room. Every pair of eyes followed him. Even Anna peeked up from beneath her fringe.

'Actually, Miss Carnaby wasn't in her room just after nine, when you heard the door bar come down. She'd been gone a long time before that.'

'How?' George Carnaby snapped.

'Let me demonstrate.' Lavender started to shut the heavy wooden door.

'Oi!'

He hastily opened it again to reveal Mistress Norris holding the tea tray on the other side. He had narrowly avoided hitting her with the door. She gave him a withering look.

'I thought I'd better bring this up, seeing as someone-' she glared at Anna, '- forgot to come back doon fer it.' The elderly woman hobbled over to the Armstrongs and held out the tray.

'Thank you,' Miss Armstrong said. She lifted a cup and saucer and sniffed the tea suspiciously before she handed it over to her father. She then did the same with her own cup.

'What the deuce…?' George Carnaby's blood-shot eyes flashed in anger.

'I think you should stay here with us for the moment, Mistress Norris,' Lavender intervened. 'You were here on the night of Miss Helen's disappearance and may be able to help.'

'Why not?' Miss Isobel said, tartly. 'Peter the manservant is downstairs – why don't we invite him up, as well?' Her voice cut through the room like glass.

'Just get on with it, Lavender,' Carnaby growled. He pulled out his silver snuff box, leaned against the flaking wall and took a pinch.

Unconcerned, the detective resumed his position at the closed door and lifted the heavy bar which leant against the wall. Everyone watched him in silence as he studied the rusty metal and tested its weight.

Suddenly he dropped it - with a resounding clang - into the staples on the back of the door. Miss Armstrong started at the noise and her tea slopped into her saucer.

Anna stared hard at the bar, trying to understand how the heavy piece of metal could drop into place without someone to move it. It looked so snug sitting in the four solid staples: the two which were widely spaced on the back of the door, and the other two placed in the walls on either side. But for the moment, that blank piece of oak was keeping its secrets.

Detective Lavender began to speak again.

'Like Anna said, she and Mistress Norris heard the bar go down on the back of Miss Helen's door just after nine. But it was not Helen Carnaby who dropped the bar into place. She'd already left Linn Hagh, and had been gone several hours.'

'Then who?' Miss Isobel demanded. 'How did the bar get into the staples? Who put it there?'

'Not who, Miss Carnaby but *what.* Do you have the two beeswax candles I requested?'

Reluctantly, she handed them over.

Lavender removed the rusty bar and stood it against the wall. Next, he put the creamy candles into the middle two staples on the back of the door. The space was slightly too large for them and they leaned forward a fraction of an inch. Carefully, he picked up the bar and balanced it on top of the candles.

Anna held her breath, fearing it would fall, but the candles supported the weight. The bar sank slightly into the wax but remained flush against the door. The staples were wide enough apart for the heavy bar to remain perfectly balanced and the wicks were exposed against the flaking metal. Significantly, both ends of the bar now hovered a few inches above the remaining two staples in the wall. Lavender gently pushed at one end of the bar, and then the other, and it glided smoothly across the tops of the waxy candles – and still it did not fall.

Now it all made sense to her. If the candles were lit and then burnt down, the bar would lower slowly into place and once its ends were in the two staples screwed into the wall, then only George Carnaby's axe would open the door.

Lavender took a taper from the mantelpiece and held it in the fire. Next, he lit the candles wedged into the door staples. The wicks burst into life and flickered happily against the iron.

'So *that's* how she did it.' Mr Armstrong's thin voice quivered with a mixture of amazement and respect.

'Well, *I* don't understand,' Miss Isobel complained, peevishly. 'What do you think you're showing us, Detective?'

'You told me the other day that these candles burn for two hours.'

'Yes, but…'

'Well, try to imagine what will happen in two hours' time when these candles have burnt down.'

'I still don't follow…'

'Let me show you,' he said.

Lavender whipped off bar again and blew out the candles. Next, he pulled out a small knife from the pocket of his black coat. The blade flashed open and he deftly sliced off the bottom inch of all the candles and exposed the wicks.

Miss Isobel groaned in horror at this vandalism.

The detective ignored her, replaced the candle ends in the door staples. He balanced the bar back on top of them and relit the candles. For a few moments nothing happened.

Then suddenly, one of the stubs fell out sideways from the staple. The bar shifted and the force dislodged the remaining candle end. It also fell onto the flagstones, rolled away after its twin and went out. Meanwhile, the bar dropped down unevenly into the four staples. The irregular thud of the metal jolted Anna's memory.

Yes, that was the noise she heard that night, she thought. Not the usual echoing clang of the bar dropping into place, but a softer, irregular thud. *Why had she not wondered about this before?*

'Good God!' Miss Armstrong exclaimed. 'What a clever idea.'

'That worked well.' The detective found it hard to hide his satisfaction. 'I believe this was exactly what happened on the night of the 21st October. Miss Helen set up the candles behind the door sometime after seven o'clock.

Of course, to get out of the room through the door, the bar had to protrude some way beyond the edge of the door, which would have made it unstable. No doubt she was very careful when she closed it behind her. To slide the metal back into position across the top of the wax candles, I suspect she stood on the landing and held the door virtually closed with one hand, and poked the fingertips of the other hand through the remaining crack of the door. It was a tricky manoeuvre, but I suspect she had practised it a few times. In the end, it worked perfectly. When the door was finally pulled shut from the landing, the metal bar was evenly balanced on the burning candles above all four staples, and it would only be a matter of time before they dropped down.

Then she left Linn Hagh. Two hours later, one of the candles dislodged from the staple before it was fully burnt out. It caused the bar to finally drop down and this noise was heard by Anna and Mistress Norris.'

Anna stared, mesmerised at the thin wisps of black smoke that still curled from the extinguished candles. Next, her eyes flitted to the door bar, now held firmly in place by the staples. But more than to either of those, her admiring gaze was drawn to the calm, satisfied face of the clever detective.

Constable Woods had promised her that Detective Lavender would solve the puzzle of how Helen Carnaby had escaped from a locked bedchamber. He had.

Now all he had to do was find her.

CHAPTER TWENTY FIVE

'So the bitch has gulled us all, damn her.' The master's voice was cold.

'Watch your, language Carnaby,' Mr Armstrong warned and turned back to the detective.

'How did you work it out?' he asked.

'I discovered a few scraps of candle wax on the bar when I examined it and beneath the bed I found this.'

Lavender pulled out another candle stub from his coat pocket and passed it across to his client. Armstrong scrutinized it before he handed it across to his daughter.

'I never found its fellow, the second stub. I assume that it was probably swept up by Anna the next day after Mr Carnaby smashed down the door.'

'You're a very clever man, Detective.' Miss Armstrong said.

'No. He ain't.' Mistress Norris' sudden interjection startled everyone. All eyes flashed towards the sour old cook.

'As I sees it, there's a big flaw with yer reasoning, Detective.'

'What would that be, my good woman?' Lavender asked patiently.

'There's only one door out of Linn Hagh and its opposite the kitchen. How did she get out of the Linn Hagh without being seen by Anna or me? Anna were up and down them stairs like a jack rabbit all night – and if the door had bin opened, the draft from the gale outside would have nithered us all within seconds.' She stopped, folded her arms and glared defiantly at Lavender.

For a moment there was silence. Then the explanation flashed into Anna's mind. 'But the door was opened!' she exclaimed. 'Don't you remember? Master Matthew opened it and were staring out into the storm.'

The defiance dropped from the cook's face. She looked flustered as she realised Anna was right.

'Ah, Master Matthew Carnaby - the missing piece of the jigsaw,' Lavender said. 'This could all have been pre-arranged with her simple-minded brother.'

'I doubt that very much,' Isobel Carnaby sneered. 'That idiot boy doesn't remember anything.'

'Failing that,' the detective continued. 'All she had to do was lurk in the shadows of the vestibule outside the kitchen door, catch

Matthew Carnaby's attention and beckon him over. Would he have gone to her if she had done this?'

'Yes, he would,' Anna said, firmly.

'She must have persuaded him to open the door, slipped outside and told him to stay where he was. Anna and Mistress Norris were busy in the kitchen. They would have felt the draught, looked up and only seen Master Matthew stood in the doorway.'

'This happened just after I'd served the main course,' Anna said. 'She knew that this course took longer fer them to eat - that I'd stay in the kitchen - and that there would be less chance of meeting me on the stairs.'

'Spoken like a true detective, Anna,' Miss Armstrong said, kindly. Anna blushed with pleasure.

'But why…' began Miss Isobel. Her face was red, her brow furrowed with anger. 'Why take six of my best candles if she only ever intended to use two in this preposterous trick?'

'I suspect she practised her escape for a while,' Lavender replied. 'She must have used up the other candles in trial and error. She probably discovered that tallow candles were too soft to hold the weight of the bar. The extra scuttle of coal was to ensure that the room was hot enough to soften, and perhaps, melt the candles if one of them blew out in a draught.'

'Escape?' George Carnaby's snarl sliced through the room like ice. 'You make it sound like my sister was a prisoner, here at Linn Hagh.'

'You have to admit, Carnaby,' Mr Armstrong said. 'It doesn't look good. Why did poor Helen feel that she had to go to such elaborate lengths to run away?'

Carnaby was silent but a muscle twitched in his bull-like neck. He glared angrily at the old man.

Anna suddenly realised that it was now becoming unbearably hot in the small room. Miss Katherine looked uncomfortable in her pelisse and began to fan herself with her kid gloves. In fact, *everyone* looked uncomfortable, except the detective.

'It's clear to me,' Lavender announced. 'That Miss Carnaby wanted to use this trick to bewilder her pursuers. She succeeded. The hysteria and confusion surrounding her 'miraculous' disappearance from a locked room, and the superstitious nonsense which has sprung up, distracted everyone from searching for her. The belief that she was still in her room at nine o'clock has also confused us. There were no late coaches from Bellingham. Everyone assumed that she was still in the area until at least the next morning. But if she left Linn Hagh at seven o'clock, she could easily have easily been on the last coach to leave the town that night.'

There was another awkward pause. Anna had the strange fancy that everyone in the room was watching everyone else for a reaction to the detective's statement. When no one said anything, he continued.

'But more than anything else, Miss Carnaby wanted to make sure that no-one discovered she was gone until the next morning, which gave her plenty of time to escape.'

'I've already told you that I don't like the word *escape*,' Carnaby growled.

'Was it necessary to put us through this?' Miss Isobel demanded, angrily. 'No one would have gone into her room anyway until the next day. Why didn't she just pack a bag and leave through the door like a normal person?'

'Are you sure about that?' Lavender asked, slowly.

'What?'

'Are you sure that no-one would have gone into her room during the night?'

Miss Armstrong gasped.

George Carnaby now moved away from the wall, his eyes fixed on Lavender's face. 'What do you mean?' he snarled.

The detective scowled back. He looked every bit as severe and frightening as he did the first time Anna met him.

'I've met those *men* you entertained on the night of the 21st October.' His voice was cold and contemptuous, his London accent alien in that stuffy room.

'Emmerson and Ingram? What about them?'

'I know about your addle-brained plan to make your sister 'compliant' and marry her off to Lawrence Ingram for five hundred guineas. Just how far were you prepared to go to sell your frightened sister, Carnaby?'

Anna gasped and Miss Katherine turned pale.

'What are you suggesting, man?' The master's eyes bulged in his red face.

'How much did she trust you and that lascivious pair of sots, I wonder? Did she fear that one or both of them would come up to her room in the middle of the night and try to despoil her?'

'The Lord save us from loose fish!' Mistress Norris exclaimed. Her hand flew over her mouth in shock.

'How dare you!' Carnaby exploded. He stepped forward. The detective braced himself for an assault, stood his ground and stared back coldly.

'How dare you come into my home and insinuate things about my guests? You're just a jumped-up bloody servant!'

Terrified, Anna shrank back against the flaking wall.

'Detective Lavender is a servant of the government, Carnaby.' Mr Armstrong's voice was still strong when it needed to be. 'He has the full authority of the law, so you can calm down.'

Carnaby paused in his aggressive advance across the room.

Mr Armstrong rose shakily to his feet. The movement distracted everyone. He looked strained. 'I think we've seen and heard enough,' he said. 'We'll take our leave now. There's no need to see us out. Come along, Katherine.'

'You've had enough?' The master of Linn Hagh was still choleric. '*I've* had enough – more than enough - of the bloody lot of you. Do you hear me?'

Miss Isobel glanced at her brother's purple face and placed a restraining hand on his lace cuff. He shook her off.

'Not only does that ungrateful jilt of a sister humiliate me in my own home with this ridiculous game, but you Armstrongs march in here like you own the bloody place. And he -' he jabbed a furious finger at Lavender '- now suggests that I run some sort of whore house and encourage my guests to dock with my own sister! Damn you, Lavender! Damn the lot of you - and get the hell out of my home!'

'Let's go, Katherine,' Mr Armstrong said firmly.

The Armstrongs left hastily, the elderly man getting down the stairs far quicker than he had come up them, with Carnaby's curses ringing in his ears.

Anna went with them to open and shut the door. For a brief moment she was alone at the top of the stone steps outside the pele tower with the Armstrongs and the detective.

'Well, that went well!' Miss Katherine laughed as she helped her father towards their coach.

Lavender held back, pulled a folded piece of parchment out of his pocket and handed it over to Anna.

'Constable Woods sends his best wishes,' he said gently.

Anna just nodded and slipped the note into her apron pocket. She would read it later. Right now she had an urgent need to speak to Mistress Norris.

'You will find her, won't you sir?' she asked.

'Yes, Anna. I will.'

She nodded again, then turned back inside and scurried off in search of the cook.

She desperately wanted to know what 'despoil' meant.

Three hours later, Lavender and Woods boarded a coach for Morpeth and set off for their pre-arranged meeting with Magistrate Clennell to discuss the new evidence which had come to light in the case of the Kirkley Hall robbery.

Lavender nearly sent word to Clennell that he wanted to cancel the appointment.

The murderous beggar who had tried to kill Helen Carnaby in St. Cuthbert's churchyard was still at large. Beddows and his men had failed to uncover any trace of the assassin in Hareshaw Woods or Bellingham. Woods' ride out to Otterburn had also failed to uncover any fresh evidence or new leads. The landlord of the Redesdale Arms and his wife were away visiting their eldest daughter in Alnwick. The remaining servants in the tavern were surly and tight-lipped when questioned by his constable.

Frustrated, Lavender knew that he needed to pursue this line of enquiry himself but until the landlord of the Redesdale Arms returned, there was not much point. Beddows' incompetence and failure to catch the would-be killer didn't surprise him but it was another source of irritation. He needed more help. He and Woods were strangers to the area and had limited knowledge of the community or the terrain. If Paul Faa Geddes was right, and the man they sought had local knowledge, then they might never find him. There were thousands of acres of countryside around Bellingham where a man like him could lie low.

In the end, Lavender resolved to keep his appointment with Clennell and use the opportunity to ask the magistrate for help from the local militia. It was the only way. He needed more men, good men, to help him flush the murderous cove out from that desolate and empty landscape. He considered leaving Woods behind to continue to search alone but then reasoned that one man alone would not make much difference in the hunt for an assassin, who could merge into the foliage of the woodland with more skill than the gypsies.

He boarded the coach to Morpeth with a deep sense of foreboding. Apart from his obvious worry about the safety of Helen Carnaby, whom he hoped was still safe in her secret lair; he also had a niggling feeling that he had over-looked some vital clue or lead. Some thing was not right.

As the coach rolled and jolted down rutted country lanes, his mind went over and over the evidence he had collected. Yes, there were still some things outstanding. The copy of Baxter Carnaby's will had not yet arrived from Mr Agar in Newcastle. Abel Knowles, the drover, had not been located, and they would have to wait until Saturday to speak to the landlord of the Redesdale Arms. But apart from these, he had diligently followed up every lead. He had solved the mystery of Helen Carnaby's escape from a locked room, and had interviewed everyone connected with Helen Carnaby and her mysterious disappearance. Even Mr Armstrong had been pleased when they all returned to Bellingham after their visit to Linn Hagh:

'You've done well, Lavender. You've got further in this case than I ever dreamed you would.'

Yet still Lavender had this infuriating sensation that there was another piece to uncover in this perplexing mystery and that bothered him.

It bothered him a lot.

CHAPTER TWENTY SIX

Friday 26th November, 1809
The Black Bull public house, Morpeth

'God's strewth.'

Magistrate Clennell stared hard at Lavender across the private parlour of the Black Bull in Morpeth. Beneath grey bushy eyebrows, his piercing eyes were wide with surprise. A look of incredulity had replaced the deep frown that normally lined his face.

Clennell, Lavender and Woods had spent the last hour listening to the testimony of the horse-thief, William Taylerson, who claimed to have new evidence against Jamie Charlton, a man suspected of robbing Kirkley Hall the previous year. Now that they had concluded this business and the gaolers were hustling the condemned Taylerson back to Morpeth prison, Lavender had started to tell Clennell about the mysterious case of the missing heiress.

'You say that you believe it was the young woman *herself* who orchestrated this elaborate ploy?'

'Yes.'

'Tell me more.'

Lavender leaned against the window frame, glad to stretch his legs after the long coach journey from Bellingham. Carefully, he explained the rest of the story about how Helen Carnaby had escaped from Linn Hagh. While he spoke, he caught sight of the gaolers dragging Taylerson across Morpeth's cobbled market square. The horse-thief blinked in the low, winter sunlight and stumbled over his ankle chains.

When Lavender finished, he closed the window reluctantly. The sickening stench of Morpeth gaol had entered the tavern parlour with Taylerson and was still trapped beneath the low-beams on the ceiling.

The room also smelt of treachery.

Lavender had serious misgivings about the use of informants, especially informants who were so desperate to avoid the hangman's noose themselves that they would say anything. At next summer's assizes, it would be Taylerson's word against Charlton's. Yet, he had no doubt that the local jury of landed gentry and prosperous merchants would convict the farm labourer, Charlton. They were desperate to hang someone for this notorious robbery and probably wouldn't be too fussy about whether, or not, they had the right man. Jamie Charlton's fate was sealed; it was only a matter of time before he was sentenced to hang for the robbery at Kirkley Hall.

The gentry must have their scapegoat for the crime committed against them at Kirkley Hall, Lavender realised, *and that wretched creature, Taylerson, is the one who will provide him.*

'I asked you why she ran away.' Impatience hardened Clennell's voice.

Lavender shook off his dark mood and brought his mind back to the current case at Bellingham.

'I believe that she fled her family home because she feared for her life.'

He told Clennell about the evidence they had uncovered including: the digitalis found in Isobel Carnaby's possession; the man who stalked the heiress through Hareshaw Woods and the comments of the servants and the gypsy girl about the atmosphere of violence and danger which hung over Linn Hagh. Finally, he told him about the attempt on Helen Carnaby's life in the graveyard.

'I need help from the militia to find and arrest this man. I'm convinced it was the same man who stalked her. The local constable is a useless fool.'

'Certainly,' Clennell nodded and turned to the dowdy little man seated beside him. 'My clerk will draft a letter to Captain Wentworth of the militia immediately.'

The scribe took up his quill and adjusted his spectacles.

While Clennell dictated his letter for Captain Wentworth and the cleric's feather scratched across the parchment, Lavender and his constable waited patiently. The smell of the roast meat began to drift into their private parlour from the tavern kitchens. Woods shuffled uncomfortably on a hard-baked chair by the door. They could hear muffled laughter from the tap room across the corridor and the slow, rhythmic tick of the long case clock which stood in the corner.

'I also require warrants for the arrest of both George and Isobel Carnaby,' Lavender said.

Clennell looked up from the table surprised.

'I'm convinced that one, or the other, of the Carnabys would confess to conspiring to murder their sister, if they found themselves in Hexham gaol for a few nights.'

'Possibly,' Clennell conceded. He scratched his head beneath the edge of his wig. 'However, this evidence – although compelling – is still circumstantial: a few shreds of snuff found in a cave on

Carnaby's own land; a button and a box of digitalis – which could have been used for rat poison. These will not get you a conviction.'

'There is also a possible case for a charge against Isobel Carnaby for the murder of her step-mother. I believe Dr Goddard would be a credible witness.'

'Yes, Robert Goddard is a good man,' Clennell agreed. 'He's a native of Morpeth. His late mother lived near my sister in Castle Square but –'

'But?' Lavender prompted.

Clennell sighed and rolled his eyes. He took off his wig and gave his close-cropped greying head another scratch.

'Normally Robert Goddard would make a convincing witness, but his mother died a few weeks ago and rumour has it that the man is distracted with grief. It's possible that Goddard is fanciful in his suspicions.'

'He seemed perfectly sane and reasonable when he treated Constable Woods for digitalis poisoning.' Lavender could feel the magistrate's resistance. His hope of acquiring a warrant for the arrest of the Carnabys began to fade.

Clennell shrugged. 'Maybe he was. I understand from my wife that Goddard's mother's death has hit him hard. He repulses all visitors and offers of help from his neighbours and friends in Morpeth. My sister tells me that he talks about leaving his practice in Bellingham and emigrating to the Americas.'

Lavender raised his eyebrows. 'Really?' This was interesting news.

'You say that you believe the girl is safe for the moment?'

'I believe she has eloped with her lover,' Lavender said.

Clennell closed his mouth into a tight line and frowned. 'Who is he?'

'Until Helen Carnaby's would-be murderer is apprehended, I'm not prepared to say.'

Woods gasped behind him and the clerk glanced up from the letter in alarm. Silence descended into the room as Clennell weighed up Lavender's defiance. The Northumberland magistrate narrowed his eyes and said:

'I'm not comfortable with the idea that a young woman's reputation and morality is in such danger – and I'm sure my friend John Armstrong won't be either. What if this rogue has not married her, or refuses to marry her when she turns twenty one? She will be completely ruined.' His voice was like granite.

'I believe that she would be in far greater danger if came out into the open and returned to the Carnaby family home,' Lavender said. 'Until George Carnaby is in Hexham gaol – along with his poisonous sister and their assassin - I'm very happy for Helen Carnaby to remain where she is. Her brother would reclaim her immediately if she came out into the open and only God knows what would happen then.'

There was another awkward pause.

'I know nothing of this fellow, George Carnaby, but it seems to me that you've already decided – without sufficient evidence – that he is guilty of crimes against his sister.'

'I'm confident that he is.'

Clennell frowned.

'I've explained the situation in full to Mr Armstrong,' Lavender lied. 'He is happy to trust in my integrity.'

Clennell shrugged, pulled on his wig and reached for his hat and gloves. The clerk handed a letter for Captain Wentworth to Constable Woods and then hurried to gather up the papers strewn across the table.

'Well, this is a private family matter, of course, not a public one. John Armstrong – not her half-brother – has employed you to track down this girl,' Clennell conceded. 'He knows what is best for his family, although, I'm surprised he agreed to this course of action.'

He and his clerk rose and moved towards the door. Woods opened it for them but the magistrate turned back before he left the room.

'Find this murderous rogue, Lavender, and maybe then you'll get the evidence you need to arrest the Carnabys. In the meantime, remember that although it's only a matter of weeks before Helen Carnaby comes of age, she is still under the legal protection of her brother.' He paused now then spoke slowly to emphasise every word. 'If you're wrong about Carnaby's evil intentions, you could be in very serious trouble.'

'I understand,' Lavender said.

'Should the girl reappear as a married woman in January, he may still bring charges against her lover – out of vengeance – and *you* may find yourself caught up in a very unsavoury mess.'

The heavy door swung closed behind them.

Woods joined Lavender by the window.

'It seems to me that Magistrate Clennell was more reluctant to condemn a member of the gentry to trial than he was when it came to condemning the common labourer, James Charlton.'

'Of course he was,' Lavender's tone was bitter. 'We have to remember, Ned, whom the law has been designed to protect – and from whom.'

He strode angrily over to the fireplace, leaned against the mantelpiece and stared down into the flames. He had expected that Clennell would refuse the arrest warrants but it didn't make his disappointment any easier to bear. Being right was not satisfying in this case.

A potman knocked on the door and came in with a message. He handed Lavender a folded letter addressed to 'Detective Lavender at The Black Bull in Morpeth.'

'Who is it from?' Woods asked.

'Armstrong,' Lavender replied, as he tore open the seal. His eyes scanned the contents and he turned pale. Bile rose in his throat.

'My God!'

'What's amiss?'

'You must set off immediately to Captain Wentworth, rouse the militia and head back to Bellingham.'

'Why? What's happened?'

Lavender reached for his hat and cane. 'I must get the next coach back to Bellingham at once…' He stared at his constable in horror and disbelief. *How could he have been so wrong? Why did he not foresee this?*

'They've found the body of a woman in a quarry near to the town...' His voice cracked. 'She's been badly burnt.'

'What! Burnt? Why burnt?'

'They believe it's the corpse of Helen Carnaby.'

Woods took a sharp intake of breath. 'Surely that is impossible, sir? If…' His voice trailed away.

'Oh, there's more,' Lavender said, bitterly. 'Beddows has arrested her brother for her murder.'

Woods' face lit up in surprise and hope.

'What? George Carnaby?'

'No,' Lavender groaned. *'Matthew* Carnaby - the family idiot. He has been arrested by Beddows for the murder of his sister, Helen.'

CHAPTER TWENTY SEVEN

Lavender leaned his head back against the wood panelling of the carriage, closed his eyes trying to ignore the jolting of the coach and the conversation of his fellow passengers. A miserable lump of dread sat heavily in his stomach.

He had been unable to get a coach back to Bellingham that day and had to settle for one back to Hexham instead. He would take a connection up to Bellingham first thing in the morning.

To return via Hexham was probably a good thing, he decided. The message from Armstrong had told him that Matthew Carnaby had been dragged off to the old gaol in Hexham. He would visit the wretch and attempt to interrogate him tonight.

Matthew Carnaby. The mute. The damaged, child-like family idiot. The man who had opened the door and enabled his sister to slip out of the pele tower unnoticed. The one member of the Carnaby family whom Lavender had consistently ignored during his investigation – at what terrible cost?

Only yesterday at Linn Hagh, he had referred to the younger Carnaby brother as the 'missing piece of the jigsaw.' Yet, even then he had still not recognised the man's significance to the case. Why had he not seen it? How had he so completely overlooked this man in his investigation?

Bile rose in his throat and he struggled to swallow. His indigestion had returned to plague him.

Ignoring Matthew Carnaby had been a terrible mistake - and now it looked like the missing heiress had paid for this mistake with her life.

After the excitement of the visit from the Armstrongs and Detective Lavender, Anna did her best to keep out of the way for the rest of the day. Both George and Isobel Carnaby were in a foul mood.

About half past four, Anna stood at the window and watched the wintery sun begin to set behind Hareshaw Woods. It had been a cold but clear day, and the sky blended calmly into vermillion and scarlet layers above the distant orb as it sank. The top branches of the skeletal trees became black silhouettes on the horizon against the vast red canvas of the sky. It was pretty; she liked to watch the sunset.

There was movement on the meandering road which led up the rise to the pele tower. In the encroaching gloom, she could just make out Constable Beddows on his horse. He led a sombre procession towards Linn Hagh. One of the beadles drove a flat cart containing a large lump covered with sack cloth.

When he arrived at the door, she showed the constable up to the master and mistress in the Great Hall and unconcerned, she returned to the steamy kitchen to help Mistress Norris with the supper.

Isobel Carnaby's scream rent the peace of the kitchen. Startled, Anna dropped her vegetable knife onto the flagstones.

The next second, George Carnaby thundered down the stairs in his shirt sleeves, trailing Constable Beddows in his wake.

'For Christ's sake!' he yelled.

He paused wild-eyed at the entrance to the kitchen and gesticulated to Peter, their manservant.

'Peter! Get a light! Move man!'

Frightened, Anna steeped back out of the way as Peter leapt to his feet from his chair at the kitchen table, grabbed a lantern and hurried to join the master.

'You, girl – see to your mistress!'

The three men left the hall. Anna regained her wits and hurried upstairs.

Miss Isobel was slumped on the chaise longue, crying into a handkerchief.

'Fetch me the smelling salts, girl,' she snapped, between sobs. 'I'm overcome – poor Helen! To think it has come to this!'

Fear crept into the pit of Anna's stomach. She froze to the spot.

'What is it…? What's happened?'

'Just get me sal volatile!'

Anna dashed into her mistress' bedroom. Her hands shook as she searched amongst the glass vials on the dresser. As her fingers closed around the small bottle of sal volatile she found herself drawn to the window.

Twenty feet below her, George Carnaby stood in a pool of white light, holding up a corner of the sacking. He peered down at the shapeless mass which lay in the cart. Jagged shadows flitted across the icy ground like knives.

She could only see the top of his head and could hear nothing. At his elbow, Peter's knees seemed to buckle. He staggered away from the group and retched into the weeds which grew against the wall of the building. The hairs rose on the back of Anna's neck.

Her feet dragged like lead as she returned to the Great Hall and gave the sal volatile to Isobel Carnaby. She heard the men returning up the stairs of the tower and watched in a trance-like state as her mistress blew her nose on her dry handkerchief and sat up.

'Is it her?' Miss Isobel demanded, when George Carnaby and Constable Beddows entered the hall.

'Hard to tell,' Carnaby said. 'She's such a bloody mess.'

'Oh, my poor sister!' Miss Isobel's head bowed over her hands and her shoulders shook as a new wave of tears overcame her.

Constable Beddows stepped forward, embarrassed. He clutched a blackened piece of cloth in his filthy hands.

'I'm sorry to disturb you at such a time as this, Miss Isobel, but we were able to get this small piece of her dress. It ain't as badly burnt as the rest. Perhaps you could identify it?'

Isobel Carnaby glanced up and blinked her watery eyes. The ammonia had made her cry.

Her hands trembled as she took the limp rag of material from Beddows.

'Why yes! Oh no! Yes, yes – it's part of one of Helen's dresses.' For a moment she was racked with another bout of sobbing. Then she turned abruptly to Anna and held out the scrap of material.

'Here – Anna. You look at it. It's my sister's, isn't it? You looked after her clothes.'

Startled, Anna jerked out of her trance and felt herself flush under the scrutiny of the adults in the hot room. She slowly took hold of the flimsy material and gently brushed the soot from charred cloth which had originally been pale blue. The outline of small spiky flowers and the winding stems of the print appeared beneath her trembling finger. She staggered and gasped for breath.

'It's alright, lass,' Beddows said. He took hold of her arm to steady her. 'It's a shock to you, I know.'

'Is it Helen's?' her Mistress demanded.

'Yes.' Her squeaky voice sounded like it belonged to someone else. 'It's from one of Miss Helen's dresses.'

The Carnabys now had heard what they wanted to hear, and they turned their attention back to each other.

'The maid's word will not be enough. We still need a doctor to identify the body if we're to claim the money,' Miss Isobel snapped.

'I've already sent Peter to fetch Robert Goddard.'

'Hmmph, Goddard is a fool. You may need to call on Horrocks in Newcastle…'

Quietly, Anna slipped the burnt cloth into her apron pocket and backed silently away towards the door.

CHAPTER TWENTY EIGHT

Hexham gaol loomed out of the gloom like a sleeping fortress as Lavender trudged up the hill. Silhouetted against the full moon, its squat bulk made it look formidable. The ground floor was solid wall. The gaol's small windows were highly-placed in its forbidding walls and they reflected the moonlight like a set of black mirrors.

The ostler at the coaching inn who gave him directions told him that Hexham was the first purpose built gaol in England. Originally built to imprison the Border reivers four hundred years ago, the building was still as bleak and inhospitable as it had been in the fourteenth century. Lavender pulled his scarf around his nose to try and protect himself from the overpowering stench of urine, faeces and unwashed bodies as he leapt up the worn steps to rap at the heavy studded door.

A nervous gaoler finally let him enter when he showed him his silver-topped tipstaff from Bow Street. 'Ay, I've heard you were in the area,' he said. 'They's sed you might turn up 'ere when they brought Carnaby in.' The man had an appalling case of acne. He ran a filthy hand through his long, greasy hair and stared uncertainly at the detective.

Behind him, Lavender could see a long ladder leaning against the rough stones of the wall and a large rectangular hole in the flagged floor. He could hear the ugly murmur of male voices that drifted up from the freezing bowels of the gaol.

'I need to see him. Is he down there?'

'Oh no!' exclaimed the gaoler in mock surprise. '*That's* no place fer our gentlemen murderers. No. Master Carnaby is in a special private room on the next floor – which we reserve fer our debtors and gentlemen criminals.'

Surprised, Lavender followed the gaoler up the twisting flight of stairs to the next floor. A few lanterns glimmered forlornly against the bleak stone walls. Shadows lurked in every draughty corner. He could smell the damp which had seeped into the rotten beams of the ceilings and the doors, but thankfully the smell of human excrement was not as strong in this part of the building.

The gaoler turned a huge iron key and pushed open the heavy door into a small, warm cell. The room contained an iron bed with blankets, a writing desk and an armchair in front of the fire which spat quietly in the grate.

'This is where we usually keep the debtors.' The gaoler explained with a nod towards the parchment, ink and quills scattered across the desk. 'That's so theys can write to their friends fer money.'

Silver moonlight poured down through the high, drapeless window but it was dark in there. Lavender lit a candle on the desk and peered around.

The sudden light disturbed his quarry. Slumped in a corner, his back pushed against the rough-hewn walls, Matthew Carnaby held his head in his hands and groaned.

'Oi! You there!' the gaoler yelled. 'Get up! This detective gadgie wants to speak to you.'

Carnaby gave a miserable howl, scrambled to his feet and scurried across the room like a frightened animal. He flung himself on the bed with his back turned to Lavender and the gaoler.

'Damn and blast him!' the exasperated gaoler cursed. 'He ain't no more than a nick ninny, anyhows. I don't know what you think you're going to get from him? He's a sap head - the man canna speak.'

'Leave him to me,' Lavender said, quietly. 'First of all, you can tell me how they found him.'

'Why next to his sister's dead body, of course. Raking around in the ashes of her funeral pyre, the grisly bastard.'

Pitiful sobbing now racked the body of the young man on the bed.

Lavender chose his next words carefully.

'Did anyone actually see him murder his sister?'

Carnaby howled and the gaoler beside him paused and scratched the pustules erupting from his cheeks.

'Why, no – not as I've bin told - but them constables up in Bellingham ses he did it.'

Lavender's lips tightened in a grim line. The say-so of Constable Beddows and his useless pack of law enforcement officers held little sway with him.

'A softer, gentler, young man you could not hope to meet,' Katherine Armstrong had said.

'He's a sweetie,' Laurel Faa Geddes had confirmed.

Constable Woods had been adamant that the murderer he had disturbed in the graveyard was not the disfigured younger brother of the missing heiress.

Was it possible that his instincts had been right, all along? Lavender wondered. Was Matthew Carnaby innocent of the charge now laid against him? He wouldn't be the first young man to be in the wrong place at the wrong time and find himself in gaol.

'Who pays for this room?' he asked. He knew it would not be George Carnaby.

The gaoler shuffled uncomfortably and cast his eyes down onto the floor. His silence made Lavender swing around to face him. His eyes narrowed. The gaoler rubbed the boils on the back of his neck and tried to loosen his stained neckerchief.

'I don't care how much he pays you to keep silent. You give me the name of the man who is paying for this private cell or I'll have you tossed down into that hell-hole below with the rest of the local cloyers.'

'I canna tell you his name!' The gaoler's head jerked up and he stared at the detective in alarm. 'He never gived me his name. He were just some toff who turned up here this morning. Gave me the money and sed to make sure the saphead were well cared fer.'

'Describe him.'

The man scratched nervously.

'I couldn't. He were swathed in scarves and had his hat pulled down.'

Lavender frowned. 'Was he dark or fair – and how old?'

'Dark. He were dark, youngish and a real gentleman, educated like. I could tell by the cut of his coat, his voice –and his boots. He had good leather boots.'

Lavender paused, incredulous. He had half expected to hear that Matthew Carnaby's benefactor had been the kindly John Armstrong - or one of his sons. But the Armstrongs had no need for such cloak and dagger secrecy. There was only one person who answered the description the gaoler had just given him: Helen Carnaby's mysterious lover.

For one horrible minute, he thought he had misjudged the man. Could this lover have been after her money as well? Did the cad entice the girl to elope with him, marry her and then persuade her simpleton of a brother to kill her so that *he* could claim her inheritance? Were these comforts in gaol part of the deal, the payment to keep Carnaby quiet?

He fought back a rising sense of alarm. No. It was not possible. No one needed to bribe Matthew Carnaby to silence, the man was a mute for Christ's sake. Besides, why kill Helen Carnaby? As her legal husband, the ten thousand pounds would be his to do with as he pleased. There was no need to kill her off.

He stared again at the poor wretch who cowered at the other side of the cell. Lavender found it harder and harder to believe that this Carnaby was a killer. He had no doubt that the simple fool had been framed by someone back in Bellingham. The real killer - the pipe smoking beggar - was still at large.

If Helen Carnaby's lover had been moved by the plight of her brother to come here and pay for a private prison cell for him, then he had been motivated by compassion. That was the only explanation.

He took the candle in one hand and picked up the hard-backed chair from the desk with his other. Then he walked slowly over to the bed, put down the chair and sat next to the distraught young man.

'Turn over,' he said, gently.

Matthew Carnaby ceased crying and obeyed. He gazed pitifully up at Lavender from the bed out of blackened and swollen eyes. Even by the dim light of the flickering candle, Lavender could see that the man had been beaten up. His nose was also bloodied.

The gaoler read his thoughts.

'He put up one heck of a fight when the beadles tried to arrest him,' he reminded Lavender. 'They had to rough him up a bit to get him into the prison cart.'

Lavender sighed, looked down at the wretched creature and tried to ignore the distorted features and silver scars which snaked across the right side of his face into the matted hair of his dark cropped head.

'Do you know who I am?'

Matthew Carnaby stared back blankly.

'I'm Detective Lavender. Mr Armstrong in Bellingham asked me to try and find your sister, Helen.'

He may have imagined it but he felt sure he saw the man nod slightly.

'You saw me once in the woods, do you remember? You were with Laurel Faa Geddes.'

A large tear rolled down the man's face from his good eye and he opened his mouth.

'La la.' The two syllables were more like growls which emanated from the depths of the man's throat. Lavender looked at him in surprise. He had thought the young man was mute. *How to progress?*

‘I need to know what happened yesterday – at the fire.’

Silence.

‘If you’re innocent, I’ll do my best to get you out of here and back home to Linn Hagh. I know that there is another man in Bellingham who has tried to harm your sister – a bad man.’

Silence.

‘Can you try to tell me what happened? Can you show me, somehow?’

The younger man just stared at him blankly. Beneath his disfigurement, he had a strong similarity to Helen Carnaby; Lavender remembered the portrait of the missing heiress. Summoning all his patience, he tried once more.

‘I’m here to try and help you,’ he said, quietly. ‘I don’t believe for one minute that you harmed your sister, Helen. ’

‘Ela.’ It was the same unmistakable throaty growl of sorrow. Lavender saw something pass across the youth’s eyes. Some flicker of recognition.

Suddenly, Matthew rose from the squeaking bed to a sitting position and swung his legs off the mattress. Lavender sat back in his chair and watched him lollop across the room towards the writing desk.

By the door, the gaoler stiffened as Carnaby approached.

‘Steady there, fellah,’ he warned, but the prisoner ignored him. He picked up the quill, leaned over the table and jabbed it awkwardly into the ink bottle. Ink slopped across the surface of the table.

Lavender didn’t move. He and the guard watched in surprise, as slowly and awkwardly, Matthew Carnaby dragged the feather across the parchment on the table. The only sound in that room was the scratching of the quill, the tearing of paper and Matthew’s laboured breathing.

What now? Lavender thought. *An illiterate man can suddenly write?* Katherine Armstrong had told him that Matthew Carnaby had never been schooled.

Lavender rose to his feet and moved across to peer over the young man’s shoulder. The letters were large, crudely drawn and splattered with ink. He couldn’t quite make them out yet but it didn’t matter. The illiterate ‘idiot’ from the Carnaby family was writing; giving him some clue about the terrible events back in Bellingham.

The answer now came to him in a flash. Helen Carnaby was a 'pupil teacher.' She had obviously spent some time teaching her brother to write.

Matthew Carnaby strained with the effort like a child with its first chalk and slate; his tongue flopped out of his slack mouth.

Finally, he stood up straight and handed the parchment to Lavender.

'La la,' he said again and with his free hand he drew his finger across his throat like he was slicing it open. In this unmistakable gesture he demonstrated murder; he must have witnessed the crime. He was showing Lavender that the girl had had her throat cut.

His job now done, the young man scrambled back to his bed where he curled up in a ball with his back to the room.

The gaoler moved to Lavender's side.

'Has he given you the name of the killer?' His gabbled voice rose with excitement. 'They never said he could write when they brought him in. 'What does it say?'

Lavender glanced down at the page and was overwhelmed with bitter disappointment.

In large, childish letters, Matthew Carnaby had written: 'BAXTR CARNBY.'

'Who's this *Baxtr Carnby*?'

'His dead father.'

At the other side of the prison cell, Matthew Carnaby resumed his plaintive sobbing.

CHAPTER TWENTY NINE

The beadles and Peter put Miss Helen's body in the barrelled vault beneath the tower. Miss Isobel would not have the burnt corpse in the house until they had got a coffin.

''Tain't right,' Mistress Norris complained as she wiped a tear from her watery eye. 'She shouldn't be lying out there in the cold on a pallet – with only the sheep and a couple of cows fer company.'

Anna stared blankly at the tearful cook and wondered why she couldn't cry. Even when they'd told her that Master Matthew had killed Miss Helen and had been hauled away to Morpeth gaol, she had felt nothing. It seemed like she was in the middle of a bad dream. She would wake up in a minute.

'Make sure you all stay away from my sister,' George Carnaby snarled at the servants. 'I don't want anyone gawping at her body, do you understand?'

Doctor Goddard arrived to examine the corpse. It didn't go well. She could see from the window that when the two men emerged from the under belly of the house they were arguing. She could hear their muffled shouts through the glass. Doctor Goddard leapt onto his horse and thundered back to town with the master's curses ringing in his ears.

The cook burnt herself on a pan and swore.

'Do you think I should bring out one of her favourite dresses?' Anna asked suddenly. The sound of her own voice startled her.

She would get out the black one with beading, she decided. Miss Helen had always liked that. The peacock blue dress was spoilt now; Miss Isobel had sullied it.

'What fer?' The cook stared at her blankly.

Anna could hardly say the words.

'To lay her out...' Her voice trailed away.

The irascible cook stopped whisking eggs, patted Anna's arm and watched at with pity in her eyes. 'I don't think there's much point, pet. From what Peter said, she's in too bad a state to wear a dress.'

Still, Anna couldn't cry.

When she began to carry the dinner up to the Great Hall a sudden wave of dizziness made her stop and steady herself against the wall.

Alarmed, she waited until the feeling had passed, then she did the rest of the journey slowly.

As she neared the entrance to the Great Hall, she heard the unmistakable sound of low laughter. Unable to believe her ears, she climbed the last few steps silently and listened outside the door.

Miss Isobel laughed again.

'This couldn't have worked out better,' she said. 'Matthew will hang, the faws have gone, and we should soon have our giddy sister's inheritance.'

'I agree.' There was a note of triumph in George Carnaby's voice.

Anna heard the chink of brandy glasses and realised that the Carnabys had just made a silent toast.

'Robert Goddard is a bloody fool,' the master continued. 'But I'll fetch Horrocks over from Newcastle – he'll identify the body - and the lawyers will have to accept that she's dead. We'll soon have the money.'

They paused and Anna suddenly became aware of her own breathing. She began to panic that they could hear her. Had she made a noise?

Oh for God's sake, did it matter? Anger welled up in her like a flash flood in a spring stream. She knew what she had to do. She walked into the room and dumped the tray on the table with a crash.

Isobel Carnaby looked up in surprise.

'Careful, girl,' she warned.

Anna didn't reply or look at her mistress as she walked out. Her legs didn't take her back down to the kitchen either. Spurred on by anger and disgust, she found new strength and leapt upstairs to her room at the top of the tower.

Within five minutes she had pulled out all her things and stuffed them into her tatty old carpetbag. At the bottom of her drawer she found the note Constable Woods had sent her:

Anna,

You must be very careful, treacle. There is a murderer in Bellingham. Take care and don't go out alone...

For a moment she paused, then she shook her head and grabbed her darning pile from the top of the dresser to stuff it into the bag.

Stick to the road... The constable had continued. *If any strange man is seen around Linn Hagh, can you send me word? And if George Carnaby meets with any men you don't know, I want to know about that as well...*

She pulled a scrap of parchment out of the drawer and stared at its fire-blackened edges. She had found this strange little note a few days ago while cleaning out the hearth in the Great Hall. She had assumed that Mr George had thrown out some old papers of his father's. This one had fallen out of the fire and she had kept it in case Miss Helen wanted it as a souvenir of her Da; it was signed by Baxter Carnaby. But there was no point in keeping it for her now. She felt sorry she had let Constable Woods down but perhaps this note might show him that she had tried?

She stuffed it into her apron pocket and felt the brittle, flaking edges of the burnt piece of cloth from Miss Helen's dress. Yes, she would give him that too. She needed to go - now.

Two minutes later, she had on her cloak and was at the bottom of the stairs. The startled cook saw her at the door.

'Where d'you think yer going?' she demanded.

'I'm leaving,' she said. 'I've had enough.'

'What, just like that?'

Anna ignored her. She opened the heavy door, walked out and slammed the door shut behind her. The cold night air slapped her viciously in the face but she didn't care.

She scurried down the icy steps and ran down the dark road, desperate to put as much distance between herself and Linn Hagh as possible. As she neared the bend in the road she threw a last frantic glance over her shoulder but no-one followed her. She rounded the corner and slowed down to catch her breath. Her chest ached with the exertion but she didn't care.

She was free.

An hour later she was sobbing in the comforting arms of her mother, in the warmth of their tiny kitchen. After she had cried her eyes out her mother made her a cup of sweet tea and she started to feel a bit better.

'Eee! I nearly forgot,' the elderly woman said. She left her chair and fetched Anna a letter from the old dresser.

Anna stared at it in amazement. *'To Miss Anna Jones,'* it read.

'It were pushed through the door yesterday. Go on,' her mother said with excitement. 'Open it and tell us what it says.'

Anna's hands trembled as she reached for a kitchen knife to break the seal.

The handwriting belonged to Helen Carnaby.

CHAPTER THIRTY

Saturday 27 th ***November, 1809***

Lavender arrived at Linn Hagh just before ten o' clock.

The manservant, Peter, met him at the steps to the tower and grasped the reins of his horse.

'The master's not in,' the servant said. 'Shall I tell the mistress yer here?'

Lavender shook his head, relieved he didn't have to see Carnaby. 'No, don't bother your mistress; it must be a difficult time for her. I'm only here to examine the body.'

'Ye'll find her in there.' The old man jerked his head towards a small wooden door at the base of the steps. Grief contorted his leathered face. 'Don't expect me to come in with you – I can't stand it.'

Lavender dismounted slowly. Woods had told him that the old man was the most tight-lipped of all the Linn Hagh servants, yet the death of Helen Carnaby seemed to have shaken the taciturn old man quite badly. Without Carnaby there, he seemed quite garrulous.

'Where's your master gone?' Lavender asked.

'He's gan to the toon. He went yesterday to fetch Doctor Horrocks so as he can identify Miss Helen.'

'Surely Doctor Goddard from Bellingham can do that?'

'Aye, he coulda…' Lavender heard the hesitation. 'He were here like, two nights ago.'

'What happened?'

The servant shook his head and led Lavender's horse away towards a stone water trough at the base of the tower. The old man had clearly said enough.

Lavender pushed open the creaking door and paused to steady himself. He had attended several house fires in the London in his time, and had helped to drag out the bodies afterwards, but it never got any easier to deal with the horror.

The gloomy ground floor of the Pele Tower had an uneven earth floor and a barrelled stone ceiling. Several animal pens lined the rough-hewn sides. The only light came from the open door behind him and two grimy deep-set windows, built low in the walls. The ancient wooden stalls were riddled with woodworm. Scattered with straw, the whole place reeked of animal excrement. He felt thankful for that. It would cover the smell of roasted flesh which would still hover over the body.

Suddenly the poor light dimmed. He turned round to see Peter stood in the doorway behind him. 'She were found in the old quarry further up the road. Him at Thrush Farm found her.'

'Thank you.' Lavender said. He sensed that the old man had not finished.

'The master had a right fight with Doctor Goddard aboot it all; they were yelling their heads off.' Then the servant disappeared from the doorway.

Lavender struck a light and hung a lantern close to the wooden table where the corpse lay covered with sacking. Next, he braced himself and lifted the cloth.

The whole of the body was badly burnt. The flames had eliminated all body hair and charred the tissue to darkened leather which stretched tightly across the bones on the young woman's face and limbs. Her remaining flesh was so taut that it revealed the contours of the muscles and skeleton beneath. Her eyes were welded shut, but her jaw and teeth gaped up at him in a grotesque grimace of agony.

He fought back a wave of nausea and tried to focus on examining the remains for clues.

There was clear evidence that someone had repeatedly hacked at her throat. The terrified Matthew Carnaby had been lucid enough when he had mimed slicing his own throat. He now knew how this girl had died. He was relieved that the poor woman had been dead before her body hit the flames.

He steadied himself again, then carried out an examination of the rest of the remains. He noted the missing piece of cloth, chopped out with shears, from the hem of what remained of her dress.

When he finally emerged from the vault he leaned back against the rough stone of the tower and took great gulps of breath to remove the stench of horror from his nostrils and calm his nerves. He walked over to the pump and washed his face and hands. The icy water refreshed him.

Now he had seen the corpse for himself, he could understand the disagreement between Goddard and Carnaby. Nothing was left to distinguish the body inside Linn Hagh from any other young woman in Bellingham. Carnaby would need an affidavit from a medical professional in order to bury the remains as Helen Carnaby and claim her fortune. It sounded like Goddard had refused to identify the remains.

For a moment he felt relieved; Helen Carnaby could still be alive. It might not be her. But his reprieve was short lived. If those remains were not those of the missing heiress, then whose were they? What had started out as an easy case to solve of a girl who had eloped with her lover had now descended into a brutal murder.

Anger flashed through him. Whoever that poor girl was - whether it was Helen Carnaby or someone else – he would bring her killer to justice. If John Armstrong refused to pay any further expenses for this investigation, then he would carry on regardless.

An awful thought now entered his mind. 'Where's the housemaid, Anna?'

Carnaby's manservant still loitered over by his horse. He looked up.

'What her?' Peter rubbed his stubble with his grimy hand. 'Oh she legged it back to her Ma's on Thursday night. They say she's not coming back. Too much fer her I reckon – all this.' He waved the arm of his tattered coat in the vague direction of the body. 'Too much fer all on us,' he added, sadly.

Lavender nodded and sighed with relief. He walked over to his horse and ran his hand gently down its flank. He knew Woods would share his relief; his constable was fond of the little maid. He decided to try a few more questions while the man was in the mood to answer them.

'How long have you worked here at Linn Hagh?'

'Aboot twenty year.'

'Has there ever been another man with the name Baxter Carnaby besides your old master - an uncle or a cousin, perhaps?'

The servant shook his head, scowled and stared at Lavender in confusion.

'You knew Master Matthew Carnaby well?'

'Aye.'

'Do you think he was capable of doing *that* to a woman?' Lavender jerked his thumb in the direction of the corpse.

The old man shook his head again and fought back a tear. 'Poor sod. He were as gentle as a lamb – wouldn't hurt a fly. In fact, manys the time I've seen him tek flies outta spiders' webs.'

Lavender nodded and put his foot in the stirrup. 'You've been very helpful, thank you,' he said.

'Are you gannin back to Bellingham?'

'No,' Lavender swung himself up into the saddle. 'I'm going to see the faws.'

Peter laughed. 'You're too late,' he said, gleefully. 'They've gan.'

'Gone? Gone where?' Lavender was shocked.

The manservant shrugged. 'Who knows? I reckon they knew they'd end up being blamed fer this lot.' He jerked his thumb again towards the ancient door at the base of the pele tower. 'I reckon they've legged it afore Jethro Hamilton and his boys come back to burn them out. They've fled to the hills, I'm thinking.'

'Did George Carnaby throw them off his land?'

'No. They's just upped and left.'

Lavender didn't wait to hear anymore. He whipped his horse into a gallop and tore across the field towards the faw camp.

Peter was right.

All that remained of the gypsy camp were the cold, blackened rings of dead fires, the empty wooden outbuildings, brown patches of grass where the tents used to stand and a broken old cart balanced precariously on three wheels and a cairn of stones.

The Linn Hagh faws had gone.

CHAPTER THIRTY ONE

Lavender rode back to the lane, turned his horse up towards the old quarry and Thrush Farm but then heard the sound of hooves thundering up the muddy road behind him. He turned back and breathed a sigh of relief. It was Constable Woods. His broad, ruddy face shone with sweat as he reined in his horse beside the detective.

'Well met, Ned,' Lavender said, quietly.

'Morning, sir. They told me at The Rose and Crown that you had ridden out to Linn Hagh. Captain Wentworth and the militia are scouring every privy and outhouse in the town as we speak – and I weren't needed, so I thought to come up and join you. If that murderer still hides in Bellingham, they'll soon flush the bugger out. Wentworth plans to move outwards into the countryside once he has finished in town.'

'Excellent,' said Lavender. 'I worked with him last year on the Kirkley Hall robbery case. Wentworth is a good man; he'll leave no stone unturned.'

'So what have you uncovered?'

'Ride with me up to where they found the body and I'll tell you what I know.'

Leaving the dense woodland behind them and the twisting road rose and dipped sharply as it traversed bleak and desolate fells. Mile after mile of ice-sharp moorland stretched beside them, broken only by haphazard stone walls flecked with lichen and moss. Occasionally, they saw a derelict, roofless stone farmhouse or a mournful flock of bleating sheep dotted on barren hilltops. Stunted alder and oak trees stretched out their bare limbs, silhouetted against the frozen sun, like sentinels of the last outpost.

Finally, they found the quarry; an ugly grey gash in the hillside. Fallen rocks balanced precariously on top of each other like demented building blocks of giant children. At the base of the quarry, their feet sank into a thick carpet of man-made stone chippings, all hewn from the rugged cliff-face over centuries of excavation. Stagnant, ice-rimmed pools dotted the site.

A large black pile of ash stood out like a cancerous sore in the flat, gravel bottom of the quarry.

Lavender dropped to his haunches then, using with a stick he poked carefully through the debris of the fire and the ground beside it. Woods mooched around the edges, his eyes scanned the weeds and the brush which was trying to reclaim the thin soil.

'There's nothing here,' Lavender called out, disappointed. 'The murderer did a good job of cremating the body, and he's left no sign of himself. Besides which that bumbling idiot Beddows and his men have trampled this entire area like a herd of cows.' He straightened up and walked over to Woods.

'There's nothing I can see that'll help us over here, either,' his constable informed him.

'Oh I don't know about that,' Lavender moved forward and stooped down to pick up a scattered handful of dark, evergreen leaves that littered the gravel. He took off his glove, stroked the leathery surface and serrated edges of the foliage then passed a few of the leaves to Woods.

'Where did these come from, do you think?'

His constable glanced around at the rocky quarry and the barren fields which fell away down to the road.

'Now, I'm no expert on the local flora,' Woods said, 'but I reckon that these don't belong here in this quarry.'

'They don't. This plant doesn't grow within miles of this place. These leaves were brought - or dragged - to this place by someone.'

'Why? What are they?'

Lavender crushed a leaf between his fingers; the aromatic scent - like crushed almonds - was unmistakable.

'Prunus laurocerasus,' he murmured.

'Eh?'

'Laurel leaves.'

'You said Matthew Carnaby had a sprig of these in his bedchamber,' Woods said.

'Yes – and Laurel Faa Geddes wore a wreath of it on her head.'

The two men stared at each other grimly.

Thrush Farm was round the next bend in the road. It was an ancient low-lying collection of farm buildings which nestled in the shelter of a small valley, screened from the road by fir trees. Only the smoke from the ornate Jacobean chimney stacks that rose from the slate roof gave the two men an indication of its presence. Shutters protected the narrow mullioned windows, which were deeply set in the weathered walls.

Lavender hammered on the heavy oak door with his tipstaff.

'This is the home of the farmer who found the dead girl,' he explained to Woods.

They heard furious barking from the nearby barn.

'I hope them buggers are tied up properly,' Woods said.

The door swung open and the two police officers were startled to find themselves face to face with the burly figure of Jethro Hamilton. Of the three men, he seemed the least surprised to find them all standing there together.

'Get yersens inside to the kitchen,' he said, gruffly. 'I've bin expecting you.' His mouth was set in a grim line and his brow furrowed with concern.

He stepped aside and Woods and Lavender entered a cold, flagged hallway. Hamilton closed the door and led them through to the back of the house.

The farm kitchen was warm and welcoming and the delicious smell of broth and baking bread assaulted their nostrils. A huge fireplace arched across the side wall where Hamilton's wife stirred a pot over the range and glanced uneasily at the strangers accompanying her husband.

'Alice, 'tis Detective Lavender and Constable Woods.' Hamilton said simply.

His wife recovered from her surprise quickly and wiped her hands on her apron. 'Would you like a cup of tea, detectives?' she asked. 'I've just made a pot.'

Lavender nodded and peeled his gloves from his frozen hands.

'That would be most welcome, Mistress Hamilton. Thank you.'

A battered old table with wooden benches and a couple of rickety, rush-seated chairs dominated the room. Three young boys aged roughly between five and twelve were seated here with slates in front of them. They gawped at Lavender and Woods, mouths wide open and chalk held up in mid-air.

'Away, lads,' their father said. The boys didn't need a second bidding. Chairs scraped back across the flag stones and in a flurry of movement and a clatter of boots, the boys dashed out the kitchen. Hamilton indicated for the officers to take their seats at the table.

'They can't allus get down to the school in Bellingham,' the farmer explained, awkwardly, as he cleared away the chalks and slates. 'I do what I can to give them a bit of schooling up here.'

'That's good,' Woods said, simply. 'I've got two lads about the same age. Schooling's important.'

Hamilton nodded and looked relieved. His wife placed three steaming mugs of sweet tea on the table then hovered by the range. The farmer glanced over his shoulder.

'You too, hinny. It's bad enough that one of us is gonna be plagued with nightmares fer months – get yerself out while I tell the detective the details.'

Reluctantly, the woman took off her apron and glided out of the room. Her reluctance to leave stemmed from genuine concern for her husband. She glared sternly at both Lavender and Woods before she left, as if daring the policemen to upset her husband further. Lavender envied them their bond.

'I first saw the smoke from the quarry at dawn on Thursday,' Hamilton said, abruptly. He slumped down into a chair, placed his elbows on the table and ran his hand through his thatch of thick hair. 'But I were out milking and couldn't get over there to check it out. It wasn't until midday – by which time the smoke had thinned to a faint wisp - that I thought I'd better gan and see. That quarry ain't bin used fer years and we rarely see other folks up here. I were uneasy all morning; I knew sommat were amiss. I just wish I'd gan sooner – I might of bin able to –'

'The girl died before she was cremated,' Lavender interjected sharply. 'Her throat had been cut. There would have been nothing that you or anyone else could have done to save her.'

Hamilton sat up straighter. The relief in his face was obvious.

'I...I didn't know aboot that. It were clear that it had been a big fire,' he continued. 'The width of it, the length of time it burned.'

'Yes, the murderer had been planning it for a while,' Lavender said. 'It would have taken some time to shift all that firewood to the place. These moors are not heavily wooded. It was a cold, premeditated act of murder.'

'The embers were still burning when I got there,' Hamilton said. 'I could see the body.' He swallowed hard. 'What was left of her - clear as day.'

'I've already seen the remains,' Lavender said, kindly. 'You don't need to describe her.

They waited for a moment; the farmer needed to compose himself before he carried on. 'There weren't nowt I could do fer her,' he finally said. 'I threw some watter from a pool on the last of the flames and went to fetch help.' He stared down at the scratched wood of the table, his mind haunted by the memory.

'When did you see Matthew Carnaby?'

Hamilton shook his head. 'He weren't there then. I never saw him until I came back with Beddows and the beadles. We found him sobbing at the side of the pyre.'

Lavender breathed out heavily. He had not realised he had been holding his breath. 'What happened?'

'Why Beddows went mad and ordered the beadles to arrest him. The lad put up a hell of a fight, but it were useless. The beadles had him trussed up like a chicken afore long.'

'In all of this, had Matthew Carnaby ever given you any suspicion that he had murdered the dead girl?'

'No, Detective,' Hamilton said. 'In fact, I'm surprised by all of this. Many a times my missus has seen that lad out walking with his sister last summer. They seemed to get along well. In fact, if truth be told, Matthew Carnaby has bin coming here to play with my lads since they were bairns. The missus and I hev never had a minute's worry about the man; the lads like him. Yes, he is a nick ninny – but he's harmless with it…' His voice trailed away and he glanced at the two policemen.

Harmless. That word again. Lavender felt relieved. The manservant Peter, Katherine Armstrong, Laurel Faa Geddes – and now Jethro Hamilton. Not one of them felt there was a shred of evil in Matthew Carnaby.

'If truth be told, Mr Hamilton,' Lavender said. 'I don't think that Matthew Carnaby murdered the girl either.'

Hamilton breathed a sigh of relief. 'I knew it,' he said.

'But I do think he witnessed the murder – although I think he was probably cowering and hiding from view when it happened. I don't know whether the murder took place in the quarry, or closer to Hareshaw Woods - I suspect the former. Even in this remote neck of the world, to carry a dead body for several miles would have attracted attention.'

'Unless it all happened at night,' Woods interrupted.

'Yes,' Lavender said thoughtfully. 'Unless it all happened at night and, as you said, the funeral pyre was not lit until dawn. I think that Matthew followed the murderer back to the quarry and hid, watching until the man cleared up and left the scene. I suspect the whole thing has been planned down the last detail, and even if he had a motive, which he doesn't, this is far too complex for someone of Matthew Carnaby's limited mental faculties.'

'We need to catch the bastard that did this and hang him,' Hamilton growled. His eyes narrowed. 'Do you think it's the same beggar gadgie you described to us before?'

'I'm convinced of it. We've fetched the militia up to Bellingham to help us in our search.'

'We'll ye'll get plenty of help from me and the boys now, Detective. We need to catch this bastard – and quick – before the sod gets a taste fer it.'

'I'm glad to know that you and the rest of the community are willing to help. Unfortunately, the murderer may already have a heightened taste for killing,' Lavender said. 'We also believe the man we seek has spent some years in the army. He is very dangerous.'

Hamilton frowned and shook his head slowly in shock and disbelief.

'What I don't get, Detective, is why burn her corpse to a frazzle? If her throat were already cut, what's the point in that?'

'I think that this was a deliberate ploy by the murderer to make identification of the corpse difficult, if not impossible, for the authorities to identify her.'

'Why?'

'Because the murderer wants us to believe that the dead girl is Helen Carnaby – but I don't think it's her.'

Hamilton and Woods stared at him.

'What are you saying?' the shocked farmer demanded. 'That the dead lass is *not* the Carnaby girl? Who is she then? Who else is missing?'

'No one else has been reported missing,' Lavender said, slowly. 'I cannot prove this – yet - but I suspect that the remains you found may be those of the young gypsy girl: Laurel Faa Geddes.'

Hamilton gasped. Woods shook his head sadly as realisation dawned.

'We've found evidence at the scene of the crime – a bunch of laurel leaves – which suggests that Laurel Faa Geddes was there. She used to wear a laurel wreath around her head.'

'What the 'young witch?' Hamilton's voice rose with surprise.

'She said she were born under a cursed moon, poor gal,' Woods murmured quietly.

'I cannot confirm it because the faws have now left Linn Hagh. Her people would not report her disappearance to the constables; they've their own ways of meting out justice. They'll never come to us for help.'

Hamilton stared at him in disbelief then shook his head.

'I can't tek this all in,' he groaned. 'The Faws have *gone*? You think the murdered lass is the one we call the young witch?'

Lavender paused for a moment to let Hamilton absorb this latest shocking revelation.

'Mr Hamilton,' he eventually continued. 'You and your neighbours need to make a decision. You say that you'll help us by rousing the community to help us track down this murderer, but you need to be absolutely clear that it's probably the body of one those hated gypsies lying in the vaults of Linn Hagh – not Miss Helen Carnaby. Do you think you – and the rest of the men of Bellingham – will still care enough to help us?'

Hamilton opened his mouth to speak but his wife spoke first.

'They'll do it,' she said from the doorway. All the men turned around, surprised. None of them had heard her reappear. In fact, Lavender realised, she had probably been listening from the hallway throughout their conversation. She looked pale.

'That murderer has got to be stopped,' she said firmly and simply. 'It could be me, or one of the bairns he kills next.'

CHAPTER THIRTY TWO

'But I don't understand, Detective,' Katherine Armstrong complained. Her eyes were red and swollen from crying.

'Why would George and Isobel Carnaby kill Laurel Faa Geddes and pretend it's our Helen? What do they hope to gain from that?'

Lavender stood uncomfortably in the centre of Armstrong's study, conscious of the incredulity in Katherine's voice and on the face of her father. Lavender and Woods had galloped back to Bellingham from Thrush Farm and immediately called on the Armstrongs. He was starving, mud-spattered and his body ached with the hard riding - but the day was far from over.

Armstrong had been angry when they first arrived. Both he and his daughter had believed what they had been told; that the dead girl was Helen Carnaby. They had felt let down by Lavender. He had promised them that Helen Carnaby remained safe in her lair. Now he had arrived and outlined yet another incredible theory. And yet again, he had no proof. They both stared at him in surprise and slight disbelief out of pale, strained faces.

'I can hardly take all this in, Lavender,' John Armstrong said, eventually.

Lavender spoke slowly, choosing his words carefully. 'I believe the Carnabys have now reached a crisis point in their evil plot to get their hands on their sister's inheritance. They needed a body, a body that no one can identify, to claim the money for themselves. The gypsies are expendable to their mind. Who would care if one of the faws went missing?'

Katherine Armstrong shuffled uncomfortably in her seat. 'The poor girl,' she muttered.

Her father continued to frown. His gnarled hands gripped the arm of his chair; their knuckles gleaming white.

'I believe that their hired assassin has provided the body by killing Laurel Faa Geddes. They intend to seek probate and claim her inheritance before her twenty-first birthday at the end of January.'

'Can they do this?' Miss Katherine swung around to face her father. 'Can they claim Helen's money that soon?'

The elderly lawyer nodded grimly.

'These things do take time,' he said. 'But if Carnaby knows the right people then he could just about make this work before the end of January. Helen would never get her inheritance back if he got his hands on it first. '

'Carnaby has gone to Newcastle to fetch a Doctor Horrocks to identify the remains.' Lavender informed them.

'Ugh! Horrocks!' Miss Katherine exclaimed. Her face wrinkled with disgust. 'According to my brothers, Horrocks is one of George's gambling friends, an unpleasant man.'

'He will give George Carnaby the identification he seeks?'

'Yes,' she said and sighed.

Silence fell in the room for a moment. The Armstrongs were still struggling to comprehend these latest developments. The fire crackled in the grate and the clock ticked quietly on the mantle. Beside him, Woods' empty stomach growled loudly.

'But surely,' Miss Katherine implored, 'but surely if Helen is still alive she *must* come out of hiding now? If she doesn't, all will be lost and these villains will get away with her fortune *and* the murder of Laurel Faa Geddes.'

'If she reappears in Bellingham,' Lavender said. 'Her delighted brother will claim her and take her home to Linn Hagh, where no doubt his assassin would soon organise some accident to befall her.'

Shock flashed across the faces of the Armstrongs.

'I cannot believe that this is happening in Bellingham – and to us and Helen.'

'This is why I want Captain Wentworth and his men to continue their search for the murderer. I believe the man is still in the neighbourhood. He has killed once and will kill again if he gets the chance.'

'Where does that idiot Matthew Carnaby fit into this mess?' Armstrong demanded, angrily. 'Beddows told us that *he* was the murderer.'

'Poor Matthew! I had forgotten about him,' Miss Katherine said.

'He doesn't fit into it,' Lavender informed them. 'Not at all. I'm convinced that this gentle young man was in the wrong place at the wrong time. I saw him last night in Hexham gaol. He was a constant companion of the Geddes girl. I suspect that he witnessed her murder and ran away. He found her burning body later and Beddows then found *him* at the scene of the crime and arrested him - probably to please George Carnaby. Now the Carnabys have a chance to claim their sister's inheritance and the family simpleton will be charged and hung for the crime '

Miss Katherine gasped. Her hand flew to mouth.

Lavender paused before continuing. His voice hardened.

'I suspect that the Carnabys have congratulated themselves on how well this has all worked out. They can claim their sister's inheritance and they've rid themselves of their nuisance brother in a single act.'

'And the faws,' Woods said. 'Don't forget that they've gone as well.'

'This is appalling,' John Armstrong declared. 'The Carnabys must be stopped.'

'I still need more time to gather evidence,' Lavender informed them. 'But I'm confident that we'll have it soon. I need to speak to the landlord of The Redesdale Arms in Otterburn.'

'If this is true, then Carnaby is trying to pervert the course of justice and is an accomplice to murder. Is there anything we can do to help, Detective?' Armstrong asked.

Lavender reached into his pocket and pulled out the ink-splattered piece of parchment on which Matthew Carnaby had written the words: *Baxtr Carnby.*

'I need your help with this,' he said, and proceeded to explain the events in Matthew Carnaby's prison cell. He shared with them his belief that Helen Carnaby had taught her brother to write.

'Has there ever been another man, besides Helen's dead father, named Baxter Carnaby?'

'No,' John Armstrong said.

Lavender's heart sank with disappointment.

'Yes, there was. Papa – you forget.'

Katherine Armstrong frowned slightly as she stared at the writing. Her capped head bowed over the parchment, grey curls bobbing beside her cheeks. The men waited politely while she tried to remember.

'There was another child at Linn Hagh, an older brother, called Baxter Carnaby after his father. I can remember Mama talking about him. I wish I had paid more attention but we were not particularly bothered about the Carnabys back in those days.'

Relief surged through Lavender. He could have kissed Katherine Armstrong at that moment. 'So George and Isobel Carnaby had an older brother?' he asked. 'What happened to him?'

'He died young, I'm afraid.'

Lavender felt his heart sink again.

'He is not buried in St. Cuthbert's graveyard.' This was a statement not a question.

‘No, he went away to school before he died.’ She paused and seemed to struggle with the memories churning around in her mind. ‘I believe he went down to Yorkshire somewhere. It was a military school for young gentlemen - near Halifax, perhaps? Or Huddersfield?’

‘A military school, eh?’ Woods queried.

‘Yes, he was about ten years old, I think. Mama said he had been a difficult boy. I expect his father had wanted to instil some discipline into him. Unfortunately, the boy died during his first winter at this school.’

‘Halifax is a long way from Bellingham,’ Lavender said. ‘Surely Carnaby could have found a suitable school closer to Bellingham for his ‘difficult’ elder son?’

‘Perhaps he wanted to put some distance between them?’ Woods suggested.

‘Excuse me, but I don’t understand,’ Armstrong interrupted. ‘Why would Matthew Carnaby write down the name of his dead elder brother?’

Everyone looked expectantly at the detective.

‘He tried to tell me something,’ Lavender said, slowly. ‘Perhaps, perhaps this elder brother is not dead after all. Maybe he is here in Bellingham and moves around amongst us all? Maybe Matthew Carnaby has seen him?’

Katherine Armstrong was the first to follow his line of thought.

‘Good grief!’ she exclaimed. ‘Do you think this murderer, this villain, could be the Carnaby’s long-lost sibling? Could George and Isobel be in league with him?’

‘I don’t know,’ Lavender confessed. ‘But this could explain why the faws felt that the murdering beggar knew Hareshaw Woods like he was born there. If it’s Baxter Carnaby then they were right – he was born there.’

‘It also explains the problems with that portrait of the nippers up at Linn Hagh,’ said Woods. ‘We said the eye colours were all wrong and that the second nipper looked like a lad. It *were* a lad. The eldest child in the portrait were Baxter Carnaby, the second were George, and the babe in arms were Miss Isobel.’

‘You’re right, Woods,’ Lavender acknowledged.

‘That sly old tabby said it were her and her brothers – but she never said *which* brothers. We just assumed it were her, George and Matthew.’

‘The answer to part of this mysterious case was staring us in the face all the time.’ Lavender said. ‘This latest discovery has taken me by surprise. I need more time to think, and we need to find out if Baxter Carnaby, the brother, survived childhood.'

'If he went into the army then there will be records.' John Armstrong announced, firmly. 'I'll contact my sons and Cecily's husband, Captain Derwent. Trust me, Lavender; if the rogue did survive and went on to join the army, then there will be records of him – somewhere.'

'I need to go and speak with Doctor Goddard,' Lavender said as they hurried down the main street in Bellingham. 'We need to split up, Ned. I'll visit Goddard, then go to the Redesdale Arms and speak to the landlord. You must go to Newcastle, find Mr Agar the lawyer and pursue my request for a copy of Baxter Carnaby's last will and testament. I must see that document. The last master of Linn Hagh had far more secrets than I ever imagined.'

'Didn't he just,' Woods said. 'This case has turned into a sack full of squirming river eels. Slippery buggers all of them Carnabys – especially the father.'

'Indeed. I hope that this document at the lawyers will shed some light on what *really* went on at Linn Hagh.'

'I'll grab a bite to eat from The Rose and Crown before I go,' Woods told him. 'Oh - and I might just call on young Anna at her mother's cottage on me way - just to check she got home safely the other night when she fled Linn Hagh.'

Lavender smiled.

'If you must,' he said.

Robert Goddard was reading in the parlour when the maid showed Lavender into the room. Goddard looked up from his news sheet and frowned.

'If you have come to search my outhouses for a murderer, Detective, then I am afraid that Captain Wentworth has beaten you to it; his men only left half an hour ago.'

Lavender smiled, but noticed that Goddard didn't ask him to sit down. Despite the helpful information he had given Lavender at their last meeting, the doctor was clearly irritated with him again.

'I'm here to ask you for some information. It won't take long. Firstly, I need to know what happened when you were summoned by George Carnaby on Thursday night to examine the remains of the dead girl at Linn Hagh.'

'Oh that,' Goddard said. He put down his paper and pointed to a chair. Lavender sat down opposite him.

‘There’s not much to report. Carnaby wanted me to identify the poor girl as his sister. Have you seen the body?’

‘Yes.’

‘Well then you’ll understand that it was impossible. The corpse is burnt beyond recognition.’

‘Did you examine the corpse and come to a conclusion about how she may have died?’

A frown creased across the doctor’s handsome forehead.

‘The light was poor and I wasn’t there very long, you understand? An argument quickly flared up between myself and Carnaby, and the brute told me to get off his property when I started to express my doubts. But I think she may have had her neck broken before she died. There was definitely something wrong with her neck, but I was compelled to leave before I could complete my examination.’

Lavender sat back in the cushions of the chair, relieved.

‘I agree. It looks to me like she may have even been stabbed repeatedly in the neck.’

The two men paused for a while in thought.

‘The poor girl,’ Goddard said. ‘What else did you want to know, Detective?’

‘My other question relates to Matthew Carnaby.’

‘No, I don’t think he is capable of murder,’ the doctor said quickly. He frowned again and stared into the fire.

‘I’m glad to hear that because that is also my impression of the man, but I’m not here to ask that question.’

‘Oh?’

‘I need to know how Matthew Carnaby came by those horrific head injuries. Are you familiar with that information?’

Goddard looked up, surprised.

‘Yes, I do know what happened to him. My predecessor, Dr Oliver, told me the story when I took over the practice on the understanding that I kept the information confidential. Baxter and Esther Carnaby – she was still alive at the time – wanted the details kept quiet.’

‘Well, they’re both dead now.’

‘It’s a gruesome tale. Is this relevant to solving this case?’

‘Extremely relevant.’

Goddard eyed him curiously then shrugged his shoulders. ‘As I recall,’ he said. ‘Matthew Carnaby received his injuries when he was about three years old. He was viciously attacked and beaten around the head with a hot fire poker.’

'God's strewth,' Lavender exclaimed. Although he had expected something like this, he was shocked. 'Who would do that to a child? Was it his mad mother, Martha Carnaby?'

'No, but I understand that she had never been a natural mother to him. Matthew had been a difficult baby, a whining child and this infuriated her. Apparently, she stood by – and laughed – while the attack took place. Her husband was outside. He heard the child's screams and the woman's manic laughter through the open window. He raced inside to find his youngest son a bloody mess on the floor of the Great Hall, his wife laughing hysterically over the unconscious child and the other children terrified.'

'What?' Lavender was appalled.

'Martha Carnaby and the culprit were restrained,' Goddard continued. 'The next day Carnaby had her committed to an asylum. Doctor Oliver was called out immediately to see what he could do for the little boy. Matthew's injuries were horrific and they didn't expect him to live but he did, although he suffered damage to his brain as a result of the attack.'

'So who did it, if it was not Martha Carnaby? Who was the culprit?'

Goddard watched him closely. 'It was the eldest son – a ten year old boy. I can't remember his name. He was egged on by his insane mother, I understand. Prone to violent rages, Martha Carnaby had become virtually impossible to control. She was a danger to herself and all those around her. The children were all wild and out of control – the eldest son worst of all. God only knows what else those children witnessed. Baxter Carnaby should have had her committed a long time before, but he didn't. He had no choice but to act now. However, rather than blame his eldest son, he decided to cover up the boy's part in all this and exile him instead. He blamed himself for not acting sooner to deal with his wife. He pleaded with Doctor Oliver to keep the details of the attack a secret. Then he sent the eldest boy away to boarding school. I understand that the lad later died there. Doctor Oliver felt sorry for Carnaby and did as he requested. Like I said, I can't remember the boy's name.'

'He was called Baxter Carnaby after his father,' Lavender said.

Goddard's eyes widened with surprise.

'And I've more news for you, Doctor. The wretched boy didn't die. He survived, joined the army and he is back in Bellingham trying to murder another one of his siblings.'

CHAPTER THIRTY THREE

Lavender was surprised to see that Woods was waiting for him in front of the hearth when he called back in The Rose and Crown.

'I thought you would be on your way to Newcastle and the chambers of Mr Agar the lawyer,' he said.

Woods shook his head, stood up and leaned forward conspiratorially.

'I had to wait for you,' he whispered. His eyes shone with excitement in his broad face. 'There's been a development.'

'What?' Lavender took off his gloves, ordered a plate of cold meats and a glass of ale and sat down at their table.

Woods clutched a brown paper parcel in his big hands. It was loosely tied with string.

'I called on Anna's mother, like I said I would, but the girl weren't there.'

'Oh?'

'Her mother said she's 'gone away for a while.''

'Gone away?' Lavender's frown deepened. 'Servant girls who have just walked out of their jobs without their wages don't 'go away for a while.' They spend every minute trying to find a new position.'

'Exactly what I thought, Sir, but the mother weren't prepared to say any more. She clammed up. I'm thinking that Anna's gone off to join the missing heiress.'

'Ah,' Lavender nodded. 'That would make sense, considering that we're convinced that Helen Carnaby is still alive. Do you think Anna knew where her mistress was from the start?'

'I don't rightly know about that, Sir, but there's more to tell.' Woods pushed the parcel across the table towards him. Infected by his constable's enthusiasm, Lavender found himself smiling.

'Tell me what it is,' he said.

Woods opened the parcel and lifted out a couple of pieces of paper, one of them badly scorched, and a piece of burnt smoke-damaged material.

'She left me a note saying as how George and Isobel Carnaby used this scrap of cloth from a dress to identify the dead girl.'

Lavender picked up the dirty rag and recognised the pattern immediately. Earlier that morning he had noted that a piece had been chopped out of the hem of the victim's dress.

‘So?’

‘Well Anna says in her note that it weren’t Helen Carnaby’s dress – not anymore.’

‘I don’t understand?’

‘Do you remember she telled us that Miss Carnaby had given one of her frocks to the gypsy girl, Laurel Faa Geddes?’

‘Yes.’

‘Well, Anna says, that this is the same dress. The dead girl *is* the gypsy. You were right. She were wearing Miss Carnaby’s cast-off dress when she were murdered.’

Lavender sat back and breathed deeply.

‘The murderer might have known this. He might have seen Miss Carnaby give the dress to the gypsy girl. You’ve done well, Ned. The time you spent building up trust with that maid was well spent.’

Woods beamed with pleasure.

‘But that’s not all, Sir.’ He now handed Lavender the charred piece of parchment which had also been in the parcel.

‘She found this when she were cleaning the hearth in the Great Hall at Linn Hagh. She thinks George Carnaby had been burning some old documents and was careless. This one must have fallen from the flames and she rescued it the next day.’

Lavender’s eyes scanned the parchment and lit up.

‘George. Meet at Redesdale Arms. Thurs. next. 18th November. Baxter.’

‘I don’t think the lass realised what she had found,’ Woods said. ‘She says something in her note about it being a letter from George Carnaby’s *father*.’

‘We have him,’ Lavender said simply. ‘The eighteenth of November fell on a Thursday *this* year. We have him, Woods. We can link George Carnaby to his murderous sibling.’

Lavender felt the excitement rise inside him and he could barely contain his satisfaction. It was moments like this which made it all worthwhile; the moments when he knew, for certain, that he could drag a criminal into the dock at the next assizes.

‘Oh and this also arrived for you about an hour ago.’

Woods lifted a bigger package from the chair beside him and placed it on the table. It was a pile of legal documents.

Baxter Carnaby’s will had finally arrived from Mr Agar.

‘I think it’s from that lawyer in Newcastle. I had a hell of a job to persuade the young lad who brought it here to hand it over. He claimed he’d been told only to give it to the Detective with the silver topped tipstaff from Bow Street.’

‘We’ll have to get you a tipstaff of your own.’ Lavender smiled as he pulled out his pocket knife and slit open the wax seal.

Woods beamed at the thought; the ornate tipstaffs with their intricate engraving and moulding were objects of envy in Bow Street. Then Woods shook his head. ‘No,’ he said. ‘They’d never give me one – and the other lads would get jealous. Just let me hold yours now and then so as I can wave it around for a bit.’

Smiling, Lavender carefully unfurled the documents.

The start of the will contained the usual small bequests of money and personal items to relatives and loyal servants. The bulk of his estate, monies and land were left to George Carnaby.

The next paragraph made Lavender smile:

‘Unto my natural daughter, Laurel Faa Geddes, I grant the right for her to remain with her people on my land at Linn Hagh for the rest of her life.’

‘I correctly concluded that the gypsy girl was Baxter Carnaby’s illegitimate daughter,’ he told Woods. ‘He gave her and the faws the right to remain at Linn Hagh in his will.’

‘D’you think that is why they’ve gone?’ Woods asked. ‘Because she’s dead? They must know that the murdered girl is one of their own.’

Lavender stopped reading and frowned. He was suddenly conscious that he had overlooked the reaction of the faws. His mistake with Matthew Carnaby had made him more cautious; he could not afford to overlook anything.

He had assumed like the manservant Peter at Linn Hagh, that the faws had vanished because they were frightened of getting the blame for the murder. If the body was that of Laurel Faa Geddes then Woods was right; they would already know this. Their silence was as worrying their sudden disappearance. He didn’t really expect them to seek redress or justice through the legal system; they didn’t trust the authorities. But it still bothered him. He had made a mistake overlooking Matthew Carnaby and he wasn’t prepared to dismiss anyone else so easily.

‘What does the rest say?’ Woods brought his attention back to the document in his hand. He continued to read the will.

‘...after all are valued and everyone knows their just part, I will that Linn Hagh be carried on in the same manner by my wife Esther and son George and all my family to continue at Linn

Hagh for as they are so long as they please, and my son Baxter Carnaby I disallow to have any right at all to the estate or monies…'

Lavender had to read the last line twice before its significance dawned on him. He hadn't expected it.

'He was alive,' he said. 'We've proof. Baxter Carnaby, the son, is mentioned in his father's will. This will was written only five years ago. The old man knew that his eldest boy was still alive and he legally disinherited him.'

'That's good evidence,' Woods said. 'Is there more?'

There was more. This time Lavender read it out.

'… and for the good behaviour of George or Isobel I appoint my lawyer Benjamin Agar to ensure that they behave themselves as they ought towards my wife, my daughters Helen and Laurel and my son Matthew, and that they carry on their business in a right and orderly manner and in case of any misdemeanour I desire the aforesaid Benjamin Agar to rebuke and admonish and pray them to do well. If either George or Isobel do not behave well towards my wife, my daughters or my son, Matthew, then I appoint constitute authorize and allow the aforesaid Benjamin Agar to turn either George or Isobel off the estate.'

'God's strewth,' Woods said. 'This old guvnor really knew his nippers. He must have been fearful about what would happen in that pele tower after his death. '

'He was right to be frightened,' Lavender commented, dryly. 'George Carnaby flayed the younger ones with his whip, Isobel tried to poison her step-mother and now the two of them have ganged up with the family outcast to commit murder.'

'Why didn't he appoint someone closer to keep an eye on his wife and young nippers though? A Newcastle lawyer is a long way from Linn Hagh.'

Lavender sighed. 'Baxter Carnaby spent most of his adult life hiding the truth about his family from his neighbours in Bellingham,' he said. 'He had a lot to hide including: the extent of his first wife's insanity; his eldest son's brutality and his youngest son's disability. In order to avoid difficult questions and scandal, he even spread the lie that his eldest son was dead. When it came time to write his will there was no-one left in Bellingham in whom he felt he could confide. No-one else knew the truth. He had to tell his lawyer the truth to write his son Baxter out of the will, but he must have died a very desperate and worried man.'

'Why did he cast off the eldest lad?'

Lavender told Woods what he had learned from Doctor Goddard.

Horror and outrage replaced the smile on Wood's face.

'Who would do that to a little nipper?' he demanded, angrily. 'What sort of evil bastard are we dealing with here?'

The sudden appearance of Mistress McMullen with a message from Katherine Armstrong saved him from replying. Lavender read the note and gulped down the last of his ale.

'We'll have to move fast. George Carnaby has returned from Newcastle with his pet doctor. Horrocks has identified the body as that of Helen Carnaby…'

'But it's not Helen Carnaby – it's the gypsy girl!'

'They plan to bury the corpse in Esther Carnaby's grave in St. Cuthbert's churchyard on Monday at ten.'

'What can we do?'

Lavender reached for his gloves. 'We'll ride out to the Redesdale Arms and try to get more information about our murderer. Then we'll travel back to Morpeth and get a warrant from Magistrate Clennell for the arrest of George and Isobel Carnaby.'

'Do we have enough evidence now?' asked Woods as the two men pushed back their chairs and rose to their feet. Lavender began to gather up the documents scattered across the table.

'I'm sure of it. If we can't arrest them for being accomplices to murder, then at least we can arrest them for trying to pervert the course of justice. That should be enough to hold them until we track down their big brother. They may know that Helen Carnaby gave that dress to Laurel Faa Geddes – or they may not. Either way, by the time I've presented the case to Magistrate Clennell, they'll sound like the guiltiest pair in England. And once I've warrants for their arrest…it's time for Miss Carnaby to come out of hiding…'

The door of the tavern burst open and Isaac Daly staggered into the taproom. The lanky farmer had been running. He was sweating, red faced and breathless. He pointed at Lavender and Woods and gestured frantically for them to follow him.

'It's that gadgie you're after…' he gasped.

'What? The murderer?'

'Aye,' Daly nodded and breathed heavily. 'Jethro and I've bin searchin' fer him. We've jest seen him – he's headed back into Hareshaw Woods…'

'Mistress McMullen! Where are Captain Wentworth and his men?'

The landlady looked up from the glass she was wiping in alarm. 'Last I heard, they're on the other side of the toon,' she said.

Daly shook his head.

'There's no time. Jethro's gan after him himself. He sent me to fetch you to help him.'

'We're coming,' Lavender said grimly. 'Mistress McMullen - send a potboy to Captain Wentworth immediately. Tell him to follow us into Hareshaw Woods!'

CHAPTER THIRTY FOUR

It was impossible to run through Hareshaw Woods. The light had begun to fade and the recent freezing rain had made the path treacherous underfoot as it rose and fell following the contours of the gorge. The three men slithered along the side of the river and headed towards the waterfall. They shouted over and over again for Hamilton. Their voices bounced back from the overhanging Jurassic rock face and echoed down the gorge.

Lavender estimated that Carnaby and the unarmed farmer were about ten, maybe fifteen, minutes ahead of them. He had no doubt that the burly Hamilton could look after himself in a tavern brawl, but these were not ordinary circumstances. The man Jethro Hamilton pursued was a vicious, knife-wielding murderer.

Lavender was also aware that Baxter Carnaby could have left the path and doubled back. He could be squatting behind a bush higher in the gorge laughing down at them as they meandered along the bank of the river. He glanced up at the tangled undergrowth and gravity-defying trees that leaned and creaked towards them. Fungi erupted like obscene cancers from cracks in the wood. Fallen ash and sycamores gaped like huge, twisted moss-coated serpents around them.

Ahead of them, the waterfall roared. They neared the hidden path, shown to them by Laurel Faa Geddes and Lavender knew they would have to split up. Following Hamilton and Carnaby alone in the dark was not a welcome thought, but at least he and Woods were armed and the militia were not far behind.

Suddenly, Woods spotted Hamilton sitting hunched and dazed on rocks by the waters' edge. Blood dripped from a head wound onto the big farmer's sheep skin coat. The three other men slithered down the bank and across the treacherous boulders towards him.

'The bastard laid in wait and jumped out on me,' Hamilton explained, ruefully. 'He bashed me over me head with a branch.'

'Thank the lord ye've got such a thick skull,' Daly said, 'or he might a hurt you.'

'You were lucky,' Lavender snapped. 'He's a killer with a knife. He could have stuck you like a pig and spilt out your guts. Which way did he go?' His mind raced. Lying in wait for Hamilton and the subsequent attack would have delayed Baxter Carnaby. He couldn't be far ahead now.

‘That way - towards the waterfall!’

‘Let’s move,’ Lavender urged. ‘You stay here, Hamilton. Captain Wentworth and his men will be along soon. They’ll help you back to Bellingham.’

‘Bugger that! I’ve come this far and I’ll see this through to the end.’ Hamilton scooped up a hat-full of the peat-black water and threw it over his head, then jammed his hat firmly back down on his drenched hair. Lavender grimaced as the icy water ran down Hamilton’s thick neck in pink rivulets. The farmer merely scowled. With grim determination etched across his pale face, he now rose unsteadily to his feet.

‘We can’t slow down for you,’ Lavender warned.

‘You won’t hev to.’

They didn’t go far. As they rounded the next bend, the sides of the gorge widened and the trees fell away to give an open view of the thundering waterfall ahead and the dark red sky beyond.

Silhouetted against the sunset, a lone man stood at the top of Hareshaw Linn, balanced precariously on the slippery rocks, calf deep in the formidable current.

‘It’s him!’ Woods shouted above the thunderous roar. Carnaby’s military greatcoat and hat identified him even at that distance.

‘What the hell is he doing?’ Lavender asked.

They hurried closer. Carnaby glanced nervously over his shoulder. He wobbled. The men below gasped as he fought to keep his balance. Daly cried out.

Carnaby steadied himself then caught sight of the police officers and the farmers forty feet below. In the fading light they could just see the lunatic grin spread across his face. He opened his mouth, threw back his head and laughed. The noise bounced off the black rocks and echoed round the narrow gorge, chilling the men to their bones.

‘He’s bloody mad!’ Daly shouted.

‘He’ll fall to his death,’ Hamilton pronounced. ‘What’s he waiting fer? Why doesn’t he back off and run fer it?’

Four other figures appeared out of the gloom at the top of the water fall. They moved stealthily towards Carnaby and encircled him. The dying rays of the sun glinted on their knives and their silver earrings. Lavender could just make out the powerful build and profiled features of Paul Faa Geddes.

The four men at the bottom of the waterfall watched in horrified silence as the gypsies moved towards their quarry. Carnaby was hemmed up against the dangerous edge of the cascade, with the surging water pressing against his thighs.

Suddenly, Geddes lashed out with his knife but its glistening point fell short of its target. Carnaby stepped away quickly and stumbled. He lost his balance on the slimy rocks. He threw out his arms to steady himself but his fingers grasped helplessly at nothing but ice cold air.

Carnaby fell headfirst, limbs flailing, onto the jagged rocks below. He landed silently. The noise of the waterfall drowned out the crack of his shattering bones. For a moment he lay still; a grotesque, lifeless lump amidst the roaring water of the living stream. Then the current took hold of the edges of his greatcoat and his legs and tugged him gently into the pool. He slipped off the rocks and floated face down towards the reeds.

Above them, the faws melted away into the darkness.

Lavender, Woods and the two stunned farmers moved silently towards the body and waded into the stream. It took all four of them to haul the sodden corpse out of the icy water. Lavender searched him but found nothing except a broken clay pipe and his gully knife. His weapon had been useless in the end, against the vengeance of the faws.

'Now I see him again, close up like,' Woods said. 'I can see that he is George and Isobel Carnaby's brother. He reached down with wet fingers and shut the dead man's blank, staring eyes. 'He's fairer of course, but he's still a Carnaby. I don't know how I missed that afore - in the graveyard.'

'You weren't to know,' Lavender said. 'Old man Carnaby kept his secrets well.'

'George Carnaby had *another* brother?' Daly asked.

'And he were in league with him to murder their rich little sister?' Hamilton sounded stunned.

'His name is – was - Baxter Carnaby. He was the elder brother of George and Isobel Carnaby.' Lavender said. 'I need your discretion, gentlemen because I must seek warrants for their arrest. Constable Woods will wait a while until the militia arrives and he will explain everything to you, but then he must go to the Redesdale Arms.'

'Alone?' Woods asked. 'They were tight-lipped buggers the last time I were there.'

'You'll have to make them talk,' Lavender said firmly. 'Take my tipstaff and rap them over their heads with it if they refuse to cooperate. I must go straight to Morpeth and get warrants for the arrest of George and Isobel Carnaby. Their assassin is dead now. It's time to bring this case to a conclusion.'

'What can we do?' Hamilton asked.

'Wait here with the body for Wentworth and the militia,' Lavender said. 'When they arrive tell them to take it to Linn Hagh. The Carnabys are responsible for the burial of this corpse.'

'What if they refuse, or deny any knowledge of him?

'I've never known anyone refuse Captain Wentworth.' Lavender smiled in the dark. He would have liked to have been there to see George Carnaby's face. Never mind. His moment would come later.

'What about them gypsies?' Woods question came suddenly. An awkward silence descended on the four men.

'They as good as drove Carnaby over the cliff edge to his death,' Woods continued. 'Do we get Captain Wentworth and his men to try and round them up? They can't have gone far.'

No, but they'll have melted into the landscape like deer, Lavender thought.

'I think that this decision rests entirely on Mr Hamilton and Mr Daly,' he said.

'What us? Why?' Hamilton's voice registered surprise.

'You see, I'm not sure that I *did* see anyone else with Carnaby at the top of the waterfall,' Lavender continued, slowly. 'The light was too dim.'

He waited. For a moment he thought that Woods was about to protest, but his constable remained silent. He could no longer see the expressions on the faces of any of the other men but he could tell by their still black outlines, that the two farmers were thinking hard as they weighed up the recent dramatic events against their long-held prejudice against the faws.

'Well, I see it this way,' Hamilton eventually said. 'There's a dead gypsy girl lying in the vaults of Linn Hagh and the bastard that murdered her is now dead at our feet. I'm thinking that justice has already bin served so there's no need to make a fuss about wood sprites glimpsed at dusk in a haunted glade.'

'Aye,' Daly agreed. 'I'm with you, Jethro.'

'And I'm with you, Detective,' Hamilton added quietly. 'It's time to bring this case to a conclusion. I never saw no faws.'

CHAPTER THIRTY FIVE

Sunday, 28th November, 1809

Lavender rapped on the door of the house in Castle Square, Morpeth. On either side of the entrance, the drapes were still drawn on the inside of the large, rectangular windows. Appropriate for a house in mourning, he thought – or for a house with a secret.

It was the startled doctor himself who answered the door. The maid must have been left behind in Bellingham.

'Detective! What a surprise.' Above his white cravat, Goddard's face assumed the frown he usually wore when he laid eyes on Lavender.

'Magistrate Clennell gave me your mother's address. I won't take up much of your time, Doctor. I've two requests to make and some information to give you. May I enter?'

Goddard stood back and Lavender walked into a spacious entrance hallway. An elaborate staircase with wrought metal bannisters led up to the first floor. Rectangular patches of darker plaster dotted the empty walls where the paintings had been removed. Packing cases stood near the entrance and he glimpsed more through the half open doorway of the parlour. Dust sheets shrouded the furniture.

Goddard followed his gaze.

'You must excuse me if I don't invite you into the parlour to sit. I'm still sorting out my mother's affairs before I close up her house.'

'Of course,' Lavender said. 'In fact, I would prefer to remain here.' His eyes glanced up the staircase to the floor above.

'Firstly, I've come to tell you some news. Baxter Carnaby is now dead.'

Goddard gasped.

'How so?'

Lavender explained, but didn't mention the part played by the faws in Baxter Carnaby's death.

'On top of this, I now have warrants for the arrest of both George and Isobel Carnaby in my pocket.'

'Why, this is excellent news!' Goddard looked relieved.

'Quite so. I intend to return to Bellingham first thing in the morning to serve them. I also have a letter for Hexham gaol from

Magistrate Clennell. It instructs the gaoler to release Matthew Carnaby from imprisonment.'

'Good. I knew the poor fellow was innocent.'

'I'm sure you did,' Lavender said, wryly. 'This brings me to my first request. I would like you to take this letter, ride to Hexham and organise the young man's safe release and return to Bellingham.'

The doctor's eyebrows rose in surprise. He looked amused.

'So I'm to be your lackey now, am I, Lavender?'

'I didn't think you would mind,' Lavender said, slowly. 'Considering how willing you were to ride out there before, and pay the gaolers to ensure that he was comfortable in a private cell.'

Goddard's handsome face flushed and his smile vanished. 'What do you mean?'

Lavender ignored his question. 'I also need to speak to Miss Carnaby. Please ask her to join us.'

'What!'

The detective stared at Goddard coldly. For a moment it looked like the doctor would refuse, or begin to strenuously deny what Lavender was suggesting.

'I don't have time to waste in an argument,' Lavender said. 'I know she has been with you, either here or at your home in Bellingham, since she fled Linn Hagh.'

A range of conflicting emotions flashed across Goddard's face.

Lavender moved past him to the foot of the staircase.

'Miss Carnaby!' he called out loudly. 'The man that threatened you in Bellingham churchyard is now dead. I've warrants for the arrest of your brother and sister. It's safe to come out of hiding now - I need to speak to you.'

'I must protest, Lavender!' Goddard had found his voice and moved beside him. 'You cannot possibly imagine -'

'I do imagine.'

'It is alright, Robert. It's time.'

The voice which floated down from the floor above was soft. A delicate white hand appeared on the upstairs banister followed by an arm clothed in black. Then she appeared. Smaller than Lavender had imagined and thinner. The oval face and the stubborn little chin, however, were those in the portrait handed to him by the Armstrongs just over a week ago. Her pale skin was as smooth as porcelain.

The missing heiress descended the stairs carefully. A borrowed gown hung loosely on her slight frame. Her white-blond head bowed as she lifted the hem of the skirts.

A dress which belonged to Goddard's dead mother no doubt, Lavender thought. She wore no wedding band.

Behind her, Anna peered down at the detective from the landing; her own face was pale beneath her freckles.

He bowed low over Helen Carnaby's hand when she reached the bottom step.

'At last we meet, Miss Carnaby.'

'The pleasure is mine, Detective,' she replied nervously. 'You've been most assiduous in unravelling the threads of this mystery. Thank you for pursuing the evidence against my wicked brother and sister.' She lowered her long eyelashes. 'What you must think of me for causing all this trouble I, I cannot imagine.' Her embarrassment was genuine.

'What *I* think of you is inconsequential,' he said, kindly. 'I'll be back in London within a fortnight. However, I know that you must have been terrified. You were right to fear for your life. Your brothers and sister are three of the most calculating villains I've ever had the misfortune to come across. But we now need to discuss your reappearance in Bellingham. It's time for you to come out of hiding.'

Her ivory skin turned a shade paler at his words but she didn't protest. She turned to Goddard.

'Shall we remove the dust sheets and light a fire in the parlour, Robert? It's chilly out here in the hall.'

The doctor jumped like an anxious puppy at her request and led the way to the darkened room at the front of the house.

While Anna removed the dust cloths, partially opened the drapes and lit a fire in the grate, Lavender took off his gloves and eyed the young couple opposite. They sat in silence, glancing at each other for reassurance. Even the confident doctor looked embarrassed and awkward.

'Did you know that the man who attacked you and stalked you through Hareshaw Woods was your half-brother, Baxter Carnaby?'

She raised her vivid blue eyes to his face.

'No. Neither of my parents ever told me about my father's first son. The first I heard about him was from Robert, yesterday. He told me about your conversation.'

'Baxter Carnaby was mentioned in your father's will.'

'I was away at school when my father died. No-one ever told me what was written in his will. I suppose that my mother must have known about this boy, but she loved my father dearly and took his secret to the grave with her. She wasn't to know that my father's eldest son was still alive and would return to Bellingham.'

Lavender nodded.

'All I knew was that I was in dreadful danger. I felt sure that the man who stalked me had something to do with George – my brother dismissed my concerns too lightly. At one point, I thought they were trying to turn me insane, like my father's first wife.'

Lavender raised an eyebrow; this was a scenario he had not considered.

'So you devised an elaborate escape from your room at Linn Hagh?'

'Yes.' She blushed. 'I had to lock the door behind me, Detective. I really was concerned that someone would seek me out before the morning and discover my bed empty.' She dropped her eyes.

'I understand,' Lavender said grimly. 'I'm aware of the lengths your brother was prepared to go to 'persuade' you to marry Lawrence Ingram.'

She flushed again.

'You do understand, Detective. I can see that. I believed that if I made my concerns public then it would all be dismissed as the hysterical complaints of a mad woman. I also knew that Izzie tampered with my food.' Her voice rose with anxiety. Robert Goddard placed a comforting hand on her shoulder. 'George wouldn't hesitate to have me committed to an asylum like our father had done to his mother.'

'In which case, he would have been able to claim your fortune,' Lavender said.

'Yes.' She bowed her head. 'One way or another, George was determined to get his hands on that money. The money is cursed. It cost poor Laurel her life.'

'No, Miss Carnaby, your inheritance is not cursed. Your murderous siblings took the life of Laurel Faa Geddes, and they'll pay for the crime – as Baxter Carnaby has already done.'

'You've enough evidence?'

'I have.'

'Thank you, Detective. Thank you from the bottom of my heart.'

'When you felt threatened, why didn't you return to Whitby or seek help from John Armstrong?'

'I did ask Uncle John for shelter but he couldn't accommodate me, and I knew that if I returned to Whitby then George or that man -' she shuddered '– would eventually find me. Then Isobel made it plain that George expected me to marry the disgusting Lawrence Ingram and I knew I had to flee.'

'Because you had already fallen in love with Doctor Goddard?'

She blushed and Goddard shuffled in his chair.

'How did you know about us, Detective?' Goddard asked. 'I thought we had managed to keep our courtship a secret.'

Lavender smiled.

'Sometimes folks fail to see what's happening beneath their noses,' he said. 'It takes someone from the outside to spot the obvious, and you two haven't been as discreet as you thought. Once we had heard from a witness that Miss Carnaby had been seen talking intimately with a gentleman on horseback, my constable and I knew that she had an admirer. It was quite simple to work out the identity of your admirer.'

'How?'

Lavender turned to face Helen Carnaby. 'The only man whose company you had regularly shared since your return to Bellingham was the doctor who attended your sick mother. I could tell by the reaction of the other women in church last Sunday, that Doctor Goddard was a bachelor – and regarded as a popular catch.'

Helen Carnaby smiled and Anna giggled. The doctor just looked embarrassed. Lavender then turned to face him.

'Besides which, when I visited you at your home you've always displayed real empathy and compassion for the plight of Bellingham's missing heiress. You also breached patient privilege on several occasions during our discussions and you were not objective about the Carnaby family, which I would have expected from a professional physician.'

Goddard shrugged. 'I gave you whatever help I could with your enquiries. We had faith in you, Detective. Helen and I quickly realised that if anyone could help us and bring George and Isobel Carnaby to justice, then it was you.'

Caught off guard by the unexpected compliment, Lavender paused for a moment.

'I've no doubt that your relationship grew out of the compassion you shared at the bedside of the dying Esther Carnaby,' he continued. His tone was gentle. 'And it developed under the ignorant noses of your brother and sister and the servants, who obviously had no idea about what was happening in the sick room at Linn Hagh.'

‘You’re right there,’ Anna interrupted as she returned with a silver tray of china teacups and saucers. ‘You could have knocked me down wi a feather when I found out.’

‘I have to point out something, Lavender,’ Robert Goddard said. He reached over for Helen Carnaby’s hand. She glanced at him with affection. ‘You must understand that everything which has passed between Miss Carnaby and I, has been entirely proper. She’s been chaperoned by my maidservant for the last six weeks, and more recently by Anna. My feelings for her are deep and genuine. We intend to marry as soon as I can get a special licence,’

‘Why aren’t you married already?’

They both sighed.

‘We planned to elope to Gretna Green the night I left Linn Hagh,’ Helen Carnaby explained. ‘We were going to marry and brazen it out with George. We knew he would turn nasty and threaten Robert with arrest but we were prepared for that.’

‘Unfortunately, my own mother’s illness took an unexpected turn for the worse that day and I wasn’t able to leave the area,’ Goddard said sadly. ‘My mother had a lingering death.’ He grimaced. ‘Helen has remained here with a maid, nursing *my* dying mother for most of the weeks since her disappearance.’

‘I only made the two trips back to Bellingham, Detective, to place the flowers on my parents’ graves.’

‘And one of those trips nearly cost you your life,’ Goddard commented.

‘Robert has been the perfect gentleman while I’ve lived in his mother’s house.’

‘I’m sure he has,’ Lavender observed wryly. ‘But it’s not me that you’ll need to convince. There are your uncle and cousin Katherine to consider, for a start. You appreciate that there will be a great scandal once you reappear? Initially, the local gossips will be distracted by the arrest of your brother and sister. Then everyone will suddenly want to know where *you’ve* been for the last six weeks. Once your marriage to Doctor Goddard is announced, the speculation will start.’

Goddard squeezed Helen Carnaby’s hand tighter.

‘We’re ready to face the consequences,’ he said.

‘We intend to leave the area anyway, Detective,’ she added. ‘I’m trying to persuade Robert that we should move to Whitby.’

‘And if Whitby isn’t far enough away from the malicious tongues, then we shall emigrate to the New World,’ the doctor announced, firmly. 'They've a great need of medical professionals in America.'

Lavender drained his tea cup. 'Well, don't go too far away,' he said. 'You'll be needed as witnesses next summer for the trial of your siblings at the assizes. However, after that your lives are your own. Whatever happens, I wish you both good-luck in the future.' He reached for his gloves.

'In the meantime, I've writs to serve and a sham funeral to stop. I expect to see you back in Bellingham at your uncle's tomorrow morning, Miss Carnaby. Doctor Goddard? You'll please be so kind as to ride to Hexham gaol and secure the release of her brother, Matthew? That's one young man who will be delighted to see his 'Ela' again. I'm sure that *he* won't ask any awkward questions. Anna -'

The little maid dropped a spoon off the tray onto the bare floorboards. It landed with a clatter. She looked up nervously at the detective.

He winked at her.

'Take good care of your mistress.'

CHAPTER THIRTY SIX

Monday, 29th November 1809

Snow fell softly onto the stone roof of St. Cuthbert's church when Lavender drew up in a carriage. With no wind, the tiny flakes danced theatricality in the still air. They muted the crumbling grey of the drunken headstones scattered amongst the weeds in the isolated graveyard and flecked the crimson uniforms of the shivering militia who waited patiently with Constable Woods at the gate.

'Have you got the warrants?' Woods asked as the detective climbed down from the carriage.

'Yes.' Lavender closed the door quickly behind him and checked that the blinds were properly drawn. 'Did you have any luck over in Otterburn?'

Woods beckoned to a nervous man who hovered at the edge of the soldiers.

'This here fellah is Charlie Peters. He's landlord of the Redesdale Arms. He has already been with me to Linn Hagh and identified the dead man as Baxter Carnaby.'

'You've done well,' Lavender murmured.

Woods' smile beamed across his broad face.

'Oh, that's not all. He also has a large amount of Baxter Carnaby's possessions and documents. The cove had been living there fer weeks, on and off, and had fallen behind with his rent, so Charlie here purloined them after Carnaby disappeared. I haven't had chance to go through it all, but I reckon there'll be plenty more evidence to tie him in to his brother.'

'Excellent work, Ned.' Lavender said. 'George Carnaby will be surprised to discover that we've made the connection to the Redesdale Arms. Where are the mourners?'

'They're still inside. I reckon that vicar is probably going on a bit. Do you intend to interrupt the service to make the arrests?'

Mock alarm flashed across the detective's face.

'I don't think so, Ned. I'd rather face a gang of silk-snatchers on a moonless night in Covent Garden than the wrath of St. Cuthbert's vicar.'

Woods laughed and the two men waited in companionable silence.

Eventually, the church doors opened and the pall bearers carried out the plain wood coffin which contained the body of Laurel Faa Geddes. Behind them walked a large crowd of mourners that included the Carnabys, the Armstrongs, Jethro Hamilton, Isaac Daly and their wives. Everyone cast curious glances at the policemen and the militia gathered on the lane beside the low wall of the graveyard.

George and Isobel Carnaby scowled.

Lavender wondered what was going through their minds. He had no doubt that the sudden appearance of Captain Wentworth with their brother's body would have alarmed them. The realisation that Lavender had uncovered one of Linn Hagh's darkest, best kept secrets – the truth about Baxter Carnaby - must have unnerved them. Nonetheless, they were still determined to continue with their charade, it seemed; even now they relentlessly pursued their sister's fortune.

'Now?' Woods asked.

'Wait until they put down the coffin,' Lavender cautioned. 'We don't want them to drop it in shock.'

He was amused to see Hamilton and Daly here and wondered how much they had neglected their farms over the last week. They, along with the Armstrongs, knew the truth about his intentions and the identity of the poor gypsy girl who lay in the coffin. He'd never seen a funeral like this, where so many of the congregation knew the vicar was about to bury the wrong body. Their discretion impressed him; this community could be tight-lipped and work together when required.

Hamilton was the last of the mourners to disappear around the buttressed corner of the church. He threw a worried backward glance in their direction.

'Let's go,' Lavender said.

With the militia following, they marched down the snow-dusted path and turned the corner.

'Stop this funeral!' Lavender instructed the vicar. 'That is NOT the body of Helen Carnaby in that coffin.'

The mourners, gathered around the open grave of Esther Carnaby, looked up in surprise.

'This is scandalous! How dare you interrupt my sister's funeral?' Isobel Carnaby screamed. 'Have you no respect?' Her face contorted with anger.

'Explain yourself, man!' the vicar blustered.

'The body in that coffin is the body of the gypsy girl, Laurel Faa Geddes, who was brutally murdered by the man known as Baxter Carnaby.'

'Who?'

'This is ridiculous, you're a blethering idiot, Lavender,' said Carnaby. Everyone else fell silent. 'I've had this corpse identified by a leading Newcastle doctor,' he continued. 'This is – was - my sister, Helen.'

'No, it's not,' Lavender said firmly. 'It's the body of Laurel Faa Geddes. I know this because I drank a cup of tea with your sister Helen yesterday afternoon.'

'What!'

Gasps escaped some of the mourners. Isobel Carnaby turned white but her brother's features flashed with vicious anger.

'You're a lying, incompetent bastard, Lavender! I'll have you thrown into Hexham gaol for this gross impertinence!'

'I don't think so, brother. I think it is you who is destined for Hexham gaol.'

The soft voice came from behind him. The stunned mourners gazed wide-eyed over his shoulder. Lavender spun around.

Helen Carnaby stood defiantly on the path behind him, a slight figure in a black bonnet and cloak. She glared at her siblings with anger.

'Helen!' Katherine Armstrong's voice was shrill with amazement.

The congregation gasped and murmured in surprise. Some threw their hands over their mouths in alarm, as if a ghost had just risen from one of the ancient tombs.

'Helen, *darling!*' Isobel Carnaby had recovered quickly from the shock and began to move slyly towards her sister. Helen shrank back from her outstretched claw.

Suddenly, Katherine Armstrong elbowed Isobel out of the way. The elder Carnaby sister stumbled and fell back in surprise as the portly Miss Armstrong raced, with surprising speed, to the side of her pale cousin and flung a protective arm around Helen's shoulders.

'Keep back, you murderous trollop!' she yelled at Isobel Carnaby. 'You keep away from Helen, do you hear me?'

Lavender turned quickly to the landlord of the Redesdale Arms.

'Do you recognise anyone, here?'

'Aye,' Charlie Peters said. He pointed at the master of Linn Hagh. 'He were the one who paid fer the room and visited that Baxter Carnaby.'

Lavender pulled out a warrant.

'George Carnaby. By the power invested in me by his Royal Highness, The Prince Regent, in the name and on the behalf of His Majesty, King George III, I arrest you on suspicion of perverting the course of justice…' The authority in his voice echoed around the graveyard and cut through Carnaby's protestations.

The militia moved forward and seized Carnaby by the arms.

'…and conspiring with your brother, Baxter Carnaby, to murder your sisters, Helen Carnaby and the gypsy girl, Laurel Faa Geddes.'

Isobel Carnaby screamed.

George, in the grip of the two soldiers, struggled and cursed. 'It's a lie!' he yelled. 'Damned calumny!'

Lavender hadn't finished. He held up the second warrant.

'Isobel Carnaby. By the power invested in me by his Royal Highness, The Prince Regent, in the name and on the behalf of His Majesty, King George III, I arrest you on suspicion of perverting the course of justice and conspiring with your brothers, Baxter and George Carnaby, to murder your sisters Helen Carnaby and Laurel Faa Geddes.'

Isobel Carnaby squealed again. Her hands flew to cover her horrified face. As the militia surrounded the woman, Lavender added:

'In addition to this, Isobel Carnaby, I also arrest you on the suspicion of the attempted murder of your step-mother, Esther Carnaby, earlier this year.'

A sudden silence fell over the shocked crowd. Even George Carnaby paused in his struggle against the grip of the guards.

'Oh, yes,' Lavender said calmly. 'Vicar? I'd be grateful if you would ask the sexton to leave Mistress Esther Carnaby's grave uncovered. We intend to exhume her body later and examine the remains for evidence of digitalis poisoning.' He took out a small silver casket from his coat pocket and waved it at Isobel Carnaby. 'The same digitalis my constable found in a drawer in *your* bedchamber.'

Isobel Carnaby went limp and collapsed, half-fainting, into the arms of the soldiers.

'Lies! All lies!' George Carnaby yelled. 'I'll have you for this, Lavender – you'll see if I don't! You incompetent bastard!'

Now Jethro Hamilton stepped forward. 'I've had enough!' he yelled.

The crowd fell silent again as the big farmer advanced menacingly towards the prisoner.

'Carnaby – you're a bastard. Is there any one in yer family, you didn't try to hurt?'

'Step away, Hamilton.' Lavender warned quickly.

'Damned if I will. By the power invested in me by the excellent ale in The Rose and Crown - I give you *this* fer what you did to yer younger brother!'

Hamilton threw a punch at Carnaby, smashing his nose and splattering blood across his face. Carnaby howled in pain. The soldiers looked at Lavender for instruction, but the detective gave them none.

'And I give you this fer what you did to that poor faw lass!'

The soldiers loosened their grip on Carnaby as Hamilton's second blow hit home. Swept off his feet by the ferocity of Hamilton's fist, the master of Linn Hagh stumbled and fell backwards. The horrified mourners screamed and leapt out of the way. Carnaby landed with a sickening crash in the open grave behind him, his boots poking helplessly out of the hole.

Isaac Daly tutted with mock irritation. 'Damn yer ruddy temper, Jethro,' he said. 'Now we'll hev to gan down there and pull the bugger out.'

It took Lavender and Woods and the militia the rest of the day to transport George and Isobel Carnaby to Hexham gaol. Once there, they had paperwork to complete and Lavender went through Baxter Carnaby' possessions and documents which had been retrieved by the landlord of the Redesdale Arms. He found several more incriminating documents in which the brothers openly discussed the campaign of terror they were to wage against their sister, Helen, but nothing about the plot to murder Laurel Faa Geddes and pretend that her corpse was that of Helen. Lavender began to suspect that Baxter Carnaby had acted independently in this instance. This would weaken the case against his brother.

But he needn't have worried.

The moment the gaoler pushed Isobel Carnaby into the private cell at Hexham gaol, so recently occupied by her younger brother, she baulked and began to squeal.

'George made me do it! He was in league with Baxter to murder our Helen! Drop that ridiculous charge against me which claims I tried to murder my step-mother and I'll tell you what went on. He forced me to help. I swear I'm innocent…'

With a growing sense of satisfaction, Lavender told the gaoler to slam the door shut.

'Let her stew for a few days in here,' he said. 'This is one for Magistrate Clennell to sort out.'

'You always said that the case against her for poisoning her step-mother was a weak one.' Woods whispered as they descended the gloomy stairs of the gaol.

'Yes,' Lavender confirmed. 'But she doesn't know this. The threat of the charge has been enough to make her confess *and* implicate her brother. He'll have a hard time wriggling out of a murder charge with the testimony of *both* his sisters against him.'

They were on their way back to Bellingham when Woods asked about Helen Carnaby. 'Where did she come from? It were spooky that - the way she just appeared out of the snow and began to throw accusations at her brother.'

'She returned from Morpeth in the carriage with me,' Lavender told him. 'When I left Goddard's house last night, she ran after me and asked to travel back to Bellingham under my protection. She and Anna were in the carriage all the time. I told them to stay there but Miss Carnaby ignored me. Quite frankly, I'm glad that she did. It removed the necessity for further explanations once she appeared.'

'I wonder what story she has told her uncle about her whereabouts over the last six weeks?'

Lavender smiled. 'During the journey back to Bellingham, Anna came up with the idea that I had discovered Helen Carnaby with an unknown friend in Whitby and sent for her to return.'

'She's a smart gal, that Anna.'

Lavender smiled again.

'I'm not sure if they'll be able to pull the wool over John Armstrong's eyes for long, especially when she marries Robert Goddard later this week, but I wish the ladies the best of luck with this ploy.'

'Do you want to go and see the Armstrongs tonight?' Woods asked when they finally returned to the quiet, snow-covered streets of Bellingham.

'No, let the family celebrate Helen's safe return,' Lavender replied. 'I'm hoping that Jethro Hamilton is The Rose and Crown tonight. I want to see him.'

'He might not be there.'

'Oh, he'll be there,' Lavender said, with a smile. 'His wife scolded him for assaulting George Carnaby when we left St Cuthbert's. I suspect he'll have sought refuge in the tavern. I want to buy Jethro Hamilton a drink. That was the most impressive right hook I've seen in a long time.'

'The first jab or the second?' Woods asked, smiling.

'Both.'

'He gave George Carnaby exactly what he deserved, in my opinion.'

'And mine, although I've no doubt the vicar will have something to say in the pulpit next Sunday about the cursing and fighting which occurred on holy ground this morning.'

'Hmmph!' Woods snorted, as they trudged across the cobbles. 'The man was resisting arrest. Hamilton were right to lay him out.'

'As I see it,' Lavender concluded, 'The Rose and Crown is Hamilton's last refuge at the moment, after upsetting both his wife and the vicar. I'm sure he'll be there. It's the one place where he won't get nagged for his behaviour. Besides which, Mistress McMullen has told me that she has never known her tavern to be so popular.'

'What d'you mean?' Woods asked.

'I think, my friend, that we've been the main attraction in this sleepy market town for the whole of the last ten days.'

'What? Like Charles Dignum down in the Vaux-hall gardens?'

'Yes, exactly like Charles Dignum.'

'We should have charged them all a shilling a piece.' Woods observed ruefully. He thought for a moment and then added: 'We've given them a good show, though, haven't we?' There was satisfaction in his voice.

'Yes, Ned,' Lavender smiled. 'We've given them a good show.'

CHAPTER THIRTY SEVEN

When their coach neared Barnby Moor on the return journey to London, Woods decided to bring up the question of the large, brown-paper parcel in the luggage rack above Lavender's head. Tied securely with coloured string, its label bore the following address: *Miss Mary Ann Elliot, Pilgrim Street, Newcastle. For a fashionable assortment of millinery, dresses, straw, leghorn, chip and willow bonnets. Imported seasonally from London.*

Before they left Bellingham, Woods had overheard Lavender ask Helen Carnaby for the name of a good dressmaker in Newcastle. He assumed that the detective planned to buy a small present for his mother or one of his sisters. However, the sheer size of the parcel bothered him; whatever it contained was large and expensive.

In addition to this mystery, Lavender had also returned from the shops in Newcastle with a selection of brand new shirts, a cravat and fashionable gold-striped, silk waistcoat. Doctor Goddard, it turned out, had also recommended a tailor.

For Constable Woods, a trained police officer with the Bow Street magistrates' court, this was a suspicious development.

Lavender sat opposite him in the swaying coach, reading a news sheet and frowning at reports of the Luddite disturbances in Nottinghamshire. Woods appreciated that the burgundy cravat suited the detective's dark colouring and the gold waistcoat gave him a look of affluence and class. But to see the detective wearing any colour at all was a new and very worrying occurrence. Lavender had always been a smart dresser but he usually favoured a black waistcoat, either striped with grey or patterned damask, with a crisp, white cravat.

'What are you staring at, Ned?' Lavender asked. He didn't glance up from his news sheet.

'You intend to leave the coach at Barnby Moor, don't you? And you'll take another one to Gainsborough to visit that señora.'

'My goodness,' Lavender smiled. 'We really must get you promoted to principal officer. Your talents are wasted in the horse patrol.'

'I knew it.'

'You knew what?'

'That gypsy girl were right – the woman's got under your skin.'

‘I only intend to make a fleeting visit, to carry out a promise I made.’

‘Magistrate Read will have you clapped in Newgate for desertion when you return to Bow Street.’

The detective laughed and folded up his paper.

‘I doubt that. I’ve worked non-stop for the last two and half years. He won’t begrudge me a few days away on personal business.’

‘Well, just be warned,’ Woods grumbled. ‘That faw girl said the señora were a ‘shape-shifter.’’

Lavender raised his eyebrows and smiled.

‘I think you’ve the bigger cause to be worried, Ned, if we’re to take the gypsy’s prophesies seriously. As I recall it, the girl said that your youngest daughter, the delightful Tabitha, will break your heart.’

‘Not necessarily,’ Woods countered.

‘How so?’

‘Well, who says that little Tabby is to be my youngest daughter?’

‘I don’t follow you.’

Woods lowered his voice and winked. ‘There’s plenty of life left in my Betsy yet. I don’t reckon that Tabby will be the last little nipper in my nest at Oak Road.’

Lavender laughed and picked up his news sheet.

Woods sat back. Lavender’s comments about Tabitha had distracted him. His thoughts turned to his boisterous family. He yearned to see them and pull them all in his lap again. It wouldn’t be long.

The irongate in the crumbling brick wall creaked as Lavender entered the grounds of the small Elizabethan manor house.

Before him, a weed-strewn path snaked through the long grass towards the dilapidated building. To his right, the ground fell away into marshy bog and a reed-lined pond. He couldn’t tell whether the pond had formed naturally through neglect or if it had once been part of the landscaping. Tall chimney stacks rose intimidatingly from the flat roof of the manor, releasing a thin trail of smoke into the cold sky above. Dark-leaded windows stared back at him across the unkempt lawn. The place was unwelcoming.

‘Detective Lavender from the British Home Department, to see Doña Magdalena Morales,’ he informed the servant in Spanish.

Above the arched entrance to the brick porch at the front of the building flared the huge stone motto of some ancient British family. He passed beneath it and entered an Iberian enclave.

The heavy smell of religious incense, burning pine logs, rich coffee, the scent of cloves, saffron and a waft of cinnamon, pervaded the gloomy house. A large selection of dark-skinned, ruffled and disapproving Dons stared down at him from gilt frames on the oak-panelled walls. The furniture was heavy and blackened with age. As he walked through the Tudor hallway he glanced through an open door and caught a glimpse of an elderly señora, dozing before the fireplace in the main parlour. Her lace cap nodded to him across the room and glass rosary beads glinted in her gnarled, limp hand.

The servant led him into a small side parlour, dominated by a magnificent cabinet which filled an entire wall. A fire crackled in the hearth, for which he felt grateful. Above it, a picture of the Madonna and child stared down at him mournfully.

Magdalena took her time.

Bored with waiting, he moved across the room to examine the intricate pattern of Moorish circles and diamonds carved into the doors and drawers of the huge cabinet. His fingers traced the outline of inlaid ivory and mother-of -pearl.

Over by the window, a messy pile of half-written letters and abandoned quills lay on a chestnut table. His sharp eyes scanned the documents. Magdalena was writing for help from other Spanish émigrés. She had even addressed one letter to Magistrate Read at Bow Street. He was curious about its contents.

'Detective, Lavender.'

Magdalena stood in the doorway and was as ravishingly beautiful as he remembered. She wore the same dress she had worn for their supper at Barnby Moor. He detected a little puffiness around her eyes from weeping, but her manner was gracious and composed.

She smiled warmly when he bowed low over her outstretched hand and kissed it. The garnet ring glinted on her elegant finger. Laurel Faa Geddes had been right.

'The pleasure is mine, Señora.'

The maid hovered in the open doorway, but this time Magdalena waved her away and closed the door. He sighed with relief.

'I've ordered coffee and refreshments, Stephen,' she informed him. Her initial formality had obviously been for the benefit of the servants. Her accented voice purred like silk; he had never heard his name sound so attractive. She gestured him towards a pair of

Baroque gilt armchairs in front of the fireplace and they sat down. Her eyes glanced curiously at the large, brown package he had placed in the corner of the room.

'How are you, Magdalena?' he asked.

Her face struggled for a moment to retain its composure.

'Alas, Stephen, I grieve and I'm frightened. The news of Antonio's death has caused me great distress.'

'I'm sorry to hear that.'

Not too distressed, he hoped. She had not seen her husband for months and he had been dead since July.

She sighed.

'I had suspected for a while that something was very, very wrong. I knew that Antonio was angry with me for leaving Spain but his silence over the last few months was unusual. Thank goodness you wrote to Magistrate Read on my behalf. Otherwise, I would still not know I was a widow. I must thank you for that, Stephen. It was thoughtful of you - an act of friendship.'

'I was glad to be of service. It must have been a great shock to learn the truth.'

Lavender sat back in the uncomfortable chair, crossed his legs and flicked a speck of mud off his boot. He didn't know where this conversation would lead but he settled down to listen. She seemed resigned to her husband's death, sad but resigned. Her glossy hair was coiled above her head and held up with a simple comb. He had a sudden urge to see her hair down, tumbling around her shoulders – preferably her naked shoulders.

'Now I'm trying to come to terms with my loss. But on Saturday, Saturday…' Her violet-black eyes filled with tears and she wrung her hands in her lap.

'Yes? On Saturday?' He tensed.

She brushed a tear from her cheek and collected herself.

'On Saturday, my son, Sebastián, returns from school and I must tell him – tell him about his father's death.' Her face crumpled with pain. 'He enjoys his life at school, and I didn't want to write to him and spoil his last few weeks there.'

Lavender paused and observed her closely. This was not grief for her dead husband. It was the prospect of causing her child distress which made her suffer. He was seeing another side of the proud and confident woman who had fought by his side against the highwaymen; this was Magdalena the caring mother.

'Why are these his last few weeks at school?'

'He cannot go back there after Christmas.' Her voice trailed away with misery.

'Why not? Surely you've paid the school fees for a full year?'

'Yes, yes. That is the one thing which Antonio didn't argue about. The fees have been paid for the rest of the year.'

'But?'

'I need this money returned to me.'

'Why?'

She bowed her head and looked down at the fire. Then she shrugged her shoulders and raised both palms in a gesture of hopelessness.

'I have nothing, Stephen,' she said simply. 'Everything I own is in the hands of the French.'

They sat in silence for a moment, listening to the crackle of the fire.

'Is your son happy at his school?'

'Very,' she said. 'And I had such trouble finding one for him in the first place. This was the only school which would take him.'

'Why?'

'Because he is a Catholic, Stephen.' She looked up and smiled wryly. 'Your country is not kind to Papists.'

'Yes,' he sighed, 'I understand what you mean, Magdalena.'

He shuffled on his seat, reached into his coat pocket and pulled out a heavy bag of coins and a folded piece of parchment.

'I've brought this for you. Perhaps it'll help.' He handed her the money bag and parchment.

She took them with a worried frown, ignored the parchment and prised open the neck of the bag. Golden guineas glinted in the firelight.

Her mood changed quickly. Suddenly, her lips tightened into a narrow line and her eyes smouldered with anger. She hurled the bag of money at his head and leapt up.

Startled, he ducked the missile, but nearly fell off his chair. He scrambled to his feet. The bag crashed onto the floor behind him and spewed its glittering contents across the floor.

'For God's sake, Magdalena!'

'What am I? Am I to be treated as your whore, now?' she yelled. 'You claim friendship – then you insult me?

She was nearly crying with rage. He had forgotten about her flaming temper.

'Damn it, Magdalena! Read the document I've given you!'

She glared at him.

'Read it!'

He thought she would refuse, but slowly she unfolded the parchment in her hands. She glanced down at the 'Wanted' notice for highwayman, Frank Smith, and her face flushed with confusion.

'Frank Smith was the villain you shot during the highway robbery we foiled.' He forced his voice to remain calm. 'The man you killed to save my life had a twenty guinea reward on his head. That money is yours, Magdalena. You've earned it through your bravery. I collected it for you at Barnby Moor.'

Realisation dawned and large, round tears rolled from her horrified eyes. She cradled her face in her hands and her shoulders shook with misery.

'My friend,' she sobbed. 'My friend – and I accuse you.'

He enveloped her warm body in his arms. She laid her head against his shoulder and cried. He held her close, relishing her softness. This wasn't how he'd imagined their first embrace would be and it was a struggle to keep his hands still. For the moment though, he was prepared to simply wait out the storm of her grief.

'You weren't to know,' he said quietly. 'I should have explained first, before I gave you the money.'

He led her back to her chair and gave her his handkerchief. Magdalena stopped crying, dabbed her eyes and smoothed down her skirts. A few moments later, the maid arrived bearing a silver tray of coffee and cinnamon cakes. He asked the maid to pick up the spilt coins before she left. The money bag was placed on a nearby table. For the moment, they both ignored it.

Magdalena busied herself pouring out the coffee, making a visible effort to regain her composure. The coffee was just how he liked it, strong and bitter.

'You must forgive my foolishness, Stephen,' she said, 'and my rudeness.'

'There's nothing to forgive.' He smiled. 'As I said, I should have explained first about the reward money. You were right, it isn't proper for you to accept gifts of money from men you hardly know.'

Again, her eyes flitted across to the mysterious brown parcel he'd brought with him, but he decided to let her wait a while and wonder. If she took offence about that and decided to hurl it at his head, he wasn't sure he'd be able to jump out of the way fast enough.

'Perhaps we should get to know each other a little better, Stephen?' she suggested as she offered him a slice of cake.

'Yes, perhaps, we should,' he said.

He finished his coffee and replaced the cup in its saucer.

'Firstly, Magdalena, you need to know that I was not born a 'gentleman' although my mother was the daughter of a vicar. My grandfather was the Dean of St Saviour and St Mary Overie in London. He was a kindly gentleman, very spiritual but not very good with money. I'm afraid, he died impoverished.'

He paused. He could see that she was impressed by this description of his genteel mother and grandfather.

'Before his retirement, my father worked as a Bow Street police officer like Constable Woods.'

He watched the smile droop slightly at the corners of her mouth.

'However,' he continued. 'My parents wed for love and my sisters and I had a happy childhood. My father was wealthy enough to pay for a good education for me. I went to St. Saviour's Grammar School in Southwark and I was destined for a career in the legal profession. I attended Cambridge University, but left there after a year to train as an officer at Bow Street. I've never regretted this decision. I did my apprenticeship in the back streets and alleys of London. I've wrestled pickpockets to the ground, chased highwaymen up the Holborn Old Road and dragged the bodies of murdered lighter men out of the Thames. I've been instrumental in sending many people to the gallows who deserved it – and probably several who didn't.'

'My job has been my life, Magdalena, for the last twelve years.'

He paused. It was her turn now.

She gave him a brilliant smile.

'I've been rude,' she said. 'I've not enquired after the success of your most recent case. Did you find your missing heiress, Stephen?'

He fought back the disappointment which rose within him, pushed against the hard back of the chair, making himself as comfortable as possible. He had hoped his revelations would draw her out, encourage her to tell him more about her own life. But if she wasn't ready yet to talk about herself, then he could wait. He was resigned to playing this game her way.

He told her the story of the Carnabys and the recent events at Bellingham.

She listened attentively as he related the details of the case. Cooped up in this gloomy house with only an old woman for company, he could see she'd been deprived of stimulation for weeks. She leaned forward towards him; her eyes never left his face. The light grew dim. Servants arrived to stoke up the fire, light the candles and to bring him a decanter of Madeira. He felt himself relax.

When he had finished his tale, she frowned.

'What I don't understand, Stephen, is how did that Matthew Carnaby, the brother without a voice, know that the murderer was his older brother Baxter? You say that Matthew was only a tiny child when they sent Baxter Carnaby away and that Matthew had been told his elder brother has died. So how did he know?'

'That's a good question, Magdalena,' he replied. Her intelligence impressed him. 'Constable Woods thinks that Matthew Carnaby recognised the man's hideous laugh, but I believe the answer is far simpler than that. I think everyone underestimated that young man. There's nothing wrong with his hearing. I suspect that George and Isobel Carnaby grew careless in his presence and that he simply overheard them talk about their brother, Baxter.'

'And this boy with no voice, will he be happy now?'

'Yes. He is to live with Helen Carnaby and her husband, Robert Goddard.'

'And that poor, poor girl – the gypsy girl.' The soft candlelight emphasised the sadness in the deep pools of her dark eyes.

Lavender grimaced.

'I wish I had been able to do something to prevent her death.'

Magdalena leaned over and patted his thigh, reassuringly. Her light touch set him on fire and he struggled to keep his hands down.

'There was nothing you could have done to prevent her murder, Stephen. Of that I'm sure.'

Her confidence in his ability made him feel better and distracted him from his un-gentlemanly urge to seduce her. He knew that this intimate companionship with a woman by the fireside, on a dark winter's night, was something which men like Woods and Jethro Hamilton took for granted. He had never experienced it before, but now he yearned for it. He wanted the love and companionship of the gorgeous woman before him - and her body in his bed. He was prepared to wait for her, no matter how long it took.

Her eyes sparkled with mischief.

'And you say that this gypsy girl read your palm - and foretold your future?'

'Yes.'

'What did she foretell?' Her head dropped coquettishly to one side. A smile flickered at the corner of her red lips and her tongue flicked briefly into view.

'She said that I was to drink coffee and take afternoon tea with a hot-tempered but beautiful woman from the continent.'

'She said all that?' Magdalena smiled.

'Oh yes, and more. She also foretold that I would leave this feisty lady a present and then come back again to drink more coffee.'

She laughed. Her eyes strayed towards the parcel.

He rose and fetched it over.

'It's a Christmas present - and a thank you present – for the woman who saved my life.'

She nodded. He could tell that her hands itched to undo the string.

'And it is not, under any circumstances, to be thrown back at me, Magdalena.'

Her eyes shone with amusement.

'I understand. Can I open it now?'

He nodded.

She tore off the wrapping paper and reached for the silk and lace of the black gown he had picked out at the dressmakers' shop in Newcastle.

'I trust that it's appropriate,' he said awkwardly, as she held it up to the candlelight. The dressmaker had assured him that it would be a suitable gown for a woman in mourning. The intricate beading glimmered in the glow from the fire.

Magdalena looked delighted. 'It is beautiful, Stephen. Thank you. You have exquisite taste.'

He rose self-consciously. It was time to leave. He reached down, picked up the discarded bag of coins and held it out towards her.

'Take this money, Magdalena. It will help you. Let your son go back to his school after Christmas, you don't need to have his school fees returned.'

She nodded.

'Thank you, Stephen. You can't imagine how relieved I feel.'

Her hand brushed against his as she took the money bag and he grasped it. For a moment they stood there, relishing the contact, the warmth of each other. Then he raised her hand to his lips.

'You must visit me in London when I return,' she said simply. 'To drink more coffee as the gypsy girl foretold.'

'I'll visit you as soon as you return to London,' he promised.

'I know you will, Stephen.' She smiled.

'You are a gentleman – a man of your word.'

AUTHOR'S NOTES

I would like to tell you that the plot of *The Heiress of Linn Hagh* is completely original and fictional. However, those of you familiar with the genealogy pages on my website may have already noticed that the contents of Baxter Carnaby's Last Will & Testament were lifted virtually word for word from one of my own ancestor's will. Yes, that dysfunctional family was mine. Although there is no evidence that the ten Charlton children of North Carter Moor Farm were violent or murderous, they were obviously a bad lot. Poor James Charlton (1700-1770) felt it necessary to admonish his children and lay down a stack of ground rules in the will he wrote two days before his death. Finding his will inspired me to create the Carnabys of Linn Hagh.

I would also like to say that all the characters were entirely fictional - but of course they weren't. Detective Stephen Lavender really was one of the Principal Officers with the Bow Street Magistrates Court in London. Following the formation of the police force by Sir Robert Peel in 1821, Lavender became the highly-respected Deputy Chief Constable of Manchester until 1833.

I first came across Stephen Lavender when researching my first novel, *Catching the Eagle*. This is the true story of how one of my late husband's ancestors was controversially convicted of Northumberland's biggest robbery back in 1809. Lavender was the detective called up from London to solve the mystery of the Kirkley Hall Robbery. Ultimately, Lavender was the man who put our ancestor in the dock but I don't hold this against him. In fact, when creating his character for Eagle I began to like the serious, intelligent and slightly melancholic Detective Stephen Lavender. I also grew very fond of his fictional sidekick, Constable Woods.

The wonderful *History of the Bow Street Runners* by David J. Cox, tells us that when London based Principal Officers, like Lavender, went out to solve difficult mysteries in the provinces, they usually worked alone. However, successful crime fiction novels usually have a pair of heroes – or heroines - resolving the mysteries. So in my books I decided to break with historical fact and stick with literary convention. I gave Stephen Lavender a partner: Constable Edward Woods.

By the time I had finished writing *Eagle,* I knew that I didn't want to let either of these guys go, and by then the first seeds of a plot for a new whodunit had begun to germinate in my head. Before I knew it, I had a Regency mystery to solve, and as far as I was concerned there were only two policemen in England who could crack this case: Lavender and Woods. I sat down at the computer and *The Heiress of Linn Hagh* was born.

I particularly enjoyed creating the female characters in this book. My first novel was dominated by men because the historical records decreed it so; they dominated the crime, the investigation and the ensuing court cases. In *Heiress* I was able to create a diverse range of women from the delightful Anna, to the tragic and mysterious Laurel Faa Geddes and the intelligent Katherine Armstrong. I loved breathing life into these women and giving them a significant voice in this book.

Last but not least, I would just like to acknowledge the help I've had with writing *The Heiress of Linn Hagh.* My grateful thanks go to: Sam Blain (locally known as His Excellency the Cultural Attaché for Boosbeck); June Thompson; Kristin Gleeson, author of *Selkie Dreams*; my sister-in-law, Yvette James, and fellow author, J. G. Harlond, author of *The Empress Emerald.*

I would also like to thank the people of Bellingham themselves, who have repeatedly welcomed Chris and I back into their lovely town with warmth, good-humour and consideration during our many wonderful holidays there.,This book is a tribute to you all. I hope that I've done you - and Bellingham - proud.

Finally, to you the reader. Thank you for reading my book. If you enjoyed it, please take a moment to leave me a review at your favourite retailer. Thanks!

Karen Charlton
1st February 2014
www.karencharlton.com

BIBLIOGRAPHY

A Certain Share of Low Cunning: A history of the Bow Street Runners, 1792 – 1839 By David J. Cox

Scottish Gypsies Under the Stewarts by David Macritchie (1894)

Also by Karen Charlton

CATCHING THE EAGLE

Book One in the Regency Reivers Series

At Kirkley Hall, the gloom had thickened; the only light came from the candles which flickered behind the casement windows of the kitchen and the servant quarters. There was a low hum of voices and occasional laughter as the skeleton staff who manned the hall during the master's absence settled down to prayers, supper and an hour of relaxation before they retired for the night. The main part of the house remained, as usual, in total darkness; white dust cloths were draped like shrouds across the magnificent furniture, priceless portraits and gilded ornaments.

Just after nine, a footman took a spluttering candle around the ground floor of the hall. His footsteps echoed eerily in the deserted building. With his itchy wig tucked beneath his arm, he checked everything was secure and tested the huge bolts on the doors.

Eventually, the laughter ceased and the conversation became interspersed with yawns. Candles were extinguished as the staff drifted off to their attic sleeping quarters. The only sounds now were those of muted snoring, distant sheep and a tiny owl who hooted softly in the drooping boughs of the magnificent cedar tree.

At the edge of the rear courtyard, a moon-shadow crept silently up towards the estate office door. With the soft ease of familiarity, it climbed deftly onto the ground floor window ledge and then pulled itself onto the flat roof above the storeroom. Hard boots scraped lightly over stone.

The nervous owlet hooted and for a brief moment the phantom paused in response.

A hundred feet above them, a large shadow glided silently across the face of the moon. The golden eagle circled slowly above their heads and landed gracefully in the topmost branches of the cedar tree. There was a flurry of terrified squawking. The other roosting birds screeched and fled. Unperturbed, the raptor drew in its huge wings and watched the human below with sharp, passionless eyes.

Confused, the intruder squatted on the flat roof and paused. He was unsure what had disturbed the creatures in the tree. He waited for a window overlooking the courtyard to be thrown up and some light-sleeping servant to cry out: ‘Who goes there?’

But the event had gone unnoticed in the slumbering manor house. The great tree, with its sharp-eyed observer, settled back down again into silence.

Now the shadowy phantom on the roof moved swiftly. The abrupt crack of shattering glass echoed around the courtyard. The sash window of the office slid upwards.

Then the mysterious figure disappeared into the gloomy interior of Kirkley Hall…

Praise for Karen Charlton's

CATCHING THE EAGLE

'Told with gritty realism, Catching The Eagle is a suspense-filled page-turner, which spares nothing in its descriptions of the hardships and injustices suffered by the poor at the turn of the 19th century.

Its ending leaves the reader poised perfectly for the next volume - for which I can hardly wait.'

Kathy Stevenson, ***The Daily Mail***

* * * * *

'It is a rollicking tale full of adultery, drinking, fighting, gambling.

Rich imagery, suspense and some genuinely likeable characters – as well as plenty of murky ones - make this an enjoyable read. Karen is particularly strong at capturing the Geordie dialect and recreating the rural Northumbrian world of the 1800s, where the wealthy lived in comfort and the poor struggled to make ends meet'

Laura Fraine, ***Culture Magazine, The Journal (Newcastle)***

Printed in Great Britain
by Amazon.co.uk, Ltd.,
Marston Gate.